Society Inciting
A Sovereign Magi Society novel
Book 3

T.J. Vensarn

i

ISBN-13:978-0-692-88146-0
ISBN-10:0-692-88146-8

Cover design by T.J. Vensarn.
Artwork by: Nadica Boshkovska
Check out author T.J. Vensarn online at www.vensarn.com
Check out the artist's gallery online at
http://theswanmaiden.deviantart.com/gallery/

The Sovereign Magi Society Series

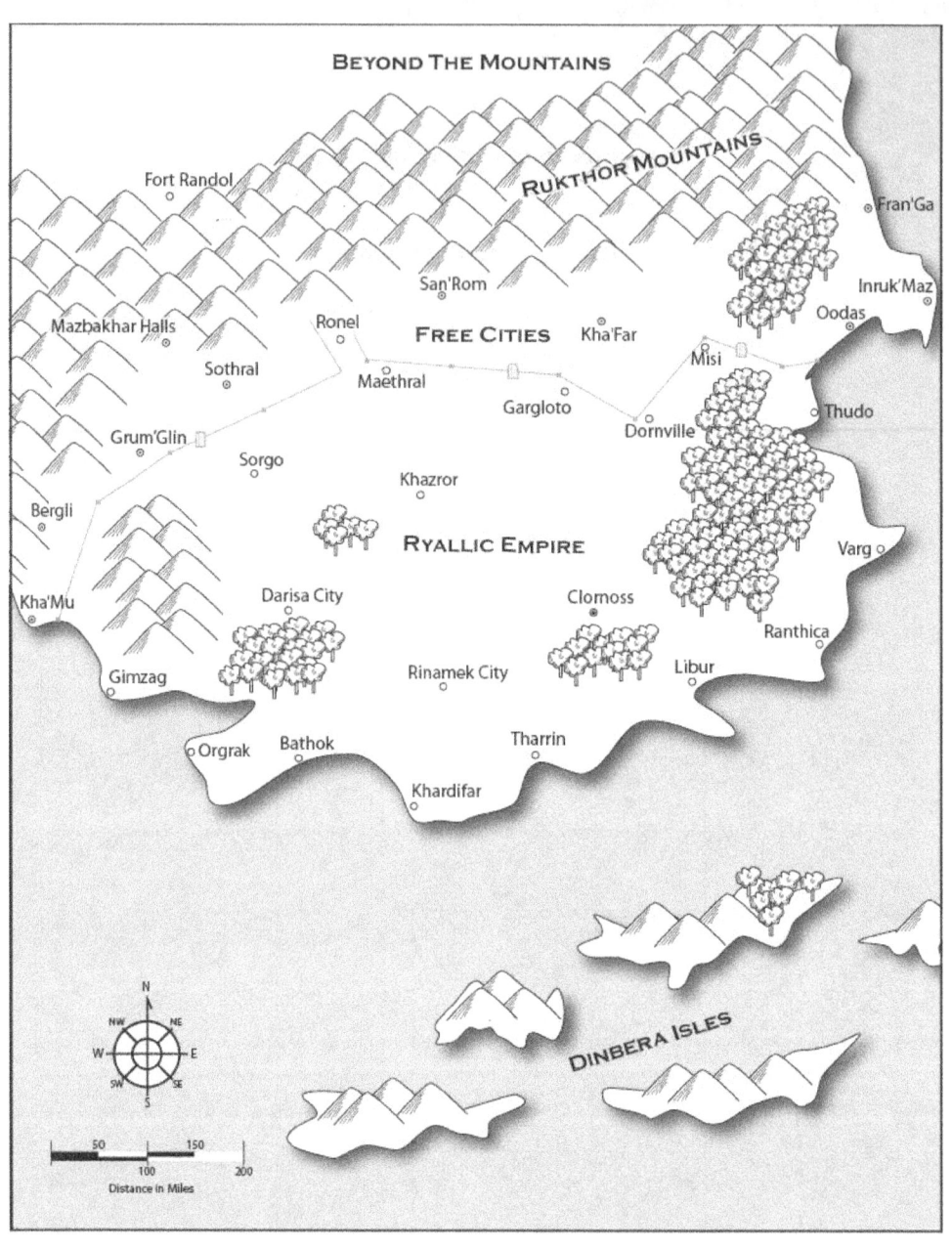

BEYOND THE MOUNTAINS

RUKTHOR MOUNTAINS

Fort Randol

Fran'Ga

San'Rom

Inruk'Maz

Mazbakhar Halls

Ronel

FREE CITIES

Kha'Far

Oodas

Sothral

Misi

Maethral

Thudo

Grum'Glin

Gargloto

Dornville

Sorgo

Bergli

Khazror

RYALLIC EMPIRE

Varg

Kha'Mu

Darisa City

Clomoss

Ranthica

Gimzag

Rinamek City

Libur

Orgrak

Bathok

Tharrin

Khardifar

N
NW   NE
W   E
SW   SE
S

DINBERA ISLES

50   150
100   200
Distance in Miles

CHAPTER 1

Jessa

"By the gods, what is that sarding thing?" Jessa stepped away from the summoning circle on the floor before her, as a creepy little creature suddenly appeared within the circle.

The creature was about one foot in height. It looked like a maniacal monkey with scorched scales instead of fur, and it had tattered bat-like wings on its back. The creature was screeching loudly and springing around within the confines of the magical circle. It slammed against the magical barrier, changed directions and sprinted until it slammed into the barrier on the other side. Each time it crashed into the invisible barrier its fury seemed to increase.

Jalinox smiled broadly. "That, my dear, is an Acarri Demon. One of the least dangerous of all of the demon types, to be sure. But this little guy is important to us because of his peculiar disfavor for Magi."

Jessa frowned, "We're going to attack the Magi with little scaly monkey-bat things?"

"No, don't be daft. We're going to use these little critters to hunt down and capture Magi, before they even know they have the potential to be Magi! These little demons can sense the magical essence within a person. All we have to do is let him loose in a crowd of people and he'll lead us right to someone with the innate ability to become a Magi."

She was starting to get annoyed, and it showed on her face. She crossed her arms and looked at the necromancer lord for a long moment. "How does it benefit us to capture random people who aren't even Magi yet?"

Lord Jalinox waited until the screams from the Acarri Demon calmed down enough for him to speak, "Because we are going to need a great many Magi, or people with the potential to become Magi, for the culmination of my greatest achievement yet! We are on the brink of something monumental, and capturing many potential Magi is key to this achievement."

Jessa kept her expression steady, and asked, "And what is this great

1

achievement?"

He put his hand on her shoulder, and said, "The tomes we took from the Magi Stronghold hold treasures of knowledge far beyond what I even dared to dream. I am now close to unlocking the key to bringing your brother back to life!"

The shock of his words hit her hard and sent a shiver down her spine. She felt her heart racing, and she took a deep breath to calm herself. Bringing her brother back to life had been her only focus when she agreed to join Jalinox, even though she had doubted that he could ever fulfill that promise.

He continued, "Dearest, we are on the verge of making significant progress towards that goal! In those tomes, I have found a ritual that can bind one of the greater demons from the lowest planes of Khalius and make it my servant! With the indescribable power of a greater demon at my command, recovering your brother's soul will be the least of my achievements. No power in the lands could stand in my way with a greater demon at my side!"

Jalinox stopped, and waited for some sort of reaction. Then he added, "The caveat is that it requires pure mana, the magical essence within the body of each Magi."

She looked at him inquisitively, "How can you extract magical essence from Magi? It's not a tangible thing, it's not like blood or urine, it's more like energy within the body."

He nodded. "That was a problem. I can't just squeeze the essence out of a Magi's body. But my research hinted at a solution. There is a delightful little creature called a Manaworm that lives deep underground in some places. Many of our Apostles have spent the last several months collecting some of these nasty little buggers. Manaworms have the intriguing capability to convert Magi into pure mana. Remarkable creatures!"

She felt excited and relieved at the same time. She was elated at the prospect of being able to bring her brother back to life. She asked, "How do the Manaworms get the essence out of the Magi?"

He laughed happily, "That's the best part! They completely consume the Magi, excreting pure mana afterwards. From my research, it seems that every scrap of the Magi will be gone, leaving only a small puddle of mana behind. How much mana we get from one Magi depends on how powerful they are, of course. A minor Magi may only produce a drop of pure mana."

Jessa felt her excitement wane a bit. "Only a drop? How much will we need to bring my brother to life?"

He held up his hands, "First things first, darling. Remember, the main goal is bind a greater demon to my will. Afterwards we'll bring back your brother."

She winced as the little demon's enraged fit grew in intensity, and then slowly waned.

She had heard Jalinox talking about the greater demon, but she had been so excited about the prospect of bringing her brother back that she barely paid any attention to that part. Lord Jalinox commanding a greater demon? She cringed at the though. It made the hairs on the back of her neck stand on end. He didn't really care about bringing Burga back to life, he wanted immeasurable power for himself. She clung to the belief that he would keep his promise even after binding the demon, but in the back of her mind she couldn't help but think that he was just dangling a carrot before her to ensure that she did his bidding.

Little did he know that she had aspirations of her own, and they had grown beyond simply wanting to bring her brother back to life. Years as a necromancer had changed her, and a thirst for power was a highly motivating force.

She smiled at him. "How many Magi do you think we'll need to achieve our goals?"

He shrugged, "Dozens at least, possibly hundreds. It's impossible to know for sure. We're going to take this little demon to the city and capture ourselves a Magi. Then we're going to let our Manaworms turn him into mana. Soon we'll have all of our Apostles spread out throughout the known lands with Acarri Demons, and they'll be bringing us more and more potential Magi. Before long we'll have more mana than we know what to do with."

He laughed and she joined in.

The Acarri Demon screamed furiously in the magical summoning circle.

Jalinox said, "If this little fellow escapes from his confinement, make sure you keep Khalius Fire between you and him. You're a Magi, and he'll come after you as quick as anyone else unless you use our fire to mask your magic from him."

- = - = -

In the days since she had learned about Acarri Demons, Jessa had spent most of her time traveling through Khalius.

The outer plane of Khalius and the underground surface of the world were closely tied, and for centuries the necromancers frequently crossed between the two. However, a recent discovery by Lord Jalinox radically changed how the necromancers used their ability to descend into Khalius.

For ages the necromancers would use a Khalius Wicket, a small magical stone, to open a hole in the ground which served as a portal into the outer plane of Khalius. Once in the hole, the necromancer's soul would leave their body behind and could move freely through Khalius without being hindered by the dirt and rock that it passed through. The necromancer could explore around Khalius, and even gather items which had been buried underground. Most commonly, they would gather remains of the dead to animate as Awakened to serve them on land. However, to exit Khalius they had to return to their body and re-emerge into the world in the physical location where they left it.

The discovery made by Lord Jalinox changed that. A tome he took from the Magi Stronghold revealed the secrets to allow the necromancers to reach from Khalius back to the land of the living and pull the Khalius Wicket down into Khalius. This allowed the necromancer to exit Khalius wherever they happen to be instead of needing to return to their physical body. When the Wicket was returned to the physical world, the necromancer's body appeared in the hole near the wicket, allowing the necromancer to emerge above ground far from where they started.

Jessa had left her body behind, and her soul moved freely through the dirt and rock. The roots and other underground features of the world were vaguely visible to her if she chose to see them, but they did not slow her progress as she flowed quickly towards her destination. She was certain that she was getting very close to the city of Gargloto. She stopped and looked at her surroundings.

There were very few roots and she couldn't see any underground structures, poles, fences, or other buried items that would indicate that she was near buildings. The underside of the stones of the road were off to her right so she knew she was still headed in the right direction. She assumed that she was in the middle of farmland, and that was as good a place as any to emerge.

With a quick prayer to Viator, she grabbed the Wicket and thrust it up beyond the surface. Her spiritual hand felt the cool wind as it emerged from the ground. She dropped the Wicket in the dirt above her and finished her prayer to the god of death.

The surface of the ground above her opened and her body appeared beside her. With a sigh, she stepped to it and suddenly she was back with her physical form. She was instantly cold, and her muscles felt stiff and awkward. For a few moments she moved her arms and legs around, then stretched her arms out wide.

When she pulled herself from the hole she looked around. She was in a farm field like she suspected. There were no buildings, but the moon was full and off in the distance she could see the road that should lead her into the south entrance of the city.

She grabbed her Wicket and then made her way to the road, brushing the dirt and grime from her clothes as she walked.

The sky was dark but it wouldn't be long before the sun peeked over the horizon. It was the early morning hour, and soon the people of Gargloto would fill the streets and marketplace, and one of them was about to become her prisoner. Jessa smiled to herself and whistled a happy tune as she walked quickly down the deserted road.

The walls and buildings of the city slowly came into view in the moonlight and Jessa picked up her pace. The city guards paid no attention to her as she walked through the gate and made her way to the bazaar. The streets of the city were mostly empty, but some people moved about on their various tasks for the day. She ignored them and continued to the busiest part of town.

Her stomach rumbled as the smells of the bazaar grew strong, reminding her that it had been a long time since she'd had anything substantial to eat.

The sky glowed orange in the east, as the sun began to peek over the horizon. She picked a fairly empty spot behind some crates, and opened up a pouch from her belt. Kneeling on the ground, she carefully poured the powders and sands from the pouch into her hand and then used that to draw a summoning circle on the ground. When the circle was perfect she stood and began her ritual.

The people around her were oblivious to her chanting, as they hurried from place to place caring only about their own worries.

The ritual was quick and within moments the summoning circle contained a small scaly monkey-like creature with leathery wings. The Acarri Demon screamed and beat against the invisible walls of its prison.

"Zortha's diddies! What's that?" A man near her stopped and pointed at the demon.

Jessa summoned Khalius Fire and held it in her hand before her, and then used her foot to smudge the summoning circle.

The demon, free from its containment, screeched in hideous laughter and rushed from the circle. It looked around quickly, and then ignored Jessa and hurried off.

People on the street shouted in surprise and moved away as the demon ran past.

She chased after the demon, darting between people as they tried to stay away from the small creature that was screeching and sprinting through the street.

The demon didn't go far before it jumped up onto a woman and latched itself onto her chest. The woman screamed and tried to knock the small creature from her, but it held tight to her clothes. It ripped at the neckline of her dress with its sharp talons and bit at her neck viciously.

The woman shrieked in terror and backed up while trying to knock the demon away. She tripped and fell to the ground, but she couldn't get away from the relentless monster.

Everyone moved away from the woman as she writhed around on the ground kicking and screaming.

As Jessa finally caught up, two men moved over to help the woman on the ground. Without warning, Jessa lobbed several purple orbs of Khalius Fire at the men. They fell to the ground lifeless, next to the screaming woman.

She chanted the final phrases of the ritual, dismissed the demon back to its own realm.

A crowd quickly gathered to see the spectacle. The shouts and cries grew louder as the woman on the ground sat up. Her face was scratched severely and blood was flowing freely from several gashes in her neck.

As she had done so many times in the past, Jessa said a prayer to Viator asking him to raise the nearby corpses to serve her as Awakened spawn. A moment later the two dead men rose from the ground to do her bidding.

The growing mob quickly backed away as she sent her newly created servants to attack the closest people.

Jessa pulled manacles from her pouch. They were made from the green garroliron that would block the woman's ability to use magic. Most likely the woman had no idea that she even had the potential to become a Magi, but Jessa wasn't going to take any chances. The woman was in shock from the demon attack, and the sight of her own blood. She didn't even fight as Jessa placed the manacles on her wrists.

Jessa dropped her Khalius Wicket on the ground next to the bleeding woman, and a large hole opened up. She ignored the cries from the crowd as the panicked people fled from her Awakened spawn. She reached down and grabbed the arm of the bleeding woman and then jumped in the hole. As she fell, she pulled the woman into the hole with her.

The woman screamed as she fell.

The hole closed around them, and Jessa reached out of Khalius to grab the Wicket from the surface above them. She moved forward and her soul easily left the confines of her physical body. Looking back, she vaguely saw the body of her prisoner. It was curled into a ball at the feet of Jessa's body.

"Let's go, woman. Follow me." Jessa's words were just thoughts directed at the woman.

Slowly the woman's soul moved from her body. Jessa saw it as a small and weak mouse that moved slowly and hesitantly.

In Khalius, the souls of other people appeared to her in the form of how she viewed that person, they didn't look like their physical form. When she first viewed Lord Jalinox within Khalius, he appeared large and powerful, with bulging muscles. He seemed eight feet tall and impossibly strong. She wondered what her soul looked like to her prisoner.

The woman moved incredibly slowly, and several times Jessa scolded her to hurry. In the land of the living it was becoming daytime, and once the sun shone brightly they would not be able to leave Khalius. Jessa had hoped to get many miles from Gargloto before darkness fell, but at this pace they would be lucky to be just a few miles from the city.

Ahead she a saw an animal burrow. In it was a partially decayed corpse of a small animal, possibly a badger. When they got close to the dead creature, Jessa said a quick prayer and called the animal to serve her as an Awakened. A life force appeared weakly within the corpse, and followed the souls of the women.

After what seemed like ages, the sun finally set. Jessa knew because the slight glow above them had faded. She was wildly frustrated at the slow pace of their journey, and she was ready to rest for a while. She stopped and thrust the Wicket up onto the surface.

She heard the woman gasp and then start yelling, as her soul returned to her body that had appeared in the hole.

"Shut up, and climb up there."

The woman sobbed. "What is that place? What happened to me?"

"If you stay in this hole, you'll be trapped in that place again all by yourself because I'm getting out."

The woman stood up and rushed to the side of the hole. She struggled to pull herself out, and finally Jessa helped to push the woman up to the surface. Then she grabbed the Awakened badger, and placed it on the surface as well. It's eyes glowed red and it was partially decomposed. Finally, she climbed out of the hole and sat casually on the ground.

The hole closed and Jessa picked up the Wicket. She pulled some deer jerky from a pouch and ate it without offering any to her prisoner.

The woman's bleeding had mostly stopped, but the wounds were covered in dirt and dried blood. The woman pulled her legs up to her chest and wrapped her arms around her knees. She quietly asked, "Where are you taking me?"

"Shut up."

"What is that place? How were we walking through dirt?"

"That was Khalius."

"Khalius? The place where evil people go when they die?" The woman looked skeptical.

"Yep, sort of. We were just in the outer plane, not in the truly horrible part. We could go to the really bad part if you want." Jessa finished her jerky and took a long drink from her waterskin. Then she pulled out a large chunk of dry bread.

"Why have you abducted me? My family has no money to pay for ransom."

Jessa took another long drink, and then put the cap back on the waterskin. She said, "You're going to be the guest of Lord Jalinox. Now shut up and get some sleep. We have a lot of travel still ahead of us."

The woman picked up her feet and stomped them onto the ground. She struggled against the manacles and then ungracefully stood up. She shouted, "I won't shut up! You can't keep me here!" She started walking away.

"If you wander off I'll have my Awakened badger eat you. Shut up and sit down."

CHAPTER 2

Konrad

Few things were as intoxicating to Konrad as having someone else's life in his hands, so he was feeling downright giddy as he stood in the common room of the *Toad Stool* tavern in Khazror.

He led a platoon of fifty imperial soldiers to do a job that could have easily been accomplished by five or six, and that was exactly the way he liked it. Nothing brought fear and insecurity to the masses like overwhelming force.

He stood in the common room of the tavern with a dozen soldiers and two Denizens. The remainder of his platoon was standing guard outside of the tavern, watching for troublemakers and spreading fear. In the kitchen area, just behind the common room, a bar wench and an old bald-headed barkeep were busily cleaning things and trying to look disinterested in what was happening in their tavern.

Konrad led the platoon in his Agent Luigey guise. He was a master of disguises, but the one where he held the most power and influence was as Luigey. In this form, he held the favor of the emperor as the hero who had twice spearheaded the capture and killing of several Magi. After the massacre south of Sorgo last year he had been awarded with medals, land, and riches beyond measure. However, the rewards that meant the most to him were the rewards of increased power and authority.

"He's lying! Pao, tell them that you made it all up! This is nuts!"

The yelling woman was one of the two Denizens in the room, and she was held tightly by two of the soldiers.

Konrad looked at her and scowled. He shook his head slowly. "If she speaks again without permission, cut out her tongue."

The woman screeched, "What!" She started thrashing and trying to break away from the soldiers. "This is insane! Pao, tell them the truth! I ain't no Magi!" She stopped thrashing around and looked to Konrad, "Sir, I ain't no Magi! Pao caught me in bed with the baker and he's trying to get revenge! You've got to listen to me!"

Konrad sighed. "Cut out her tongue."

One of the soldiers drew his dagger and the woman began screaming hysterically.

He gave the soldier a dirty look and held up his hands. In a loud voice, he said, "Not here, you idiot! Take her out into the street so I don't have to listen to her scream, and so the people of Khazror can see the punishment for lying to an imperial agent."

As the soldiers dragged the woman out of the tavern, Konrad looked to the other Denizen in the room. He was a middle-aged man with an unkempt beard and greying hair. The man looked nervous as he watched his wife being dragged out into the street.

Konrad gave the man a stern look. "Pao, don't tell me that you're now starting to re-think your original report. Lying to an imperial agent is a serious offense, and if I found out that you lied about your wife and her lover being Magi then I'm afraid you'd surely suffer terribly."

Pao shook his head vigorously. "Oh no! I saw them all right! They were locked in a lover's embrace, gyrating and casting disgusting sex magic right there in my bed! The man was using magic to-"

"Shut up, Pao." Konrad put his hand over the man's mouth. "Save the depraved details for your testimony to the magistrate, I don't need to hear them."

He knew that the man was most likely lying, and he didn't care in the slightest. As long as the fool would stand before a magistrate and testify that his wife and the baker were Magi, it would mean two more scores for imperial agent Luigey.

The emperor's most recent decree stated that anyone accused of magic use by at least one credible witness would be prosecuted as a Magi. The decree didn't bother with pesky details like proof or truthfulness. Not surprisingly, the number of reported Magi sightings were blossoming nicely as people used the current fervor as an excuse to get rid of old enemies and new rivals.

Outside, a crowd was starting to form as Denizens came out onto the street to see what was happening to the woman.

Konrad smiled, he had hoped to have a good crowd when his soldiers dealt with the baker. He looked to Pao, "You're sure that the baker who was using magic in bed with your wife is in that shop across the street?"

"Yes, that's him!"

"And his family lives there with him?"

"In the rooms above the shop, yes."

Konrad turned to one of the soldiers, and said, "Sergeant, it's time to round up the whole nest of them. Be careful, they're all probably Magi and if you give them the chance they'll fry your entire company without a second thought. I've seen it happen. Bring them out and line them up in the middle of the street. If any of them resist in the slightest they must be killed quickly before they can attack."

The sergeant saluted and hurried out of the common room. Most of the other soldiers in the room followed him.

"Your part in this is done for now, you can go. Be sure to be at the magistrate's office first thing in the morning to give your statement." Konrad watched Pao leave and rush down the road. After a moment, he exited the tavern as well.

He stood on the top step for a while, watching the baker's shop across the road. He could hear yelling and crashing from the building but no one had emerged yet. The crowd in the street continued to swell.

He felt something bump up against his right shoulder. He stepped to his left and turned to face whoever dared touch him. He laughed out loud when he saw that it was only the tavern's sign swinging on its support bar in the breeze. There were no words on the sign, just a carving of a large frog sitting on a bar stool with a big tankard of ale in his hand.

Konrad slid his sword back into his scabbard and looked back to the baker's shop. He didn't recall drawing his sword, but he was happy to note that the drunk frog would have been dead in an instance if it had meant him harm.

The soldiers walked out of the baker's shop pushing four Denizens before them. The first Denizen was a middle-aged man dressed in the white tunic and apron of a baker. Behind him was a middle-aged woman in a dress that had been patched and mended many times. Last out of the door were two adolescent boys in overall breeches and no shirts. The soldiers had all four people bound with their hands behind their backs.

The four Denizens were led to the middle of the road and forced to their knees.

Some soldiers brought Pao's wife into the middle of the street and forced her to kneel next to the others. Her mouth, neck, and blouse were covered with blood from where her tongue had been removed. She was sobbing heavily as she knelt on the ground, casting her eyes down and refusing to look up.

Konrad walked out to the road and stood before the kneeling and bound Denizens. He spoke loudly and clearly, so that the gathered crowd could hear him. "Kreg Bogguns and Sibil Cullans, you have been identified as Magi by a citizen who witnessed you using magic. By imperial decree you shall both be prosecuted as Magi. These three accomplices will hang beside you to pay for your crimes."

The baker's wife stood up and started shouting, "No! Not my boys! They've done nothing wrong! If this good-for-nothing man has been sarding that chippie again then he deserves to hang! But that ain't got nothing to do with my boys!"

The soldiers shoved the woman back to her knees, and other soldiers drew their weapons and stepped towards the five captives.

The baker stared at the ground before him and said nothing, but Konrad could hear the sobs coming from the weak man. He felt his contempt growing at a man who could allow something like this to happen to his own family and mistress and just kneel there and cry instead of at least dying in an attempt to defend them. In his mind, Konrad was convinced that the pathetic man deserved worse than the gallows.

"No! This can't be happening! They've done nothing wrong!"

Konrad looked to his left to see who dared speak against him. He saw a young man of perhaps twenty years rushing forward.

Someone tried to pull the man back into the crowd, but he pushed his way forward. He walked through several soldiers to stand between Konrad and the prisoners. He said, "This is not justice! These boys did nothing wrong, I know the family and they're not Magi!"

Konrad could hear a low murmur coming from the crowd and he knew if he showed weakness that things could become messy. The soldiers were now outnumbered at least three to one as the crowd in the street continued to grow. He looked to the platoon commander, and said, "Lieutenant, read the imperial decree on aid and support."

One of the soldiers standing near the tavern pulled a scrolled parchment from a pouch. He unrolled the parchment and read loudly, "By the order of his imperial majesty, Emperor Ryal III Supreme Commander of the royal forces of the empire and the one true imperial overlord of these lands. Let it be known that all persons who provide aid or support to any Magi shall immediately give up their rights as a person and be thereby given as a Dreg to the chancellor of the city of their residence or to the emperor himself if outside of any city limits. So sayeth the emperor!"

After a brief pause to let the lieutenant's words sink in throughout the crowd, Konrad said, "Son, are you attempting to provide aid or support to these Magi?"

The crowd grew silent and he could almost feel the weight of the situation pressing in around him. If the young man refused to back down, it would likely end in a small riot with dozens of Denizens dead at the hands of these soldiers. That would mean no end of paperwork and annoying meetings where Konrad would have to explain the fiasco to one bureaucrat after the next.

A moment later the young man hurried back into the crowd, and Konrad felt the tension lift some. He looked to the platoon sergeant and said, "Sergeant, lead the prisoners away."

He watched as the soldiers ushered the prisoners down the street. Before long, all fifty soldiers were formed in a long column and they walked down the road together. He fell in stride next to the platoon commander walking beside the column near its rear.

As he walked, the young commander began singing out a cadence song.

He sang, "Hey there people look this way."

As one, the entire platoon of soldiers echoed him. "Hey there people look this way."

The platoon commander sang, "Imperial troops move through today."

The soldiers echoed, "Imperial troops move through today."

"With our long swords in our hands."

"With our long swords in our hands."

"No braver warriors in the lands!"

"No braver warriors in the lands!"

The sound of fifty warriors singing in deep and foreboding voices was eerie and awesome to behold. The song was almost hypnotic and it drew him in. Soon Konrad found himself echoing the commander along with the rest of the soldiers.

"Woo Ooh Ooh Oo"

"Woo Ooh Ooh Oo"

This wasn't a song that he knew, but that was the beauty of cadence songs, the soldier didn't have to know it. He just had to echo it. When the second verse started, Konrad sang at the top of his lungs along with all of the other soldiers.

The commander sang, "Hey there people look this way."

The soldiers echoed, "Hey there people look this way."

"Magi gonna die today!"

"Magi gonna die today!"

"Emperor says to kill them all."

"Emperor says to kill them all."

"Run them through and watch them fall!"

"Run them through and watch them fall!"

"Woo Ooh Ooh Oo"

"Woo Ooh Ooh Oo"

Konrad loved the second verse and sang it proudly. He knew he'd be singing that in the bath for years to come.

CHAPTER 3

Rissyl

"Yes, you look fabulous in your new red and black cloak, Grand Evoker Rissyl!" Cynia laughed, but he knew that her mocking tone was meant to be playful and not hurtful.

Rissyl turned to one side and then the other as he looked at himself in the large mirror. He was a young man who had recently turned twenty. He was average height and slightly more than average girth, although his new training schedule had helped him slim down a bit. His curly light-brown hair was longer than he liked it and it was getting wild again already. As he looked at himself in the mirror he decided that she was right, the new cloak did look great and he was extremely proud to wear it.

Dalen threw a small pillow across the room at Rissyl, but it missed. Because of his aggressive training schedule, and the long hours that he spent working as a blacksmith and weapon enchanter, Dalen had gained a significant amount of muscle over the last year or two. He had been a big and intimidating man for as long as Rissyl had known him, but now he was downright scary looking. He frequently wore tunics with the sleeves completely removed because his bulging muscles were just too much for most shirts. Dalen said, "By the gods, Cynia. Does he wear that cloak to bed too? We got our new cloaks over a fortnight ago!"

Rissyl was a bit surprised to hear that it had been more than a fortnight since the ceremony installing him, Cynia, Dalen, and Sarasa officially as the grand officers of the Sovereign Magi Society. Things had finally settled down enough to hold an election, and the four of them were elected to formally hold the positions that they had been filling for well over a year.

He shook his head as he walked over to the large and comfortable chair next to Cynia. Time had been going so quickly. It had been over a year since they had claimed the Stronghold, and well over two years since the four of them had started the daunting quest of trying to rebuild the Magi Society.

Cynia was wearing a low-cut green blouse with dark green leggings.

The blouse showed too much of her ample breasts, like always, and the ends of the blouse extended low below her waist. She had it wrapped with an elaborate, but dainty-looking, metal chain around her waist. He smiled at her as he sat down, and he noticed again how great her light blond hair looked when she let it grow out.

"He only wears it to bed on nights when he ain't wearing his sexy serving wench outfit for our depraved lovers' games." She gave him a mischievous grin.

Rissyl's face turned red and he groaned, "Geez woman, must you tell all of our secrets?"

Sarasa said, "Eww! No. We really don't need that much detail."

He wished that Sarasa was being playful, but her voice sounded genuinely annoyed. She had changed since her experience at Randol's house when the imperial troops attacked. She had always been driven to learn as much as possible and she had enjoyed training in a fighting guild since she was a young girl, but these days she was even more focused on learning to be a more powerful Magi and a better fighter.

She was just as gorgeous now as the day he met her. The difficult choice between Cynia and Sarasa had come to a head a couple of years ago, and he rarely regretted the choice. Yet, it would probably always be difficult to look at the beautiful red-head and not wonder what it would have been like to be with her. They'd gone through a lot together, and at least he no longer felt awkward in her presence.

Brandam sat next to her, in his customary position at her side. Cynia liked to call him Sarasa's boyfriend, but boyfriend was a bit of a stretch since both of them insisted that their friendship was not physical. Brandam had been an imperial soldier, but he had been Sarasa's friend and training partner long before that. She brought him into their group and the man had quickly proven himself as a dedicated and loyal Magi. He had recently taken the oath and donned the red and white cloak of an Order of Evokers Magi, so he and Rissyl had been spending more time together lately.

"I'm sorry, Rasa. I was just joking." Cynia turned to Rissyl and winked, and then said, "He don't wear the whole sexy wench outfit, just the pretty under garments."

"That's so freaky." Sarasa rolled her eyes.

Dalen said, "I ain't surprised at all, I suspected that all along."

His sister gave him a dirty look, and said, "Dalen, you're such a troll."

Firana wore a huge grin. She was a comely woman in her mid-twenties, with long dark brown hair which contrasted strongly with the extremely light complexion of her skin. She said, "Riz, I'm sure you look sexy in your pretty little undies!"

She sat next to Dalen, and from the position of her head against his shoulder and her hand in his lap it was clear that their relationship was much more physical than that of Sarasa and Brandam.

"Yes, ha ha, very funny." Rissyl was sure that his cheeks were bright red. "My wife is quite the jester, she should entertain for chancellors."

Tiberos barked in his unusual high-pitch yap, which sounded like it should come from a much smaller dog. He was Rissyl's Rolimi dog, and like all Rolimi in human lands he appeared to be made out of pure light and each hair looked like a single strand of red light. However, it didn't glow brightly and it wasn't entirely transparent. It was rather short and squat for a dog, with a long body, short legs, and long floppy ears. Next to Tiberos was Skamp, Cynia's Rolimi dog. Skamp was a thick fuzzy dog that glowed green and had short ears, a thick body, and a short snout.

It was uncommon for the Rolimi dogs to be around these days. He hadn't seen Dalen or Sarasa's dogs in a month or two. Given the uncertain relationship with the various Rolimi castes, the fact that their Rolimi dogs still chose to come around at all was probably a good sign. If the Rolimi were actively planning a war against the humans, Rissyl expected that the Rolimi dogs would stay in the plane of magic all of the time.

Suddenly the doors to the room burst open and Asha rushed in, looking much more excited than Rissyl had ever seen her.

She was average height and very muscular, with dark skin. Her black hair was pulled up tight along the sides of her head and bound at the top and down the back so the large tightly curled hair looked almost like a bushy mohawk across the top and back of her head. She wore breeches and a tunic of dark grey, and over that she wore her newly earned white and grey cloak of an Order of Shadows Magi.

When Rissyl first met her, he knew her only as the Magi from Ferth's coterie in Maethral who was a bit of a loner and preferred to live among nature instead of within a house in the city. Since the Magi had all relocated to Fort Randol, Asha had proven herself to be a hardworking and intelligent Magi. She had a natural affinity towards Order of Shadows magic, and she was highly skilled in the disciplines of hunting, forestry, and woodlands navigation.

17

Although she had been assigned a home within the walls of the Stronghold, as far as Rissyl knew she spent almost every night sleeping outside of the walls in the nearby woodlands.

Asha was almost always introspective, quiet, and reserved. So, to see her visually excited about something was highly unusual. Rissyl stood up as soon as he saw her enter.

She said, "Come quickly, Ferth made a discovery!"

Rissyl followed the others out of the room, and out into the courtyard outside of the building they'd been using. He took a moment to take in the sight of the Stronghold, which he had renamed to Fort Randol. They'd been here for several months, but he was still trying to get used to the idea that it was now their home and the headquarters of the Magi Society.

The building they were in was called Summit Hall. It was an impressive three-story stone building in the middle of the fort. They had been relaxing in the largest room on the first floor, a room they had named the Lounge because it was filled with comfortable chairs and couches. Its original purpose was not known, but Rissyl assumed that it was designed to be a comfortable place for Magi to relax and chat before or after formal coterie meetings.

The second floor of Summit Hall was filled with small offices and reading rooms. As far as he knew, no one had yet had time to go through any of the rooms on that floor so they sat undisturbed. The third floor consisted entirely of the most impressive room for coterie meetings that he had ever seen, they called it the council chambers.

Fort Randol was built in the shape of a square, and a large portion of the middle of the square consisted of buildings for the brown and white cloaked Society Magi who had not been selected for one of the four Orders, or buildings that were used by all of the Orders. The buildings in that section included homes and dorms for Society Magi, as well as libraries, training halls, taverns, and other common buildings that folks would expect to find in any small town. The vast majority of these buildings sat unused and unexplored, until the society grew enough to have the manpower and need of them.

The northwest quadrant of the fort was built for the Order of Shadows. All of those buildings featured a placard with that Order's emblem, two crossed fists holding daggers on a grey background. The Order of Shadows specialized in *Illusion* and *Enchantment* schools of magic. The quadrant included many homes for Shadow Magi, as well as a number of other buildings marked for the use by that Order. The quadrant featured a large stone building named Shadow Hall. It was the command center for the Order of Shadows.

The northeast quadrant was built for the Order of Champions. The buildings all featured a placard with that order's emblem, a horizontal sword crossed with a vertical battleax on a blue background. *Abjuration* and *Artificing* were the schools of magic that the Order of Champions specialized in, so they focused on crafting magical weapons and their spells focused on protection and augmenting their already impressive martial combat expertise. The command building in this quadrant was named Champion Hall.

Over in the southeast corner was the Order of Diviner's quadrant. Their placards displayed the Diviner's emblem of a hexagon with an eye inside on a green background. The magic specializations of *Divination* and *Transmutation* were the focus of Diviner Magi. These schools gave the Diviners access to spells having to do with changing shape, controlling nature, and those affecting the mind. The command building in that section was aptly named Diviner Hall.

They were not headed to any of those quadrants. Asha led them quickly through the grid of buildings and into the quadrant for the Order of Evokers. Rissyl was extremely familiar with this section. He had spent a great deal of time exploring the buildings in this area.

As an Evoker, he specialized in the magical schools of *Conjuration* and *Evocation*. Like all Evokers, he commanded the potent combat magic of the elements, such as the always useful *Fireball* and *Lightning Bolt* spells. He also had teleportation magic at his disposal. He knew a few conjuring spells, but he had not yet spent the time to learn many spells in that discipline.

Within a few minutes, they all arrived at the front door of Evoker Hall. As they walked up the stairs he glanced at the placard near the door with the streaking fireball on a red background that was the emblem of his Order.

He wasn't sure what Ferth could have discovered in this building that hadn't already been found. Rissyl had searched this building countless times and he knew exactly what was inside. The second floor had a series of offices and meeting rooms. Rissyl had claimed a large room in the southwest corner, with several windows. His office was right next to a large meeting room where he sometimes met with the other Evokers to talk about plans and strategies for the upcoming confrontation with the empire and the necromancers. The first floor, like the main floor of all of the other Order Halls, was a huge open room with marble floors, marble walls, and in the middle of the room was a lifelike statue of a group of Evokers in a battle pose. Other than that, the first floor was empty.

When they entered the room, it looked just like he expected to find it. The room was brightly lit with several sconces on the walls around the room, each of the sconces housed a bright magical light orb. Ferth turned to face them when they walked in the room, he was standing near the statue.

He said, "Rissyl, how many times have we stood in this huge room wondering why they built it? We've searched for hidden doorways, and we've even placed fire orbs in the palms of some of the Magi in the statues."

Rissyl nodded impatiently, "Many times. What did you find?"

Ferth looked like he was going to explode with excitement. He said, "I decided to cast the Evoker portion of the spell that we using during the opening of a meeting of coteries. But, instead of casting it on my weapon, I cast it on this statue. Watch this." He hesitated for a moment. Then he placed a hand on the statue and said, "*Vaelth*. The first principle of the Society is truth. We will be true and loyal to ourselves, our fellow Magi, and to the Society."

As soon as he finished the spell, many of the marble stones that made up the floor in the middle of the room began to sink. They moved and rearranged themselves, forming a wide staircase leading down to a lower room. The stairs wrapped around both sides of the statue and met on the other side as they descended into a room far below.

Firana squealed.

Dalen exclaimed, "By the gods!"

Rissyl held tight to Cynia's hand as they slowly walked down the stairs. The stairs went down at least two stories before opening into a huge room. The wall sconces around the room lit with light orbs as they walked down into the room.

It was filled with display cases, statues, shelves, and pedestals. All of the surfaces were filled with magical artifacts and items. He walked over to a life-size statue of a Magi that held an actual wooden staff in its hand. A sign at the base of the statue said, "Alinundor's Staff." Rissyl had no idea who Alinundor was, but he carefully picked up the staff from its holder on the statue. The staff was slightly heavier than Rissyl's, and the top was adorned by an eagle holding a small red gem in its talons. The staff had runes up and down the shaft.

He placed the staff back on the statue and walked over to the nearest display case. Under the glass were dozens of different rings, each intricately engraved with shapes and runes. There was a small sign next to many of the rings telling of its name or previous owner.

Movement caught his eye from his left and he noticed that a small shelf extended across the walls around the entire room, slightly above eye level. On the shelf were dozens, if not hundreds of small statuettes. Each one depicted a Magi, and they all moved around as if they were all alive. The signs above them listed them as the former Grand Evokers, and listed their names and the years of their reign. He looked around the room and saw that there seemed to be a little statuette of every Grand Evoker of the Sovereign Magi Society going back hundreds of years. The sight of the tributes to all of the past powerful Magi who held the position made him feel grossly unqualified to wear the red and black cloak that he now wore.

Rissyl leaned against the wall and put one hand on his forehead. He was filled with a rush of different emotions. In the months since they'd captured the Stronghold, his biggest disappointment was that they couldn't find any of the vast trove of magical weapons and artifacts that they expected to find. They had been afraid that either the Magi had cleared them all out before abandoning the place, or the necromancers had stolen them all.

He looked around the room again. Display case after display case, and shelf after shelf, all filled with magical artifacts. It was beyond anything that he dared to hope. If the Order Halls for the other three Orders housed a cache of items nearly this impressive, then the Magi Society had gained a very powerful and much needed resource.

Sarasa pulled him from his thoughts, saying, "Riz! Look at this!" She was turning the pages of a large book that was sitting on a pedestal near the stairs. "I think this book describes each of the items in this room. Check this out." She paused for a second and then continued, "Here is the entry for the staff that you were holding. It's written in Menelian of course. It says, 'Alinundor's Staff was the primary weapon carried by Grand Evoker Alinundor throughout his reign from 3,245 to 3,248. The weapon was enchanted to deliver a unique combination of a deep freezing attack followed immediately by a blunt force attack which had the potential to shatter weapons and body parts.'"

Rissyl stared at Sarasa, and then at the staff, for a long time. Finally, he said, "This is phenomenal. It's the kind of thing I dreamed we'd find."

Ferth said, "That's not all, Riz. Check out these doors."

There were several doors around the perimeter of the room. Rissyl walked over and opened the door that Ferth was standing near. Beyond the door was a long hallway that seemed to go on forever. Spaced irregularly down the hallway on both walls were many more doors.

"I've only looked in a few of them. There are libraries and reading rooms, large rooms with targets for practicing offensive spells, other rooms filled with even more weapons and artifacts. We could spend several lifetimes studying and practicing down here, and we'd probably still never learn all there is to discover."

From behind him, he heard Dalen say, "This is great Riz. I've gotta go check Champion Hall!"

Cynia squeezed his hand, and then released it, "And I've gotta check out my hall. This is amazing." She kissed him quickly, and hurried up the stairs.

Before long, the others had all rushed off to check their own halls, leaving only the Evokers to continue exploring the vaults beneath Evoker Hall.

Rissyl walked solemnly into the large library. His eyes were wide and his hands shook slightly in excitement and anticipation. Many of the bookcases were labeled with headings such as History, Philosophy, Magic Theory, Society Law, Theology, and much more. He walked along the space between bookshelves looking for one topic in particular. Finally, towards the back of the room, he found it.

Spellbooks.

CHAPTER 4

Sarasa

"No, I'm not saying that we shouldn't meet with these people. We're just so busy, and now that we have finally found the Order Vaults there is even more to do! I'd much rather be back at Fort Randol learning and discovering." Sarasa brushed some hair out of her face, but the wind quickly blew it right back there.

Sarasa, Dalen, Firana, and Brandam were walking through the streets of Khardifar, heading towards the appointed meeting place where they were supposed to talk to a man named Favin who ran a local thieves' guild. The man had contacted them months ago, claiming to have information vital to the Magi. With everything going on after capturing the Stronghold, and because of a general distrust of thieves' guilds, the meeting was very slow to come to fruition.

Dalen sighed, "We've been over this, Rasa. I agree with you, but they sounded like this was important. We gotta hear them out."

She bit back her response when she saw a man sitting on the low stone wall near a patch of red and white flowers. The man was playing a recorder and tapping his right foot.

Firana said, "There is our contact. He's tapping his right foot, so that's the sign that it is safe to make contact."

"Keep your eyes open." Brandam slowed down a bit and allowed the others to move in front of him. Sarasa knew that he was taking up a position in the back to watch for a sneak attack from that angle.

The Magi slowly walked up to the musician. When they got close, Dalen said, "Hail friend. Have you seen a one-legged man running by here?"

The man on the stone wall stopped playing. He replied, "A one-legged man with the earless dog?"

Sarasa grudgingly admitted to herself that Favin's group had a pretty good system to help keep themselves from being discovered by rivals or imperial troops. The earless dog question had two possible answers. If the Magi were confident that they were not followed then they would say anything about the man having an earless dog, if they suspected that they were being followed then they were to respond that the man had no dog and then they could give the musician a message to pass to Favin.

Dalen replied, "Yes, the man with the earless dog. Seen him?"

The musician nodded. "Yeppers, please follow me."

He led the Magi down a dark alleyway, and then through a door that was mostly obscured by barrels and crates. They walked through an abandoned building and then down some stairs. The hallway came to a four-way intersection of underground passages, and the man turned to the left and continued. At the end of a long hall was a small room with a couple of seedy looking guards.

Sarasa summoned a small amount of magic and called her Magi Cloak from its storage location within the plane of magic. Instantly the grey and black cloak, identifying her as the Grand Shadow, appeared on her back and she pulled the hood over her head. The cloak was made from incredibly light material and it flowed easily as she walked. Along the front edges, and around the seam of the hood, were intricate runes embroidered in silver. She did not summon her weapons yet, but they were available in an instant if she felt that she needed them.

When the other Magi saw that she summoned her cloak, they also summoned theirs. Within a second Dalen was wearing his blue and black cloak of the Grand Champion, and Firana and Brandon were both wearing their red and white cloaks of the Order of Evokers.

The guards didn't say anything as their guide led the Magi through a door and into a large storeroom. At the far end of the storage room was a desk with a man behind it.

The man raised his head, and then stood when he saw who had entered. He smiled and walked towards them quickly. As he got close, he said, "Well met, I'm Favin. I was beginning to wonder if you were going to accept our invitation to chat."

Sarasa started to reply, but Dalen stepped forward and shook the guild leader's hand.

Dalen said, "Well met, Favin." He made introductions to each of the Magi by name and title.

The guild leader was short, coming only to Dalen's chin, but he was broad shouldered and carried himself like a man who was accustomed to combat. His long brown hair was pulled back into a single pony tail at the nape of his neck. He had multiple bladed weapons of various shapes and sizes at his belt, on his legs, and tucked into his boots.

After introductions, Favin led the Magi to the other side of the room. He said, "Please make yourself comfortable." He sat down on the opposite side of the desk.

Dalen and Firana sat down near the desk, and Brandam sat behind Dalen. Sarasa moved to the side of the room where she could see Favin and the door. She did not sit.

The guild leader said, "I'm sure you're all very busy, so let's jump straight to the point of this meeting. Several months ago, my associates and I found ourselves in possession of an Imperial Army officer. After a great deal of persuasion the officer revealed some information that I am sure you will want to know. It has to do with what the emperor knows and what his army is planning to do."

There was a pause, and after several moments Dalen asked, "Yes? Gonna tell us?"

Favin looked at each of the Magi, "This is the negotiation portion of the meeting. How much are you willing to pay my guild in exchange for this vital information?"

Sarasa hissed a curse. "Not a lousy copper falcon! Come on Dalen, I told you this was a waste. They're simply trying to squeeze coins from us. That's what these kinds of people do." She started walking towards the door.

The other Magi stood and started towards the door as well. Dalen pulled his hood over his head as he walked.

Favin stood up. "Wait! Stop. Please come back and listen."

They turned to look at him.

The guild leader motioned for them to sit back down. He said, "Please sit, this really is very serious. I will tell you the information that we have for you. At the end, if you feel it was valuable, then perhaps you will consider a donation to my guild for our services but that is up to you."

Reluctantly, Sarasa turned around. All of the Magi returned to their previous spots.

Favin sat down and continued, "According to the army officer, the emperor knows about your Stronghold and he knows how to get to it. The officer said that a large force is being prepared to march on the dwarves and then on to your Stronghold to finish off the Magi once and for all."

She sat in stunned silence. This was dire news, but she couldn't understand how Favin or the emperor would know about the Stronghold.

She had a thousand questions.

Dalen beat her to the first question. "How'd you get an Imperial officer?

Favin shook his head, "That information is irrelevant to this conversation."

Sarasa said, "Fair enough. Why were you interrogating him about the army's activities against the Magi? Surely a thieves' guild on the southern coast of the empire has more important things to worry about when it comes to city and imperial military?"

The guild leader was quiet for a long time. After a bit, he said, "Magi, I am an agent of The Shrouded, an ancient and secret guild. Our business is our own, but let's just say that The Shrouded was interested in him."

Dalen sounded skeptical, "The Shrouded? I ain't never heard of it."

Favin smiled mischievously, and replied, "Secret guilds are often unknown by most people."

"Rasa, you heard of The Shrouded?"

Sarasa shrugged and said, "I know of dozens of different secret guilds that have existed over the years. Those are just the ones I've read about in books. By their very nature, secret guilds are secretive and it's plausible to think that there have been countless others that weren't written about."

Dalen turned to Favin, "Can we talk to the imperial officer?"

"Sadly, he no longer lives." Favin shook his head slowly as he answered.

"Dammit." Dalen looked to Sarasa, and then back to Favin. "Was that it? Did he say how many soldier's they're bringing? When they'd be attacking? How they found out about the Stronghold?"

Favin answered, "He didn't know about troop strength, other than to say that it was a force larger than the one that captured Ronel last year. He made it sound like there were many logistical issues to take care of before the army could march, and that the campaign wouldn't begin until spring. He also said that a Magi came to the emperor and offered the location of the Stronghold."

That brought a gasp, various grumbles, and exclamations from the Magi.

Sarasa said, "Baeldin." It wasn't a question, she knew in her heart that it was the cowardly bastard who killed Uli and almost got her killed as well. She had sworn to herself that she'd kill the man with her own hands.

From his raised eyebrow, it was obvious that Favin was surprised at her response. He said, "Yes, that was the name that the officer gave."

She said, "We've got to warn the dwarves that the emperor's troops are going to attack."

Dalen nodded his agreement, "I agree."

He stood up and walked over to Favin. He offered his hand for a farewell handshake, and said, "Favin, you've given us good information, thanks. We'll contact you soon."

"I look forward to it." Favin held Dalen's handshake much longer than normal and they looked at each other. After a moment, Favin said, "You look so familiar and I just can't figure out how I know you."

Dalen nodded. "I've been thinking the same thing."

They released the handshake and both men stood there looking at the other for several long seconds.

Favin stomped his foot and said, "Blood Night! You competed in Blood Night a few years ago in Maethral, didn't you?"

"By the gods! Yes! You kicked my arse in the second round!" Dalen smacked the guild leader on the shoulder.

Favin smiled sheepishly, "I don't remember the details. But, yes, I have fought in Blood Night many times."

Sarasa wouldn't have recognized him if Dalen hadn't pointed it out, but now that they were talking about it she remembered Favin from that fighting festival. She said, "If I remember right, didn't you win the whole competition in Maethral?"

"I should have. There was some controversy about me not fighting fairly in the final match. Fighting fairly is against my better judgement. The whole idea of rules in a fighting competition makes me want to spit."

Blood Night was an annual fighting festival organized by the various fighting guilds throughout the empire. Each guild was an independent group, and dozens of them got together in a secret location that changed each year. The fights were illegal, but some cities were more aggressive in trying to stop them than others. Once the location was chosen, the information was spread throughout the various fighting guilds. Somehow the word got out to hundreds of spectators who were eager to watch the matches and bet on the outcomes.

Sarasa had hated the Blood Nights for years. Dalen started competing in them when he was young. Even though the matches between the children rarely led to actual bleeding, they were still quite brutal.

Favin added, "Are you planning to attend the Blood Night in DC? It's just a few days from now."

Dalen raised an eyebrow, "Darisa City? No, I'm outta the loop. I didn't even know it was coming up. I gotta check it out."

"Oh yes, that'd be great. We should be leaving now." Sarasa pulled on Dalen's shoulder to get him moving.

CHAPTER 5

Vendino

The emperor's atrium had one of the nicest flower gardens that Vendino had ever seen. He rarely had a chance to view it, since it was a private space reserved for the emperor and his family. However, when he was invited by the emperor to accompany him to the atrium, Vendino gladly accepted.

Prince Edal sat at a marble table in the middle of the atrium, playing a game of goblin squares. His opponent was the young waif named Tali, the daughter of Jalinox's assistant.

The prince was the emperor's oldest child. He had grown several inches recently, as do all children as they approach their teen years.

Vendino snubbed his nose at the young girl and turned his attention to the beautiful flowers and marble statues throughout the atrium.

The emperor sat down in a large chair, and motioned for Vendino to sit next to him.

The offered chair was luxurious and extremely comfortable. He settled in and accepted a glass of wine offered by a servant.

When the Dreg left, the emperor said, "Thorli says that two more divisions should join the main army within a fortnight. I ordered the main force to begin its assault on the dwarves immediately."

Vendino raised an eyebrow in surprise. He took a drink to consider his reply carefully. "How did Minister Thorli respond? I believe he wanted to wait until several more divisions arrived, as well as some supplies and support troops."

The emperor waved his hand dismissively. "You know how generals are. If they had their choice, they'd sit and plan endlessly and nothing would ever get accomplished."

"That reminds me, our troops have searched the countryside all around Clornoss and they can find no trace of any dwarves near here. The reports of dwarves sneaking around at night must be drunken babble, or outright falsehoods."

"Have them search again." The emperor watched his son take a move in his game, then he said, "Several of the dwarven Dregs have vanished from their owners, and we know that's not drunken babble. I want them found. If they had help then they all need captured and returned to the Dross. I won't have filthy dwarves wandering around my lands."

"Yes, My Lord."

The two sat in silence for a while and watched the children play their strategy game. The emperor smiled proudly each time his son captured one of Tali's pieces.

"Any updates on the hunt for Magi in our cities?"

Vendino groaned on the inside. The topic of increased hunting of Magi within the cities was something that made him uncomfortable. It was one thing to go after genuine Magi, but allowing Denizens to implicate their neighbors with little or no evidence was another matter entirely. He cleared his throat, "We have received reports from most of our cities that the number of Magi hangings continues to increase."

"Most? Which cities haven't reported increased progress?"

"Khardifar has only reported a handful of hangings in the last two months. Misi has not reported a single hanging of any Magi."

The emperor grunted. "How is it that Misi doesn't have a single Magi, when they're so wide-spread throughout the rest of the empire?"

"I have no idea, My Lord."

"Agent Luigey is still in Khazror, isn't he?"

Vendino nodded. "Yes, My Lord."

"Send word to him that I would like him to go to Misi. Maybe he can help the Misi Chancellor capture some Magi."

Before Vendino could answer, he heard a commotion coming from the entrance to the atrium. He looked that way and saw three people walking down the path towards them.

Two guards were walking beside Lord Jalinox, and they were pleading with him to stop.

"Please, Lord Minister. The emperor is busy and shouldn't be disturbed in his private atrium!" The guard reached out like he was going to grab Jalinox's shoulder, and then he withdrew his hand.

Jalinox ignored the guards and walked briskly towards the emperor. In a bright and cheerful voice, he said, "Ryal, there you are! I've been looking all over for you. I must say, your guards and servants are less than helpful when it comes to locating you!"

The guard looked at his emperor with fear in his eyes. He said, "Your

Majesty, he wouldn't stop! We tried to keep him from bothering you."

The emperor waved the guards away.

Jalinox walked over to the table and looked at the children's game board. He said, "A grand strategy, Tali! Our young prince probably thinks he's about to win. You're learning this game wonderfully, keep it up!"

Vendino stood up and stepped over to Jalinox. He said, "Jalinox, what do you want?"

"I've come to talk to our emperor, I have a small favor to ask."

The emperor laughed a quick and humorless laugh. "What could you possibly need now? I just gave you a new compound outside of the city, I've put you on my council, and I'm paying you a woefully large pile of coin each year. You already have everything you've demanded. Have you come to ask for more virgin Dregs?"

"Well I…" Jalinox began to answer and then paused. "I certainly won't turn down more Dreg virgins if you're offering them, but that's not why I've come. I want the Magi named Baeldin. I'd like to take him to my compound. I'd also like the other Magi that were captured in Libur last year."

Vendino returned to his chair. He was surprised by the creepy alchemist's request. The Magi named Baeldin had been in the dungeons since the day he arrived offering information about the whereabouts of the Magi Stronghold. The emperor gave him audience, and then tossed him in the dungeons. He was surprised that Jalinox even knew about the Magi captured in Libur.

Emperor Ryal said, "Baeldin claims to have more information about the Magi, but won't give the information unless I agree to grant him freedom. That's not going to happen."

Jalinox smiled, "I can help with that, oh great and wise one. Let me take the Magi and I'll extract his secrets."

"Fine, take him. Don't set him free, I don't want him returning to the other Magi. Take the other Magi prisoners as well, as long as they're all killed eventually."

With a small laugh, Jalinox gave the emperor a wink. "You have my word that they won't be set free."

"Yay! I win!" Tali squealed and stood up with both fists in the air. She bounced a little and waved her arms around in victory.

Prince Edal started putting the pieces back in their original spots. He said, "Come on, let's play again. I'm not gonna go easy on you this time."

31

CHAPTER 6

Rissyl

Peke and Bull entered the meeting room and took a seat near Ferth along the wall next to the exit.

"Now that everyone's here, let's get started." Rissyl looked around the room while he waited for everyone to quiet down.

They were gathered in the council chambers on the third floor of Summit Hall. All of the Order Magi were in the room, and even with eighteen Magi in the room it still looked mostly empty.

He continued, "As you've probably heard, Dalen and others met with a Khardifar rogue named Favin who claims that the emperor is planning an attack on the dwarves and then on us."

Sarasa interjected, "Asha and I did some scouting this morning, and there is a large imperial force gathering a few miles from the entrance to the dwarven kingdom."

Ranik, an Order of Champions Magi from the Free Cities region, sat forward in his chair. In a strong voice, he said, "The dwarves would not be in danger now if they hadn't given us assistance. We have an obligation to come to their aid."

Several Magi started talking at once, and things quickly grew loud as everyone attempted to get their point across more pointedly than the next person.

Ferth stood up and held his hands out for silence. He shouted, "Listen!" He waited for a moment for the volume to lower somewhat, and then he continued, "If we get in a direct conflict with a huge force of imperial soldiers, we're going to suffer catastrophic casualties. We're not ready for that kind of battle yet! We need to grow our numbers and our power first!"

Once again pandemonium broke out. Over the roar, a few comments stood out to Rissyl.

"Better to fight the imperials on the other side of the mountains than at the gates of our Stronghold!"

"Let the dwarves handle this, it is their battle!"

"We should attack the army from the rear while they're fighting the dwarves!"

He let the argument continue for a while, to give everyone a chance to get the bickering out of their system.

Then he noticed Brandam standing in front of his seat, patiently looking at Rissyl waiting to be given permission to speak.

Rissyl rapped his gavel several times, until the room started to grow quiet. Once he had everyone's attention, he said, "Yes, Brandam. You have something to add?"

The newest Order of Evokers Magi nodded, and said, "Maybe this is a bad time to bring this up, but I must admit, I don't know what happened to the original Magi Society. How were they defeated by Ryal I? It seems as though a large society of magic users should be able to easily defeat an army of non-magic-using soldiers."

Rissyl was surprised by the question, but he was happy for any excuse to redirect the conversation for a bit. He looked over at Sarasa and gestured for her to tell the story.

She began telling the history of events. She went into great detail about the Betrayal and the fall of the Magi Society about a century ago. She explained how the Magi had been betrayed by one of their own, and how complacent the Magi had grown. She also emphasized that since all Magi have a limited pool of magical essence at their disposal, a small group of Magi facing a massive number of standard troops would eventually run out of magical essence and need to rest while the soldiers could simply press on as long as they continued to breathe. Mostly, she stressed that the Magi were defeated because the insane emperor was willing to cause the death of tens of thousands of soldiers and innocent civilians to see to the death of a few hundred Magi.

"So, it seems to me that nothing has changed." Brandam, who was normally quiet and respectful, appeared unusually defiant.

Dalen looked perplexed, "What do you mean? Everything has changed. Unlike the Magi Society of old, most of our Magi are novices and we don't just have to deal with the imperials. We also got the sarding 'mancers to worry about."

Brandam nodded. "Good point. The situation is much worse now than it was for them. Yet, we still insist on following in their failed path. If it led to destruction for them, why do we think it will serve us any better?"

Sarasa could tell that Dalen was getting frustrated. She answered

34

before he could, "What failed path is that, Bran? We're dealing with things as best as we can as they arise."

Brandam stomped a foot on the ground for emphasis. Loudly he said, "Yes! That's exactly the problem. We are allowing the emperor to dictate the battles. He chooses when to attack, and how to attack. Then we have to try to fight his troops at their strongest. I'm not a tactical expert, but it seems to me that this is a terrible approach. We need to force the emperor and his people to fight at a disadvantage at every opportunity."

Dalen stood up, and at first Sarasa thought he was going to explode at Brandam.

He said, "Bran, you're a sarding genius! This is kinda what they teach in our fighting guild, force the enemy to fight to your advantage." Dalen paused briefly, and then added, "I like it, Bran. What ideas do you got to put the imperials on their heels?"

Brandam grinned sarcastically, "Well, the obvious suggestion is to avoid any direct attack by large numbers of imperial troops. If they have time to plan, establish supplies, and launch a large-scale attack then we're probably doomed."

Sarasa thought back to recent encounters against huge numbers of imperial troops, and she couldn't help but nod in agreement.

Brandam continued, "It's no secret that I was an imperial soldier. What we need to remember is that a large army needs to eat. They need to be paid. They also need armor, weapons, and countless supplies. All of those things take time, and many of those supplies travel the open stretches of country roads with very little armed protection."

Dalen was grinning wickedly, "Oh, Bran, this is brilliant. You just might be my hero."

Everyone laughed, and the tense mood from earlier completely vanished from the room.

Brandam said, "Another thing to consider is that for as long as the emperor sees us as a single target on the other side of the mountains, he can combine all of his troops for a large-scale attack against us. But, if we launched a bunch of attacks on the troops garrisoned in individual cities around the empire, the army would be forced to spread the troops back out to protect the garrisons. With the portal stones we could attack an area and then fade away before re-enforcements arrive. We could ambush their supply wagons, and other important shipments while they're alone and less of a threat. They'd never know where we'd strike next."

Dalen let out a growl, "Sarding right! It'll be awesome, and I'd love to capture their supply wagons and starve the bastards into giving up."

Rissyl felt a huge sense of relief. Cynia reached over and squeezed his hand, and he smiled at her. The change of tactics seemed like a fantastic idea, and he felt his spirits raise significantly. He said, "Great! After this meeting we'll break into small groups and discuss specifics."

"Speaking of small groups, I have something else to propose." Sarasa looked around the room, and then continued. "A few centuries ago, Grand Evoker Mellentinos issued an order that all potentially dangerous missions be conducted with at least one Magi from each Order present. He referred to these groups as a Cadre. His reasoning was that a full Cadre of Magi would ensure that each group was adequately equipped to handle every situation since they'd have access to the full spectrum of magical spells. I thought this had merit."

Rissyl listened as a handful of Magi discussed her idea. Overall the comments were supportive and no one had anything negative to say about it. He thought it was a good idea. "Great suggestion, Rasa. Simple patrols and other routine things can still be handled by Society Magi or mixed groups of Order and Society Magi. But, let's do our best to follow this example as we take on more dangerous missions to harass the imperials."

The room was quiet for a few seconds, and then Zahr stood up. He said, "Riz, what are we going to do about the 'mancers? They ransacked our Stronghold and stole... we don't even know what. We've pretty much ignored them for a year, and if we're not careful they're going to spring up and bite us when we're most vulnerable. I don't trust that they just vanished, they're up to something."

With that, Rissyl's newfound optimism dipped sharply. He'd tried to push the problem with the necromancers to the back of his mind, since they hadn't been an immediate threat. He replied, "I'm not sure there is anything we can do, right now. We don't even know where they're hiding?"

The Order of Diviners Magi from the Libur Coterie, Eleyne, stood up and said, "Riz, I've heard several rumors of people being abducted by 'mancers. Sometimes people have been abducted right in the middle of cities, with several witnesses. The rumors come from different cities all around the empire."

Several gasps from around the room told Rissyl that he wasn't the only one in the room that was shocked. However, some of the other Magi had heard rumors as well, and soon several people were comparing rumors and stories that they'd heard.

Rissyl sighed, "Do we have any ideas what they might be up to this time?"

No one offered any suggestions.

He continued, "Me either. All we can do is keep our eyes open. If you can intervene, do so. Especially if we can capture one of the 'mancers and figure out what is going on."

Thon, the fighting guild master from Sorgo, stood for his turn to talk. He asked, "What about the Rolimi? Have they decided against retaliating against all humans for the necromancer attack on their people?"

Rissyl's optimism continued to drop. He shook his head, and said, "No, there has been no word from them at all. They might have decided to shun us, or there could be a large army of gods-blessed creatures from the plane of magic on their way to destroy us all. It's been over a year for us, but time works differently in the plane of magic and for them it's only been a little over a month. As slowly as they debate things, there is no telling how long it will be before they even come to a decision. It'd be nice if they choose peace, but knowing our luck they'll show up ready for battle at the worst possible moment."

He looked out across the room and saw the expressions of concern on the faces of his fellow Magi and knew that he needed to find a way to end the meeting on a good note.

He said, "We can't focus on the things we can't control. Let's break into small groups and discuss positive tactics to deal with the emperor's army. If anything changes with the Rolimi or the 'mancers then we'll deal with that as it comes. Now, let's talk about good news. What exciting and useful magical artifacts have we discovered since our last meeting?"

The sudden smiles on several faces told him that he picked the perfect topic to end the meeting.

The door opened, and Ayris came running into the room. She sprinted at Rissyl and jumped into his lap.

Ayris came into the picture around a year ago. She was orphaned after the imperial invasion of Ront'El, and she had been rescued by Rissyl and Cynia. Several months ago, Cynia asked Sarge to perform a ceremony binding them as her parents in the eyes of Kelegar. Ayris had become a loving and attentive sister to her new brother Chardy, and she was quickly adjusting to her new life.

He held her close and watched as several of the Magi began talking about new artifacts that had been discovered in the Order Halls.

CHAPTER 7

Sarge

The early morning sun shined in through the colored glass windows, casting light on an altar in the middle of a large dais. Several candles were burning on the altar, and Madalyn knelt before it. Her fists were clinched at her chest, her elbows were pointed straight to the sides, and her head was bowed in the solemn attitude of prayer to her deity.

The girl had matured considerably since Sarge had first recruited her to be Kelegar's cleric, a little over a year ago. When he first met her, Sarge questioned whether she was old enough to face the challenges that would surely fall upon Kelegar's first cleric. Over the last year she had grown into a young woman and she had grown significantly in her faith.

The divine-sire had given her wisdom and guidance, and granted his powers for her use. Since becoming his cleric she spent much of her time with her head bowed in prayer. When she wasn't praying or sleeping, she was usually learning to read the ancient Menelian language and doing research in tomes on ancient theology that she found in the libraries at the fort.

Rissyl had given them the choice of any of the temples in the Stronghold to use as the first Kelegarian Temple in modern times. Sarge let Madalyn choose, and she chose the largest temple with the simplest features. The building didn't have many pillars or flourishes, but it was spacious and could house a few hundred worshipers.

Madalyn's bright blond hair was left loose and it hung low, well past her shoulders, as she knelt with her head bowed. She was dressed in long silken robes of white, trimmed in silver and blue. They found the robes in the basement of the temple and she worked late into the nights for a fortnight to embroider Kelegar's symbol on the left breast area.

The months had flown past very quickly, and Sarge knew that the time for preparation was drawing to a close and the time for action was upon them. He felt a chill creep down his spine as he thought about the hard times ahead. He'd grown to care deeply about the young cleric and he feared what would become of her in the impending war. He didn't have any children of his own, but in his heart the young woman who knelt at the altar before him was as dear to him as any daughter could ever be.

He knelt before the front pew in the temple, facing the altar. For an hour or more he joined her in quiet prayer and devotions to Kelegar.

When he stood up his muscles were stiff, and he stretched his back and sides. Kneeling for hours in prayer was rewarding spiritually, but it was awful for his poor old back and knees.

He was a middle-aged warrior and Magi, who had spent most of his youth exploring the countryside north of the empire throughout the lands of the Free Cities. A little more than a year ago, he answered the call of the divine-sire and became the Azure Paladin.

For most of his life he had wandered from place to place just trying to make a living. Over the years, he fought for many causes and he patrolled the countryside as a Magi looking for necromancers, but, although he didn't realize it at the time, his life had little direction or focus.

Now, as the Azure Paladin, he knew what he was meant to do. During his weeks on the islands with the Kelegarian Zealots many truths were revealed to him by the divine-sire. With the young cleric at his side, he was meant to spread the word of his divine-sire while helping the cause of the Magi.

He grumbled to himself as he twisted back and forth at the waist and tried to work the kinks out of his old bones.

Madalyn stood up quietly and turned to him. "Something wrong?"

"Nothing, just bellyaching. I'm too old to kneel for so long." He sat down on the pew, "We should have some time today, do you want to stop by the training hall and practice some hand to hand combat?"

She shook her head and sat down beside him. "We've discussed this a bunch. I won't fight people."

He sighed, and it came out more like a low growl. "Some folks ain't gonna give you a choice. You've gotta learn how to protect yourself."

She gave him a genuinely confused expression. "Why would I need to fight when I have Kelegar to protect me?"

Sarge rubbed his palms down his face in frustration. "Kiddo, it don't work like that. Kelegar ain't coming here to protect you himself. He's given you the skills to learn to protect yourself."

She patted him on the shoulder, "And he's sent me a strong Azure Paladin to keep me safe."

Turning to look at her, he started to protest.

She shook her head again. "Theo, I'm not gonna hurt people. My destiny is to heal, not to harm. If anyone should understand that, it should be you."

A few months ago she had started calling him Theo. She had asked why everyone called him Sarge, and then asked his real name. When he told her that his given name was Theodonis, she decided to start calling him Theo. He wouldn't admit it, but he liked that there was a name that only she called him. It wasn't like she was calling him father or papa, but it was different than what others called him and he liked that.

Before he could respond to her, the door to the sanctuary opened behind them. He turned to see Rissyl and Cynia walking in.

Sarge stood up and moved to meet them halfway down the row of pews. "Well, if it ain't the Grand Evoker and Grand Diviner, descending from on high in their fancy new cloaks to mingle with us lowly folk in the temple."

Rissyl laughed and met the gruff warrior's strong handshake, placing his other hand on Sarge's shoulder. "It's good to see you, Sarge. It looks like things are coming along nicely in your new temple."

Madalyn stepped over to the group, smiling greetings. She said, "It's ready for you to devote your soul to Kelegar, if that's why you've come."

"Wow, no. Actually, ah..." Rissyl stammered, and then cleared his throat. "Cynia and I have been talking, and we have an idea. With the imperials increasingly harassing and persecuting the Denizens while looking for Magi, it is likely that many people are starting to grow tired of this treatment. Many of them may already see the emperor and his men as the villains. If we can make the people view the Magi Society as the heroes, that would be helpful."

Sarge nodded, "Not a terrible idea. How wouldya do it?"

The Grand Evoker smiled. "I was hoping you'd take on that task."

Sarge laughed boisterously for a bit. When he calmed, he said, "If I was gonna pick someone for that task, I'd be the last guy I'd pick."

Rissyl shrugged, "You're planning to heal people and spread the word about Kelegar, right? Are you almost ready to begin? You could start now, and do it in the name of the Magi Society."

Sarge started to respond but Madalyn beat him to it. She said, "We're more than ready. But we'll do it in the name of Kelegar, with the Magi Society's help."

Rissyl looked like he might protest, then he said, "That would be great.

When you leave, please take Asha, Brandam, and Peke with you so you have a full Cadre."

Sarge grunted. "Have I mentioned that I prefer to work alone? I don't really like people all that much."

Madalyn gave him a stern look.

He sighed. "Fine, they can tag along."

- = - = -

The next morning Sarge, Peke, Asha, Brandam, and Madalyn were walking through the streets of Khazror. None of them were wearing their Magi Cloaks. They were all wearing simple traveling garb except for Sarge who was wearing his Azure Paladin armor under his traveling robes and Madalyn who insisted on wearing her white clerical robes which were trimmed in silver and blue.

They'd been walking through the large city for nearly an hour.

"Do we have a destination in mind? Should we ask someone how to get there?" Peke had been impatient to ask for directions since they'd first passed through the gates after taking the portal stone and arriving just outside the city.

The young cleric shook her head. "Kelegar will lead us where we need to be."

Brandam and Peke glanced at each other, and Sarge bit-back his sarcastic comments. He was anxious to get started as well, so he understood the other Magi's impatience. However, he didn't want to hurt the girl's feelings and he was proud of her growing faith so he held his tongue.

They continued to follow her through the maze of streets. Eventually, she turned and walked up the stairs of a large temple. To the side of the door was a large sign with the symbol of Kason, the deity that most people worshiped.

Before becoming the Azure Paladin, Sarge had never been a very religious man. However, on holidays and such when he did attend religious services, they were almost always services held at a Kasonite temple.

Madalyn walked through the door and entered the temple without waiting to see what the other Magi were going to do. Sarge followed her in, and the other Magi entered after him.

42

The benches of the sanctuary held a few dozen worshipers, and a Kasonite preacher stood on the dais in the front of the sanctuary. He was in the middle of a sermon.

The preacher continued his sermon, saying, "On that day, the farmer went out into his fields with his threshing scythe in hand, leading a group of fifty-seven servants. Through his hard work, leading by example, and by relentlessly pushing the fifty-seven servants to work hard the farmer reaped the rewards of yet another large harvest season that were graciously provided by Kason."

Even though the preacher tried to carry on with his prepared sermon, most of the worshipers turned their attention to the new arrivals. Madalyn walked all of the way to the front of the sanctuary, with Sarge at her side. The other Magi stopped along the outside of the sanctuary near the front benches.

Without being invited, Madalyn walked up onto the dais and approached the preacher. Sarge walked quietly beside her.

Once they moved onto his dais, the preacher finally turned his attention to the new arrivals. He said, "Children of Kason, I must ask you to take a seat among the congregation. The time to approach the altar to ask for salvation will come after my sermon." The preacher motioned for them to move down to the benches.

Madalyn nodded briefly to the preacher, and then turned to face the worshipers. She said, "People of Khazror, I have traveled far to spread the word that the divine-sire has returned! Kelegar has returned from his solitude and he will open his arms to all who worship him above all other deities!"

"Blasphemy!" The preacher moved to grab Madalyn, but Sarge reached out and gently pushed the preacher back. In a loud voice, the old preacher shouted, "This is a house of worship for Kason, the most revered of the Pantheon of Nine! I will not tolerate heresy in this holy place!"

Madalyn continued as if nothing had happened. "Kelegar is the sire of five of the Pantheon of Nine, and he reigned supreme for eons. Long ago our ancient ancestors turned from him to a life of avarice and debauchery. But this is our chance to make amends and devote our souls to the one true creator of life!"

The people in the crowd sat in stunned silence, while the preacher turned bright red with rage.

A young man in the front row stood up and shouted, "Wench, get off

43

the stage before I come up there and drag you down! We came to receive the blessings of Kason, not to hear this blasphemy."

Madalyn walked to the front edge of the dais and knelt before the young man, so that her face was on the same level as her heckler. She pointed at the middle-aged woman sitting next to the man. She asked, "Is that your mother?"

The mother sat quietly and stared at the floor, as she had the entire time that Sarge had been on the dais. It was obvious that the woman was dim-witted or somehow not completely well.

The man sounded annoyed, and said, "Yes, what about her?"

The young cleric asked, "What's wrong with her?"

There was a long pause, as the man looked at his mother. Finally, he looked back to Madalyn and there was a tear streaming down his cheek. He said, "She ain't been the same since Pa passed. She locked herself away inside. Won't talk or work around the house. We can barely get her to eat sometimes."

Madalyn hopped down from the stage and knelt in front of the woman. She placed her hands on the woman's shoulders, and said, "Blessed Kelegar, I ask you to bring peace to this woman. Fill the void left in her heart by the passing of her husband with the love and joy of your divine grace. You are the sire of gods and the one true creator of life. If it is your will, please grant me this prayer."

Several people from the crowd moved forward so they could better see what was happening in the front. For a moment it was silent throughout the temple.

The quiet was broken by the woman sitting before the young cleric. In a raspy voice she said, "What gift have you given me, child?"

The young man said, "Mother? You spoke!"

Several people in the congregation started whispering and murmuring to each other.

The woman looked at her son, "This girl speaks the truth, I can feel the warmth of Kelegar in the depths of my soul. While she prayed for me, I had a vision of your father. I see now that it makes him sad that I've retreated from my family, and he wishes for me to make the most of the time I have left to live."

Madalyn stood up, "Ma'am, I hope you've found peace. The divine-sire wants us all to enjoy our time alive and make the most of this gift before the day of his judgement."

44

"You have given me peace, and understanding."

The young cleric shook her head, "I have given nothing, the blessings come from Kelegar. I must ask, did you feel the presence of Kelegar within your heart? Do you feel the presence of Kason when you pray to him?"

The preacher grumbled, "This is an outrage! Someone summon the sentinels!"

No one moved to follow the preacher's orders, as they were all captivated by what was happening in front of the dais.

The woman stood up and raised her hands. "Yes, girl! I feel the power and joy of Kelegar deep in my heart. I've come to the Kasonite temple all my life, and I've never felt anything like this! I can feel that Kelegar loves me and wants me to devote myself to him. There is a sense of warmth and peace within me."

Madalyn climbed back onto the dais and moved behind the altar. She said, "If you truly wish to give yourself to Kelegar, the time is at hand. The divine-sire insists that all followers faithfully adhere to his three Divine Directives. First that you will worship no god above him, and that you observe a sacred Sabbath Day every fifth day dedicated to worship and prayer. Second, that you will not lie, steal, cheat, or murder. Third, that you will live as a shining example of purity, morality, charity, honesty, and modesty. Those who accept him and live by his directives will be graced with an eternity in a paradise like no other!"

She motioned for the woman and others to form a line in front of her. She bowed her head, placed her fists at her chest with her elbows out to the side, and said a silent prayer.

When she finished, she carefully removed all of the Kasonite items from the altar and set them aside. Then she pulled a simple silk cloth from a pouch and draped it over the altar. On the front of the cloth was an embroidered symbol of Kelegar.

Then she pulled several candles, small pots of incense, and single blue rose from the pouch and spread them around the altar. Finally, she pulled out a scroll and unrolled it carefully. The parchment was ancient and tattered, and on it were written some of the holy words from ancient Kelegarian writings.

Sarge and Madalyn hadn't found very many of the Kelegarian writings yet, and they treasured each one they had. Madalyn insisted that they bring this one page so they'd have the holy words on the altar when she gave Kelegar's blessings.

Madalyn encouraged the woman to kneel before the altar, and then the young cleric knelt behind the altar. Both of them faced each other. She led the woman through a lengthy prayer of devotion and promise to serve and evangelize.

For over an hour, Sarge stood on the dais and watched the girl lead every member of the congregation through the blessings and devotions to Kelegar.

The preacher leaned over to Sarge, and said, "The girl must be some kind of Magi. She's enthralled my entire congregation!"

Sarge looked over at the frustrated preacher. He said, "We are Magi, but she is truly a cleric of Kelegar. The two things are separate, and what you see here is the work of the divine-sire."

"You really are Magi?"

He nodded to the preacher.

For a long while, the preacher watched the events at the altar. Then he said, "If you're truly Magi, maybe you can help my niece? They're going to hang her this afternoon because she was falsely accused of being what you say you are. I've talked to several magistrates, and no one else will help her."

CHAPTER 8

Ferth

"The compound is large and could probably hold hundreds, or thousands, of soldiers!" Kyoso, a Shadow Magi, spread his arms wide dramatically to drive home his point. He spoke quickly as if the excitement was almost too much to bear.

Kyoso took a deep breath, and let it out slowly. When he spoke again it was more composed, almost disappointed. "But now it looks mostly empty. There's only about twenty soldiers in there. Most of them were cleaning and working on general maintenance." He sat down in the grass next to Bull.

Ferth tossed a biscuit to him, and then pulled another out of a bag for himself.

Kyoso was a young Magi from the Free Cities region. He was shorter than most men, and of slight build. His light brown hair was long and wild. Ferth guessed that the man was in his late twenties. When the other Free Cities Magi answered the call, and joined with Rissyl and the Magi from the empire, Kyoso stayed away. He didn't answer the summons until just a few months ago, and the Magi Council quickly selected him to join the Shadows.

Ferth was surprised that the council didn't leave him as a Society Magi for a while, if for no other reason than as a punishment for ignoring the earlier summons. However, he had to admit that the young Shadow Magi had some impressive skills. He was also more than a little odd.

With a groan, Bull stood up and wiped the biscuit crumbs from his clothing. He tied his bag closed, fastened it to his belt, and then looked down the gentle hill towards the imperial army compound far off in the distance. "Well, let's go storm the gates."

"The council wants us to spread chaos." Ferth stood up, and held out his hand to help Zahr to his feet. "Let's go spread some chaos."

"Wait! Kyoso has a plan!" Kyoso did a backwards roll from a seated position, and ended on his feet with his arms out to the sides. He beckoned the other Magi closer like he was going to share an important secret. In a slow and quiet voice, he said, "We should use..." After a brief pause, he said loudly, "The rings!" As he finished, he pointed both hands towards Ferth.

Looking down at the two rings on his hands, Ferth smiled. Originally, they planned to use the rings as a quick escape method, but Ferth had to admit that the eccentric Shadow Magi had a good idea.

The rings were a pair of magical artifacts that they had discovered in Evoker Hall. Each ring could create a magical portal, one serving as a gateway to the other.

He took off the destination ring and handed it to Kyoso. "We'll wait here. Make sure you activate your ring someplace safe, I don't want to port right into a fight."

The Shadow Magi placed his hand on Ferth's shoulder, and said, "Kyoso will not fail you!" Then he took off running towards the army compound. After a few strides he made himself invisible.

The remaining three Magi stood in silence for quite a while, watching the compound.

Bull asked, "Why does he refer to himself by name? It's weird. We know he is Kyoso, he doesn't have to tell us."

The other two Magi looked at him briefly, and then they both started laughing.

Zahr said, "Of all of the peculiar things that he does, that's the one you point out? Earlier today, I saw him talking to himself as we walked here."

"Actually, he wasn't talking to himself. He carries a little river rock in his shirt pocket and he claims it's a sentient rock named Barthalamu."

Taking a step away from the others, Ferth held up his right hand and summoned a small amount of magic to activate the ring. A large portal appeared in front of his palm. It was about six feet tall and three feet wide, shaped like an oval disk standing on end. The portal was made entirely from swirling light of all different colors, the light swirled mainly counter-clockwise although there were many small vortexes of swirling light scattered about the portal that were circling clockwise.

"Very impressive." Zahr smiled. "How do we know when Kyoso is ready with the portal on the other end?"

"Oh, you'll know. Trust me, there is no mistaking when the portal on the other end has been opened." Ferth put his hand down, and moved away from the swirling portal.

The Magi stood for several minutes watching the mesmerizing swirling

48

colors.

Bull plopped down into the grass ungracefully. He said, "It's a long way to the compound, it'll probably take him a while. I should sit." He rolled onto one side and propped his head with his hand. "How long will this portal stay here?"

Ferth took a step closer and sat down next to his friend. "I'm not sure. When we tested them we saw that the source portal will vanish shortly after the person wearing the source ring steps through it. The destination portal also vanishes shortly after the person with the source ring steps through it. But we didn't activate any portals and just let them sit until they vanished on their own, so I'm not sure. Maybe a few minutes, maybe for centuries?"

The conversation died down and for well over half an hour the three Magi stared at the portal, as if transfixed by the ever-evolving patterns.

Then the swirling colors began to change. The spinning colors around the outside border of the portal remained the same, but the middle of the portal morphed into a shimmering image giving a glimpse of what the destination looked like. Ferth could see what looked like a narrow path between a couple of long rows of small buildings.

He stood up and motioned for the others to use the portal.

Zahr got to the portal first. He reached out and pushed his hand into the portal without hesitation. Instantly the Magi seemed to be pulled into the portal, and his body appeared to become elongated and started to rotate in conjunction with the colors swirling around the outside of the portal.

"By the gods, did you see that?" Bull jumped up. "Is he dead? It twisted him like a noodle!"

"He's fine, Bull. It's your turn."

For a moment, Ferth thought that Bull might refuse to touch the portal. After a little bit of coaxing, the big Magi reached out and touched the portal. As soon as Bull was through, Ferth touched the portal as well.

After a moment of slight vertigo, he was in the middle of the army compound, next to the other Magi. As he expected, the portal had vanished as he stepped through it. The familiar dizziness of teleporting was flirting around in his head, but it wasn't nearly as bad as when they used the portal stones.

He removed the teleporting ring and held it out to Kyoso. "Trade me rings, so we're prepared to make a quick exit if needed."

As an Evoker, Ferth could teleport without needing portal stones or rings as long as he could visualize his destination. Their exit plan, if things got ugly, was for Ferth to teleport somewhere safe and then activate his portal ring so the other Magi could join him using the portal ring that Kyoso was putting on his finger.

Ferth asked, "So, how are we doing this? Wandering around and killing imperial soldiers indiscriminately? Do we give them the opportunity to surrender?"

Bull and Kyoso looked at each other and shrugged.

Kyoso said, "You're the Evoker. Lead us."

He felt someone tap him heavily on the shoulder. He turned and Zahr held a bracelet out to him.

Zahr said, "Hold that for a minute." As soon as Ferth took the bracelet from his hand, the Diviner muttered something under his breath. Ferth couldn't hear exactly what he said, but he could tell that it was Menelian and he assumed that it was the verbal trigger for a spell.

His assumption was proven as Zahr quickly transformed into a large bird of prey. Ferth wasn't an expert on bird species, but he was pretty sure that Zahr was now some sort of large eagle.

Zahr the eagle stood almost four feet tall from talons to the top of his head. He was dark brown all over, had a dark brown beak, and dull yellow talons. The eagle reached over and took the bracelet out of Ferth's hand with its beak. Then it leaned forward and carefully pushed its talons through the bracelet.

The eagle jumped up, spread his huge wings, and gracefully flew into the air. Ferth noticed that the bracelet was still upon the eagle's right leg as it climbed high into the air.

The other three Magi stared at the eagle as it soared into the sky.

"Wow." Bull placed a hand on one of the small buildings as he tilted his head back to follow the eagle's flight into the sky.

"Kyoso should have chosen a green cup. Would be fun to fly like a bird!" The Shadow Magi kicked at a dirt clod on the ground. Then he dropped an *Invisibility* spell on himself.

Ferth said, "Let's go." He led the way through several buildings until they came to a large open area. As they stepped into it, he saw several soldiers standing around the grassy area. Some were doing yard work, and some were doing some sort of maintenance on a few of the buildings.

Only Ferth and Bull were visible, and they were both wearing their

Magi Cloaks as they stepped into the open area. Ferth had his staff in hand and Bull had his sword drawn but the tip was pointed at the ground.

One of the soldier shouted, "Sarding Khalius! Magi! Right over here! Get them!"

"Wait! Stay where you are, no one needs to get hurt!" Ferth held up his empty hand, palm forward, urging the soldiers to stay where they were.

From his left, Ferth heard the unmistakable TWANG sound of a bow being fired. That was followed immediately by a streak of light and a scream from one of the soldiers.

The soldier who ordered the others to attack stopped in his tracks. He looked down at his chest and there was a magical arrow deep in his chest. The arrow was mostly transparent, and traced in magical light much like the Rolimi. The arrow quickly vanished leaving a large gaping hole in the soldier's chest. The man screamed and grabbed at his chest, as he fell to the ground.

Kyoso, who was once again visible, pointed at the fallen soldier and said, "Except that one. That one needed to get hurt. So, Kyoso hurt him." The Shadow Magi drew back his empty bow, and a magical arrow like the last one appeared in the bow as the Magi brought the bowstring to a full draw. He aimed and fired the magical arrow.

A scream from another soldier verified another hit.

"And that one. Kyoso hurt him as well."

The soldiers drew their weapons as they charged the three Magi.

Under his breath, Ferth muttered, "Dammit, Kyoso." As he did, he raised his left hand and pointed the index and pinky fingers at the closest soldier. He said, "Krol'Fe." A small mint green orb of magic shot forward towards the soldier. The magical sphere of force slammed into the soldier's face, knocking him backwards as his feet flew out from under him. The man landed on his head first, and dropped awkwardly to the ground.

A screech from high in the sky drew Ferth's attention upwards. He saw Zahr, the eagle, diving quickly towards the ground. His long wings were stretched wide and his talons were extended forward. The bracelet flashed briefly as the sun gleamed off of it. With another screech the eagle changed the pitch of his dive and turned slightly. Several magical spheres of fire shot from the eagle's talon. Ferth knew that the Magi was using the bracelet as a focus for his spells.

One after another, a dozen large balls of fire smashed onto the ground. The first several fireballs missed the soldiers as they rushed towards the Magi on the ground. The next few spheres hit their marks, and several soldiers met a fiery death in the midst of the terrible fire spheres.

The remaining soldiers dove for cover, looking to the sky for the bird to circle back around.

Ferth watched the battlefield carefully, waiting for the right moment to strike. He saw Kyoso fire a continuous storm of magical arrows at many of the soldiers.

Bull stood near the Evoker, waiting for an adversary to move into melee range. He hollered, "Surrender is your only option if you want to live! Drop your weapons and surrender!"

"No! Don't surrender! Kyoso wants to shoot you! Come out where I can see you!" Kyoso laughed maniacally.

One soldier shouted, "Everyone rush the Magi archer!" He jumped out from behind a barrel and rushed towards the Magi.

Just as other soldiers left their hastily selected places of cover, Zahr landed next to Ferth. One moment he looked like a large bird, and the next moment he was man-shaped once again. In his natural form, Zahr raised his right hand and said, "Raeln'Esti."

Immediately the lead soldier froze in his tracks, his feet had become solid stone and they were rooted in the ground. The stone condition quickly spread to the man's legs and then his torso.

The soldier screamed in terror, begging someone to help him as he thrashed around the parts of his body that would still move. The petrification continued to spread quickly, and within moments only the man's head remained flesh. The screaming stopped abruptly as the soldier turned completely to stone.

The whole area grew eerily quiet as the remaining soldiers slowed to a stop and stared at their leader in disbelief.

Kyoso laughed, and then said, "Very nice! Kyoso's impressed!"

Ferth lowered the tip of his staff and pointed it at the stone soldier. He quickly summoned magic and focused it through the staff. A series of greyish rings sped from the tip of his staff and rushed towards the immobile soldier. A low humming sound rang out from the grey rings as they pulsed rhythmically on their way towards their target. When the first grey rings struck the soldier, his stone skin started to crack. The pulsating grey rings pounded the man one after the other, the cracks widened, and quickly the man started to break apart. Even as the soldier's body began to break up, the steady stream of humming and rhythmically pulsating rings continued to bombard him.

Suddenly the petrified man shattered. His entire body, including the parts that were falling to the ground, exploded into a huge cloud of tiny stone chunks.

The Evoker ended his spell, and the grey rings stopped shooting from the end of his staff. He placed the end on the ground, pointing the tip to the sky, and looked around at the rest of the soldiers.

Several of them had fallen to the ground to retch, and some stared in shocked horror. All of them dropped their weapons and surrendered.

Kyoso groaned and caused his magic bow to vanish back to its storage place in the plane of magic. He drew a dagger, and dropped an *Invisibility* spell on himself once again.

Bull walked towards their captives with his sword drawn. He said, "Everyone form a line over here, with your hands on your head. If you move, I'll let those two turn you into a pile of stone shards!"

Ferth looked over to the place where the stone soldier had stood. Now it was just a layer of rubble covering the ground for several yards in every direction, and a pair of stone feet were still anchored to the ground. He and Zahr had talked about combining those two spells, but he had no idea that they'd work so well together. He thought that perhaps he should feel some sort of regret or remorse about the death of the soldier. Fortunately, he did not.

He walked over to the line of captives. There were nine of them. Ferth said, "So, Magi, what should we do with captives? I never really expected to be in this situation."

From somewhere behind the captives, the voice of Kyoso said, "Kill them!"

Zahr stepped towards the line of imperial soldiers. "Let me read them."

Ferth nodded. "Very well. You will be judged by the Diviner. If you are found to not be a threat to the Magi, you'll be released unharmed immediately. If you are found to be a threat to the Magi..." He paused, unsure how to proceed.

Predictably, Kyoso finished the statement. "You'll be killed!"

As the captives began to complain, Bull held up his hand.

Bull said, "Ferth, what about the dungeons? Asha found a very large series of cells below one of the guild buildings at Fort Randol. We could take them there and lock them in the dungeon until the council decides what to do with them. We can't just release them, and it don't feel right to kill them in cold blood."

"Yes, she showed the dungeon to me, but how would we get the prisoners there? I'm not walking all the way."

"With the portal rings? The portals don't require magic once they're created. Maybe we can use the rings to get the prisoners there?"

Ferth rubbed his chin. After a bit, he said, "Fine. If you're found to be a threat to the Magi you will be confined to the dungeon at Fort Randol until the Magi Council decides what to do with you."

Pandemonium broke out as the captive soldiers all began to protest and shout.

One soldier tried to run. He quickly screamed out, as Kyoso reappeared from his invisibility in front of the fleeing soldier and smashed his dagger into the imperial's chest. The soldier dropped to the ground holding his bleeding chest, and Kyoso looked around smiling.

He said, "Someone else run, please!" He laughed wildly.

The remaining eight soldiers grew quiet once again.

One of the many new spells that Ferth had discovered in his research in Evoker Hall was a spell called *Create Mundane Item*. It was a fairly intricate spell, and it used a large amount of the magical essence from his Magewel, but he knew as soon as he discovered it that it'd be a very useful spell to memorize. It allowed him to create some simple object from thin air.

He cleared his mind and began summoning the magic needed for the spell. Then he molded and formed the magic into an intricate pattern in his mind, the exact shape was influenced largely by the item being created. He'd practiced it a few times, but each time the spell was formed differently as he created different things.

When the spell was ready, he said, "Mayl'ozi."

Fizzle.

Ferth cursed under his breath. There were few things that he hated as much as the fizzling sound of a spell failing. There were actually only fifteen things he hated more. The fizzle sound was sixteen on his Sarding Grubby Chippies list.

Bull and Kyoso both laughed out loud at the sound of Ferth's spell failure.

Kyoso said, "Don't feel bad, Ferth. Lots of novice Magi fizzle their spells."

He felt about as amused as the prisoners looked, but the other Magi laughed at Kyoso's joke. Ferth gave Kyoso an annoyed expression and flashed rude gestures at him with both hands.

He started the spell over. The magical essence used for the spell that failed was simply lost. So, he'd have to spend another large portion of his remaining magical essence to try casting the spell once again. Once the spell was ready, he whispered the trigger word, "Mayl'ozi."

A long portion of rope appeared in his hand. Ferth held the rope up, pointing at Bull and then Kyoso while giving them both a big grin. He tossed the rope to the Shadow Magi and said, "Cut this up and bind each prisoner's hands behind their back."

When Kyoso finished binding the first prisoner, Zahr walked over to the man. He asked, "If we let you go, will you retire to a peaceful life or will you seek out ways to further battle the Magi?"

The man didn't answer and Ferth could tell that Zahr had opened his Magesight. As a Diviner, Zahr would be able to see deep into the man's soul. When he finished, there would be no doubts about the man's past, his desires, or his future intentions.

Almost a full minute passed as Zahr stared quietly into the soldier's eyes. When he took a step back, he looked to Ferth. He said, "This man will always be a threat. If we release him, he'll stop at nothing to rejoin the emperor's armies to hunt us down."

Ferth nodded once, "Thank you, Zahr. Bull, place that man over there and make him sit until we're finished."

Bull led the man to a place near one of the small buildings and said, "Sit. Don't move."

Moving to the next prisoner, Zahr asked him the same question he'd asked the first prisoner. The man remained quiet.

He stared into the soldier's eyes for a short time, then he turned to Ferth. "This man is a murder and a psychopath. He bullies and blackmails his fellow soldiers, and has a burning desire to kill even more people. I say we should kill him now."

Ferth looked at the soldier for a moment, and then said, "The Magi Council will decide his fate. Place him with the other, and we'll take him to the dungeons."

The interrogations dragged on for much longer than Ferth would have liked. Before long he sat down on a low stone wall as things progressed. As all eight of the remaining soldiers were judged by Zahr, they were separated into two different groups. There were five soldiers to be teleported back to the Stronghold, and three soldiers set to be released.

Zahr rubbed his temples as he stepped away from the last prisoner, Ferth could tell that reading the prisoners had taken a lot out of the Diviner.

With a quick nod, Ferth instructed Bull to release the prisoners who were to go free. Once they were untied, Ferth walked over to them.

He said, "Go in peace, and spread the word if you wish. The Magi are going on the offensive, and we will treat any threat without mercy. You've seen what we can do, and the four Magi before you are not even the strongest Magi in our Society. If you care for your friends and neighbors, encourage them to reject the emperor's unethical war against the Magi. We don't want to fight, and we don't want to harm anyone. However, we will not sit quietly and allow the emperor's people to hunt us wherever we go!"

The three men thanked him profusely for allowing them to leave unharmed, and soon all three of them rushed away from the Magi on their way to whatever new life they desired. As Ferth watched them hurry away, he felt a sense of happiness. He wished more people were like those soldiers, and could just be sent away to live peacefully.

He turned his attention to the five remaining captives. He sighed to himself, and then said, "I'll port back and open a portal for you, directly into the dungeon. If any of the prisoners give you any problems at all, kill them."

"Kyoso will be most happy to kill them!" The unusual Shadow Magi smiled sincerely.

Ferth stepped away from the prisoners and quickly summoned the magic for his teleportation spell. When it was ready, he said, "Kur'Gezbar."

Instantly his scenery changed, as he arrived within the heart of the Stronghold. He waited for a moment for the dizziness to pass, and then quickly made his way to the guild building that housed the stairs down to the dungeon. Once inside, he went down the long, steep, and narrow stairway into the dungeon.

He tossed a few light orbs at the walls as he walked through the cold and dank corridors. The narrow corridor opened into a large room that served as a guard post.

On the far side of the room was a small window and a large metal door which stood ajar. The room contained a small cluttered desk with a chair in front of it, a large weapon rack along one wall, and a shelf with a number of sets of manacles sitting on it. In the middle of the room was a large wooden table with several chairs around it, and a dusty old deck of cards spread across it.

He walked over to the desk and moved some of the papers and other abandoned clutter, looking for cell keys. Not finding them, he pulled open the top drawer. Sitting on top of a big pile of junk was a large metal ring with a single key.

Grabbing the key, he headed through the metal door and down the corridor. It was lined with small cells on either side. He walked to the end and turned the corner. The cells continued on for quite a distance, and then the corridor turned again. He didn't know how many cells were within their dungeon, but just the first corridor had twenty of them. That was more than what they'd need for the five prisoners.

He activated the magic ring, causing a swirling portal to appear within the hallway. Within a few moments, Bull came through the portal followed by all five of the prisoners. Finally, Zahr and Kyoso stepped through, and the portal closed behind them.

The Magi quickly ushered the prisoners into cells, and Ferth walked around locking each cell door behind them.

CHAPTER 9

Sarge

When the Magi entered Khazror's bazaar, Sarge was shocked at how many people were gathered around the gallows. The crowd stretched back to the houses around the east side of the bazaar, and people fanned out to the north and south trying to get close enough to see the show up on the gallows.

On the platform was a large contraption designed to allow several people to be hanged at once. There were five people on the gallows, standing on barrels with the hangman's noose securely around their necks and their hands and feet bound tightly.

Two imperial soldiers stood guard on the platform, and the hangman stood near one of the victims who was to be hanged. His attention was on the man standing quietly on a barrel before him.

One of the condemned was a woman who was not content to die quietly. She struggled against her restraints and screamed fiercely.

"Let me go! I ain't no Magi! If you kill my sons I'll haunt you 'til the day you die! If I was a sarding Magi, I would've already killed you all!"

The hangman ignored the woman, and continued checking the restraints and the noose on his first victim.

For the most part the crowd stood silently. There were a handful of hecklers who called out taunts and encouraged the hangman to hurry and begin the spectacle, but most of the people seemed too stunned to do more than stand and watch.

Sarge watched Peke and Madalyn veer off to the left and Asha turn to the right to blend in with the crowd, while he and Brandam pushed their way through the throng of people to make their way up to the platform.

He followed Brandam up the stairs and onto the platform, as a low murmur moved through the onlookers.

The nearest guard moved towards them with his hand on the hilt of his sword. He said, "Get down off the stage, Denizens!"

Without warning, Brandam whispered the trigger word to a spell and several rings of fire appeared around the nearest guard. The fiery rings were stacked one above the other, and the guard was trapped inside them. He was not yet harmed, but the intense heat could be felt by all of those near the rings.

Sarge and Brandam both summoned their Magi cloaks, as the crowd gasped at the fiery display of magic before them.

Brandam stepped over to the hangman, with the cowl of his red and white cloak pulled low and hiding his face in shadows. He said, "These people are not Magi, release them immediately."

With several long strides, Sarge moved to intercept the other guard and prevent him from interfering with Brandam. The guard drew his sword and moved towards them. Sarge held up his hand and pointed at the approaching guard. The man took a step back quickly.

"If you take another step, I'll break your face. Got it, bub? Now, set the sword on the ground very slowly." The Azure Paladin's blue tinged armor shined brightly in the winter sun, and his blue and white Magi Cloak flowed smoothly in the light breeze.

The guard slowly placed his sword on the ground, and raised his palms to the sides.

"Who are you people? What's going on? Someone cut us down!" The woman's face was covered in a burlap bag, and she continued struggling against her restraints.

The hangman stood motionlessly and stared at the Magi before him. He did not respond to the Magi's command.

Brandam lobbed a fire orb above the head of the nearest prisoner, and it hit the rope and burned through it quickly. The severed end of the rope dropped over the man's shoulder. The Magi then launched a fire orb at the rope of the other four condemned people and severed each of them. The ropes smoldered as they dropped.

With the immediate threat to the prisoners eliminated, Brandam turned his attention back to the hangman. He said, "Get out of here before I cook you where you stand."

Without waiting for further prompting, the hangman rushed off of the platform and faded into the crowd.

Sarge glanced over at the guard trapped in the fiery rings, and he could see that the man was about to do something stupid. He was half tempted to warn the man not to try it, but instead he stood quietly and watched the display of stupidity as it happened.

The guard wrapped his arms in front of his face and let out a war-cry as he rushed through the intense heat of the magical fiery rings before him. The man didn't even make it entirely through the rings before he fell to the ground lifelessly. His char-blackened skin and clothes smoked and burned, and both Magi covered their noses from the sickening smell that filled the air.

The other guard stared in horror at his friend, and then slowly backed away from the Magi. When he got to the stairs he rushed as quickly as he could away from the platform.

The crowd cheered as the Magi helped the people from the barrels and removed their bindings.

Sarge looked to Brandam, and said, "We've gotta get outta here. The guard will be back with buddies, and the sentinels are already starting to move this way."

The vocal woman hugged her sons tightly and sobbed.

Sarge pulled the noose from around the other woman's neck and removed the bag from her head.

Blood was dried on her face and neck, and all down the front of her clothing.

He asked, "What happened to you?"

The woman opened her mouth, and he could see that her tongue had been crudely cut from her mouth.

He said, "Let's find Madalyn and see what we can do about that."

He led her down the stairs and away from the platform, and the others followed behind. Sarge moved in the general direction that he'd seen Peke and Madalyn going. At first, he wasn't sure how he'd find them quickly in the writhing mass of people.

Then a commotion broke out before them, and the crowd dispersed in a wide circle in front of him. As he got closer he saw the cause of the panic. Peke was walking towards him with the young cleric at his side. Peke had transformed himself into a large bear, which had apparently caused the swarm of people to quickly retreat and made it much easier to find them.

When they got close, he said, "Let's find Asha and get out of here."

Right on cue, Asha dropped her invisibility and placed her hand on Sarge's shoulder. She said, "I'm found."

Sarge said, "Hide the cloaks, let's see if we can get out of here in one piece."

Brandam held out his hand, showing off two rings. He handed one of them to Sarge and said, "Portal rings. I'm told that they'll work for non-magical folk too."

Sarge shrugged, "Anything that gets us outta here safely." Then he looked to the people that were just rescued from the gallows. "Looks like you're going on a trip to a magical fortress. Unless you'd prefer to stay here."

- = - = -

A few hours later, Sarge entered Champion Hall and looked around the large and mostly empty room on the first floor of the building. He exhaled a cleansing sigh of relief to finally have a bit of time to himself, as he walked over to the large statue in the middle of the room. He rested his hand on the statue and said, "*Kolpassil.* The third principle of the Society is compassion. We will strive to help those less fortunate who are worthy of such consideration."

When he finished the spell, the marble stones of the floor began to sink. They rearranged themselves into a wide staircase leading to the basement, and wrapped around both sides of the base of the statue meeting on the other side far below.

He slowly descended into the vault beneath the hall of the Order of Champions. He'd spent many hours looking through the weapons in this room, over the last fortnight since the secret to the hidden stairway was discovered.

Most of the items in the room were weapons of various shapes and sizes, all were enchanted with one form of magic or another. He'd selected a beautifully crafted longsword, and a handful of daggers in a variety of lengths, all of which were enchanted with the element of electricity. He hadn't needed to use them against an enemy yet, but according to the descriptions the elemental enchantment should add an additional level of damage to his opponents. If the book was to be believed, the electrically enchanted weapons would damage his opponents even if they were able to block his attack.

Sarge reverently caressed a few of the remarkable magical weapons as he passed them, admiring the beauty and breathtaking craftsmanship of each and every one.

On the far side of the room he opened one of the doors to a maze of rooms of Champion Hall's vault. He walked past the meditation rooms and library, past several other doors until he came to his favorite room in the complex.

Even before he opened the door, he could hear someone else in the room. With a slight sigh of disappointment, he tossed the door open and walked into the training room.

Alin was in the room, practicing with a halberd against a dozen magical practice dummies. Sarge didn't know the new Order of Champions Magi all that well. He knew that the man used to be in Keta's coterie, but he hadn't spent much time with him.

He watched as Alin skillfully spun the halberd and ended the deadly spin with a strike to the side of the head of one practice dummy. With almost no pause, the Magi moved and used the bottom end of the weapon to block incoming attacks from three different practice dummies virtually simultaneously.

Sarge could see that the kid did have some skill with weapons. The room's magical practice dummies were impressively challenging magical opponents, and some new Order of Champions Magi might have difficulties facing one or two of them. Sarge hadn't taken on a dozen of them at once yet, but he was confident that he could if he chose to.

He watched Alin finish his battle, and then he applauded. "Nice work, that's some impressive halberd skills you've got."

"Thanks Sarge. I'm all done, you can have the room."

The middle-aged Magi nodded his thanks, and slapped the younger Magi on the back in congratulations as he walked past. He said, "What have they got you doing these days?"

"We've been hitting some of the roads leading to Clornoss, ambushing troops and seizing supplies. It's kind of scary how successful we've been so far. If you get them in small groups, the troops don't put up much of a fight when they realize we're Magi."

Sarge laughed, "They're scared. We saw the same thing in Khazror today."

Alin looked thoughtful for a moment, and then said, "You know, I was in Khazror almost a month ago, and I saw some imperial troops marching down the road. I was almost certain that I saw Konrad with them, in an officer's uniform."

"Konrad? Wasn't he one of the Magi from your coterie, one that died with Keta at Randol's place?" Sarge never knew the man, but he'd heard the stories.

"Yes, but we never found his body. It might not have been him, but I'm pretty sure that it was."

"Have you said anything to Rissyl or the other Order leaders?"

Alin shook his head. "No, I wasn't certain it was him. I'd feel stupid bringing it up if I'm wrong."

"I think you should probably tell them anyway, just in case."

"Good point, I'll tell them. Thanks."

Sarge watched him leave and then waited for the Magi to close the door. He walked over to the statue of a warrior standing guard. He summoned the magic to activate the practice dummy spell twelve times. Each time he did, another magical practice dummy appeared in the room. They were full sized warriors that seemed to be made out of wood, but they moved as gracefully as any person. The twelve opponents circled him and waited for him to make the first move.

He pulled his sword from its scabbard and rushed at the first magical opponent.

CHAPTER 10

Rissyl

The large corridors of the dwarven kingdom were every bit as impressive this time as they had been the first time that Rissyl had walked them. The stone work was unbelievable, and he couldn't help but stare at the finely carved details in all of the surfaces that they passed. The walls and columns were solid stone, and many of them were covered with detailed patterns and symbols from the floor to the ceiling.

He would have liked to stop to look more closely at some of the gorgeous carvings on some of the pillars, but the group had pressing business to attend to and their escort through the corridors was walking briskly.

In sticking with his own mandate of having a Magi from each Order present for missions when possible, he had teamed up with Cynia, Dalen, and Sarasa for this trip to the Mazbakhar Halls. Dalen and Sarasa hadn't been with them the last time that Rissyl was here, and he could see the wonder and awe on their faces as they took in the unexpected beauty of the dwarven subterranean fortress.

While the corridors looked the same, the dwarven people looked and acted differently than during his first visit. Previously, the vast majority of the dwarves were dressed in casual clothes, and they all were going about the routine activities that one would expect to see in any city. He had seen very few guards, even at the front entrance to the underground fortress. Laughing and good-natured smiles were common.

This time it felt more like walking through a massive military complex. Almost every dwarf he saw was wearing armor, and they were all armed. His group hadn't traveled more than a hundred yards without seeing a squad of guards walking or standing watch at corridor intersections and doorways.

Even as he considered this, his point was accentuated by a squad of dwarven soldiers mounted on large lizards making their way down the corridor. The armored warriors looked impressive sitting upon the large creatures, and everyone moved to the sides of the corridor to give the dwarven cavalry room to move through the hall unimpeded. Rissyl looked to each mounted soldier to see if he recognized any of them, since he had traveled with some lizard riders during his last visit, but they were all wearing helms and he couldn't get a good look at their faces.

The winding corridors seemed endless, and it didn't take long for Rissyl to become hopelessly lost. After dozens of twists and turns, and four long ramps to levels deeper underground, the group entered another busy section. This area was filled with dwarves breaking down game and preparing food.

The guide walked over to an older dwarf who was skinning a large elk. The dwarf wore simple working clothes and no armor. His greying black hair was pulled back into a simple braid at the nape of his neck and his beard was braided in two sections.

"Sire, there's Magi 'ere to see you." The guard bowed low as he spoke.

Rissyl looked at the old dwarf again, and he was shocked to realize that the simple laborer before him was the high king of the dwarven lands. Even knowing who it was, he still barely recognized him.

The king motioned towards the floor near him. "Have a seat, Magi. We can talk while I work, there is much to be done."

Rissyl was prepared to make formal introductions, but that seemed silly given the circumstances. So, he sat down near the elk, and watched the high king skillfully skin the animal. The other Magi sat down on the hard stone floor next to him.

Without looking up from his work, the king said, "So, Magi, why'd ye come to me kingdom once again?"

Rissyl leaned forward and clasped his hands together. From the changes around the dwarven halls, he was pretty sure that the dwarves already knew about the threat from the empire. What he didn't know was whether they blamed the Magi. If it hadn't been for the Magi, and the assistance given to them by the dwarves, the dwarven kingdom would not be facing this threat. To make matters more complicated, Rissyl was not willing to commit Magi to assist in the defense of the dwarven home because he was dedicated to pushing forward with their plans to take the attack directly to the empire instead of reacting to what the emperor planned.

He took a deep breath, and said, "We have heard that the emperor intends to invade your kingdom, in hopes of breaking through to the other side to attack the Magi at our Stronghold."

The king glanced up from his work. Looking back down, he said, "Aye."

Rissyl wasn't sure what else the king wanted him to say. "Ah, we're sorry that your aid to us has brought a threat to your kingdom, but right now we can't offer to assist in the defense of your kingdom."

For well over a minute the king laughed raucously, eventually holding his side and visibly attempting to calm himself. When he finally caught his breath, he looked over to a younger dwarf who sat next to him, skinning a different elk. He said, "Ye hear that, son? The Magi can't keep us safe from our enemies!" He started laughing once again.

When he looked over, Rissyl saw that the younger dwarf was Prince Khatohar, the king's eldest son.

The prince looked amused as well, but he was able to contain his mirth better than his father.

Rissyl wasn't sure which part of his statement was so funny, and he looked over to the other Magi to see if they could clue him in.

Dalen and Sarasa shook their heads, and Cynia just shrugged.

When the king calmed his laughter enough to allow conversation, the prince said, "We are well aware of the empire's impending attack. Their armies are gathering several miles from our gates even as we speak. Our last scouting mission estimated about a thousand soldiers currently assembled. That is not nearly enough to even break through the outer gate, so clearly it will be many fortnights before they're ready to attack."

Dalen said, "I wish we could help, but -"

The king burst out into giggles once again.

"I don't get the joke." Sarasa looked more annoyed than amused.

The prince bowed his head slightly to her. He said, "Telling dwarves that we need humans to keep us safe from other humans is insulting or comical. Luckily, father took it as a joke. Dwarves don't need help from Magi to keep our kingdom safe. We've been scouting their buildup for over a month now, and we'll be ready if they decide to attack."

Rissyl felt a bit insulted that the dwarves would think so little of the assistance that could be offered by the Magi, but he could see the prince's point. Looking to his fellow Magi, he wasn't surprised to see that Dalen looked furious. He decided to try to defuse the situation as much as possible.

"We only learned about the threat a couple of days ago. How did your people learn of the emperor's plans?"

The prince smiled proudly. "We have elite units stationed just outside of Clornoss, and they've been there for almost two years. They've remained undetected by imperial troops the entire time, while carrying out missions to free dwarven citizens who have been captured and enslaved by the emperor. During that time, they've dug a series of tunnels in and around Clornoss, and have managed to setup a system for learning imperial secrets."

Rissyl was genuinely impressed. He grudgingly admitted that he might have underestimated the stout folks. He said, "That's quite impressive."

"Yes, very nice. How long can you keep them outta your kingdom?" Dalen no longer looked angry, as his attention became redirected to military strategy.

The prince replied, "The gate has never been breached."

"And it ain't gonna be breached on my watch!" The king returned to his task of skinning the elk.

Cynia asked, "Sire, how come you are skinning an elk? Surely you've got people who do this?"

"Aye, but they're training to be warriors now. This task's gotta be done, and me arm's fit as the next dwarf's. Besides, I've gotta have something to make me feel useful."

Rissyl stood up, "Well, your majesty, we should be leaving."

Drilzad looked up, and started to wipe his hands on his clothes. He said, "Before ye go, there's something we'd like ye to have."

A bell started ringing off in the distance. It wasn't too loud and it echoed down the corridor. Moments after the first bell sounded, several other closer bells began ringing as well.

High King Drilzad stood, as did the prince. Several other dwarves, who had been working on various tasks nearby, also stood and hurried over to their king.

The other Magi stood as the king began issuing orders.

"Denoz, get me lizard ready." The dwarf turned to obey, and the king grabbed his arm and added, "And prepare lizards for the Magi."

The dwarf rushed off down the hall.

The king looked at the next dwarf before him, and said, "Rhenny, I want all of the stewards in the war room in ninety minutes ready to report."

With a nod, Rhenny rushed off to inform the stewards.

"Boz and Brunte, help us with our armor and then go to the war room to help the stewards." The king walked out of the room and around the corner.

Prince Khatohar motioned for the Magi to follow him. When they got around the corner they saw the king beginning to don his armor. The prince joined him, and with assistance from other dwarves they were soon fully armored.

Rissyl was impressed with how quickly they were able to get the full plate armor strapped on and ready. The dwarves no longer looked like laborers, they looked every bit as regal as the first time he'd seen them. Rissyl said, "We really should be going."

The king motioned for the Magi to follow him, and without waiting for them he started walking quickly down the hall.

Khatohar patted Rissyl on the shoulder as he passed, then he hurried off in the other direction.

The Magi hurried to catch up with the king.

Without looking back at them, the king said, "Imperial army's attackin' sooner than we thought. Yer departure's gonna have to wait."

Rissyl's long strides quickly brought him beside the dwarven king. He asked, "Where are we headed?"

"Goin' to the Eye o' the Gods."

He regretted asking, and decided to simply follow quietly. He didn't know what an Eye of the Gods might be, and he wasn't sure that he wanted to know.

The king led them quickly through a maze of corridors, passing through countless intersections and archways. The vast majority of dwarves that they encountered were travelling in the other direction, many of them mounted on lizards of various sizes and all of them well armed and armored.

The warning bells continued to echo through the stone passages, but at times it was drowned out by the shouts and chants of large groups of dwarven soldiers as they hurried through the halls singing and getting each other pumped up for the anticipated conflict ahead of them.

They turned yet another corner and suddenly they were in a huge room containing many pens filled with large lizards. There were many different types of lizards, some of them tall and narrow and others shorter and wide, and they ranged in color from greys and browns to greens and reds.

Denoz hurried over, and said, "Sire, yer lizards are ready." He turned and hurried deeper into the room.

When they got to the pen with the king's lizards, several dwarves were there to help the Magi get mounted on their lizard's back.

Rissyl and Cynia didn't have much trouble getting mounted, after spending a few days traveling by lizard-back a couple of years earlier.

Dalen grumbled as two dwarves helped to get the muscular Magi onto the lizard's back and situated properly in the saddle.

"Well, this should be fun." There was no humor in Sarasa's voice.

Without warning, the king urged his tall green lizard out of the pen. He said, "Gotta hurry, try to keep up. We've a long way to go, don't get lost."

The pace set by the king was not nearly as fast as some of the riding they'd done when Rissyl travelled by lizard previously. So, he quickly fell into the rhythm of the ride. He looked back periodically, and was pleased to see that the other Magi appeared to be keeping up without much difficulty.

They hurried through the passages and before long they were in a section where they saw very few other dwarfs. The lizards seemed anxious and occasionally added leaping and jumping to their lumbering gallop through the halls.

He didn't notice the gradual incline of the corridors at first, but eventually the incline became much steeper. They travelled up in a wide spiral.

For well over an hour they continued to follow the spiral rise higher within the mountain.

"By the gods, how high are we gonna go? I didn't think the Eye of the Gods would be up so high." Dalen cursed and continued to grumble under his breath.

Rissyl couldn't make out the rest of his comments, but he got the general point, and could identify with his grumpy companion's complaints.

Sarasa asked, "Are we going to the very top of the mountains?"

If the king heard her question, he didn't answer. They just continued their long trek up.

Dalen asked, "My ears hurt a lot. Is it just me?"

Now that he brought it up, Rissyl was starting to feel pain inside his ears. At first he thought that he was imagining it, but soon he noticed that his hearing seemed like he was wearing ear muffs.

The pain got gradually worse as they continued to climb, and he began to worry that his head might rip open at his ears. He'd never known anyone who had climbed mountains, and didn't know if maybe it was dangerous for people to be up this high.

In a loud voice, trying to talk loud enough to at least hear himself clearly, he said, "Your highness, why do our ears hurt so much?"

The king looked back, and shouted, "It'll feel better when yer ears pop."

Cynia exclaimed, "Pop?"

"What do you sarding mean, pop? Pop off? Pop open?" Dalen sounded genuinely afraid.

"Chew on yer tongue or somethin', it'll help."

With the talk of ears popping and chewing on tongues, Rissyl was starting to think that perhaps the king was crazy.

Sarasa exclaimed, "Oh sweet Nalria, that's so much better!"

Eventually Dalen and Cynia both voiced their relief, but for some reason Rissyl still felt like his head might burst apart.

After what seemed like an eternity of riding up, the corridor levelled off. The king led the group into a large open cavern that looked like a naturally occurring cave.

On the far side of the cave was a huge opening to the sky.

Without warning, Rissyl heard a loud popping sound in his ears, followed by a series of crackling sounds. Finally, the pain subsided and he breathed a sigh of relief.

The king stopped and dismounted. He said, "We'll hitch the lizards over there."

The Magi followed and tethered their large mounts to hitching posts mounted near one wall, well away from the opening to the sky.

Rissyl walked slowly and carefully towards the large cave opening. The dwarves, or someone, had built a low stone wall at the cave opening. However, as he got closer to the opening and began to look down at the ground so very far below him, he started to feel an irrational fear that he might unexpectedly topple up and over the wall and plunge to his death far below.

When he got close enough, he grabbed the wall which came up to his belly. Leaning over slightly, he marveled at how impossibly high up they were. Far below him he saw birds flying high above the ground. The road leading away from the entrance to the dwarven fortress looked like a thin line on a parchment.

King Drilzad walked over to the low wall and leaned against it casually. He said, "There they are, out yonder, but it's a while still b'fore they're in crossbow range."

Dalen, staying far back from the wall, said, "By all the sarding gods, we're up so high! How far can we see? I can almost see Clornoss from here."

The king laughed, "Nay, not that far, but we can see fer many miles. Our lookouts could see the army when it was still in imperial lands."

The Magi spent a while staring in awe at the breathtaking view before them, and watching the slow approach of the imperial army. Eventually Dalen and Sarasa sat down on a bench, far from the opening to the sky.

As Rissyl and Cynia walked over to sit in a bench near the other Magi, several dwarves arrived. They were sitting in a large cart being pulled by one of the huge lizards. Rissyl didn't recognize any of the dwarves, but from their sashes and fancy armor he assumed that they were clan leaders or other high level members of the dwarven military.

Several other lizards entered the massive cavern, carrying other dwarven soldiers. They dismounted and took up positions guarding the entrance to the room.

Rissyl looked at the other Magi and raised an eyebrow. "Well, I certainly feel safe from the imperial troops up here."

Sarasa shrugged, "I don't think they'll even breach the outer doors."

"I'm surprised that Prince Khatohar ain't up here with his father and the other dwarven leaders." Cynia nodded towards the group of dwarves near the wall overlooking the side of the mountain.

Rissyl shrugged, "I got the impression that he'd be leading the troops into battle."

The Magi were quiet for a while, and Rissyl listened to the dwarves talking strategy.

After a while, Sarasa said, "Speaking of fathers and sons, Chardy sure is getting big!"

Cynia nodded, "Yes, he's huge! He's grown so much."

"Riz, have your parents even met him yet?"

Rissyl looked over to Dalen, and frowned. The man always knew the wrong thing to say.

He shook his head. "No, they might not even know that they have a grandchild."

Sarasa asked, "Do they even know that they have a daughter-in-law?"

Dalen added, "More importantly, do they know their old Dreg is their new daughter-in-law?"

He laughed at his own question, but the others didn't laugh. The Magi all sat in awkward silence.

"Thanks for that, Dalen." Rissyl looked out towards the sky. "No, they don't know yet. I need to get to Misi and talk to them. We need to take Chardy out there so they can meet their grandson, but we have had so much to do."

Cynia placed her hand on his hand, and said, "We gotta visit them soon."

He shook his head, "No, I should visit them first. I need to tell them about us and give them time to adjust to the new situation before we both go there, otherwise they're likely to do or say something that will hurt everyone."

Dalen slapped his hand down onto his knee. "That's sarding trollshit. You gotta be proud of your wife, and stand up to your parents if they ain't gonna accept a new daughter that used to be a Dreg!"

Rissyl felt his anger rising, but before he could reply Cynia answered for him.

"No, Riz has a point. It is a big change for them, they should have a chance to absorb new ideas before they have to react to them."

"They're almost in crossbow range!"

Rissyl looked over to the dwarven king, who was pointing out towards the ground.

He stood up, and walked over to the wall to look down at what was going on below. The first line of the imperial army was much closer, but they weren't quite to the doors yet. From this high up, the army didn't look all that big. However, he knew it would seem much larger and more dangerous if he was down on their level.

The king looked back into the room, and said, "Someone bring me a beetle."

Rissyl looked over at Sarasa, and she shrugged. He felt better knowing that she was just as confused as he. He asked, "Beetle?"

One of the younger dwarves rushed over and handed the king a shiny silver cage that was about the size of a helmet. Inside the cage was a giant green beetle, with long antenna and pincers. It scurried around the cage looking for a way to escape.

King Drilzad looked out at the approaching army.

One of the old dwarves next to him said, "They're within range, Sire."

Still the king watched the army. Well over a minute later he held the cage up near his nose, and in a loud voice he said, "Attack!"

With a shocked expression on his face, Rissyl looked at the king. He was now sure that the old king was crazy.

The little beetle started making noises. At first the noises just sounded like random animal sounds, but the more that he listened it almost sounded like the creature was saying, "Attack" over and over. It was not very clear, and it was mixed with other clicking and snapping sounds.

Cynia elbowed him and motioned for him to look out at the ground below. When he looked down he saw crossbow bolts being fired from dozens of different places below him. So, the cavern they were in obviously wasn't the only place where the dwarves could look down from their mountain and see the approaching army. They must have squads of archers stationed in many such caverns. He was impressed, and became even more confident that the army wouldn't be able to breech the dwarven defenses.

However, that didn't address the curious behavior with the beetle. He said, "King Drilzad, did you just speak to that bug?"

"Aye."

"And did it just reply to you?"

"Nay, it repeated me. It's a Mimic Beetle."

Rissyl raised an eyebrow, but did not reply. He turned his attention back to the killing grounds below.

Sarasa ask, "Why did you talk to the Mimic Beetle? This seems like an odd time to talk to a pet."

The king chuckled, "They repeat words. All the Mimic Beetles from a brood are connected and when one makes noise, all o' them from the same brood make the same noise if they ain't far apart. All me marshals have a beetle from this little guy's brood, and they all said 'Attack' when this one did."

She grinned, "Remarkable! It's really impressive how you dwarves have adapted to your mountainous home. You use the creatures from this place in ways I never even imagined."

Rissyl was reasonably impressed as well, but he didn't express it. The dwarven ways seemed to work for them, but they weren't nearly as handy as being a Magi.

He looked back down to the scene below. Judging from the large number of motionless forms on the ground it looked like the army was taking a huge number of casualties from the dwarven crossbows. A group

73

of soldiers were huddled around a large wooden machine of some sort, and they held their shields up to protect themselves from crossbow bolts as they pushed the contraption forward. It looked like a huge log suspended on a wheeled frame, and he assumed it was a siege weapon designed to smash down the fortress door.

The main part of the army, including the siege machine, were almost to the gates, and the trailing archers finally got within range to fire. The imperial archers could fire further than the dwarven crossbowmen, so he worried that the dwarves would start to take some casualties in their crossbow squads. However, the cave where the Magi were observing from was high enough that they were well out of range of the imperial archers. So, there was no threat in their cave.

"Pitch!" The king spoke to the beetle again.

When the beetle started making sound, Rissyl thought it sounded much more like "itch" than "pitch". He looked down and saw several chutes sticking out from overlooks below them, and soon a black mass of ooze slid down the chutes and spilled onto the soldiers below.

The king yelled at the beetle, "Fire! Fire! Fire!"

As the talkative beetle mimicking "Fire", or a close approximation of it, over and over, Rissyl saw several streaks of fire launch from below. The dwarves started shooting flaming crossbow bolts at the pitch-covered soldiers below.

Almost immediately the ground below them exploded into a massive ball of flame. The fire quickly spread around a huge area. Soldiers near the door no longer moved, and he assumed that dozens of them died in the sudden blaze. Dozens more rushed around on fire, and the siege machine burned brightly.

He was happy that he wasn't close enough to smell the horrible stench that he assumed filled the air down there. As he looked at the death and devastation below, he felt no sympathy. It was horrible and tragic, possibly even inhumane, and he just didn't care.

For a moment he wondered if that made him a bit of a monster. Somehow he was losing compassion for his fellow man. That moment passed quickly. They were trying to kill all of the dwarves, so they could come to Fort Randol and kill him, his family, and all of the other Magi. Rissyl was glad they were dead.

Trumpets began sounding below, signaling a retreat of the imperial army.

He looked to the king and said, "You mentioned that you wanted to give us something before we leave?"

The king walked towards him, "Aye! Let's get yer elk meat!"

Elk meat? He expected something useful or meaningful, not dinner. If he would have known that it was just elk meat they could have ported home long ago.

He resisted the urge to sigh, and forced a smile, "Thank you, your highness. Yes, let's go get some elk meat."

CHAPTER 11

Kimly

"The first client should be ready in a few minutes, Mrs. Watters." The guard announced, and then closed the door as he walked back out of the small room.

Kimly closed her eyes for a moment, intent on fully enjoying the occasion. Over the past several months, when she was not travelling to expand The Shrouded, she was becoming more involved in some of her husband's business dealings.

When she first found out that Cletis was a Dreg Broker, she was shocked and a bit taken aback. She had since discovered how profitable, and even enjoyable, the underworld career could be.

The term Dreg Broker referred to the aspect of the career where Cletis would arrange for a Denizen to be sentenced as a Dreg, and this was typically followed by the new Dreg being purchased by the client who originally arranged the deal. She had found that this activity was actually very uncommon, and the vast majority of their business came from people who wanted to buy existing Dregs, were hoping to find someone who had become a Dreg, or wanted to free one from his or her owners. There were, of course, many other miscellaneous services that a Dreg Broker could provide to those with the resources to pay for them.

For the last year Kimly had frequently sat with her husband as he dealt with clients. After much discussion Cletis had finally agreed to let her meet with some clients alone. She implored him to let her get more involved, saying that she wanted to be able to help him and that it would eventually allow them to work with more clients and continue to expand the business. Really she didn't care about coins or expanding the business, she just saw a chance for a taste of power. She wanted to experience what it was like to hold the power that she frequently watched Cletis wield.

She opened her eyes and looked around the small room. It was just like most of the rooms where Cletis conducted his business. It was furnished with just two chairs and a desk. The walls were recently cleaned and there were no portraits or decorations around the room.

When the doors opened, she felt her heart start pounding faster. The first client that she would deal with alone was about to walk through the door. It would be Mrs. Sauthers, a mother who killed her own husband and allowed her daughter to take the blame for the crime. The daughter became a Dreg and Mrs. Sauthers hired Cletis to rescue the girl. Kimly though it was fitting that the first time she sat alone with a client that it should be this woman, since Kimly watched the exchange between the woman and Cletis just over a year ago.

The door opened, and the guard led a blindfolded Mrs. Sauthers to the chair in front of Kimly's desk. The guard removed the blindfold and left the room.

The woman said, "Where is Mr. Watters?"

Kimly ignored the woman, and pretended to look through her file for several minutes. She had already memorized all of the info in the file, but she wanted to keep the woman waiting while she composed her response.

When she looked up, Mrs. Sauthers looked annoyed.

Kimly smiled on the inside, and said, "My husband is attending to other matters. I'll be handling your business today."

The woman crossed her legs, leaned further back in her chair, and crossed her arms. She remained silent.

"I have good news, Mrs. Sauthers. You've successfully paid for our services."

She looked shocked, and she sat up straight in her chair. "Seriously? I don't have to endure those depraved parties for your warped friends anymore? When will my daughter be freed?"

"Indeed, your unconventional repayment program has concluded. We actually freed your daughter months ago, and she has been a guest at one of our facilities. She is travelling with a merchant caravan now and should be in town in a few days. I hear that she is in good health and spirits."

Mrs. Sauthers buried her face in both hands and started crying quietly. After a moment, she composed herself and dried her eyes. She cleared her throat, and said, "Thank all the gods, maybe this nightmare will finally end!"

Kimly smiled, and she felt like it was a pretty convincingly sincere smile. "It's been a pleasure, Mrs. Sauthers."

She pulled the lever beneath the desk and the guard walked in almost immediately.

She watched the guard escort the woman from the room and then she picked up the next file in the stack. The next client was a merchant named Loyd Krazni. Mr. Krazni was born and raised in Khardifar, but spent much of his youth traveling with merchant caravans. He now had a crew of traveling merchants who made regular trips throughout the empire, selling wares and bringing merchandise back to the south for sale here. He was ranked as one of the top ten wealthiest merchants in the city. The dossier went into great detail about the man's personal life and business dealings, but Kimly skipped over those sections.

She turned the page and continued reading. Mr. Krazni originally met with Cletis on the 26th of Late-Fall in the year 110 RY. He stated that his brother had been a Khardifar sentinel until he got into a bar fight and ended up killing a Gentry craftsman. Mr. Krazni wanted Cletis to help find his brother who had apparently been sold outside of Khardifar. The brother's name was Chyak Krazni.

The most recent case update said that Chyak had been transferred to the Clornoss Dross, but that he never made it there. Instead he and several other Dregs were taken to the Dross in Misi.

Kimly closed the file feeling a little disappointed. This was going to be a dull case. She sighed. This wasn't at all the type of fun and excitement she was looking for when she told Cletis that she wanted to help with the business.

The door opened and the guard brought the blindfolded Mr. Krazni into the room, removed his blindfold, and bid him to sit down.

He looked surprised to see a woman behind the desk, but he didn't comment about it. He was younger than she expected, and he looked strong and proud. She wouldn't have guessed that he was a merchant, he had more the build of a dock worker.

Kimly nodded her head slightly, and said, "I am Mrs. Watters, and I'll be handling things today. So, Mr. Krazni, you're here about your brother Chyak. Is that correct?"

The merchant replied, in a deep voice, "That's right. Did you find him?"

"Yes, your brother is in the Dross in Misi."

The strong merchant took a deep breath and then leaned forward and rested his forehead on his hand, with his elbow on his knee. He remained in this position, rubbing his temples with his thumb and middle finger, for a short time. When he looked up, she could tell that the man was fighting an internal conflict. He said, "I want you to kill him."

She didn't know what to say. Her husband didn't deal in assassinations and this was far outside of what most Brokers would handle, but she was confident that she could do it with Favin's help. As she began to consider possibilities, it sounded like a remarkably exciting adventure. There would be danger, but that'd make it more exciting.

She pushed the folder to the side, and said, "My husband and I are Brokers, not assassins. I think you've come to the wrong place." What she meant to say was that the cost was about to go up significantly, but she thought this approach would accomplish the same thing in a friendlier manner.

He said, "Money is no concern, name your price."

Kimly leaned closer to the man. "I don't want your coins. But you have quite the widespread enterprise at your disposal. I could use more eyes and ears on the streets, possibly the occasional pair of hands to perform small favors? Shall we enter into a mutually beneficial friendship?"

He stood up, "Chyak has a distinctive tattoo on his chest of an animal with an object in its mouth. Bring the tattoo as proof, and you'll have my enterprise's undying loyalty and support for five years."

She wanted to squeal in excitement, but she pushed it down. In a straight face, she said, "Make it seven years and you've got a deal."

The door opened and the guard returned.

Loyd didn't look at the guard. He said, "Six years, and not a minute longer."

The guard held out the blindfold. "Put this on, please."

Kimly nodded. "Six years it is."

Without another word, the guard tied the blindfold over Loyd's head and led him out of the room. As they walked out of the room, her husband walked in.

He didn't look happy.

Cletis said, "We can't help that man, Kimly. We don't assassinate people!"

She sat down, leaned back in the chair, and placed her feet up on the desk. Quietly she said, "You were watching me?"

"We can't help that man."

"No, you and your people can't help that man. I can help that man."

He stopped in mid-stride. "What do you mean? How can you help him?"

"That's my business. Me and my people will handle this. Arrange for your driver to take me home, I have things to do to prepare for this contract."

At first she thought he would insist on answers to his question, but after a very brief hesitation he turned and walked out of the room.

She exhaled audibly. Now she just needed to convince Favin to travel to the other side of the known world to help her. She was confident that she could kill a Dreg on her own, but it'd be more enjoyable with some assistance.

- = - = -

"Why does The Shrouded need us to travel to Misi? Aren't there Shrouded agents in Misi that can take care of this?" Favin looked annoyed, and stressed.

Kimly knew that he had been under a lot of pressure lately, as his thieves' guild continued to grow. It seemed that every day brought a whole new batch of more complicated problems.

She was more frustrated with him than she probably had a right to be, because she just assumed he'd jump at the chance to tag along and help. She'd always relied on herself and she found it annoying to ask someone for help.

She replied, "This ain't your mission, Favin. It's my mission. If you're too busy to help, that's fine."

Viper was walking into the room as Kimly turned to leave. She hadn't heard him enter, but that wasn't surprising. The little man was uncannily quiet and sneaky, even without magic. Since he'd learned some basic Magi skills for stealth and concealment he'd gotten significantly more adept at going unnoticed.

He was a small thin man, noticeably shorter than Kimly. He kept his tightly curled black hair cut short, and his dark brown skin helped to give him some natural camouflage in dark places.

As he walked into the room, he said quietly, "I'll help. What's the mission?"

Kimly replied, "There is a Dreg in Misi, we need to break into the Dross and kill him."

Viper nodded. "Sounds like fun, boss. You should treat yourself. Take a break from pushing papers and get out there and act like a rogue for a change."

Favin shook his head, "I can't, it'll take ages just to get to Misi. I can't be away that long."

Kimly turned back to Favin. She smiled mischievously, "Maybe it's time that I tell you about portal stones."

The two agents of The Shrouded looked genuinely intrigued as she described the system of portal stones and how they worked.

Favin asked, "And the Magi don't mind that The Shrouded use these artifacts?"

With a shrug, she said, "I'm sure that no one has asked, but I've never had any problem using them. I just try to avoid the Magi. We're The Shrouded, sneaking is what we do best."

It suddenly dawned on her that she had never used the Misi portal, and she had no idea what number it was. She cursed to herself.

"What's wrong?" Favin looked around the room in alarm.

She realized that her curse wasn't as concealed as she intended. She said, "Nothing. I have some things to do. Let's meet back here tonight to make final plans."

Both men nodded their agreement, and she made her way out of Favin's compound. As she walked, she fidgeted with the nexus gem in her pocket.

Once she got outside, she walked towards the bazaar. She hated the idea of contacting the Magi to ask the portal number for Misi, but there was no other way to find it. Well, she could travel to Misi the slow way, and look at the inscription on the stone, but she didn't have time for that.

She pulled the nexus gem from her pocket and summoned enough magic to activate it. She prepared it to send her message to all other nexus gems. She said, "What is the portal number for Misi?" The magical artifact glowed red for a moment, and then went dark.

Within a couple of seconds the gem glowed green softly. She held it up to her ear and activated it. She heard the voice of a male Magi say, "Twenty-Six. Tov Zaeks." She didn't recognize the voice, but she mentally wished him well for assisting without asking a bunch of questions.

Kimly put the nexus gem back into her pocket, and looked around the sprawling marketplace. She could smell some kind of meat being cooked, and it smelled delicious. She headed towards the smell. Preparing for a new adventure always made her hungry.

CHAPTER 12

Jessa

"A cauldron? You're actually putting a sarding cauldron inside my cell? Is this some sort of sick joke? Surely you don't plan to eat me?"

Jessa tried, and failed, to suppress a laugh.

Lord Jalinox didn't even attempt to restrain his mirth. "Baeldin, you are truly quite clever. To be honest, I didn't expect much in the way of smarts, coming from a Magi who knowingly wandered into the palace of the emperor who wants all Magi dead. But here you've got the whole plan figured out on your first guess."

The large boisterous Magi moved to the back of his cage, as two large soldiers pushed a huge cauldron into the cage with him. Two other soldiers stood near the cage with crossbows aimed at the Magi as the cauldron was moved. When the cauldron was fully inside the cage, the guards closed and locked the door of the cage. Jalinox dismissed them, and all four soldiers left the room.

They were in the lower level of one of the buildings in the new compound that the emperor provided to Jalinox. The compound was old and seemed to have been unused for decades. However, it was in a secluded area north of Clornoss, it contained several buildings, and it had a small wall around the perimeter. Jalinox had been pleased with the accommodations, particularly when his hired soldiers arrived to guard the place.

The Magi crossed his arms at his chest and sneered. "You don't really think I'll allow you to hurt me, do you? I've been patient thus far, because I understand the politics involved in this game. I'm willing to play the game, but very soon I expect to see my rewards."

Jalinox placed his hands on his hips, and regarded the Magi with amusement. "My friend, I hope you realize that you're not in control here. You're the rat in the cage, and I am running things."

"You made your fatal mistake when you removed those cursed manacles, Necromancer! Now all of my magic has been restored and I can destroy you any time I desire. So, let's start talking about my reward."

82

Lord Jalinox ignored the Magi's bravado. He said, "Baeldin, it is time for you to get into the cauldron."

"Go sard yourself, 'mancer. Let me out of the cage and fetch my reward, and I'll be on my way."

"I really must insist that you get into the pot, I've got a great many things to do today and I can't waste the whole day with you."

Baeldin growled in anger as he brought his hand up and pointed his palm at Jalinox. He said, "Krol'Tu." A small orb of fire shot from the Magi's hand and sped towards the necromancer, but it didn't even get past the bars of the cage. As the fiery sphere got to the bars, it quickly vanished.

The Magi roared his surprise and frustration, as he launched a series of fiery orbs at Jalinox. Each one dissipated at the bars of the cage.

Jessa had wondered if the Garroliron enhancements on the cage would be as effective as Jalinox had predicted, once again he was correct. She wasn't sure if it could block all of the Magi's spells, but it was certainly stopping the fire magic.

Lord Jalinox shouted, "Stop wasting your magic!" He stepped forward and brought both hands up and extended them to his sides with the palms facing Baeldin. Suddenly purple Khalius Fire shot from both of his hands. This Khalius Fire wasn't the normal purple magical spheres that Jessa was accustomed to using. Instead, Jalinox had unleashed two steady beams of Khalius Fire that crackled and sparked as they streaked to the Magi. The deadly necromancer magic engulfed the Magi and swirled around him, and still Lord Jalinox continued to pour more power into the two streams.

In mere moments the impressive display was over. Baeldin was slumped in an unnatural heap in the corner of his cell. Jalinox smiled evilly as he stepped over towards the door and called the soldiers back in.

He said, "Kindly place the Magi in the pot, and then you can leave."

All four soldiers entered the cage, and struggled to lift the rotund Magi up and into the cauldron.

When they left the room Jalinox grabbed a large fox-hide bag from the corner of the room. He said, "It's really a pity that he wouldn't get into the pot on his own. I was really looking forward to seeing the Manaworms consume him while he was still bragging about how powerful he was."

Jalinox walked into the cage and motioned for Jessa to stay back. "Don't get too close, my dear. It would be unfortunate if any of these little devils jumped over there and started eating you."

She scowled at his unamusing joke, but she did back up.

Her annoyance was quickly replaced with fascination as she watched Jalinox empty the bag of Manaworms into the cauldron with Baeldin's body. They instantly began consuming the traitorous man, and within seconds the cauldron seemed to be filled with some sort of gory blood soup.

After a few minutes Baeldin's body completely disappeared. All that remained were several dozen engorged worms, violently writhing around in the otherwise empty cauldron.

Lord Jalinox clapped his hands together once, and flashed Jessa a huge smile. "What a remarkable show! I've never seen a human body so quickly and completely disposed! Now we'll leave these fantastic creatures alone to digest their meal. Soon they'll all excrete pure magical essence for me! Tomorrow we can let them eat the wench you picked up in Gargloto."

Jessa smiled, the woman was annoying and she was looking forward to seeing the woman eaten by Manaworms.

Jalinox continued, "Our apostles have captured over a dozen Manaworm meals from all around the empire, and more are being brought in each day. We also have the Libur Magi that the emperor so graciously gifted to us. Our plan is coming along nicely! Which reminds me, in the morning I have something very special planned and you will play a key role in it."

- = - = -

The next morning, Jessa was riding a horse slowly down a long and deserted rural road outside of Clornoss. She wished that Jalinox would come up with plans that didn't involve her needing to wake before the chickens and gallivant around the countryside on a cold Early-Winter morning. Of all of the twisted and evil plans made by the necromancer lord, she felt that this was probably his most wicked. A tiny part of her, that part that was still a normal person, already regretted what she was about to do. However, most of her simply didn't care. It was just another mission, and the means to an end. She didn't yet understand what that end would be, but she didn't need to. She just needed to follow her lord's simple instructions.

After several hours of dull and uncomfortable riding on horseback, she finally saw her target. Far ahead of her was a chariot being pulled by a pair of white stallions. She road casually onward and pretended not to be interested in the chariot as she passed it. The opulent chariot and prized stallions were guarded by four well-armed and armored soldiers, who ignored her as she passed them.

Once she got well on the other side of the guarded chariot, she stopped her horse and dismounted. With a tiny bit of magic she summoned her brown and white Magi cloak, and pulled the cowl low over her head to help mask her face. It had been a long time since she had used it, but the cloak was key to Jalinox's plan. The whole ambush needed to look like it was done by the Magi. She hoped he was right about who was inside the chariot, or the plan was wasted.

As she rushed at the chariot, she shouted, "For the Sovereign Magi Society!" She summoned a series of fire orbs and started launching them at the chariot and the two nearest guards. The relentless swarm of magical fire overwhelmed the two guards, and they dropped before they even got their weapons drawn.

Jessa heard the unmistakable sound of a crossbow bolt being loosed, and she barely threw up a magic shield in time to deflect the deadly bolt before it ruined the whole plan. Not to mention causing an annoyingly fatal hole in her head.

She turned her attention to the crossbowman, and several fire orbs later that guard was dead as well.

The final guard screamed a battle cry as he approached her with his sword poised over his head to cleave her in two. She stepped to the side quickly and unleashed a huge amount of Khalius Fire, sucking the life from the man as he was still swinging his sword. She wasn't supposed to use any necromancer attacks in this ambush, because it was supposed to look like the Magi attacked them. However, she panicked when the guard got so close.

She looked to the chariot to make sure it's occupants didn't see her mistake, but they were just exiting the chariot with their hands covering their heads as they tried to escape the smoke from the blazing fire that was consuming the expensive vehicle.

She lobbed a few fire orbs at the already dead guard at her feet, to make it look like a Magi attack, and then she turned her attention to the occupants of the chariot.

Prince Edal and little Tali coughed and gagged as they tried to get the smoke from their lungs. A nursemaid stumbled out after them.

Jessa sent a stream of fire orbs at the stunned nursemaid, causing her to stumble back into the burning chariot.

Jessa then walked over to Tali and grabbed her by the head.

The young prince held his hands up and pleaded with her. "Please Magi, have mercy! Tali is just a little girl, please don't hurt her! I'll give you riches and land! Anything you desire will be yours, I am the prince of all of these lands!"

"Your father's war against the Magi will bring the death of every last imperial! We're gonna kill you all!" Jessa kept her voice at a whisper, to try to disguise it.

With both palms on either side of the little girl's head, she sneered and whispered, "Krol'Tu!" She sent several fire orbs from both hands directly into the girl's skull.

Prince Edal's expression turned to shock and terror as he watched the fire burn out his sweetheart's eyes and erupt from her nose and mouth. Her face withered and blacked as Jessa let her body slump slowly to the ground.

The prince screamed in despair and horror, and he looked around for somewhere to run.

In her whispery voice, Jessa said, "Don't run or I'll make your death slow and painful!"

She hadn't heard Jalinox arrive, but she expected him to come at this point to save the prince and secure his place in the young prince's mind as a friend and savior.

In a bold and commanding voice, Jalinox shouted, "Not while I'm alive! The Magi shall not harm a prince of my beloved land!"

Jessa turned to face him, and just saw a glimpse of the purple necromancer magic streaking towards her.

In an instant everything went dark.

- = - = -

When Jessa woke, she felt terrible. She opened her eyes slowly, and looked around. She was inside a tent, and Jalinox stood over her with some woman who was wearing Jessa's black robes.

She closed her eyes and laughed to herself. Everything seemed to be going exactly the way that he had planned it. However, she wasn't ready to get up. She felt like death, or just a hair better than death, and she wanted nothing more than to take a very long nap.

Jalinox kicked her solidly in the side, and said, "Sleeping time is over, up and at 'em."

When she looked up, she saw him place a hand on the woman's shoulder. A brief flash of purple glow appeared and sucked the life from the woman next to him. The woman fell without a word. He wasted no time, quickly undressing the woman.

Jessa groaned and started stripping as well. With his help she exchanged clothes with the dead woman, so that woman would appear to be the prince's attacker.

After they positioned the woman on the cot, Jessa followed him out of the tent.

Jalinox led her to another tent, positioned on the other side of the road near a wagon and a team of horses. Several of Jalinox's guards stood near the tent and two guarded the entrance.

When they got to the tent, Jalinox said, "My prince, may we enter?"

A few moments later the prince stepped out of his tent. His eyes were red and puffy like he'd been crying, but they were dry and he stood proudly. His expression was angry and he said, "What do you need, Lord Jalinox?"

"My prince, the Magi assassin has died."

"I wish to see the Magi's body."

Jalinox turned and Jessa fell in beside the prince as they followed the necromancer lord to the other tent.

"There she is my prince." Jalinox held open the tent so the prince could look inside.

At first it looked like the young prince would start to cry once again, but he choked back his tears and Jessa was sure that his anguish and dismay was already turning to hatred.

The prince stared at the body for a long time, and eventually said, "Why did she do this? I can understand the Magi attacking our army, but why murder a little girl?"

Jalinox put his arm around the young man and led him away from the tent. He said, "Let's take a walk, my prince, and I will explain some things."

They walked for a half an hour or more, until they came to a small stream. Jalinox sat down on a large rock on the edge of the stream, and motioned for the prince to sit on a rock near him.

"You must understand, my boy, that the Magi crave power more than anything else. They feel that their Magi Society is more powerful than any king or emperor. They are above the jurisdiction of nations and kingdoms, because they want to rule even monarchs and imperial sovereigns, and they will kill anyone who threatens their power and influence. That's what makes them so dangerous, and that's why your father and your great grandfather have risked so much to battle them. I know it's a lot for a young man to understand, but you must now realize that none of us are safe and there can be no peace until every Magi has been slain."

The prince nodded. "Yes, I see that now. But I must ask..." He hesitated, looking for the right words. "That purple light that you used to kill the Magi..." He let the question dangle for a moment. "Did you use magic to kill her? Are you a Magi too?"

Jalinox shook his head slowly. "No, my prince, I am not a Magi. What you saw was not magic, it was the power granted by Viator, the god of death. Now you know my secret, my prince. I am what you would call a necromancer, and my power is at your command."

"I don't understand. A necromancer? You worship the god of death?"

"For centuries the only force that could stand against the vile Magi have been the humble followers of Viator. The unenlightened call us necromancers, but we refer to ourselves as Dark Apostles of Viator. My ancestors secretly served your great grandfather, and now I secretly serve your father."

Prince Edal looked shocked, "My father knows that you're a necromancer?"

"Absolutely not, and he must not! Your father wouldn't understand, because his zeal for wiping out all magic users consumes him. Alas, we must serve him secretly, otherwise he would turn his forces against us as well. It is the curse of serving the god of death, but it's a curse we gladly accept so that we can aid in purging the world of the vile Magi."

"How can you serve the god of death?"

Jalinox laughed, "How can you worship Kason, the god of order? It's simply a matter of faith, and choice. My devotions go to one god, and yours goes to another. There are few differences, except the details. Let me ask you this, what does your god give you in return for your faith?"

The prince shrugged, "Peace of mind, I guess. The knowledge that in death I will ascend to a better place."

Jalinox scoffed, "Worthless gibberish! My god grants me the power to slay my enemies with Khalius Fire! I can raise the dead and control an undead horde with just the power of my faith."

Edal looked repulsed.

The necromancer lord pressed his argument harder, "How well did that 'peace of mind' assist you when the Magi melted poor little Tali's face right before your eyes? Your worthless god left you powerless to even save the life of your beloved! What good is faith in a god like that? You scoff at my god when you worship a god that gives you nothing!"

The prince's brows narrowed in anger, and for a moment Jessa thought he might lash out. He said, "I accept your offer of assistance. When I am emperor, the necromancers will be welcomed to serve our empire openly."

Jalinox bowed his head respectfully. "Your wisdom and grace is far beyond your years, my prince. I am overjoyed to hear this wonderful news."

"There is more. I wish for you to teach me the ways of your necromancers. I never again want to stand at the mercy of those wretched Magi!"

"I can do more than that, my prince. I believe that I can make you one of the most powerful men in the known lands."

He raised an eyebrow in interest. "And how would you do that, Lord Jalinox?"

"During my devotions, Viator has spoken to me. His father Wirmyntas has once again taken an interest in the lands of the living. He desires a mortal to become his warlock, the first of many, who will serve the ancient god in life like few have done in a millennium. Viator has called on me to guide his father's warlock to the service of the patron-god."

"The ancient gods are not truly dead?" Edal looked shocked.

"They were never dead they simply withdrew, but they are once again interested in the lands of people. Viator demands that I deliver the future warlock to Wirmyntas, and you are to be that warlock! The ancient god longs for you to give yourself to him in eternal service! If you freely give your soul to him, the gifts and powers you would receive would be without measure!"

Prince Edal turned white as snow. He softly said, "This Wirmyntas is a huge fiery creature with many arms and horns?"

Jalinox's widening eyes revealed his surprise, "The ancient god has come to your dreams?"

"Yes. Not often at first, but lately he haunts my dreams almost nightly. I have known that he was coming for me, but I had hoped that it was simply a bad dream."

"War is already here, my prince. It is time that you take sides. The awful god of magic, Nalria, and her father the ancient god Kelegar are on the side of the Magi. Only Viator and his father Wirmyntas can stand against them, but they need faithful and powerful humans to act as their hands on earth. You, my prince, must raise the banner for Wirmyntas and stand against the Magi!"

Edal crossed his arms at his chest. "If the ancient god will grant someone wonderful powers, why don't you serve him yourself?"

"I have pledged my soul to Viator, it is not an oath that can be retracted. I can pray to Wirmyntas, and the ancient god does grant some minor prayers. But my loyalty and devotion must always be to my lord Viator. Wirmyntas' followers must be willing and able to pledge their soul to him."

He exhaled audibly, and then said, "So, I'm to become a necromancer then?"

Jalinox shook his head, "Followers of Viator are called necromancers. You, my prince, are to become the Archwarlock, the first of many warlocks who will serve Wirmyntas. Viator grants his faithful the power to control the undead, but Wirmyntas grants his faithful control over the demons themselves!"

"Demons?" The prince was clearly stunned at the thought of controlling demons.

"Yes, my prince! How can the Magi possibly stand against us if you have an army of demons to do your bidding?"

Jalinox stood and started walking back to the camp. Jessa walked behind the prince, and followed them both. When they finally arrived in the camp, Edal went straight to his tent without saying another word.

She followed the necromancer lord to the other side of the road. When they were well out of earshot of the prince, she said, "How can you give all that power to the boy? Isn't there a way that you can keep it for yourself?"

"Mortals are the grunts of the gods, but like in Goblin Squares even the grunts can defeat the king with a little luck and a great deal of strategy." He smirked smugly. "Besides, the patron-god has chosen the boy."

"I still don't see what's in this for us. The boy gets great powers, the throne of the empire gets even stronger, and what are we left with?"

"We are left with a dead emperor, a powerful warlock on the throne who answers to me, and I will be in command of a greater demon. The future couldn't be more wonderful!"

She still wasn't convinced. "You told the boy that the warlocks are given power over the demons, while the necromancers control undead. If he commands demons, and you use this ritual to bind a greater demon to your will, couldn't the boy simply take your pet demon from you?"

"Foolish girl!" Jalinox practically spat the words. "Hundreds of people with magic potential will give their lives to provide us enough mana to cast this ritual! The power to control a greater demon is without equal! Even the most powerful warlocks couldn't hope to control a greater demon without a ritual such as this! Sure, the boy will have a whole army of lesser demons to serve him, but he will never be nearly powerful enough to control a greater demon! The boy and his demons will be one more tool in my arsenal of power."

CHAPTER 13

Sarasa

The layout of Darisa City was the same as the other major cities of the empire. The Garden District, where the rich and powerful lived, was situated to the east along with the Chancery District which held the chancellor's palace and various government buildings. On the west side of the city was the Dross, a nice name for the highly-guarded area housing most of the city's Dregs. Nestled between these two extremes, and conveniently separated by large walls, was the Commons District where the Denizens lived, worked, and shopped.

In general, as you travel further west in a city you were likely to encounter progressively worse living conditions, more clutter, more dangerous streets, and seedier people. The warehouse that was chosen for Blood Night in Darisa City was as far west as one could go without passing the gate into the Dross.

When Sarasa walked into the warehouse she was disappointed to smell that the stench of the streets outside was significantly better than the stench of a few hundred reeking people crammed into a large, but poorly ventilated, abandoned warehouse.

She covered her nose as she pushed her way through the crowd and attempted to find an empty bench. The term bench was actually a bit of an overstatement, really they were just wood planks resting on large rocks. Eventually she found a small section of bench open in the middle of the crowd, about halfway between the caged arena in the middle of the warehouse and the outer walls of the building.

There was very little space beside her, but it didn't take long for some massive, and rather dirty-looking, fellow to approach and ask if anyone was sitting beside her.

The man didn't even wait for her to reply before he shoved his rotund butt into the miniature space between her and the next person. By the time Tiny got situated, she was sitting with only one butt cheek on the plank and she had to plant one foot in the isle beside her to keep from falling to the floor.

Tiny brought with him a new and impressively worse smell than the already rancid stench that filled the place, and Sarasa desperately wanted to get up and find a new spot. However, looking around the packed warehouse she saw that most people were standing and there was not even much space left for walking around. So, she decided to tough it out and retain her seat next to the man that she sarcastically thought of as Tiny.

The low roar of the crowd was already beginning to give her a headache, and the competition hadn't even started yet. She was starting to remember why she always hated these things. This event was much more crowded than the competitions that she'd been to in the past, but it had been many years since she'd attended any.

Sarasa looked around the crowd, hoping to spot the other Magi. They had split up and entered the warehouse separately. Dalen should be with the other competitors, preparing for the competition. Firana and Eleyne would be in the crowd somewhere, but she couldn't see them.

The constant roar of the crowd calmed slightly once the competition started and the first fighters stepped into the arena, but it was replaced by various periods of significantly increased shouting and cheering as the fighters scored brutal hits on one another.

She paid very little attention to the matches between the people that she didn't know. Even though she trained in Thon's fighting guild for many years, she really had no interest in this sort of vicious competition. Her fighting guild master had stressed that fighting guild students should focus on learning to keep themselves safe from assailants, they should not train to compete for money or glory.

Dalen, on the other hand, had always loved the money and glory side of competitive fighting, and he had competed in Blood Nights on several occasions. He had left Thon's fighting guild at a young age to join a rival guild that specialized in this sort of glory fighting.

Someone pushed past her, and she looked to see that it was one of the many bookies who walked around and took wagers from the people in the crowd. Normally there weren't many wagers placed on the early fights, but the bookie that pushed past her seemed to be a very busy man.

Sarasa was starting to wonder if she had missed Dalen's first match, but finally she saw him strut into the arena. He had always been a ham when it came to this kind of thing. A few years of learning magic, and a number of bloody battles, had fed his ego a bit too much. She watched him bounce around the arena and play up to the crowd, working them into a loud frenzy as the judge tried to get the two competitors to square off.

Finally, Dalen sauntered over to his opponent and stood with his guard down. His opponent was a large and slow-looking ogre of a man with huge fists and no shirt.

The judge shouted, "Begin!"

Apparently Shirtless assumed that Dalen was at a disadvantage with his arms down around his waist, and he quickly pressed that perceived advantage. He lunged in with a sloppy horizontal punch with his right hand. The wild haymaker was extremely slow, and Shirtless stepped towards Dalen as he attacked.

The Magi stepped towards the attack and easily blocked it using both forearms and jammed them into Shirtless' clumsy strike.

Sarasa knew what was coming next, and she already felt bad for the shirtless man.

Dalen's block instantly stopped his opponent's attack, knocking the man off balance. He quickly captured the man's attacking arm with his left arm, and then leaned forward and delivered a devastating back-fisted punch to the side of the man's face at the base of his jaw with his right fist.

A loud popping sound carried all of the way from the arena as Shirtless' jawbone snapped, and the crowd groaned and cheered at the same time.

Shirtless grabbed his jaw with his left hand and leaned forward in agony.

Dalen didn't even hesitate. As the opponent leaned forward, Dalen grabbed the back of the man's head and pulled him down into a crushing knee strike up into the face.

From the way the man dropped to the floor, Sarasa didn't know if he was knocked out or dead.

The Blood Night officials didn't wait to find out. Three men rushed into the arena to remove Shirtless, as the judge declared Dalen the winner.

The next match started almost immediately, and Sarasa went back to focusing her attention on other things.

She looked around some more, trying to catch a glimpse of Firana or Eleyne. She wondered if Firana was nervous seeing Dalen fighting in the Arena.

Thoughts of her brother and his lover made Sarasa think about her own love life, or lack thereof. She often spent time with Brandam, and many of her friends assumed that they were lovers. As much as she enjoyed spending time with him, they both knew that they weren't meant to be together. They were great friends, but her heart belonged to someone that she would never have and she had made that very clear to Brandam.

Long ago she had asked Rissyl to make a choice between her and Cynia. He had made that choice, and Sarasa accepted it. What she didn't expect was that her love for him would grow so much after being denied by him. It was a tragic fact that she desperately tried to keep from Rissyl and Cynia both.

Over the last year or so, Sarasa's relationship with Rissyl had evolved and changed. At first, he seemed infatuated with her, even after he made the choice to be with Cynia. Since then they had grown closer as friends and he seemed to view her more as a beloved relative and confidant and not as a love interest. This arrangement had worked out well, as it removed much of the awkwardness that existed between them for too long.

It was often said that people want what they can't have, and that had certainly been true for Sarasa. The more unobtainable he seemed, the more her need for him grew. The desire was exasperating, but she felt that she'd been doing a commendable job of keeping it contained.

Unfortunately for her, that meant a lifetime of loneliness and a general lack of physical affection. Perhaps someday she would find someone to pique her sexual curiosity, but it seemed unlikely.

The surprise sensation of a hand resting on her inner thigh brought her thoughts back to the present. She looked down to see Tiny caressing her leg with his pudgy hand.

She snatched his hand by one finger, and pealed that finger backwards until it was in danger of dislocating. She shoved the finger and hand against her leg, trapping it and, hopefully, causing a tremendous amount of pain.

Tiny squealed a high pitch scream, that was mostly drowned out by the cheers of the crowd as they responded to whatever was happening in the arena. He tried to remove his hand from her leg, but she kept it trapped there with his third finger bent back at a terrible angle and at risk of breaking.

She said, "If you touch me like that again, I'll break every bone in your hand."

Releasing his hand, she tried to brush his grime from her clothes.

Tiny clutched his sore finger with his other hand, and pulled it completely away from her. He muttered something under his breath about overly-sensitive people.

From that point her mood grew even more sour. She passively watched the matches, but paid little attention to them. Even when Dalen came into the arena, she barely watched the match. Instead she let her thoughts dwell on situations of love and war, and pretty much anything else that she could focus on that would feed her anger and frustration.

She thought back to the horrible day at Randol's place, when she had watched the beloved old sage get killed by the imperial army's twisted wolf-like creatures. She thought about how the battle had quickly gotten out of control, and the despicable soldiers who had pulled her into the woods behind Randol's home.

A huge cheer erupted from the crowd, and pulled her attention back to the present. When she looked to the arena, she saw the judge holding Dalen's arm in the air.

The judge shouted, "The winner of Blood Night for the year 110 RY." He paused for effect, and then added, "Dalen Dodisen!"

Again the crowd went wild, and she saw several bookies roaming the area handing coins to participants who won their wagers. She was surprised to see that the entire competition was over already.

Dalen walked to the edge of the arena and raised his hands bidding the crowd to be quiet. When things calmed down, Dalen started to speak.

She groaned on the inside. They hadn't talked about him making a speech and she hated it before he even began.

He shouted, "Gents and lasses, I won today with just my power and skill. I didn't use any magic!"

Laughs rang out from around the room, as most of the spectators thought he was making a joke.

Then he caused his blue and black Magi Cloak and his weapons to appear. The crowd gasped as he drew his sword from the scabbard. Lightning danced up and down the blade brightly, causing the crowd to murmur and buzz with nervous chatter.

Sarasa noticed someone on the far side of the room slip over to the door and exit quickly. The door closed heavily behind him, and she knew that the man's sudden departure promised an unpleasant remainder to the day.

She stood up and started walking towards the back of the room. As she walked, she dropped an invisibility spell on herself. If anyone around was paying any attention they didn't indicate that they saw her vanish. Most likely everyone was paying more attention to Dalen in the arena.

He continued, "The sarding emperor's been hunting the Magi and it needs to stop! Innocent Denizen and Gentry have been falsely accused and punished for too long because of the emperor's insane bloodlust for the Magi!"

As she got near the back of the room, she looked around the warehouse. She didn't see any city sentinels in the room, which wasn't too surprising since the whole event was officially outlawed. She did see several men standing guard around the room, and they were probably employed by the people hosting the competition. They were stationed there to keep the peace, and deter theft since most of the attendees carried a good deal of coin to bet on the fights.

The crowd cheered at Dalen's comments, and he seemed bolstered by their approval.

He said, "The Sovereign Magi Society is now recruiting! War has come to us, and we're looking for Magi warriors! If you wanna take a stand against the emperor, and if you're ready to stop the practice of turning people into Dregs, then join with us!"

The rowdy cheer suggested that most of the crowd was at least supportive of his statements, even if they weren't personally willing to take a stand to help.

Dalen continued, even louder, "If you got a magewel, the potential to use magic, you can come with us! We'll teach you to use your power and be a Magi!"

The crowd went wild, and several people started moving closer to the arena.

Dalen added, "Even if you ain't been blessed with the ability to be a Magi, you can still help us by staying here and opposing the emperor's men when they're hunting Magi and making people into Dregs! If you wanna be tested, come down here to the arena!"

Many people in the crowd begin pushing their way to the arena cage. Sarasa saw Eleyne enter the cage and stand next to Dalen as several people lined up in front of them. Eleyne had summoned her green and white Magi Cloak and she held her staff casually at her side.

The door burst open on the far side of the warehouse and, before Sarasa could take a step, another door opened on the side near her as well. City sentinels and imperial troopers started pouring in through both doors.

Mayhem quickly erupted throughout the warehouse, as the emperor's men blocked the only two exits from the building and more continued to shove their way through the door.

The soldiers began stabbing and cutting down everyone they got near, ruthlessly killing anyone they could. Several of the imperial soldiers shouted comments about all Magi deserving to die, and that the hands of the emperor had arrived to kill all Magi and their supporters.

The death screams were deafening, and Sarasa was blocked from even getting close to the soldiers, for the time-being she was helpless to stop the killing. She couldn't even lob simple fire orbs, because they were just as likely to hurt a spectator as they were to hit a soldier.

As the emperor's troops moved away from the door and further into the warehouse, they slaughtered everyone in their path. The few guards in the room who were hired by the competition coordinators were quickly cut down by the advancing soldiers.

The soldiers pressed forward and left room for more soldiers to move into the warehouse behind them. The new troops were armed with crossbows, and they wasted no time in randomly shooting anyone that caught their attention.

Sarasa desperately tried to push her way towards the door, so she could engage the soldiers in combat. She was already having a miserable day, and some life or death combat sounded like exactly what she needed to brighten things up. However, if anything, she was losing ground. She was probably the only person in the room trying to move towards the soldiers. Everyone else was panicking and the terrified mob was swarming towards her. The more she tried to push through in the opposite direction, the more she was at risk of getting knocked down and trampled.

She heard someone shout, "Just torch the sarding place and kill them all!"

It wasn't long before she first smelled smoke, and the fire swiftly took hold on the old boards of the warehouse.

The soldiers quickly retreated and shut the doors. The crowd that had been shoving away from the exits suddenly turned and rushed towards them. Panicked screaming and crying mixed with the pitiful cries of the mortally wounded victims of the soldiers' attack.

People pounded on the doors and pleaded with the soldiers to let them out, but the doors were shut and the soldiers had barricaded them. The walls were on fire in several places, and the fire had started to climb to the rafters. More deadly was the black smoke that was beginning to fill the ceiling and started growing thicker throughout the room.

Down in the arena she saw a brightly glowing portal near Dalen. He was shouting and pushing people through the portal, trying to get as many people out of the warehouse as possible.

It was a good plan, but it would take time for people to go through the portal one at a time and there was no chance that everyone in the warehouse could escape through the portal before the smoke became too much to bare.

The soldiers weren't content to let their victims die in the fire. One of them had a crossbow and was firing at random people through a small opening of one of the boarded-up windows. Sarasa saw the window as a potential escape route, if she could take out the soldiers on that side of the building to give the people a chance to slip away in the confusion.

Pushing through the chaos of terrified people, she summoned one of her new weapons as she got close to the window. The remarkable weapon was one of the many artifacts that she discovered in the vault below Shadow Hall. It was a compact crossbow that fired bolts of magical energy and once she cocked the firing mechanism, the weapon would magically reengage and another bolt of magical energy would appear without needing physical movements from her. The result was a magical ranged weapon that didn't need reloading or quarrels and could fire dozens of shots in a minute.

She moved the slider on the side of the weapon, which armed the firing mechanism. A small magical bolt appeared on the weapon, and glowed a soft yellow as she raised the weapon towards the little hole in the boarded-up window. The trigger pulled easily, and the screams of a guard on the other side of the wall hinted that her bolt hit its mark.

Sarasa looked towards the crowd. She shouted, "Someone get over here and start ripping these boards off the window. I'll deal with the soldiers, just get this window clear!"

Not a person in the crowd moved to help.

She summoned her grey and black Magi cloak. She clipped the crossbow to her belt and then, in dramatic fashion, she waved her hands and smacked them together over her head. As she did, she said, "Taln'Foish!"

A loud explosive sound was accompanied by a bright flash of light from her hands. The whole thing was an illusion, but the sounds and bright light seemed real enough to everyone nearby.

The illusion caused a collective gasp from the people near her, and everyone turned to look in her direction. She said, "I'm a Magi, and I'm going to try to get us out of here. You've got to do your part! Start pulling the boards off this window. I'll deal with the soldiers."

Several people rushed over to her, and started yanking on the boards covering the window from the inside.

It was becoming more difficult to breathe in the heavy smoke that was quickly filling the room. If they didn't work faster, most of them weren't going to make it out of the building alive.

She glanced down at the arena cage, and saw Dalen and Eleyne trying to rush people into the portal. The sea of people around the arena cage were coughing and covering their faces with cloth, their hands, or anything they could find to try to keep from breathing smoke.

The first board finally gave way from the window with a crash as the people slammed it on the ground and started on the next board. Within seconds the next board was yanked down.

Sarasa saw two soldiers rushing over to assist their fallen companion. She grabbed her crossbow and cocked the firing mechanism. Aiming quickly, she loosed the magical bolt and watched it streak into her target. As the man fell, the weapon was ready to take out his partner. The second streak hit the soldier in the side of the head as he turned to find the attacker who killed his friend.

Once the first board was removed, the helpers had made quick work of the remaining boards.

She held up her hand for the helpers to get out of her way, and they quickly complied. "Follow me!" She shouted.

As she climbed out the window, she dropped an invisibility spell on herself. She didn't stop to see if the people complied with her command, but the sounds behind her confirmed that people were ungracefully climbing out the window.

There were no other soldiers on this side of the burning building, so she hurried towards the front where she saw a dozen or more standing near the main doors to the building. The soldiers were laughing and pointing.

One of the soldiers shouted, "Burn Magi lovers, burn!"

Sarasa shot him first.

Without waiting, she began firing at one soldier after the next. Each magical bolt streaked with deadly accuracy to its target, and she methodically took down one target after the next. Five of the enemies were dead before any of them even drew their weapons and turned to engage her. By then it was too late.

The fire in her soul burned brighter than the warehouse she stood next to, and she prayed to any god who would listen to bring her more soldiers. Each of them deserved far more than the quick and merciful death that she gave them.

A tremendous crashing sound came from the building beside her, and jarred her from her murderous fury. She half expected the building to be in ruin, but it was still standing.

Small bits of rock and wood debris fell on her from above, and she looked up to see bits of wood and rock raining all around the area.

She hurried over to the main doors to the warehouse, and shoved some large barrels and crates away from them. The fire on the walls had moved to some of the crates that were barring the door, and she kicked those out of the way.

When she threw open the double doors she saw that some of the smoke had cleared from the room.

She looked towards the arena and saw Eleyne standing with her hands above her head. A large rock appeared above her and it shot towards the roof of the warehouse. The rock crashed into the ceiling and shattered a huge hole in the roof above. It shattered into smaller pieces as bits of debris cascaded down into the room.

The people scurried around, trying to avoid the larger pieces of falling boards, rock, and burning embers.

The fire covered the walls, and most of the ceiling, but the two large holes in the roof along with a magical wind, flushed much of the smoke outside at least making the air breathable. The down-side was that the wind was fanning the flames causing the fire to burn hotter and faster.

As the people noticed Sarasa standing with the doors open, a sudden surge of people sprinted towards the relative safety of the city streets.

Sarasa moved out of the way of the flood of people heading towards the doors. She skirted along the outer edge of the flow of people and headed towards the Magi in the arena cage.

"Nice of you to join us, Rasa. Done screwing around?"

She flashed a rude gesture at her brother and he squeezed her shoulder.

Eleyne continued to usher the final few people through the portal.

With the main doors open, the warehouse quickly emptied. Some of the people opted to wait for a chance to go with the Magi through the portal, but most ran for their lives out the open doors.

A large flaming board fell near them, and smashed benches near the arena cage.

Eleyne shouted, "The roof ain't going to hold long, hurry up!"

The last two people stepped through the portal, and they were quickly followed by Eleyne, Sarasa, and finally Dalen.

Sarasa had no idea where Firana had teleported and opened the exit end of the portal. So, when she stepped out of the portal she was surprised to find herself standing at the edge of a city. There were no walls around the city, so clearly it was not any of the major cities within the empire.

A large crowd of people were standing in a clearing.

Firana stood near the portal, shouting, "Keep going people! Step out of the portal and move far over there to make room for the next people to exit!"

Sarasa slapped the dark-haired Magi on the bottom, and said, "Nice job, Firi. You saved a lot of people today."

Firana turned and gave her a strong hug, "I was scared you wouldn't make it out of there. I hated porting out with all of you left in that place!"

"We each have a part to play, today your part was to port somewhere and open the portal to bring all these other people to safety. Speaking of safety, where are we?"

"I just ported to the first safe place that came to mind when I knew we needed to flee. We're outside of Kha'Mu, where I grew up."

Sarasa had never been to the Free City of Kha'Mu, but she knew it was on the far west coast near the sea.

Dalen interrupted them by grabbing Firana and embracing her in a fierce hug. Sarasa walked away as the hug turned into kisses and muffled sobs.

She walked up next to Eleyne and smiled at her. "Nice job back there. I don't know how much more smoke those people could have taken.

Knocking holes in the roof and creating a magical breeze to flush the smoke from the place was brilliant."

"Are you kidding me, if you hadn't gotten those doors open we'd still be there with the roof falling on us."

Dalen walked up, clapping slowly. "Yes, you're all heroes. We'll be throwing a sarding parade for you next week. If you could take a small break from patting each other on the arse, maybe we could deal with these people?"

For the second time in a few minutes Sarasa flashed a rude gesture at her brother. The two of them walked over to the restless crowd of people, with the other two Magi closely behind.

Dalen said, "Listen up!" His blue and black Magi Cloak flowed smoothly in the cool gentle breeze.

Sarasa took a moment to enjoy the relative warmth of the land so close to the western sea. Early-Winter was about to give way to Mid-Winter and the weather had been cold and snowy in the lands north of the mountains where Fort Randol was located.

The people standing around in the clearing stopped talking and turned their attention to Dalen.

He said, "If you wanna stand up and fight the emperor who sent his soldiers to burn innocent people alive for just being with Magi, stay right here. We'll take a quick peek to see if you got a magewel."

A low murmur spread through the people as they commented, or complained, to each other.

"If you want us to return you to Darisa City so you can take your chances with those soldiers, go stand by those trees and we'll open a portal soon."

Most of the people in the clearing moved over to the small copse of trees.

One of the women walking towards the trees stopped and turned to Dalen. She said, "Where are we? Can we just stay here?"

He nodded, "That is the Free City of Kha'Mu, and if you wanna live there I ain't gonna stop you."

"I grew up here." Firana stepped towards the people, and pointed at the city off in the distance. "This is primarily a fishing city and most of the jobs support fishing in one way or another. Shipwrights, lightermen, fishmongers, coopers, netmakers, porters and the like. If you're willing to work hard, you'll be welcomed here."

After a brief discussion, several of the people left the trees and started walking towards the coastal city of Kha'Mu.

Dalen turned back to the group of people waiting to be tested to see if they could become Magi. There were a couple dozen people standing there, and most of them looked pretty uncomfortable. He said, "If you got the gift to be a Magi, we'll tell you to stand by that rock and if you ain't then you'll go stand by the trees with the others."

With a quick gesture from Dalen, the Magi started checking to see who possessed a magewel.

Sarasa stepped up to a fairly tall man. She said, "Look me in the eyes."

When the man looked down, she opened her magesight and gazed beyond his eyes and into his soul beyond. What she actually saw was the view of his soul as seen by her magesight, and the sensation always made her feel uneasy. It took only a moment to see that the large man did not possess a magewel. She closed off her magesight and said, "Go over by the trees, please."

She stepped over to a woman who had been standing next to the large man. She quickly saw that the woman did not have the blessing from Nalria and could not become a Magi. Sarasa pointed towards the trees.

In just a few minutes the Magi had checked everyone who wished to be checked. There were four good Magi candidates standing near the rock, and everyone else had moved over to the trees.

Four out of about twenty-five people was a pretty good ratio. Sarasa had found that only about one in ten people possessed a magewel, so it had been a good day when it came to expanding the number of Magi. Unfortunately, thanks to a traitorous spectator and a group of imperial soldiers who were willing to kill innocents to get at Magi, the new Magi candidates had come at a tragic price.

She followed Dalen over to the trees to help bring those people back to Darisa City.

As they approached, one of the people stepped forward. He said, "What if we still wanna help you? What happened today ain't the first time innocent folks have died because of the emperor's stupid war against you. I wanna help."

Dalen nodded, "Of course! When you get back to your city, tell people that we ain't the enemy! Work from the shadows to hinder them when they try to hunt us."

Another man stepped forward and his wife stepped up with him, holding his arm. They looked at each other, and then the woman spoke. "We're merchants in Darisa City and everyone there knows us. Lots of folks saw us in the warehouse, even some of the soldiers. If we go back, they'll label us Magi supporters. Couldn't we go with you and help somehow? Perhaps we could serve as cooks or laborers?"

Sarasa looked to Dalen and he shrugged his shoulders at her.

She looked back to the people, and saw some of them nodding and pleading. She couldn't think of any good reason why non-magical folks couldn't live at Fort Randol. The woman was right, there were many tasks that needed to be done that didn't require magic. As the number of Magi increased they would probably need even more help. She held up her hands for quiet, "That is true, we could use a good cook and other skilled laborers. If you want to join us, and live and work at our Stronghold, then go stand over by the rock and you can go with us."

Before the people started moving, Dalen added, "I can't promise any pay right away, but you'll be welcomed to live, eat, and labor alongside the Magi."

More than a dozen people walked over to stand with the new Magi candidates near the rock.

Without waiting any longer, Firana whispered, "Kur'Gezbar." She vanished instantly.

Dalen opened a portal with his ring, and a few seconds later the swirling colors of the portal faded into a scene near the marketplace in Darisa City. He said, "If you're going back to DC, get over here and go through the portal one at a time."

CHAPTER 14

Rissyl

He'd been dreading this day for almost two years, and now that it was here he realized it was going to be much harder than he feared. When he was with his Magi friends, his marriage to Cynia seemed like the most natural thing in the world. When he was together with his wife, it never even crossed his mind that she used to be a Dreg. However, as he walked towards his parents' beautiful villa he had no idea how he was going to explain to his parents that he'd married the woman who used to be their property.

Before his life exploded into the whirlwind of change and chaos that had existed since he'd become a Magi, his world was one of order and routine. He grew up in a nice Gentry family living in a beautiful home in the Garden District of Sorgo. Just like all of his friends and relatives, his parents owned a couple of Dregs to do the cooking, tend the grounds, and take care of other menial tasks around the home.

His father had been the Magistrate of Live Property in Sorgo, but most people referred to him as the Dreg Dealer. Criminals and other undesirables were sentenced to a period of time, frequently until the end of their life, as a Dreg. Dregs were not human, they were property. Well, at least that is what had been stressed to him since he was a little boy. In his early life it was just understood that Dregs were Dregs for a reason and they got what they deserved. The concept of feeling sorry for a Dreg was as unusual as the idea of feeling bad that a chair wasn't a cow or a horse.

His understanding of Dregs, and much of his understanding of the world in general, began to unravel when Cynia introduced him to her cousin Dalen. Even after years of being married to a woman who used to be his family's Dreg, Rissyl still wasn't completely convinced that the concept of sentencing people to a life as property was an entirely bad idea. He acknowledged that oftentimes the empire had used it as a weapon and innocent people got sucked into the system. He'd even helped to free many Dregs who'd suffered that injustice. However, quietly he still held to the belief that there were evil people who needed to be subjugated for the good of the decent people.

It was because of this deeply held belief in the inherent benefits of the Dreg system that he was so apprehensive about telling his parents that he had married their former Dreg, and that their grandchild was conceived with their former property.

He was certain that it would be scandalous for his family, and he wouldn't be at all surprised if his parents simply disowned him as a family disgrace.

Rissyl took a deep breath as he walked up the steps to the front door of the main building of the villa.

Sarge patted him on the shoulder lightly. "Breathe, Riz. It'll be fine, these are your parents."

He wanted to tell the old paladin that he had no idea what he was talking about, but he decided to keep his mouth shut. The man had been surprisingly supportive, and was just trying to encourage him. He looked back at the other Magi.

Madalyn stood next to Sarge, like normal. She insisted on wearing her Kelegar cleric robes, even though he encouraged her to dress more casually to better blend in.

It didn't help that Sarge wouldn't compromise, and wore his ornate Azure Paladin armor.

Behind them were Asha and Zahr, who followed his request and wore simple traveling clothes.

Really, Rissyl had wanted to come alone. It would be awkward to drag all of these people into his parents' home and try to explain who they were without explaining that they were all Magi. Since both of his parents were high ranking officials in the Misi city government, knowledge that their son and his travelling companions were enemies of the empire would make an already difficult conversation all the more unpleasant.

When he told Cynia that he'd be visiting his parents alone, she insisted that he take other Magi with him. Against his better judgement he brought a Magi from each Order. He wasn't sure that visiting his parents qualified as a dangerous mission. It was silly to come with so much magical power on a simple trip to visit his parents, but in the end he decided not to argue with her about it.

He knocked on the door, took a deep breath, and let it out slowly. A short time later the door opened and an attractive young woman smiled at him.

She said, "Greetings."

"I am Rissyl Sokigo, and I've come to visit my parents."

The woman opened the door further. "Please come in, milord, and have a seat in the foyer. I'll let milady know that you've come."

The Magi made themselves comfortable in the large, and lavishly furnished, room.

When Rissyl sat down, Tiberos climbed out of the floor, plopped down next to him, and leaned against his leg. He reached out and scratched the Rolimi dog behind the ear. Even though his hand passed through the mostly transparent dog, Tiberos moved its head closer to his hand like it was enjoying the scratches.

When his mother walked in the room, he stood up and she rushed over and embraced him at length.

"I'm so glad to see you, it's been far too long!"

"I know, Mom. I should have come to visit a long time ago, I've just been very busy."

She looked to the other people in the room, and asked, "So, who are your friends?"

"This is Sarge, Madalyn, Asha, and Zahr." Then he motioned to his mom and to the Magi he said, "This is my mother, Amalia."

She sat down and the group exchanged pleasantries for quite some time. Mostly they talked about the weather and other topics that strangers might discuss when first meeting. She filled him in on gossip about extended family and their new friends.

The Rolimi dog leaned on Rissyl's leg once again, but his mom didn't even look down at it. Few people could see the Rolimi dogs.

When the conversation grew quiet, he said, "I figured that Dad would be home by now. Aren't ministers done working by the noontime bell?"

He laughed at his own joke, but his mother didn't join in. His father had been a high level official in Sorgo, and he was then promoted to the Council of Ministers reporting directly to the chancellor of Misi when that city was newly populated two years ago. Rissyl hadn't had a chance to speak to his father about his new job, but he assumed that the prestigious job would be much less stressful than his previous position back in Sorgo.

His mom shook her head, "Politics have been a messy business lately. I don't want to get into the details right now, but I'll just say that he's been working many long hours lately."

Rissyl wanted to press for more details, but decided to leave it alone for now. Instead he said, "Where is Brielle? I'm guessing that she's found a bunch of potential suitors by now?"

His little sister had been growing up quickly when she and their parents moved to Misi, and she was now an adult so she might even be married already. He feared that he might have even missed her wedding, but the expression on his mother's face suggested that he hadn't.

With a single shake of her head, she said, "Brielle has gotten mixed up with some undesirable friends. She doesn't come home all that much these days."

He thought his mother might start crying, but she wiped a tear from her eye and smiled.

She said, "Let's talk about something happier. How have you been, what's new?"

Rissyl was taken off guard by the sudden change of topics, and all of the gentle ways of breaking the news to her abruptly fled his brain. He said, "Well, I got married last year."

Her shock was apparent, and she covered her mouth with both hands. She looked from Madalyn to Asha and back. "So, which of these lovely young ladies is my new daughter?"

He stood up and said, "Mom, let's go for a walk."

She led him out of the room, and away from the other Magi. He still didn't know how to explain it to her, but however he did it he didn't want his friends to see how uncomfortable he was about the topic. Mostly he didn't want them to see his mother's reaction.

They walked through a large study and into an even larger library. He walked over to a set of massive windows overlooking the splendid view of rolling meadow covered with a thin coating of snow. Without looking back at her, he asked, "Do you remember Cynia?"

There was a long pause. "You mean the large bosomed Dreg that you begged your father to leave with you in Sorgo when we moved to Misi? Oh Riz, please tell me you haven't."

He turned to her and nodded.

Amalia sat down in one of the room's many reading chairs. "Plenty of people enjoy the company of their Dregs more than might be proper, but this? She is still a Dreg, Riz! Your father still has her papers. How could you have been married? It's not possible."

"We have a son named Chardy. He recently turned one."

His mother sobbed, "Oh by the gods, Riz, what have you done? My grandbaby is a Dreg!"

He put his hands on his hips. "Chardy is not a Dreg!"

She let her hands drop heavily to the arms of the big chair. "You know the law, Rissyl! All children born to Dregs are Dregs! Your father was Magistrate of Live Property for most of your life, you know how these things work! How could you have done this?"

Before he could try to explain things to her, he heard the front door open and crash into the wall behind it.

His father's voice boomed through the front part of the house. "Amalia, where are you? We have a problem!"

She stood up and he followed her through the study.

Before they got to the foyer, he heard his father say, "Who are you?"

His mother answered for them, saying, "Those are Rissyl's friends. What is the trouble, Tuknor?"

Tuknor reached out and squeezed Rissyl on the shoulder. He said, "It's good to see you, boy. But you've picked a rotten time. Brielle is in trouble."

Rissyl had never seen his father cry, so he was stunned to see that his eyes were bloodshot and his cheeks were wet and red. Whatever was going on, it wasn't good.

Amalia crossed her arms at her chest, "Now what's she done?"

Choking back his tears, Tuknor said, "She's been found to be a Magi. They're going to hang her in the morning with several of her friends!" His voice broke and the last several words were barely audible.

His mother slowly melted to the floor in anguish and tears, and her husband knelt next to her and put his arm around her.

Rissyl looked at them in stock and disbelief. He said, "But you're a minister! Just order them to release her!"

Without standing, his father said, "It doesn't work like that, Riz. The emperor sent his agents here, and they've accused her. She's already a Dreg and she's been in the Dross for a day or more. The sentence didn't even go through our office. The emperor's agent carried out the sentencing himself. It's a miracle that I even found out before they administer the punishment in the morning."

Rissyl took a step towards the door. He said, "We've got to go there, now! Surely you can order them to release her?"

His father stood up and shoved Rissyl hard enough to knock him back several steps. Tuknor followed him, shaking his finger in his face as Rissyl caught his balance. "Don't you think I've already tried that? Do you think I want to let my own daughter be hanged? I've spent most of the day pleading with the chancellor to interject somehow! The imperial agent speaks with the authority of the emperor himself! There is nothing to be done!"

"Maybe for you, but I'm not going to let them kill my little sister. The emperor has done enough killing in the name of this stupid war against Magi!" He pushed past his father and motioned for the other Magi to follow him.

The door was still wide open, from when his father entered, and Rissyl stormed out of the doorway with the other Magi close on his heels.

Tuknor rushed out the door after him. "What are you going to do?"

Rissyl didn't look back. As he walked, he said, "I'm going to go and bring Brielle home."

Tiberos padded along beside him.

Tuknor warned, "If you interfere, they'll tattoo you and toss you into the Dross next to her! Please stop and think!"

When he got to the wagon Rissyl turned to face his father. "There is no time to stop and think. Go back and comfort mother, she needs you right now."

"How do you expect to get her out of the Dross? It's guarded even more now than normal, since the emperor's agent showed up with a squad of elite troopers."

Rissyl was furious, and he didn't have patience to argue. In a perfect world, he would have liked to break the news to his father in a gentler way. "Because I am a powerful Magi, and no one can stop me from getting her back."

Tuknor looked like he wasn't sure if his son was trying to make some sort of sick joke. "That's not funny, Riz. It's that kind of crazy talk that got your sister in trouble! She hangs around with her freaky friends pretending to be Magi! Look what that got her!"

"Zahr, drop the portal right here. I'll go set up the other end." Without even trying to explain things to his father any further, he said, "Kur'Gezbar."

He teleported as close to the entrance of the Misi Dross as he could get, while still in a relatively secluded spot. When he found someplace safe, he used the magic ring to drop the exit portal.

His father was the first person to step through the portal. He blinked and grabbed for the wall of a building to steady himself. "By all the sarding gods."

Sarge was the next one through the portal. He said, "Sorry, Riz. He insisted on coming along."

The others stepped through the portal quickly, and it vanished as soon as Zahr stepped through.

Rissyl said, "It's fine, Sarge. Let's just go and get my sister."

They walked down the length of the wall separating the Dross from the Misi Commons.

As they walked, Tuknor asked, "So, what's the plan? How do we get in, and how do we get your sister out?"

Rissyl shrugged, "I haven't gotten things planned out that far. I figured I'd just blast my way in and find Brielle, and blast my way out."

His father stopped walking and pulled Rissyl around to face him. He said, "I have no idea what powers you've got. But if you blast your way in they might kill her and the other Dregs before you even get through the door. Let me use my rank to get us in. Once we find her, you can do your thing."

He stood there and looked at his father for a long moment. "If you go in there with us, you'll have to flee the city. They'll hunt you down, and mom too."

"Let me worry about that. Let's go."

When they got to the gate, they found it guarded by several stone-faced Dross Lions, the specially trained troops assigned to guard the Dross.

Tuknor approached them, and the Magi followed closely behind. He was still dressed in his extravagant Council of Ministers robes. He said, "I am Minister Sokigo, and I would like to see my daughter."

One of the Dross Lions stepped over to better situate himself between Tuknor and the gate. He said, "I'm sorry, minister, you can't enter."

"Son, get your commander here. Now."

The soldier hesitated, and then motioned for one of the other soldiers to summon the commander.

A short time later, a tall and lanky soldier came through the gate. He wore the usual Dross Lion tabard with fancy embroidery around the edges to denote his rank. The man said, "I am Lieutenant Molanders. What is the problem?"

"Greetings, lieutenant. I am Minister Sokigo, and I would like to see my daughter who is being held in there."

The lieutenant shook his head. "I'm sorry minister, but Dregs are not allowed visitors."

Tuknor placed his hands on his hips. "Who is your commander's commander, lieutenant?"

The lieutenant obviously saw where Tuknor was going with the question. He shifted uncomfortably from one foot to another. "The Magistrate of City Safety."

"Ah, yes. Magistrate Fullerto. And who does Fullerto report to?"

Growing more uncomfortable, the lieutenant said, "Ah, she reports to you."

Tuknor shook his head. "Wrong. Magistrate Fullerto reports to Junior Minister Zool. Zool reports to me. The point, lieutenant, is that I am so far above your station that your commander's commander fetches my morning coffee. I don't like to pull rank, but I really must insist that you let me see my daughter. Don't make me start making unpleasant threats about the future of your career."

There was a brief period where the lieutenant seemed to be debating whether to comply, and finally he said, "Who are all these people? If I permit you a brief visitation, all of these people need to wait out here."

He shook his head once again, "These people are my family and friends. We wish to say a final goodbye before..." His voice broke, and he stopped talking.

Everyone stood in uncomfortable silence, until the lieutenant turned to one of the other soldiers. He said, "Sergeant Pyal, take these people to the Mist-Bear building."

The gate opened and the lieutenant walked off to the left quickly.

Pyal walked through the gate and to the right. Tuknor and the Magi followed closely behind. Tiberos walked right next to Rissyl, as if guarding him.

Rissyl could feel his heart beating heavily as they walked through the Dross. He'd never been inside one, and he never really had any desire to see what was in them. The place was immaculate. There wasn't a blade of grass out of place, and he didn't see any discarded trash on the ground. The buildings looked new, but there was a depressing feeling throughout the entire area as they passed by windowless building after windowless building.

Off in the distance he could hear voices, but they were too far away to make out what was being said. He got the impression that there were cries mixed in with abrupt laughter.

The more they walked, the louder the voices sounded. Soon Rissyl could clearly hear the sounds of a man crying out in pain, and that was immediately followed by more laughter.

Rounding another turn they could finally see the source of the noises. Off in the distance were four soldiers, each armed with a wooden practice sword. They were standing around a naked man who stood motionlessly with his fingers interlaced behind his head. The soldiers were all standing in various combat stances with the naked man clearly their intended target.

One of the soldiers gave a command and simultaneously all four soldiers attacked the naked man with their wooden swords. One of the soldiers did a single attack against the base of the man's neck, another slammed his weapon into the man's groin. The soldiers to the sides each executed multiple hits with their weapons in quick succession. The naked man cried out in pain and dropped to one knee.

The soldiers laughed and one of them kicked the naked man. He said, "Stand up, Dreg!"

Slowly the naked man stood up and interlaced his fingers behind his head once again. His body was covered in long welts from where he'd been hit by the wooden swords over and over.

When they got close, Tuknor said, "What's happening here?"

One of the soldiers turned to him and sneered. "Target practice, old man. Gotta keep the troops battle ready!" All of the soldiers started laughing once again.

Tuknor placed his hands on his hips, and then pointed at the soldier as he talked to him. "In Misi we don't torture or harm our Dregs! It's the law!"

The soldier made a mocking face, drawing further laughs from the other soldiers. He said, "I don't care about your laws. We report to the emperor, and your laws don't apply to us!"

From his right, Rissyl heard a very weak voice, "Dad?"

He looked over and he saw a young woman crawling towards them. Near her, huddled in the shadowed corner where two buildings met, were half a dozen naked Dregs. Some of them might have been dead, or perhaps they had passed out from excessive abuse. Their bodies were black and blue, and completely covered in long welts like the ones on the naked man between the soldiers.

It wasn't until the young woman tried to stand up, reaching towards Tuknor, that Rissyl realized that the wretched Dreg kneeling naked before him was his own little sister.

Rissyl and his father both rushed over to her at the same time. He wanted to gather her into his arms to protect her, but her body looked fragile and broken. She was bruised from her neck to her knees, and savage welts crisscrossed everywhere. Many of the welts leaked small streams of blood down her body.

He and his father were afraid to touch her, for fear of harming her further. She held out her hand to Rissyl, who took it gently.

Tuknor tore off his robes and draped them carefully over her.

Fury grew and intensified deep within Rissyl as he looked at the beaten and badly damaged body of his sister. He squeezed her hand softly, and she howled in pain. He silently begged her forgiveness for not being there to protect her.

Behind him, he vaguely heard one of the soldiers say, "Go get Agent Luigey. Now!"

Rissyl stood up and turned to face the soldiers. He saw Sarge physically restraining Madalyn to keep her from rushing over to Brielle.

"I am already here, Captain. What is the problem?"

Rissyl knew that voice, but he couldn't place it. He turned to his left and saw an imperial officer walking up behind him.

The officer looked at him and muttered, "Rissyl?"

As he looked at the officer he thought the man looked familiar but he couldn't figure out where he'd seen him before.

Agent Luigey shouted, "This man is a Magi! Kill him! Kill them all!"

The realization hit him like a ten-ton hammer. The agent standing before him was Konrad, the Magi who supposedly died alongside Keta at the battle at Randol's place last year. The Magi had been an imperial spy all along. He was responsible for the death of Randol, Keta, and so many other Magi. Now, he had captured and encouraged the savage torture of Rissyl's sister.

The white-hot fury that Rissyl had felt at seeing what had happened to his sister intensified into a blinding rage like he'd never experienced.

Some tiny part of him noticed that the entire area exploded into chaos and motion. The Magi armored themselves with their cloaks and summoned their weapons, soldiers dropped their practice weapons and moved to draw real ones.

However, none of that mattered. None of these imperials would live to harm someone else, and Rissyl fully intended to be the one to see to that.

In a deathly quiet voice, he hissed, "Krol'Tu Nari."

It was a spell he'd used to kill a spectre when they were fighting to claim the Stronghold, but over the last year he had practiced and refined the spell so that it was a much smaller column of fire that used much less of the magical essence in his magewel.

However, he thought of none of those things as he watched the first column appear where Konrad stood. His mind was void of anything besides murderous rage. In rapid succession, fiery column after fiery column appeared and engulfed each of the soldiers. No sooner did one appear when the previous one disappeared. The victims had no warning and no chance to defend themselves. One moment they were there, preparing to attack, and the next moment they no longer existed.

In the span of less than a second, a series of six fiery pillars had appeared and vanished. In the places where the pillars appeared, six enemies were quickly turned to ashes and some of that ash still floated in the cool evening breeze. For a brief moment, the heat from the columns was intense, but that quickly vanished leaving nothing but a deathly calm.

The calm was pierced by the maniacal wailing of the naked man who cried out in panic and shock, as he huddled in a ball in the middle of six scorch marks on the ground around him.

The man's screams seemed to thrust everyone out of their stunned silence, and they all burst into movement. Rissyl and Tuknor knelt beside Brielle, but Madalyn pushed her way in and rested her hands on the young woman's shoulders.

Rissyl vaguely heard Sarge shout, "You two, guard over there and there. I'll take this side!"

Asha said, "Sure thing."

Something large, most likely Zahr in the form of a gorilla, let out a guttural roar. Rissyl didn't look up to see. If something large was going to eat him, it was just going to have to wait until he knew that Brielle would be alright.

He listened to Madalyn's prayer, as she whispered, "Blessed Kelegar, I ask you to heal this young woman. Mend her broken body and comfort her traumatized soul. You are all-knowing and all-seeing, the sire of the gods and the true creator of life. In your blessed name I pray, and humbly plead, that you grant me this prayer."

116

There were no trumpets or brilliant displays of lights. Nothing happened and for a moment he feared that Madalyn's god had chosen to ignore her in Brielle's time of need.

His sister's bruised and battered body didn't change, but she looked up at Madalyn with wide eyes. She gently moved her arms and then pressed carefully against the ribs just below her neck. The expression on her face showed that she expected blinding pain, and then she smiled weakly.

The smile brought a huge sense of relief, and Rissyl let out a long sigh.

"Company's coming!" Asha's voice sounded almost excited.

"Riz, get out of here and give us a portal destination or prepare for more killing!" Sarge drew his sword, which gave off a metallic hum.

Rissyl stood up. "Sarge, I want all of these injured people taken with us."

"We don't have time for that, Riz. We're gonna be flooded with troops in seconds." Sarge didn't look back at him.

Pointing the palm of his hand towards the soldiers rushing at Sarge, Rissyl said, "Krol'Tu Salindi." A large ball of fire sprang from his outstretched hand and streaked towards the soldiers. He didn't wait to see if it hit any of them. It didn't matter, it just needed to scare them and hold them away briefly.

He turned and faced the soldiers rushing towards Asha. He launched another large ball of fire in that direction.

Then he turned to Sarge, and grabbed him by the shoulder. He turned the tough old warrior to face him, and said, "All of these wounded go with us."

Rissyl looked back to Brielle, and saw her standing up slowly. He whispered, "Kur'Gezbar."

He reached out and grabbed hold of the railing at the base of the stairs of his parents' villa. No matter how many times he teleported, the brief moment of vertigo was always present and it was even worse if his magewel was getting empty.

He didn't have time to let the dizziness pass, so he held the rail with one hand and activated the portal ring on the other hand. The swirling colors of the portal appeared instantly.

Madalyn came through first, followed almost immediately by Brielle. He rushed over and helped his little sister away from the portal so the others could step through.

She seemed too small and frail, and she shivered as she stood in the cool breeze wrapped in her father's robes.

Brielle smiled slightly and leaned into him, as he enveloped her in a gentle embrace. She said, "I've missed you so much, Izzy. I've been stupid since we moved here."

He held her close and tried to keep her warm. In the whole world, she was the only one who called him Izzy, and normally she did it to pester him because she knew it was a name he disliked. At this point in time he couldn't think of anything he'd rather be called.

Sarge stepped over by them. "One more port, Riz. Let's go home."

He looked to the door of the house and saw his father leading his mother down the stairs. As she saw her daughter, Amalia rushed over to her.

Tuknor said, "That man is right, Riz. Let's get someplace safe. The emperor's men won't take long to get here." He turned and looked at the servant who originally answered the door for Rissyl, and said, "Hesha, get the others, you're coming with us."

Rissyl stepped away from his sister, as his mother gathered her into her arms.

He said, "Kur'Gezbar."

CHAPTER 15

Kimly

"By the gods, why is it so cold? Is this normal?" Favin wrapped his scarf around his face another time, and then crossed his arms in front of himself trying to keep warm.

Kimly laughed quietly, shaking her head. "It's really not all that cold out here. We're only a few days from Mid-Winter, it could be much colder this far north. I grew up in northern cities, trust me this ain't bad."

He was quiet for a time, shivering and keeping his thoughts to himself.

She turned her attention back to the road. They were sitting in a thicket near the road leading southwest out of Misi, waiting for a group of Dregs to return from their daily labors. On the other side of the road, Viper sat in wait.

They had arrived in Misi two days ago. They bought an old abandoned shack next to the wall separating the Misi Commons from the Dross, and they used that place as their base as they gathered information about their target. After dozens of scouting missions around the area, including two dangerous missions into the Dross itself looking for information, they found that their target was assigned to a Dreg work group called the Frost Weasels.

Further investigation revealed that the Frost Weasels were assigned to road maintenance, far to the southwest along this road.

The sun was dipping low in the western sky, and within an hour or two it would be dark. Their observations of the various work groups showed that the group leaders always had their groups securely back inside the Dross before darkness fell unless they were away for several days.

So, Kimly expected to see the Dregs and their guards walking down the road on their way back to the Dross at any minute.

Favin stood up and started rubbing his rear-end with both hands. "It's like all of the warmth in my body is being sucked out through my arse!"

"Get down, troll brains! You're gonna give us away! I told you to find some large sticks to sit on. You don't wanna sit right on the ground, or it'll pull the warmth from you."

"Dying in a failed ambush is better than freezing to death in a frozen patch of weeds and thistles."

She watched him pile together a small nest of sticks and branches, carefully avoiding the ones with the largest thorns.

When he finally got settled, they resumed their quiet observation of the secluded road. She was beginning to get a little worried that the Frost Weasels had changed their plans or decided to return to the Dross on some other road.

"Do you think the Magi made it out of the Dross alive?"

She was a bit surprised by his question, although she'd been wondering the same thing for hours.

Earlier that day Kimly, Favin, and Viper were sitting in their newly-acquired shack when they saw Rissyl, Sarge, and four other people walk past their building. She had been half-tempted to go out and talk to them as they passed, but she couldn't think of a plausible excuse to explain to Rissyl why she was in Misi. While she was still debating, the Magi walked right up to the main gate of the Dross. They were even crazier than she remembered.

The Magi talked to a guard at the gate, then a different guard, and soon they walked right in the main gate of the Dross. She was extremely curious what would bring the group of Magi to the Dross in a remote city on the edge of the empire. Only a few minutes after the Magi entered, Kimly saw several shafts of fire streak into the sky from somewhere behind the Dross wall.

Whatever brought them to the Misi Dross apparently needed burned to the ground, and she didn't particularly care what it was. The Magi's attack in the Dross created exactly the kind of distraction that Kimly and her group needed to slip out of the southwest gate of the city without being noticed or questioned.

Within minutes of the Magi attack the emperor's elite troops and Misi sentinels began rushing to the Dross. If the Magi didn't make a quick escape, it was unlikely that they made it out at all.

Kimly nodded, "Magi are deceptively tricky, and they have so many magical spells in their arsenal. If they walked in the front gate of that place in broad daylight, they went in with a plan on how to get back out."

She hoped she was right. A tiny part of her felt guilty that they didn't make any effort to see if the Magi needed help. It wasn't that long ago that Rissyl and others risked a lot to rescue her and Jessa from the Motlite compound.

With a shiver, she pushed those thoughts away. For the most part, she didn't like dwelling on bad memories, and that was one of the worst.

She continued, "That's why The Shrouded have been paying the heaviest price in the emperor's war on the Magi."

"What do you mean?" Favin looked baffled.

For over a year she'd been lying to these people about The Shrouded, claiming that there was an elaborate network of spies and assassins and Favin and his group were just a small part of a secret and ancient brotherhood. She'd made up the entire thing. Over the last year, Favin recruited people in Khardifar and she'd recruited people in several other cities. They recruited only people with a magewel, and she'd taught them all some simple magic spells and tasked them with missions occasionally. Mainly the missions were simple thievery or extortion tasks that made them all a great deal of money.

However, the falsehoods were becoming more difficult to hide and some of her new agents hinted at wanting to meet her superiors within The Shrouded. Some even desired promotions within the brotherhood and aspired to work in the secret headquarters and help to oversee larger portions of the group's business.

It was all starting to get a bit out of hand, and it was time for her to do something about it. This line of conversation gave her a nice little lead-in for a new lie to bring to close a bunch of other lies.

She said, "Right before we left to come here, I received word that the emperor's people raided The Shrouded's home base. It looks like none of our top people survived." She put her face in her hands, pretending to be upset over the tragic news.

Favin placed his hand on her back and rubbed it gently.

Kimly looked up and said, "We've been taking heavy losses for months. It seems like each fortnight I get word of more of our agents being killed by Magi hunters. The sarding Magi have gotten us sucked into their war with the emperor, and we're the ones paying the heaviest price. They have a huge arsenal of powerful spells to fight off the emperor's troops, but the magic available to The Shrouded is much more limited."

He looked at her with concern in his eyes, and after a moment he said, "So, the death of the people at our home base. Where does that leave us, as far as leadership and power within The Shrouded? Do we know which high level agents will take over operations?"

121

She shrugged, "I just don't know yet. I'm starting to suspect that I might be the most senior agent left alive, but it will take time to know for sure."

Favin looked thoughtful, "That's bad news for those who died, but perhaps we can turn the group's misfortune into a bit of an opportunity for us? Could you take over the entire operation? Would the remaining agents follow you?"

Since she'd recruited all of the agents who weren't working directly for Favin, she had no doubt that they'd follow her. However, he didn't need to know that. She shrugged, "I suppose there is only one way to find out. There could be agents who are senior to me who are still alive, we'll have to see how things shake out."

Favin looked back to the road. He whispered, "Here they come!"

Looking back to the road she saw that the Dregs and their guard were getting close. The conversation would have to wait until later.

Somewhere in the group of Dregs walking towards them was Chyak Krazni, and today was his day to die.

The unmistakable sound of a crossbow bolt being launched and zipping through the air announced that Viper had decided that the group had gotten close enough.

She stood up threw a dagger at the nearest guard. With a tiny bit of magic and a whispered trigger word the dagger streaked remarkably fast and true towards it's victim. It sunk deep in the neck of the guard, just behind his jaw.

When she brought her hand up to throw the next dagger, all of the guards were already dead. She sighed in disappointment and slammed the blade back into the leather scabbard on her left forearm. Favin and Viper were too fast, and it spoiled some of her fun.

In the middle of the road were two large wagons each attached to a pair of oxen. The wagons were each filled with a dozen or more large metal balls. The balls had several large chains attached to them. Surrounding the wagons were around one hundred Dregs, who were all chained to the large metal balls in the wagons. The Dregs stood cautiously, looking at their ambushers. Some of the Dregs looked hopeful that they were being rescued, and others looked fearful. A few looked at Kimly with more lecherous thoughts clearly on their mind.

As she and Favin walked slowly towards the Dregs, Kimly heard Viper's crossbow several more times. She wasn't sure if there were more guards on that side of the road, and then she saw the oxen fall to the ground one at a time.

She raised an eyebrow and looked at Favin.

He shrugged, "Well, now we don't have to worry about them getting away. Those wagons aren't going anywhere fast." As he walked, he kept his crossbow aimed at the Dregs.

"Chyak Krazni!"

Hearing Viper yelling on the other side of the road prompted Kimly to follow his lead. She echoed, "Chyak Krazni!"

A murmur spread around the Dregs, and many of them looked around but none spoke up.

Kimly shouted, "Chyak Krazni! Your brother hired us to find you! Chyak Krazni?"

Off to her right there was a commotion. She looked in that direction and one of the Dregs was standing with his arm raised.

As they got close to the man with his hand raised, a different Dreg reached out and seized Kimly's left arm at the bicep. His vice-like grip felt like iron and he yanked her towards himself as if she were a rag doll.

While she was still moving towards the beast of a man, she smoothly drew a long bladed dagger from her belt sheath. The man leered at her, and she smiled up at him as she quickly rammed the long razor-sharp blade deep into his lower abdomen.

The massive man let out a high-pitched screech and crumpled to the ground, taking her dagger with him. He was balled up on the ground and holding his stomach. The man's wailing dragged on, and all of the nearby Dregs backed away from her quickly.

She reached down and grasped the hilt of her dagger. "I'm gonna need that back." She yanked the blade forward as she withdrew it from his body, greatly widening the vicious wound in the process.

When she stood back up, Favin and Viper were both standing protectively at her sides. Although she didn't need them to keep her safe, she was happy to know that her companions were at her side.

They turned their attention back to their intended target.

She said, "Chyak Krazni, where are you?"

The man held his hand up slightly and stepped forward. The rest of the Dregs moved as far from him as they could, while the grievously wounded Dreg continued to scream in agony.

Kimly stepped closer to Chyak. "I'm going to need to see your tattoo, to know it's you.

The Dreg lifted his thick wool shirt, to reveal an elaborate tattoo of a tiger with a large bone in its mouth. The colors of the tattoo were remarkable and the picture was well-drawn. Clearly this was a tattoo created by a very talented craftsman, and it must have been obscenely expensive. It was certainly the best tattoo that Kimly had ever seen.

She was impressed. "Chyak, this really is a —"

A crossbow bolt exploded into the Dreg's face suddenly, and Kimly stepped back in momentary shock.

Kimly turned to face Viper as he reloaded his weapon. "Dammit Viper! I wanted to tell him how great his tattoo was before we killed him!"

"I'm sure he knew how great it is." Viper kept his eyes on the other Dregs and swept the aim of his crossbow around the area, keeping the remaining captives at a safe distance.

Favin stepped over to Chyak's body, and began the unpleasant business of removing the tattooed skin so they could give it to her client to prove that the job was done.

She placed her hands on her hips in annoyance. "Just because we are here to kill him, doesn't mean we can't be friendly."

Viper began backing away from the wagons slowly. "I'm hungry, and I wanna get back home. Besides, he's too dead to care whether we were friendly before we killed him."

When Favin finished his grisly work, he shoved the skin into a bag and stood up. The three Shrouded began walking away from the wagons.

After about 50 yards, Kimly stopped and tossed the bloody long-bladed dagger into the ground at her feet. The hilt stood higher than the brown dead grass. Looking back to the wretched Dregs still chained to the wagons, she called out, "If you can get to this dagger, maybe you can find a way to free yourselves."

"Or kill each other." Viper unloaded his crossbow, and stored the bolt in his quiver.

"Come on, it'll be a long walk back to the portal stone. I'd like to get there before it's too dark. I've been away from the guild too long." Favin picked up the pace.

CHAPTER 16

Vendino

He took another deep breath, and let it out slowly. Vendino loved the unique mixture of herbs and plants that were burned in the chambrium. It wasn't overpowering or overwhelming, and sometimes he didn't even notice the smell until his mind was free from the stresses and worries of the day and he entered the calm state of relaxation created from a long session of cheirapsia. The gentle music being played by a small band on the far side of the room added calm to yet another of his senses.

He opened his eyes and looked to his left to see that Minister Thorli looked about as blissful as Vendino felt. Thorli was laying on his stomach on a thick and fluffy mat filled with wool and goose feathers. He was surrounded by six cheirapsians, who were enthusiastically massaging, hitting, pressing, rubbing, and hammering on various parts of the minister's body simultaneously. One cheirapsian knelt near his head and used her thumbs to dig into the muscles at the base of his skull. Two women, one on each side, were working on his arms with strong kneading motions on his triceps. Two others were aggressively working on his calf muscles. The final cheirapsian was straddling his rear-end, and slowly but powerfully massaging the muscles along his lower back.

The woman at Vendino's head grabbed his head firmly and repositioned it so that she could continue working on his temples. She purred, "My lord, I can't do a good job if you keep moving. Relax, close your eyes, and let your worries melt away in my hands."

Vendino did as he was told. The pain between his shoulder blades was almost enough to make him moan out loud, and the rhythmic hammering up and down the backs of his legs was a pleasure that no one could comprehend without experiencing it for themselves.

The ancient art of cheirapsia combined the pain and pleasure of rough massage, varying in intensity and location, and happening in many places of the body simultaneously to bring the recipient to a level of peaceful euphoria unimagined by commoners. It was a luxury reserved for the Aristocrats of the empire, and one of the many perks of making it to the top of the social ladder. It was also one of the few things that made the extreme stress of his job a little more manageable. Each session cost him a small fortune, and he was happy to pay it.

It was a pleasure that he only had time for every two or three days, and those days when he wasn't able to make it to the chambrium for four days or more were almost unbearable. If he were to suddenly become a commoner, the cheirapsia sessions would probably be what he most missed about his life as an Aristocrat.

"By the gods, man. I forgot how amazing this is. Why do I only come here a few times a year?" Thorli whispered

Without opening his eyes, Vendino whispered, "Because you're a fool."

"No, because I really can't afford to come more often than that."

"Oh, but it's worth every raptor."

The rapid slapping sounds of bare feet walking quickly on the stone floor alerted him that he was about to be scolded.

He heard the footsteps stop near him, and he knew that the cheirapsian overseer had knelt down between him and Thorli.

Her voice was warm and soothing. "Hush, my lords. Others are also trying to find their peaceful place."

Vendino didn't respond, and he soon heard the overseer walk slowly away.

The art of cheirapsia had been practiced since before written records, and the men and women who devoted their life to learn and perfect the ancient art were highly sought after by Aristocrats throughout the empire. They were all members of the cheirapsian guild, which carefully monitored the living and working conditions of its members. Clientele who failed to provide a lavish environment for their cheirapsians, or who did not treat them with reverence and respect, quickly found themselves without the powerful guild's services.

All cheirapsians were basically nudists, wearing only the unique garment called a cheirapol. It was essentially a loin cloth with a thin strip of fabric that ran up the middle of their torso in front and back and had a simple collar around the neck. When they walked through the palace or down the city streets, they were easily recognizable since their chest and rear end were effectively bare. However, within the chambrium they didn't stand out at all since all clientele were required to wear only a loin cloth if they wore any clothing at all.

Commoners might assume that all of this nudity and intimate physical contact meant that a chambrium was a room for sexuality or lewd behavior, but nothing could be further from the truth. All chambrium clientele knew that sexual behavior, lewd actions or comments, and anything else that might be deemed sexual in nature was strictly prohibited. It was considered tacky and improper to even show physical signs of arousal while within the chambrium, however some leeway was given on this matter as long as the client was equipped with an adequate loin cloth. This wasn't a shortcoming that Vendino struggled with, thankfully.

A soft bell chimed.

He heard rustling sounds to his left and knew that Thorli was trying to gracefully extract himself from the soft thick mat. It wasn't an easy task, especially after becoming so completely relaxed.

He was a bit surprised that Thorli only signed up for a one hour session. Vendino still had an hour of bliss left to enjoy.

Commotion from far to his left was the first sign that his enjoyment was about to come to an abrupt halt.

"Get out of my way!"

It was as bad as he feared, and it certainly was not going to go away. The emperor had entered the chambrium, and he sounded furious.

"Thorli! They took my son!"

The emperor was much closer now, and his announcement was most dire. Vendino tried to stand but couldn't with one of the women still straddling his back. When the cheirapsian slid gracefully from him, he slowly sat up and then stood up.

More emphatically the emperor shouted, "The sarding troll suckers took my son!" He stomped a foot onto the stone floor.

The cheirapsian overseer rushed over to the emperor with both hands held before her. Softly, she said, "Please hush, Your Majesty! This is a place of harmony and peace."

Vendino fully expected the emperor to lash out at the woman who dared to confront him. He finished standing and gingerly stretched out his muscles. He saw that Thorli was doing the same thing, as the emperor's attention was turned to the overseer. He had no idea who had taken the young prince, but whoever it might be, the situation was surely dire.

As the emperor stared at the defiant woman before him, a quiet tension fell over the room. All eyes were on the two as they glared at each other.

Abruptly the emperor pointed at Thorli, and then made a sweeping gesture with his arm and pointed towards the door. He turned and stormed out of the room without waiting to see if the minister would follow.

Thorli hurried after the emperor and Vendino fell in behind.

Vendino had hoped that the emperor would at least move to the bath so that he and Thorli could grab their clothes before the outburst continued. Unfortunately, he did not.

Instead, the emperor rushed right past the bath and out into a long hallway. He and Thorli followed him, naked, into the crowded passage. He felt extremely uncomfortable standing in the hall in such an indecent state, but there was nothing he could do.

The emperor turned and placed his hands on his hips. "The sarding Magi attacked the carriage and took Edal!"

Minister Thorli modestly crossed his hands before his genitals, and asked, "Do we have any idea where he is now?"

"No! A squad of sentinels patrolling the road discovered my chariot, destroyed along the road north of here. The guards are all dead, as is Edal's little playmate. I want every last Magi dead, and I want my son returned immediately!"

"Majesty, are we sure it wasn't brigands or random ruffians?" Thorli sounded nervous.

The emperor stepped closer to the old minister, and for a moment Vendino thought the enraged monarch might strike him.

"Talk to the sentinels yourselves. Do whatever you must to find my son! The report that I got moments ago described scorch marks on the dead guards where the Magi attacked with fire. The sentinel stated that the commoner girl's head was burned from the inside out. Tell me how brigands and ruffians did that!"

"Majesty, the Magi will all be captured or killed, and we will find Edal, but it is going to take time." Thorli spoke quietly.

"No!" The denial came out more like a bestial howl than a human voice, and the emperor looked like he might be on the brink of a maniacal breakdown. He stomped his feet and made broad sweeping motions with his hands. "I want my son found! Now! By imperial decree I demand that a conscription be implemented for all able-bodied adults of my lands under the age of thirty! Every last one will report immediately to the imperial garrison of their nearest city. I also demand that all sentinels from every city be conscripted into the imperial army, and they have one day from the time they receive this decree to train replacements to guard their city from among the Denizens remaining who are above the age of thirty!"

Thorli looked incredulous, "Even the women?"

"And the Gentry?" Vendino was more shocked than Thorli.

"Yes! The women and the Gentry! They can carry a sword, can't they?"

The ministers didn't respond. Vendino had nothing constructive to add, and anything he might say was likely to just anger the emperor further so he kept his mouth shut.

"Make sure it's known that anyone who defies the conscription decree is to be cut down on the spot for cowardice and treason! Furthermore, I will offer a bounty of ten raptors for every dead Magi! They must be able to present the Magi's cloak or magical weapon as proof to claim the reward."

Vendino bowed. "Yes, Majesty!"

The emperor looked from one minister to the other. "Why are you still standing here? Get my son back!"

CHAPTER 17

Edal

The cavernous room felt oppressive and ominous. Edal shivered and pulled his robes closed at his chest to try to ward off the chill in the air.

It had been several days since the Magi attack, and he had spent the entire time with Jalinox and his people at a compound north of the city. He worried that his father might be angry that he'd been gone so long. However, Jalinox promised him a chance for true power and he didn't want to pass up the opportunity. Besides, the god Wirmyntas had been coming to his dreams nightly and he was certain that the god wasn't going to let him get a good night of sleep until he went through with this.

After breakfast, two soldiers escorted him to an underground passage and encouraged him to enter this huge room alone. The echo of the door slamming closed behind him was still fresh in his ears.

He hadn't seen Jalinox or any of the apostles since he woke up this morning. This was the day when he was supposed to begin his journey towards becoming a warlock, and he rather expected Jalinox to be there to guide that journey.

Near the middle of the room was a small table with some items upon it, and not far from the table was a drawing on the floor. The room was illuminated by several candles in sconces on the walls, and the flicker of the candles' flames caused the shadows to dance and shimmer throughout the room, adding to the creepy feeling of the place.

There were no couches or cushions to sit upon, so he walked towards the middle of the room to investigate the items on the table. He wasn't sure if Jalinox was indisposed and expected him to wait patiently for the lessons to begin, or if being alone in the room was part of the lesson. His teachers back at home had always given him more guidance on their expectations. He was rarely left alone to simply figure things out on his own.

Even when he wanted to be alone there were always guards, nursemaids, or servants around and usually several of each. Then there was his little sister, who seemed to grow more annoying with each passing year. Being alone was an unusual feeling, and he suddenly felt vulnerable. He suppressed a shiver and looked around the room.

Upon the table were two books, several thick candles, and a handwritten note. He picked up the note and looked at the precisely crafted lettering. Whoever wrote it had much better penmanship than he did, that was for sure. It simply said 'Read.'

Edal sighed, dropped the note back onto the table, and picked up the first book. It was thick and looked expensive. The hard cover was elaborately decorated with symbols and pictures on every inch. He turned it over in his hands looking at some of the designs and then held it upright to read the title. His eyes grew wide with shock as the realization hit him of what he was holding. The title said *Holy Kasonite Bible – Emperor Ryal I Edition*. He sat the book down on the table, quickly but reverently, so as not to offend anyone.

It was sacrilege for anyone except a Kasonite clergyman to possess that book, and he felt like he'd accidently broken a major law. He looked around the room to make sure that no one saw what he'd done, and then he carefully pushed the book further away.

For several minutes he stood nervously, halfway expecting to burst into flames or perhaps for a Kasonite priest to hurry into the room and smite him for his outrageous actions.

When nothing horrible happened, he turned his attention to the other book on the table. Using the sleeves of his robes, to avoid touching the book, he pulled the second one closer so he could read the title. This book looked ancient, and he was afraid that it might break apart simply by sliding it across the table. The cover was plain and tattered. The title simply said *Zyrmyntas Zult*.

He had no idea what zyrmyntas zult might mean. Literature had never been his favorite topic to learn, but he felt that he was a fairly competent reader most of the time. He was certain that these words had never appeared in his vocabulary assignments.

Very gently he opened the ancient book and turned to a random page somewhere in the middle. The pages weren't made of parchment, they were thicker and almost felt like thin pieces of animal hide. The words on the pages were neatly written but faded, and to his dismay he couldn't read any of them. It wasn't that they were too faded to read, it was that the order of the letters didn't form words that he knew. Some of the letters were unusual as well. He turned the page several times, and on each one he saw a jumble of letters that didn't make any sense.

He closed the book and looked at it in annoyance. Who would print an entire book of gibberish?

At one point, long ago, one of his teachers had mentioned something about another language used long before the foundation of the empire. That teacher was scolded severely by one of the other teachers, and when Edal had asked about it he was told not to worry himself about silly details from a time of darkness and ignorance. He had dismissed the whole thing and hadn't really even given it any more thought until now. One would think that if it was a time of darkness and ignorance, that there wouldn't be books or other written things.

He looked down at the book once again. Clearly it had been written long before his great grandfather established the empire, and for some reason it was written in words that Edal had never seen.

He opened the book again to see if he might be able to figure out what it said. He flipped from one page to the next, and some of the words did look similar to words that he knew but it was no use. He wouldn't be able to read anything in the old book.

With a quick flip of the front cover, he closed the book again. He sighed in disappointment, and looked around the room. Still he was alone, and now there was nothing to do.

The note said to read, but how could he read something filled with words he didn't know? He crossed his arms and paced around the room. When he got tired of walking around he moved over to the side of the room and sat on the floor, leaning his back against one of the bare walls.

Several minutes turned into hours, and still no one came to the room to give him any guidance.

Annoyance turned to anger, and angry thoughts made him think about the day that the Magi killed Tali right in front of him. He'd struggled with feelings of rage and regret since the Magi attack.

Several tears rolled down his cheeks and his inability to stop them fueled his anger further. He tried to push the sight of pretty little Tali's death from his mind, but once it invaded his thoughts it was stuck there.

Edal stood up and resumed pacing. As his anger grew, he clinched his fists and wished for something to throw or smash. With nothing nearby he settled on stomping his foot.

The stomp sent a loud bang echoing around the room. Again he stomped and again he heard the satisfying banging echo through the room. With each stomp of the foot he could feel the anger build.

He jumped in the air and stomped both feet to the ground, over and over. Each stomp banged louder, and with each one he jumped higher and smashed his feet to the ground harder.

No matter how hard he stomped he couldn't get the banging as loud as he needed it, so he added a scream to the stomping.

The Magi had murdered his lovely Tali right in front of him, and he'd been weak and powerless to stop it. His insignificance had never been as pronounced as it had been that day.

For what seemed like ages he stomped, jumped, screamed, and flailed his arms around like a savage. Finally, the rage fled with his screams leaving him feeling empty. He allowed himself to crumple to the ground as one of his jumps ended.

He breathed heavily, and curled into a ball to sob.

"I apologize, my prince. I didn't expect you to finish reading so quickly."

The sound of Jalinox's voice startled Edal. He hadn't even heard anyone enter the room. He wiped his eyes furiously and took several deep breaths to try to get his emotions in check. Even as he stood, he continued to try to dry his eyes.

He felt ashamed to stand before the necromancer with tears streaking his cheeks like a baby. He was even more ashamed to think that the man had probably witnessed his tantrum. Edal prided himself on being mature and composed. He had recently turned twelve, but he didn't want people to treat him like a child. So, he always tried to act more mature than other kids his age.

Today he had failed, and his new mentor had seen it.

He wiped his eyes again as he walked towards Jalinox. His cheeks were probably red, and his eyes surely looked like he'd been crying.

The sound of a door closing caused him to look in that direction, and his heart sunk when he saw her walk into the room. The dark apostle Jessa walked in confidently.

Edal groaned on the inside. The woman was dark and beautiful, and she made him feel things that he really couldn't explain. He thanked all of the gods that she hadn't walked in earlier to see him acting like a child. He stood a little taller and tried to compose himself.

As he got closer to Jalinox, he said, "The words are a mystery, how could I read that book?"

"They haven't taught you to read Menelian yet? Whatever do they teach you all day long if you aren't even learning such an important language?"

Jessa walked up and stood next to, but slightly behind, Jalinox.

Edal looked at him inquisitively, "Menelian? I don't even know what that is."

"Fear not, my boy, you'll be reading it like a scholar in no time. Still, it's amazing that you were able to finish the entire Kasonite Bible in just a few hours! It took me days to get through it. Most of that thing is incredibly dull, especially the Emperor Ryal edition. This language simply doesn't have the poetic flow of Menelian, and the whole work loses much of the rhyme and dynamics in translation. You truly are a remarkable reader to tear through it so quickly!"

The prince shook his head. "I didn't open the Kasonite Bible, that would be blasphemy."

Jalinox laughed raucously. "Nonsense, boy! Who has the authority to declare that a book can't be read? By a prince, none the less? The emperor, perhaps?"

"It's just something that everyone knows."

"Why?"

Edal didn't know what to say.

Jalinox put his arm around him, and led him slowly towards the desk. "I'll tell you why. Control. The Kasonite temples want to control the holy book so only the preachers know what it says. It's not just the Kasonites, all of the modern temples do the same thing. If the people don't know the words of their gods, then they must depend on the temples to guide them towards salvation."

"Why do the temples need to control things?"

"That is a complicated question for another day. The simple answer is wealth and power. But let's turn our attention to *Zyrmyntas Zult* which means the *Word of Wirmyntas*. This is one of the oldest books in existence, it was written even before our people learned to make parchment. Even for those of us who fluently read Menelian it is difficult to read because it is written in an archaic version of the language from a time before it was common to write words. It is a treasure from a time long-forgotten about a god who has been silent for ages. It is your key to power beyond imagining."

He felt a rush of pride and excitement hearing the necromancer promising him such power. As much as he wanted to embrace and pursue this power, he questioned whether it was a wise thing to do.

The god had been appearing to him in his dreams for many days. The dreams were troubling and the god seemed scary.

Like he'd done so many times over the last few days, Edal questioned whether he should allow Jalinox to lead him down this path. The necromancer promised him ultimate power. He knew that the cost was his soul, but what he didn't know was whether the reward was worth the price.

He wished he could talk to his father about the dreams and get his advice, but he knew that his father's hatred for all things magic would skew his answer. The dreams might even cause his father to turn against him. So, it was best not to mention them at all.

The point of no turning back was fast approaching. He looked from Jessa to Jalinox, and said, "In my dreams, Wirmyntas looks vicious and scary. Am I about to give my soul over to an evil god?"

The necromancer shook his head, and smiled warmly. "My prince, people don't truly understand the concepts of good and evil. They fail to realize that right and wrong or good and evil are constraints and expectations established by the gods. What is good to one god may very well be evil to the next. As creations of the gods, it is our duty to live within the rules and boundaries of our own deity and not the concepts created by people."

Edal was already confused. "I don't know what you mean?"

Jalinox thought for a minute, and then pointed to the table. "Open the Kasonite Bible to the book of Epochs. It's the first book of that bible. Chapter two, start reading with verse one."

Edal nervously reached out and pulled the book closer to him. With great care he opened the cover and flipped through the pages. They were thin and finely crafted. He was surprised to see scribbles and notes written in the margins of many of the pages. The book of Epochs was a very small section of the thick book.

He read, "In all things the divine brothers competed, but they had to compromise in the days of the creation. Wirmyntas created the earth and Khalius, while his brother created air and the heavens. Kelegar then created water and nature, and his brother created fire and time. Back and forth the brothers worked and compromised. When Kelegar created light, Wirmyntas created darkness.

"With each creation, the brothers tried to outdo the other. Then it came to pass that Kelegar created life. Determined not to be bested by his brother, Wirmyntas created souls and demanded that each living creature be inhabited by a soul, that the life be limited by time and then given over to death, and the souls allowed to exist eternally.

"Kelegar agreed to the demands, but countered that he be allowed to choose where the souls would reside after death. Those souls he desired would be allowed to live with him in one of the levels of paradise he'd created in the heavens. The others would be given to Wirmyntas to reside in Khalius.

"Wirmyntas felt trapped and stewed over the complication for a time. Finally he agreed to the terms, with the caveat that all intelligent creations be given the free-will to worship the deity of their choosing, even so much as to promise their soul to the deity of their own choice. Kelegar agreed to the first part, but demanded that no soul would be permitted into his heavens without his blessing, regardless of their choice.

"Determined to ensure that his beautiful paradise was filled with only the worthiest souls, Kelegar sent a host of seraphim to the peoples of the lands with a list of three Divine Directives by which his people were to always abide. I) You will worship no god above the divine-sire Kelegar, and will observe a sacred Sabbath Day every fifth day dedicated to worship and prayer. II) You will not lie, steal, cheat, or murder. III) You will live as a shining example of purity, morality, charity, honesty, and modesty. The seraphim promised that all who worshiped Kelegar and followed his Directives would be granted entrance into paradise for all eternity when their life was over.

"Seeing this, Wirmyntas sent forth demons with three Commandments of his own. His Commandments were as follows. I) You will worship Wirmyntas above all other deities, and will devote one full hour per day for prayer and worship to him. II) You will live a life of honor, but will remain strong, proud, and powerful at all times. III) You will not tolerate weakness, lies, or dishonor in your own life nor suffer the same in those with whom you associate. The demons swore that the loyal followers of Wirmyntas would be granted luxury, honor, and power for all eternity as the lords of Khalius, ruling over the pitiful and discarded souls who were damned by Kelegar to an eternity of suffering."

Edal stopped reading at the end of the chapter and looked to the necromancer. His head was spinning and he struggled to absorb all of the information he'd read. He asked, "Why have my teachers never taught this? This explains so much."

Jalinox nodded. "Indeed it does. The preachers have known this, and they keep it from the people. Now you know divine truths that most people simply don't know."

He looked back over the chapter, and reread it a few times. When he'd finished, he looked back to Jalinox. "Kelegar seems weaker. I like Wirmyntas' Commandments, especially the one about honor, pride, and power."

"Very good, my prince. Very good indeed. Because if you dedicate your soul to him, you must agree to live by those Commandments. Now, skip forward to chapter twelve in the book of Epochs, and start reading with verse one."

Edal turned a few pages, and then read, "The fury of the divine-brothers simmered hotter than the fires of Khalius. The blasphemous ways of the people knew no bounds, and the number of worthy souls dwindled as the people abandoned the houses of worship for the halls of pleasure and vaults of wealth. Sabbath days, hours of worship, and even the acknowledgement of the existence of the gods themselves became scarce.

"In those ancient days, the divine-offspring were infants and even the blessed Kason still suckled from the bosom of his celestial matron. Having not yet matured, the nine progenies were powerless to intervene on behalf of the people of the world.

"Kelegar unleashed powerful storms and tidal waves. Wirmyntas caused wildfires and earthquakes. Still the people refused to repent or turn from their profane ways. For a century and then another, the wrathful divine-sires rained vengeance upon the vile people and still they grew even more irreligious.

"As their rage escalated, the divine-sires eventually concluded that their only choice was to destroy all life and start anew. Only the pleading of their celestial mistresses stayed their mighty hands.

"A bright light was seen in the skies on that day, and that was followed by shadow. For twenty-six celestial days, shadow reigned throughout the lands. There was no light of day, nor dark of night. The sun shone as dim as the moons and it refused to move across the sky. And so ended the Second Epoch."

When he finished reading, he released the book letting it thump onto the table and looked to Jalinox. "What was the bright light?"

"No one knows. The book of Epochs is the only record we have of that event, and we know only what is written. The book of Epochs is the only book that is included in the bible of each of the deities of the Pantheon of Nine, and in each one it's identical. Preachers in the modern temples use Epochs 12:5 as the basis for their lessons that the ancient gods turned their backs on us or that they are dead."

Edal didn't fully understand what the passage meant, but he didn't want to encourage a lecture so he kept quiet.

"We've dallied long enough, are you ready to begin your path toward ultimate power?" Jalinox smiled pleasantly, and motioned towards the tattered old book.

He took a deep breath, and let it out slowly. After a slight pause, he nodded once.

Jalinox closed the Kasonite Bible and pulled *Zyrmyntas Zult* closer. He opened it to one of the first pages. In a slow and deep voice, he read, "Omnipotent Wirmyntas, make me your servant and grant me the power of your portentous blessings. My heart and soul belong solely to you. You are all-powerful and eternal, the sire of the gods and creator of souls. In your omnipotent name I pray, and proudly entreat, that you grant me this prayer."

When he finished reading, he looked at the prince.

Edal felt excited and extremely nervous. His heart beat loudly in his chest.

Jalinox said, "That is the prayer, and you must learn it precisely. Say it with me."

For several minutes the two said the prayer over and over. Each time he made a mistake, Jalinox corrected him and they started over.

Eventually he had it down so he could say it perfectly.

"I think you have it." The necromancer placed his hand on Edal's shoulder.

Jessa turned wordlessly, and walked from the room.

Jalinox continued, "Once I leave, you need to assume the proper Posture of Pride, for the prayer."

"Posture of Pride?"

"Yes, the Posture of Pride. *Zyrmyntas Zult* describes it this way. You will stand with your feet shoulder width apart with both legs straight. Both hands formed into fists and placed proudly against your waist. Chest out, stomach in, and chin held high. Assume that position, inside of that sacred circle on the floor over there, close your eyes, and say the prayer. And, whatever you do, do not leave the circle until I return."

He felt a sense of relief. "That's all there is to it? Once I do that, I'll be done?"

The old necromancer laughed once again. "No, once you do that, you will have begun. Good luck."

Edal watched the old man walk out of the room, and close it loudly. Once again he was alone in the large room.

He looked back to the drawing on the floor. The sense of relief he'd felt a moment ago had completely vanished. In its place was a sense of foreboding and more than a little self-doubt. He pushed that aside and tried to focus on thoughts of strength and pride.

Walking over to the circle, he stepped inside. He placed himself in the Posture of Pride and took a deep breath. He closed his eyes, and with his heart and his mouth he spoke the prayer he'd just learned.

As he finished the prayer, the room became unbelievably hot. He was slammed with an uncontrollable wave of reverence and terror. He tried desperately to appear proud and strong, but in reality he wanted to flee in horror. He kept his eyes tightly shut, so he didn't gaze upon the unfathomable power and strength of Wirmyntas. He had no idea if the god was actually in the room with him, or if the phenomenal power that he sensed before him was simply a projection from somewhere beyond.

The explosive and deafening sound of Wirmyntas' voice tore through his mind. It said, "Open your eyes, and take my hand. Enter into the domain of your god. You have much to learn."

The heat was almost unbearable, but he stood his ground. He opened his eyes slowly, initially blinded by the intense light radiating from the deity before him. Wirmyntas was huge, impossibly fitting into the room that now seemed much larger than ever, or perhaps he was even smaller than before. The horned deity looked much like he appeared in Edal's dreams, with many arms and a powerful tail. The deity's expression was one of pride and contemplation as he gazed upon the young prince before him.

Edal reached his hand out of the circle, and took one of the outstretched hands offered by his deity. Immediately he felt like he was plummeting down and away from his own body.

CHAPTER 18

Rissyl

"This man is a Magi! Kill him! Kill them all!"

Rissyl looked at the officer and he looked vaguely familiar. The voice gave him away. Konrad!

The rage of months of warfare, death, and suffering by so many people that he cared about filled his soul and boiled over. Rissyl looked at the traitorous Magi in imperial agent clothing and he didn't see a human, he saw a monster.

He didn't remember saying the trigger word for the spell, but he must have said it because the fiery pillar erupted on top of Konrad.

The agent started dancing.

As quickly as the pillar of fire formed, it abruptly disappeared. Konrad pointed and laughed at Rissyl's failures.

Bringing both hands up, Rissyl furiously launched wave after wave of deadly lightning into the hated man, yet it had no effect. Still the mocking and laughing continued.

Rissyl rushed over and grabbed the agent by both shoulders. He gave a fierce yank with his right hand, and Konrad's left arm popped off! Candy and treats spilled out of the hole in Konrad's torso where his arm used to attach.

He yanked on the agent's right arm, and it popped off just as easily. Rissyl held the arm by the wrist like a giant club and started beating Konrad in the head with his own arms. Every time he slammed the arm into the side of the agent's head, more and more candy sprayed around the courtyard.

Still Konrad mocked him.

"Rissyl!"

He was shaking and he didn't know why. Someone was holding him back, and keeping him from hitting Konrad with the arm. Everything started to fade.

"Dammit Riz, wake up!"

Someone was screaming, and it was hurting his head. After a moment,

142

he realized that he was doing the screaming.

Cynia stroked his hair and wiped his face with a warm wet cloth.

"Where's Konrad? He's bleeding candy pretty badly, but he won't die!"

"Konrad's gone. Sarge said you killed him."

He sat up and looked around. He was in his room at Fort Randol. Swinging his feet over the side of the bed, he reached over to grab the bedframe to keep from tipping over. "Argh. I feel like Khalius, and I was having an awful dream."

She sat next to him and put her arm around him for support. "Yes, draining your magewel down to about nothing and spending the next four days in bed will do that to you."

A very attractive young woman walked into his bedroom without knocking. It took him a moment to recognize her as Hesha, the Dreg from his parent's house.

She looked at Rissyl and Cynia sitting on the bed, and she stopped walking. "I'm sorry, milady. I didn't know that Lord Rissyl had risen. Should I come back later?"

"No, Hesha, it ain't a problem. The chamber pot's over there, and please take out that pile of rags too. Thanks." Cynia smiled at her pleasantly.

"Yes, milady."

Rissyl watched as the woman cleaned his room quickly. Over the years he'd had many different servants clean up after him, and it had seemed like the most natural thing in the world. Now, it seemed wrong somehow. After seeing how those soldiers treated the Dregs, his little sister, it was almost enough to make him sick to his stomach.

He looked at his wife. It suddenly struck him as odd that Cynia could sit there and let a Dreg work for her, after being in that position just a few years before. The whole thing seemed wrong.

When Hesha finished, she left the room quietly.

Rissyl said, "How can we sit here and watch someone else do our chores? We won't have Dregs in our fort. I'm not going to allow it."

She shook her head, "Hesha ain't a Dreg no more. Bran already removed her tattoo, and the tattoos from the others. She ain't property, she's working as our maid and we're gonna pay her."

"So, she doesn't have a tattoo and she'll get a few coins, but she's doing the same work? How has her life changed? I don't want servants toiling within our Stronghold."

Cynia laughed as she stood up. "Oh, look at the mighty Gentry, growing a conscience somehow." She held out her hand to help him up. "Come, milord. Lots of folks wanna see you. We shouldn't keep them waiting."

He followed her out of the bedroom and down the hall. The stairs took him longer than normal, because he was still weak. However, when they got to the common room he was astonished to see how bright and wonderful the room looked. The curtains were mended and opened wide, letting the sun bathe the room in its glow. The furniture was dusted and polished, and the debris had been cleaned from the floors.

A man that Rissyl had never seen was hard at work spreading varnish on one of the large chairs, and the fumes brought back many memories from his childhood of walking through his home as a boy.

She grabbed a heavy robe from a hook near the door, and he grabbed his as well. The cold wind hit him hard as they walked out into the winter air.

The two Magi walked quickly through the thin coating of snow, and she led him towards the middle of the fort. Summit Hall didn't seem like a very long walk when the weather was nice, but in the frigid winds of winter it seemed like a very long trek.

He opened the large door quickly, and rushed into Summit Hall with Cynia right on his tail. She pushed him playfully and made a comment about him being too slow.

It took a bit for the warmth of the room to push the chill from his bones. As he removed the heavy robes, he heard someone rushing up beside him.

"Izzy!"

His sister slammed into him and pushed him against the wall, as she hugged him tightly. When she finally let go, he held her at arm's length and looked at her.

She still looked fairly tattered, but the smile on her face and glow in her eye set his mind at ease a bit.

"Bri, I'm so happy that you're alright. I was scared that you'd been broken."

"I'm too tough for them to break. Especially with Madalyn around to fix me up."

She hugged him again, and he closed his eyes and rubbed her back. Soon he felt someone else pile onto the hug and he opened his eyes to see his mother holding her children tightly.

His father slapped his hand onto Rissyl's shoulder heavily, "It's good to see the family together, and in one piece. Let's sit down, there is a lot to discuss."

Rissyl walked into the lounge and looked at the place in surprise. Someone had cleaned and fixed everything. The furniture was cleaned and repaired, and the room looked like a posh sitting room in a large villa instead of a dilapidated relic from a century ago.

Then he noticed several servants working around the room. Some were cleaning and others were tending to various repairs of the furnishing.

Cynia beamed, "Don't it look great, Riz?"

He was embarrassed that so much work had been done to make the room look pretty, when there had been so much killing and suffering in the name of the emperor's war against the Magi. It seemed like a pretty stupid thing to waste time doing, when there was so much else to be done.

Rissyl nodded, "Yes, it's a room fit for Aristocrats." He gave his father a disapproving look.

Tuknor sighed and motioned towards the furniture. "I didn't furnish the place, Riz. I just arranged for staff to make it more like a place for people and less like a barn."

A man walked up with a tray of drinks. Most of his family accepted a cup, but Rissyl refused.

"Fort Randol will not have Dregs serving us."

His mother put her hand on his knee, "These are not Dregs, son. They're all paid staff now."

"What's the difference, they're still acting as our servants and it's not right. I see that now."

"You're looking at things wrong, son." Tuknor used his father-voice.

Rissyl shook his head, "I was, but now I see that I was wrong. If these people want to help the Magi cause, then we need to teach them to fight."

His father took a long drink and then leaned back on the soft couch. He said, "Who cooks the food and cleans the dishes in the fort?"

"We all pitch in and take turns with that."

"And who deals with animal carcasses and other refuge?"

He saw where his father was going with the questioned, but he answered anyway, "All of the Magi take turns with that."

Tuknor took another drink, and then asked, "You have a war to fight against the emperor. Every day more innocent people like your sister are killed or sentenced to a life as a Dreg. As far as I see it, the Magi Society just might be the only ones who can put a stop to that. I assure you, the emperor and his soldiers aren't taking a break from their efforts to wash their dishes and take out their own trash! The Magi have important things to do, and you need help with mundane things so you can focus on the important things."

"Yes, yes, I see that. But we need all the soldiers we can get, even folks who can't use magic can battle with a sword or a staff! Something more useful than sweeping and mopping."

His father pointed at the servant who brought the tray of drinks. "That is Rulgur. The man faints at the very sight of blood, and jumps at every loud bang. He is a bit of a coward and the thought of hurting even a small animal is enough to make him cry. He'd rather go hungry than kill a rabbit for food."

Rissyl looked at Rulgur, who hurried away to do something in the other room.

Tuknor continued, "Is Rulgur the man you want guarding your flank in the middle of a fierce battle? No. He isn't strong enough to do hard physical labor, and doesn't have the skills to run a blacksmithy or woodcraft shop. But he is a hard worker, and he has a heart of gold. He wants to make a difference, and he can be helpful by doing some menial tasks around the fort that free-up others to better use their skills."

He looked around, and everyone seemed to be nodding along with his father. It wasn't something he wanted to fight about, so he conceded. "Fine."

Rissyl sat in uncomfortable silence for a bit, and then decided to change the subject. He looked to Cynia, "Where are we on raids? Are we having any impact?"

She nodded, "Yes, we're doing three to four of them a day. I dunno how much it's helping, but we hit them hard and haven't take many injuries. Madalyn and Sarge have set up a medicinal house, and over the last few days your parents got a bunch of non-magical folks to work as medics and nurses."

"How many non-magical people do we have working at the fort now?"

"Four hundred."

Rissyl's jaw dropped and he looked from his parents to Cynia and back.

"Four hundred? In four days?"

Amalia smiled, "We've been busy. Sarge and Thon have been a big help too! Most of the new residents were from Misi and Sorgo, because that's where we know many people."

"By all the sarding gods, Cynia! How are we going to pay all of these people? We're almost out of money."

His father answered, "The woodlands north of here is going to be a money machine. We've recruited hunters, trappers, tanners, and leatherworkers. We've also brought in loggers, mill workers, carpenters, and woods crafters."

"Don't forget the foragers, herbalists, alchemists, and apothecaries." His mother beamed with pride, and he assumed those were her additions.

Rissyl's head was spinning. "Mill workers? We don't have a mill."

Cynia laughed, "Not yet, but construction should be done in the next fortnight on our mill."

"You see, son, you're sitting in virgin country with valuable resources all around you. We've recruited some of the best merchants that I know, and they'll be making regular trips from here to all of the cities in the known lands. We've already made good profits in just a few days, and everything is still in the early stages of being set up."

He couldn't believe what he was hearing. "Where will all these people live? Fort Randol is big, but it's really designed to be a Magi fort not a major trading center."

His mother smiled proudly again, "We've got that covered as well. Craftsmen are hard at work building homes and shops just outside of the Stronghold walls, to the north. In time, it will become a large town, I'm sure!"

"We're calling it Randol City." Cynia smiled at him, and he knew that she had some influence on the name, to further pay tribute to the old Grand Diviner.

He thought for a moment, and then came to a troubling realization. He asked, "Who is going to lead this new town? Certainly not the Magi, we have plenty of other things to worry about."

His sister spoke first, "How about dad? He was on the Council of Ministers in Misi? Only the Chancellor was above him. He could be the Chancellor of Randol City!"

Rissyl shook his head, "Absolutely not. Okay, I'm not opposed to father leading the town, but we're not going to use imperial titles. We need to think of something else."

Cynia nodded in agreement, "I think that's smart. Maybe we should go back to the old ways, and use the old Menelian titles and such?"

Brielle thought for a moment, and said, "So, he'd be king?"

"Actually, it would just be baron since there is only a single town to lead." Tuknor shook his head, "But I don't know how I feel about adopting titles of nobility. It seems a bit archaic, and more than a little presumptuous."

"Why not let the people choose?"

Rissyl looked over at his wife, and smiled. "I like that, how would we do it?"

Before she could answer, Tuknor said, "Leave the details to us, Riz. We'll find out what the people prefer, and we'll make it happen. You focus on running this war, and we'll handle stuff with the town and supporting the fort."

"Thanks father, I appreciate that. I'm sorry I kept all of this from you for so long, but it sure is great to have your help now." He paused for a second and looked to his wife, and then back to his father. With a sigh, he said, "We should talk privately."

Tuknor followed him out of the lounge and into a small room down the hallway.

When they entered, Rissyl closed the door behind them. He didn't know how to start. He'd already had this conversation with his mother, and it hadn't gone well. He stood there for a moment, collecting his thoughts.

"Riz, we don't have to do this. Yes, you married our Dreg and no your mother didn't handle the news very well. I've had time to think about your choices, and you don't have to explain yourself." Tuknor placed his hand on Rissyl's shoulder, and squeezed.

"You're not angry?"

Tuknor released his shoulder, and crossed his arms. "I wasn't surprised. Cynia is a very attractive woman, and I suspected that there was something between you two when you begged me to leave her in Sorgo."

Rissyl stood proudly, almost defiantly. He said, "Cynia is no longer a Dreg, and Chardy has never been one. The Magi Society will see an end to the practice of owning Dregs."

"I don't doubt that, son. I've been involved with overseeing a small portion of the Dreg establishment for many years, and I've grown to

148

despise the system. I've been working to undo it since moving to Misi. The chancellor in Misi is a good man, and he is also turning against the Dreg system. For the last few years we've been trying to make changes in Misi, but it hasn't been something we could do quickly. Obviously, my loathing of that system has grown stronger since your sister was dragged into it. I fully support the Magi in their efforts to end it."

He let out a breath that he hadn't realized he'd been holding. Rissyl didn't know how to respond, so he just said, "Thanks, that means a lot."

Without any further comment, he opened the door and led the way back to the lounge.

As soon as they entered the room, the door on the other side of the room opened and Sarasa came rushing into the lounge. She brought a large gust of frigid air with her. Out of breath, she said, "By the gods, you're hard to find! Come quick, Riz! The Rolimi are here, and they want you!"

His heart dropped to his feet. "Have they started killing yet?"

"Not yet. Mr. Pyllis is with them."

Rissyl smiled slightly and stood up. "Well, that's good news."

"Who are the Rolimi?" Brielle stood up, and her parents followed her lead.

Cynia stood as well, "They're magical creatures that were our allies and teachers."

"Now they might want to kill us. We're about to find out." Rissyl quickly hugged his parents, "I've got to run, I'll leave administrative affairs in your capable hands."

Brielle stepped in beside him as he and Cynia started walking towards the door.

"Where are you going, Bri? You should stay with mom and dad."

"No sarding way, I'm going with you! I'm gonna be a Magi soon, Cynia said!"

He looked at his sister, and then looked at Cynia in disbelief.

Sarasa reached out and grabbed Rissyl's hand. She gently pulled him towards the door. "Come on, Riz! We can argue about that later. Let's go find out if the Rolimi want war!"

He grabbed his heavy robe and put it on. He followed Cynia out the door, and said, "This isn't over. I've almost lost her once, I can't go through that again."

They followed Sarasa quickly through the Stronghold, to the Evoker quarter and then to Evoker Hall.

Rissyl hurried up the steps, and led the others into the room. He summoned his staff and cloak as he entered the main room of the building. If they wanted war, he wasn't about to show up unarmed.

The others closed the door and fanned out behind him, as Rissyl slowly walked into the room. The stairs had not been activated, so the large statue in the middle of the room was the only feature taking space in the huge marble room.

Standing near the statue was Mr. Pyllis and a dozen other Rolimi. They hadn't attacked yet, which was probably a good sign, but he refused to let down his guard.

Each of the Rolimi were traced in thin lines of bright light, and they came in a variety of different shapes and colors. He knew that they only appeared that way because of how they projected themselves from the plane of magic to the domain of humans.

Mr. Pyllis was the only one that Rissyl recognized. The Rolimi in the hall represented seven of the twelve Rolimi castes, and there were several members of the large and intimidating caste of guardians.

Rissyl walked casually to the middle of the room and stopped before Mr. Pyllis. "Have you come to a decision?"

In his fast and unpausing manner, Mr. Pyllis said, "Rissyl Sokigo, after a long and contentious debate in the Synodus, the castes have made the decision that we will not wage a war against the humans. The final vote was seven castes against war and five castes in favor of it. Your presence was able to sway two castes to change their position."

One of the very large Rolimi took a step forward. In a deeper voice, but still fast and difficult to understand, the Rolimi said, "Magi, I am Vrinythorikan the elder of the Warder Caste. I was also the most vocal in favor of war with the humans. Warders respect bravery and assertiveness, and your display in the Synodus exhibited both. You changed my position in the vote, and I would like to offer warders from our caste to serve as guardians of your Stronghold once again."

Rissyl almost missed what the Rolimi was saying, because he spent the entire time repeating the name over and over in his mind so he could say it correctly. "Elder Vrinythorikan, I appreciate your generous offer. We would consider ourselves fortunate to have your warders to ensure that our walls remain safe, however before I formally accept the offer it would only be prudent for me to bring the matter to our council for a formal vote."

The Rolimi bowed his head slightly, "It would seem that bureaucracy is a universal hindrance, but one that I can appreciate. I will await your council's decision."

When Vrinythorikan stepped back another Rolimi stepped up.

She had very long legs and a tiny body. Her long and thin arms extended all of the way down to her knees. Her face was oval shaped and much wider than it was tall, with her eyes positioned wide apart. She smiled, "Magi, I am Mistress Ammazoorithal, the elder of the Beneficence Caste. I was also in favor of war against the humans. Your kind has a long history of violence and suffering, but your concern and compassion for your injured friend demonstrated a side of human-kind that I didn't expect. You succeeded in swaying me to vote in your favor."

Rissyl bowed slightly to her. "Elder Ammazoorithal, I am extremely thankful for your vote."

Pyllis said, "The matter is settled, but there is more. When we first met, I informed you that you must earn our respect and trust if you are to earn our loyalty on your own merit, as your forefathers did before you. The elder of the Cognoscente Caste, Meligoricko, has instructed me to inform you that our caste is prepared to offer our services for your magical training once again. Additionally, Meligoricko has authorized that we include advanced training in Order Magic as well."

He was almost speechless. He hadn't considered that the Rolimi could teach advanced classes about Order Magic. Rissyl smiled broadly, "Mr. Pyllistacaillian, I am overjoyed to hear that. Of course I need to talk to the council before I accept, but I am extremely excited to get started with these lessons. You've all brought the most wonderful news. The outcome of the Synodus was much better than I thought possible."

CHAPTER 19

Kimly

As she walked into Favin's office, Kimly was surprised to see the room filled with people.

She was in a fantastic mood, having just enjoyed a lengthy and particularly raucous session of love-making with Cletis. He had grown even more amorous, and adventurous, recently and she found that the frequent physical release typically put her in a pleasant mood. She suspected that his increased attention to sexual games was meant to distract her from her more nefarious endeavors, and in some ways it had. This was the first time, in the days since returning from her tattoo acquiring quest, that she had visited Favin or the other Shrouded.

It was common to find Favin in his office at his guild's headquarters until the wee hours of the morning. Running a guild of thieves meant working long hours, typically while everyone else was sleeping. However, it was uncommon for his office to be filled with people during the prime hours when those people should be out and about making money, taking stuff, and doing other things that go bump in the night.

There were at least thirty people packed into his office, and none of them were talking. Everyone had their attention fully on Favin, who hadn't noticed Kimly's entrance. People were sitting on barrels, standing next to the walls, and scattered all around the room. Some were sitting on the floor.

Most of the members of Favin's guild were not part of their select group of rogues who could use magic. The Shrouded were limited to just a handful, and they were careful not to reveal themselves to the rest of the guild. It was almost a guild hidden within the larger guild. Those who were involved with The Shrouded knew Kimly as a high level agent of that group. The rest of Favin's guild knew her simply as Favin's trusted friend.

From the looks that she got, she was certain that many of the members assumed that she was one of Favin's lovers, and she was fine with that reputation. It helped to justify in their minds why Favin let her come and go within the guild headquarters, and it also kept most of the guild members from venturing a wandering hand in her direction as she walked through the hallways.

As she started to weave her way through the people, she said happily, "Good morning, riff-raff! Why didn't I get the party invitation?"

People made way for her to pass as she walked towards Favin's desk.

He looked up and saw her approaching. "Skoots is missing. She hasn't checked in for several days."

Rath was standing directly behind Favin, and leaning against the wall. He was a wiry man with unkempt brown hair and many old faded tattoos. He was one of the leaders of the guild, and a member of The Shrouded. Tossing a dagger into Favin's desk, he said, "Eight days. It's been eight days since she last checked in. That's far too long, something's wrong."

Skoots was also a part of The Shrouded, and Kimly had grown to admire the woman's skills at gathering information. If it was scandalous and worthy of an impressive pile of coins through blackmail, Skoots could dig it up.

She squeezed between two men who were sitting on a crate near the front of the room. "Maybe one of her marks thought it was easier to eliminate the source of some juicy bit of information rather than to pay to keep it quiet?"

Favin nodded, "Yes, that's what we've been discussing."

"Skoots and I work together all the time. She's been on a dry spell lately, it's been months since she had a good mark. She mighta been working on one, but I'm pretty sure I woulda heard about it. I think something else happened."

She didn't know the rogue who spoke, but that wasn't uncommon. Favin had well over a hundred thieves, pick-pockets, racketeers, and the like working for him these days.

"What if it was another 'mancer napping?"

Several people around the room started talking, mocking, and scoffing at the man's suggestion. Kimly had no idea what he was talking about.

Favin's expression showed that he was as doubtful as the rest of the room. He said, "Alright, let's not start with paranoia and crazy things. All that nonsense of 'mancer nappings is just people jumping at their own shadows because of the emperor's war against the Magi. Those people were probably dragged off by imperial agents or something."

The room got quiet again. Everyone in the room knew someone who had been affected in one way or another by the emperor's new edicts. The

Shrouded had the added worry of being targeted because technically they were magic users and the emperor's men would be delighted to kill one of them given the chance.

Suddenly Kimly felt a little less mirthful. Skoots seemed like a nice woman, and Kimly would be a bit bummed if she had gotten herself killed because of her involvement with The Shrouded.

Another random rogue said, "Maybe she answered the emperor's edict, and joined the imperial army like Floppy did?"

Rath grabbed his dagger, and yanked it from the table. "Nope, Skoots was already missing for days before that edict came down."

"Wait, Floppy joined the imperial army?" Kimly was shocked. Not only was he another member of The Shrouded, he was the last person she would expect to enlist to serve the emperor. He hated rules and the emperor.

Favin looked at her like she was crazy. "Have you been hiding under a rock the last several days? The emperor has demanded that all men and women under the age of thirty report to the nearest garrison for conscription into the imperial army. You, my dear, have been drafted. You should have already reported, like Floppy did. We've lost almost one third of the entire guild to the conscription. Imperial soldiers have been searching the streets for days, anyone caught defying the conscription orders are being executed. I am a bit surprised to see you here, I thought you'd be hiding out somewhere or marching with the army."

"Well, I'll be a troll sarding chippie! I guess that explains the soldiers who chased me for half a mile tonight. By the gods, has the emperor lost his mind completely?" Kimly stared at Favin in utter disbelief.

Standing up, Favin looked around at all of the gathered rogues. He said, "Get out there, and find out what happened to Skoots. All other routine missions and heists are on hold until I have some answers."

"Ah, boss, I've still got a number of merchants to shake-down in the morning for their protection fee."

Favin kicked the desk, hard. He took a deep breath, and then said, "One of our people has vanished, and I don't like not knowing what happened. So, everything is on hold until I get answers about Skoots. Find her, or find out what happened to her. If another guild is sarding with us, or if she's floating in the sea somewhere, I want to know. Now, go get us some answers!"

The room was suddenly filled with noise and motion as everyone

154

moved to leave at once.

When the room finally cleared, Favin turned to Rath. "I want you and Viper to make some quiet inquires with the leadership of the other guilds. Not just thieves guilds, but merchant and crafters guilds as well. Any group responsible for several people. I want to know everything you can find out about these 'mancer nappings. If that happened to Skoots, then things are worse than we may think."

Kimly repositioned herself on the crate, now that the others had left and she had all the room she wanted. "I thought you said the stories of nappings was hooey?"

"Of course I did! We can't have the guild jumping at their own shadow, but we have to look at all possibilities." Favin repositioned his desk, and began straightening the things that he disturbed when he kicked it.

Rath walked out of the room, with Viper close behind.

When the door closed behind them, Kimly and Favin were alone. He continued to fix the items on his desk for a bit, and then he sat down and looked at her. "I've got a dinner appointment with the chancellor tonight, care to join me?"

She smiled mischievously, "You troll, you know that I'm a taken woman. Are you asking me on a date?"

He looked annoyed, "Sorry, Kimly, I'm really not in the mood for your games. Do you want to spend some time with the chancellor or not?"

"Oh, Favin, you're no fun at all when you're stressed. Don't worry about Skoots, she's probably just hiding out somewhere or something."

"I don't think so."

She looked at him for a long time. "You two involved?"

He shrugged, "No, it's nothing like that. I'm just worried."

Kimly wasn't entirely sure that she believed him, but she left it alone. "Fine. I'm gonna go and see what kind of trouble I can dig up while the night is still young."

"It's morning already, sun will be rising in just a few hours. Be careful out there, the imperial troops are as thick as flees on a dog's arse. They won't hesitate to slit your throat for treason if they think you've skipped the conscription order. It's happened several times already."

"I ain't worried about troops, Favin." She stood up.

"I know, just be careful."

She turned away from him and walked towards the door. "I'm always careful. I'll be back tonight to be your date for dinner."

As she walked out of the door, he said, "We need to leave by six bells. Don't be late."

- = - = -

Four imperial soldiers passed directly in front of Kimly as she stood near some bushes on a main street leading into the Khardifar bazaar. She was concealed by her *Shadow Shroud* spell, and the soldiers had no idea that they were passing within inches of a Magi who was also defying the conscription decree. The danger sent a shiver of pure joy all the way down her spine.

She couldn't resist reaching out and touching the sleeve of one of the soldiers as he passed by her. The touch was very slight, but she saw the man reach up and touch his shoulder in the very spot where she had brushed him. He looked around briefly, as if looking for the branch that had touched him, but the troops did not even slow down.

Kimly giggled to herself and slinked down the road looking for something fun to do. Far off to the east the sky was just starting to brighten, and it wouldn't be long before the sun peeked over the horizon. The bazaar was busy with people setting up their shops for another hectic day of selling things.

Up ahead, a man carefully stacked a large pile of melons on a table. He pulled an armful from the back of his wagon, and placed them carefully onto the table next to the others. Over and over the man pulled melons from the cart, and she watched him stack them neatly for a few minutes. Finally she could resist no longer, and when he turned to grab more melons from his cart she reached out and grabbed the corner of the table. With a quick lift of one corner, she caused the large pile of melons to go crashing to the ground at the merchant's feet.

The man was so startled by his product spontaneously smashing to the ground around him, that he turned quickly to see who had sabotaged his hard work. His sudden movements caused him to slip and fall in the broken goo of his melon pile. The man cursed and struggled to get up off of the sloppy ground.

Kimly walked quietly to the mule that was tied to the man's wagon, and she yanked several hairs from the donkey's ear. The mule went nuts, kicking and squealing, and then bolted down the street causing several melons to spill from the cart and land on top of the furious merchant as the wagon jerked forward and followed the crazed donkey down the street.

She rushed away from the area before her uncontrollable snickering and giggling gave her away.

It was childish, and she didn't care. What good was it to have access to magic, risking her life because of the emperor's stupid war on Magi, if she couldn't at least have some fun sometimes?

Without a great deal of thought, she moved from one merchant stall to the next, looking for her next bit of amusement. A group of tables across the road and to her left showed promise, so she headed that way. Two hired goons stood guard, and the tables were covered with display cases. She couldn't see the contents of the cases yet, but she imagined they were filled with gems or jewelry. Really, she didn't have any need for more money, and she could buy any jewelry that she might desire. However, the enjoyment wasn't in the gaining of more wealth, it was in the thrill of the hunt.

The goons were impressively attentive, and extremely well armed. They both looked like experienced mercenaries, so she would have to proceed with more caution than normal.

She approached carefully and quietly, even though her *Shadow Shroud* spell would ensure that people wouldn't see her unless she screwed up and did something to break the spell.

Her heart pounded wildly in her chest as she got close enough to see the contents of the display cases.

That's when the screaming erupted behind her.

The screams startled her so badly that she almost wet herself a little. At first she assumed that the screams had something to do with her, but that was silly. She turned to see what was going on, and she saw that most of the people nearby were running.

Screams and shouts filled the area, along with the sounds of crashing as people knocked over tables and entire stalls in their frantic attempts to flee whatever had startled them.

When she first saw the creature, she thought it was a monkey. It was about a foot tall and it had scorched scales instead of fur, tattered wings on its back, and it was screeching like a crazy thing.

It turned towards her, and sprinted in her direction. She moved to her right, and it changed course so it was still headed right for her. Whatever it was, it could see right through her *Shadow Shroud* spell.

She rushed backwards, but it caught up quickly. Just as it leaped at her, she backed right into one of the large goons. She spun around, grabbed the goon, and pushed him slightly towards the freakish creature as it flew through the air at her.

The monkey thing grabbed the goon with its claws and prepared to pounce at Kimly once again. She was on the verge of panic and was about to resort to magic to kill the thing, when it unexpectedly vanished.

No sooner did the creature vanish, when a single purple Khalius Fire orb slammed into the goon, knocking him to the ground.

A necromancer rushed up, and the other goon moved to attack him. The second goon didn't even get close, as the necromancer tossed five deadly spheres of the purple fire at the man. He collapsed on top of the table, shattering the display case and spilling the contents on the ground.

The necromancer didn't even bother to look at the man again, he turned his attention back to the goon who had been clawed by the monkey-creature. The necromancer pulled manacles from a pouch, and said, "Don't move, Magi! If you give me any trouble, I'll kill you like your buddy. Jalinox will be just as happy with a Magi corpse!"

The goon shouted and reached for his weapon, but he didn't even get his hand close to the hilt before the necromancer tossed a volley of necromancer magic on his face, killing him.

The necromancer was preoccupied, and Kimly was curious about what was going to happen next, so she moved closer quietly. She knelt down next to the goon on the broken table.

The whole area was mostly abandoned as everyone had fled for their lives and they all seemed hesitant to return while the necromancer was still around. The necromancer stood up and looked around, as if waiting for something or someone.

As long as it wasn't another one of those creatures, she didn't care who happened along.

Before long, two more necromancers walked over, each dragging a prisoner behind them.

From far off to the right, she heard someone yelling, "You're not gonna take my wife, you sarding bastards!" The man was old and looked more like a baker than a warrior, but she admired his determination.

One of the newly arrived necromancers said, "Can I kill this one?"

"Do it quick, we need to go! I had to kill the Magi, at least you two kept yours alive!"

As the woman moved to take care of the attacking baker, another necromancer dropped a wicket on the ground and Kimly watched the hole open.

When she was a captive of Jalinox, she had traveled the outer plane of Khalius with him, and she knew exactly what the necromancers were about to do.

She watched patiently as they placed their captives, both the dead one and the alive ones, into the hole. Then one at a time they climbed into the hole as well, and it closed over them.

Kimly assumed that they planned to hide underground until darkness fell once again, and the bazaar was more safe, and then they would appear from the hole and flee with their prisoners. She knew that if she stole the wicket that opened the hole, which was now sitting vulnerable on the ground near where the hole had opened, the necromancers would be trapped. Sure, the prisoners would die but they were goners anyway and three dead necromancers would be a win in the long run.

She moved over to the wicket and bent down to pick it up, and then jumped back when she saw a hand reach out of the ground and grasp the stone. The hand pulled the wicket right down to Khalius.

"Sweet ugly chippie humpers!" She exclaimed, as she scooted backwards.

It seemed that the necromancers had new tricks up their sleeves. This changed things a bit. For some reason the necromancers were abducting people they thought were Magi, and taking them through Khalius to Jalinox? If she hadn't tossed that goon at the little creature, they would have been dragging her through Khalius. Somehow the creature knew where she was standing, and she guessed that it was able to sense her magic.

She now had no doubt that Skoots was in a lot of trouble. It was entirely possible that she had been abducted by necromancers after all.

She reached down and scooped up a large handful of gems from the broken display case.

- = - = -

"Are you sure the creature could sense that you can use magic? Maybe it was just running at random people?"

Kimly shook her head, "No, it followed me and I was shrouded."

159

Favin looked around to see if the servant was returning yet, then looked back to her, "And they said they were taking their prisoners to someone named Jollynix?"

"Jalinox, and yes I'm certain of it."

"I don't know who that is."

"He's the leader of the necromancers."

He laughed, "Yes, I gathered that much. How do you know his name?"

"It's a long story, let's just say that I've been his guest just like Skoots is probably his guest now. I don't know what he's doing with Magi, but I promise you it's not good."

Favin was quiet for a long time, simply staring at her. Eventually he patted her on the thigh. "You're an intriguing person, Kimly. Do you have any idea where we might find this Jali-something person?"

"When I ended up with him, it was near Clornoss." She paused for a moment, unusually somber. "This man is a special kind of twisted. If you want to see Skoots again, you need to find her soon."

"Can you reach out to whatever Shrouded contacts we have left and see if they can help us locate this Jalinox guy?"

There weren't many people involved yet, but she did have a few members spread out in a handful of cities throughout the south. She nodded, "I'll make some inquires and see what we can come up with."

A door opened at the end of the hallway, and one of the chancellor's servants walked in. He said, "Mr. Favin, the dining hall is ready for guests."

He stood up, and held his hand out to Kimly.

"You look stunning, by the way. You really do clean up well."

She giggled, "You flirt! Are we on a date after all?"

"Nonsense, but we do have to play the part for the chancellor."

Kimly grabbed his arm and held him close as they walked into the dining hall. She whispered, "I'll do what I can to make it believable."

The chancellor was sitting at the head of the table when they entered. He extended his hand, motioning for them to sit in the chairs to his right. On the other side of the table was a rough looking older man, who was clearly a soldier of some sort.

She reached out and squeezed Favin's hand. All of a sudden she felt like they might be walking into a trap. The chancellor and Favin had been meeting for dinner for many months, and he trusted the man. She, however, hadn't met the city leader and didn't like that some soldier had been invited to join them.

Favin smiled at her, as he pulled out her chair and bid her to sit down. "My darling, may I introduce Lord Bernold the Chancellor of Khardifar. Lord Bernold, this is my lady-friend, Kimly."

"I've heard much about you, Kimly. He really is quite smitten with you."

She forced a smile but didn't reply, her attention was fully on the soldier sitting across from her.

The chancellor said, "Where are my manners? Favin and Kimly, this is Marshal Andraes, he is in charge of my private militia forces."

The marshal smiled and nodded, as the servants began passing around plates of food.

Kimly found that she didn't have much of an appetite as she kept her eye on the marshal. She wasn't a scholar when it came to city military organizations, but she'd never heard of a chancellor with a private militia.

As Favin filled his plate, he said, "Private militia forces? I haven't heard of such a thing."

Between large bites of dinner, the chancellor laughed. "Of course you haven't heard of it, few people have. It's a little contingency that I implemented shortly after I took over as chancellor, and the force has grown slowly over the years. Sometimes they're integrated with the palace guards, and sometimes they work as a part of the sentinels. Marshal Andraes has earned a great deal of autonomy over the years, and since what's good for me is good for him, he knows he'll have my full support in operational matters."

She was beginning to trust the old soldier even less. If the chancellor had any clue that she and Favin could use magic, they could be looking to cash in on a bounty. She asked, "Why are you telling us about this?"

The chancellor didn't answer, instead he looked over to the marshal.

Andraes put down his fork and finished his bite, then said, "Several days ago a member of your guild was seized by imperial agents, and charged as a Magi. She was found guilty and sentenced to hang on the following day."

In a low voice, Favin said, "Skoots."

The marshal nodded, "Yes, her street name is Skoots."

Kimly raised an eyebrow in surprise, "Is? She wasn't hanged?"

Between bites, the chancellor replied, "Andraes visited with Skoots several times in the day before her hanging and, after she made certain concessions, Andraes arranged for her to be removed and brought here.

All of this was done clandestinely, of course, and at great personal risk to the marshal I might add."

"Why wasn't she returned to us immediately? What concessions?" Favin sounded extremely agitated.

Andraes said, "Several witnesses told the emperor's agents that Skoots appeared out of thin air, in the middle of a busy street. Skoots claims that she is not a Magi. To this day, she still insists that she's not a Magi. Instead she claims to be a part of some group called The Shrouded. Some kind of secret magic using underground guild that is not associated with the Magi at all. But, she says that you know how to contact the Magi. Is this true?"

Kimly was on the verge of standing, or attacking. She had a number of spells on her tongue, and Favin reached under the table and squeezed her leg reassuringly.

"Chancellor, I know you well enough to know that if you were going to double-cross me, it would already have happened and it wouldn't be done in your palace. So, help me understand your angle. What's in it for you whether we're Magi or if we can contact the Magi? If you just wanted a bounty we wouldn't be having this conversation."

She let out the breath that she hadn't realized that she'd been holding. Favin's comments made sense, but she still wasn't ready to lower her guard.

The chancellor looked at one of the servants, and said, "Guard the door, and make sure no one enters."

When the servant turned to leave, Kimly noticed a pair of daggers at the man's waist, and another in his boot. If he was just a servant, then she was a goblin.

The chancellor continued, "The emperor is robbing me blind. Not only has he raised the taxes on each city, now he is stealing our young men and women! My entire force of sentinels! His troops and agents flood my streets, and they're killing my people at will! If they're not killing them, they're dragging them away as Dregs. They've emptied my Dross, and still they conscript and kill even more. It's terrible for morale, and even worse on my profits!"

She remained silent and let the chancellor take another bite from his still overly full plate.

"I'm completely fed up. If I can get a commitment from the Magi that they'll back us up, I'm ready to declare Khardifar an independent province. It would be suicide if we attempted it alone, but with the support of the

Magi we might be able to make it work."

Favin dropped his napkin onto his plate. "You're a madman, you know that right?"

"Do you know how to contact the Magi?"

"Where is Skoots?"

"She is safe, and will remain where she's at until I can sit down and talk to actual Magi."

Slightly above a whisper, Kimly said, "I'll arrange a meeting."

CHAPTER 20

Sarge

He closed the door as quietly as possible, and brushed the snow from his cloak. The newly debuted Kelegarian Temple within Fort Randol was so large that even with several fireplaces it was difficult to keep it warm enough to be comfortable.

Sarge pulled his cloak tighter, walked down the main aisle between the benches, and stopped in the front of the sanctuary. As he expected, Madalyn was kneeling before the altar in prayer. She was accompanied by Rissyl's sister Brielle, and Rissyl's adopted daughter Ayris.

Brielle and Madalyn were very close in age, and the two young ladies had quickly become close friends. The friendship started as Madalyn tended to Brielle's wounds during her first full day at the Stronghold, and it grew stronger as Brielle began to take an interest in Madalyn's responsibilities as a cleric of Kelegar. Her initial desire to become a Magi soon shifted to an interest in becoming a cleric like her new friend.

When Brielle arrived at the Stronghold, Ayris latched onto her immediately and suddenly she wanted to be just like her Aunt Brielle. She'd been tagging behind Brielle since then, and recently she'd spent a great deal of time at the temple with the older girls.

He sat patiently, waiting for the young ladies to finish their devotions. It filled him with pride to see them taking their prayer time seriously.

When Madalyn concluded her prayers, she stood up and the others followed her lead.

Brielle saw him first, and she hurried over to him. She said, "Sarge, look at what Madalyn made for me! My very own robes!"

Ayris rushed over too, and turned in circles showing off her new white robes. "Me too!"

"That's great, girls! You look official now." He smiled at them, genuinely delighted to see their excitement.

"Theo, I've been thinking." Madalyn walked over, and sat down next to him. "Everyone's bringing their family to Fort Randol. I'd like to go to Khardifar and get my mom and sister, so they can come live here before something bad happens to them. I keep hearing people talk about how dangerous it's getting for the Denizens, and I worry for them."

He shook his head, "We've talked about this. It's not safe for you in the empire right now. The emperor's new edicts say that you are subject to his conscription. Even if I don't see you as an adult, you are one according to the emperor's laws. If you go walking around an imperial city, you'll be a target for every soldier and guard we see because you ignored the conscription decree."

She started to argue with him, and he placed his hand on her knee.

He continued, "Don't worry, I'll go to Khardifar and bring your mother and sister here. But you're not coming with me. Besides, don't you have plenty to do right here at the Stronghold?"

She stood up and nodded, "Yes, I should already be in Randol City. I told Tuknor that we'd open a healer's shop in the city, and we'd come by once a day to tend to illness and injuries that happen. There are so many people building things and moving stuff around now, and they keep having accidents and end up injured in one way or another. We were there for a few hours yesterday and it was really busy the whole time. Brielle and Ayris have been a big help!"

Sarge stood up and gave her a fatherly hug. "I'm proud of you, keep up Kelegar's great work. I'll go to Khardifar today and bring your family here."

He followed the young ladies towards the door and waited as they pulled their winter robes from hooks near the door. Before they got bundled up, the door opened quickly.

Firana and Bran hurried in.

The right side of Bran's clothing was scorched, and his right arm was pretty badly burned. Firana helped him sit down.

Madalyn walked over to him calmly, and gently raised his arm examining the wounds. She asked, "What happened to him?"

"We were trying out new spells, something went screwy and I blasted him accidently." Firana looked like she was about to start crying.

With a heavy sigh, Madalyn said, "You Evokers really need to stop blowing up each other, one day you're going to get hurt worse than I can heal."

Bran shouted in pain as she softly pulled pieces of clothing from his wound.

She looked at Brielle, "Would you two mind going to the healer's shop in the city? We're already late. I'll catch up with you when I'm done here."

"Sure!" Brielle and Ayris hurried out the door.

Sarge watched the young cleric do what she had gotten quite skilled at doing. His heart swelled with pride, and he mussed her hair on his way to the door.

Another shout of pain from Bran made him regret messing with her as she worked. Not very much, but he regretted it a little.

She growled, "Dammit, Theo! Not while I'm working. Sorry Bran, now try to hold still."

He stopped and turned to face Firana. "If you're not busy today, could you go to Khardifar with me? I told Madalyn that I'd bring her mother and sister to the Stronghold and I need an Evoker and a pair of portal rings to do that."

"Sure, anything for Madalyn! Let's go get a pair of rings, and we can go right away."

- = - = -

An hour later, the pair of Magi were walking down a secluded side-road in the commons district of Khardifar.

Firana said, "I'm sorry I couldn't port us closer to the gate."

"Don't worry about it, but keep your hood pulled up and try to walk like a kid. If anyone asks, tell them you don't reach the age of majority until Mid-Spring. The last thing we need is some soldier asking why you didn't report for conscription."

She laughed, "And just how do I walk like a kid?"

"I dunno, dance around every once in a while or something? It's only been a couple of years, hasn't it? Walk however you walked when you were a kid. It's been ages for me, so I don't remember it. I'm an old man."

"Or we'll just blast them."

He laughed, and looked around to make sure they weren't being noticed. Now that they were here, he wished that he would have asked a different Evoker to join him. She was a fine Magi, but her age would make them a target if any soldiers noticed them.

Sarge felt naked walking down the streets of an imperial city without his armor. He had been working on the enchantments to tie all of the pieces of his blue-tinged armor to the plane of magic, so that he could summon and dismiss the armor just like he did with his cloak and weapons. The process had been long and tedious, but now that he was finished, it was worth the work. He could now walk around completely unencumbered by the armor, and without the unwanted attention that the armor could generate. However, in an instant he could summon the armor back from the plane of magic and he would be protected by it. Not only was it handy in battle situations, it also saved him almost an hour a day of the time it used to take to put on and take off the heavy armor.

They walked for quite a while, until they finally arrived at Madalyn's house. He knocked on the door, and Madalyn's mother answered while holding her toddler.

"Ms. Chardwil?"

The woman looked at him for a long time, and then recognition shown across her face. "Blessed Kelegar! It's the paladin, please come in! Where is Madalyn, is she well?"

He let Firana enter first, and he followed in behind.

He said, "Yes, yes, she is amazing. Your daughter is becoming a skilled cleric and healer. I'm here because she wants you to come to the Magi Stronghold to live with us. A small town of non-magical folk is being built right outside of the Stronghold, in a place safe from the emperor. It's still under construction, but it's safe."

Tears swelled in her eyes, and quickly streaked her cheeks. "You were right about Kelegar, he truly does answer prayers! I did what you said. I've been trying to spread the word of the divine-sire to all who would listen. We now have about thirty people who meet down the road at an old abandoned house."

She started crying harder, and placed the child on the ground so she could dry her eyes with a handkerchief.

"There's no need to cry, you don't gotta leave your friends and home if you don't wanna. Madalyn asked us to bring you to safety, but you're welcome to stay here if you want."

"Oh no, that's not it at all. The other day, soldiers started asking questions about why we were all meeting in that house. Worshiping any deity other than the Pantheon of Nine is illegal, and we've been very afraid of the soldiers showing up to drag us away. We're trying to remain faithful to Kelegar, but it's terrifying to see people dragged to the gallows on a whim each day, and we know that they could be coming for us next. We've prayed for a solution, and here you are. Is the offer only for me, or could others come to the Magi place also?"

Sarge sighed to himself. He'd hoped to gather the mother and child, and then be back at the Stronghold quickly. Bringing a large group of people, and waiting for them to set their affairs in order and get things situated would take much longer. Things were never as simple as they should be. However, he forced a smile. The woman did keep her promise and had spread the word of Kelegar, and this was his chance to reward her.

"Of course they can come. They need to understand that they won't be able to easily travel back here, so moving to Randol City will be a long-term deal. The city is still being built, so many of the niceties that they're used to may not be available right away. Also, they can only bring what they can carry."

The woman hugged him abruptly, and he returned the hug reflexively.

Once she'd released him, she said, "But, they won't have to worry about being hanged for no reason? It sounds like an easy choice. I will spread the word and tell people to meet at our temple at dusk. How will we get out of the city, do you have a wagon?"

He gave her a sarcastic smirk, "We're Magi, ma'am. We won't be using a wagon. We'll use a magical portal."

She looked surprised, and then reached down to pick up her daughter, who had been tugging on her dress and whining for attention. Softly she said, "Magic portal, really?"

Firana smiled and tickled the toddler. "Yes, it's quite fun. You'll love it!"

CHAPTER 21

Bull

"Maybe everyone should declare a truce until spring? I need a warm fire and a large mug of ale. It's much too cold for wars tonight." Bull pulled his robes tighter around his neck and then rubbed his hands together to generate some warmth.

Firana stood up and started walking around. "It's probably dropped twenty degrees since the sun set. I'm about ready to call it a night so we can go home." She shivered.

"Actually, this winter has been noticeably warmer than normal. We should all be glad it's not as cold as it was back in 103 RY." Peke stared out the window and didn't look at the others as he spoke.

Bull looked over at Asha, who was sitting in the corner doing some sort of meditation and didn't seem to be bothered by the cold at all.

They were in a small building that was designed to be an animal shelter. It was out in the middle of a pasture and far from other buildings. It gave the Magi some shelter from the wind and kept them mostly hidden as they watched the nearby road for imperial army patrols or convoys. They were a few miles north east of Clornoss, at the end of another patrol.

They had been doing a lot of these ambushes recently, but this was the first one they'd done so late at night. Typically, the imperials were considerate enough to wander by while it was still light so the Magi could be back at Fort Randol for dinner.

The imperial troops hadn't been that considerate this time.

They had been waiting all day to spring their ambush, and thus far they'd seen only farmers and lonely merchant caravans.

He turned to the Evoker, "Dinner's been calling me for hours, Firi. I say you're right. The imperials will just have to wait for another night to get ambushed."

"Hold on a minute, Bull. There's a group of something headed this way." Peke whispered as he pointed to the east.

"Oh dammit!" Bull moved to one of the windows so he could see also.

The moon was full and the sky was clear, so the night sky was abnormally bright. Far off in the distance, he could see something headed their way. As they approached, their shapes slowly became clearer.

Firana swore quiet, "By the gods, what is that?"

"Are those lizards?"

"Those are lizards, with dwarves on their backs!"

Bull looked at her, "What are dwarves doing so close to Clornoss? Should we greet them?"

She summoned her Magi Cloak, "Yes, let's go. Riz mentioned that there are a group of dwarves near Clornoss. This must be them."

He and the other Magi summoned their cloaks as well, and followed her out of the building and down to the road.

The lizards were running extremely fast, and it didn't take long for them to get near the Magi. There were eight large lizards, and each one had a single dwarven rider.

The dwarf on the first lizard climbed down from his mount, and walked up to Firana.

He took off his helm, and bowed slightly. "Greetin's Magi. I'm Marshal Gruknor, commander of the Spike Head Cavalry, second son of King Drilzad, and second heir to the throne of the Mazbakhar Halls."

Firana bowed awkwardly, "Ah, I'm Firana Aestelya an Evoker in the Sovereign Magi Society of Menelia. Well met, Marshal Gruknor."

She then introduced the others, and pleasantries were passed around.

When the formal greetings were over, she said, "We've heard that the dwarven kingdom had a special force working around Clornoss, but I don't know the details. How goes your mission?"

Gruknor grinned, and pulled out a small flask. "Many months ago, yer emperor threw a dozen of me clansmen in shackles as slaves! They were merchants and came here to trade. Me unit's been 'round here over a year buildin' our tunnels, spying, and rescuin' me shackled dwarven brothers."

Peke asked, "Have you had much luck in rescuing them?"

The dwarf finished a long swig from his flask, and then replied, "Aye! We've rescued 'em all, but two! We're goin' fer those two right now."

"That's fantastic!" Firana looked genuinely excited for them. She asked, "How have you managed to live so close to the imperial capital for so long without the emperor's troops capturing you?"

"Tunnels!" Gruknor raised his flask, and the rest of the dwarves cheered. "We've been buildin' tunnels all 'round Clornoss fer more than a year now. Openin's in some woodlands east of the city, and our tunnels go under the city and all about. We can even sneak right into the palace from its basement."

"That really is remarkable!" Peke looked at the dwarves and their mounts and his admiration was apparent in his expression.

"We're goin' to get the last two captives now. Wanna tag along?"

Firana shook her head, "Thanks for the offer, but we should be getting back to the Stronghold."

Bull stepped forward, "Not so fast, Firi." He looked to the large lizard before him, and then looked to Gruknor, "Could we ride on your lizards?" He felt like a child waiting for a turn to ride a pony. He clasped his hands together, in a pleading gesture.

"Aye! Of course! Climb on up, behind me!" Gruknor climbed onto his lizard, and held out his hand to pull Bull up behind him.

Firana sighed, but she moved over to another one of the lizards, and the other Magi did the same.

Soon the cold night breeze was rushing past Bull's face, as he clung tightly to the dwarf seated before him. The lizards raced through the darkness at a frightful speed, and the feeling was exhilarating.

Bull had ridden a few horses, but that was nothing like the experience of riding on the back of a huge lizard as it sprinted and bounded through the countryside. They followed the road for a while and then turned to the north. He had no idea how far they travelled, but far too soon the ride was over.

The dwarves led the lizards up to a farmhouse out in the middle of the country. The farmland north of Clornoss extended for hundreds of miles, and they had traveled far enough that the farms were scattered widely apart.

Gruknor brought his lizard to a stop near the house, and tied the reigns of his mount to a hitching post. The other dwarves dismounted and each tied their lizard's reigns to a nearby lizard.

One of the other dwarves moved over next to Gruknor, and said, "Gruk, we sure this here's the right place?"

The dwarven marshal smacked the other dwarf against the side of his head with a heavily gloved hand, and gave him a dirty look. "Aye, this is it! Let's go in!"

All of the dwarves drew large battleaxes and rushed to the door of the house.

Firana motioned for the Magi to follow her, as she tailed behind the dwarves.

Gruknor didn't knock, he simply crashed through the door with his large ax. He pushed through the remains of the door, and stormed into the house yelling. "Get up, imperials! Dwarves on a rescue mission!"

The dwarves split up, some going north and the others going south through the house. As they split up, each group began shouting.

Bull followed Gruknor and two other dwarves through one room and down a hallway. He didn't look to see if the other Magi followed them. He summoned his swords, but didn't draw them. He didn't plan to battle farmers in their home, but he wanted to be armed just in case he suddenly needed to defend himself.

A door opened at the end of the hall and a man walked out, wearing only undergarments. The man looked terrified and he held his shaking hands above his head. In a squeaky voice, he stammered, "What do you want?"

Bull thought the poor old man looked like a kind farmer, and he felt bad bursting into the man's house late at night.

"Yer keepin' two of me dwarven brothers as yer servants, and we're here to bring 'em home!"

Another door in the hallway opened, and two young ladies peeked their heads out. One of them said, "What's going on, papa?"

The farmer shouted, "Get back in your room, girls!"

Gruknor slammed the hilt of his battleax onto the floor heavily, and held onto the neck just below the double-sided blade. In a gruff voice, but slightly less than a shout, he said, "Listen, pal. Gimme yer dwarven captives, and we'll leave yer family in peace."

"Follow me out back." The farmer motioned back down the hallway, grabbed a heavy robe, and the dwarves let him lead the way.

They all followed the farmer through the house, and around to a small shed nearby. He opened the door of the shed, and Bull could see a dwarven man asleep on a cot in the little building. There was a large chain binding the dwarf to the floor. He was covered with a thin blanket and was shivering in his sleep.

The farmer said, "You can have him, dwarves make terrible Dregs! I sold the other one weeks ago, I don't know where he is now."

The dwarven rescuers swore and complained loudly, and at great length, as the farmer unlocked his Dreg from the chains.

When the dwarven Dreg was unchained, Gruknor grabbed the farmer by both shoulders and pulled him close. The human was about a foot taller than the stout dwarf, but Gruknor was easily three times the farmer's girth. He pulled the thin human down until he bent low enough to look directly into the dwarf's eyes.

Gruknor growled, "Think carefully. Who has me dwarven brother now?" His hands slowly moved from the farmer's shoulders to rest at the base of the man's neck. The dwarf didn't squeeze, but the threat was clear enough.

With both hands on the dwarf's powerful arms, the farmer tried to pull Gruknor's hands away. But the attempt was pointless. After a moment, the farmer said, "Some rancher down near Tharrin bought him. That's all I know, I swear!"

The dwarf glared at him at length, and then released him with a small shove. "If you don't mind, we'll take a peek 'round yer house just to make sure yer not mistaking 'bout me brother bein' here."

"Do I have any choice?" The farmer recovered from the shove, and stepped away to put more distance between himself and the dwarves.

"None. Dwarves, check the house quick then we'll be goin'."

One dwarf stayed behind to care for the rescued Dreg, and the others hurried into the house. The farmer followed behind them.

Gruknor walked over to the Magi, who had been watching from a few feet away. He said, "Well we ain't done yet, dammit. Was hopin' to be done with this and headin' back to the mountains."

Firana smiled at him, and placed a hand on his shoulder, "Well, you rescued one more. You'll be home soon, I'm sure. And on that note, we should get back to the Stronghold. Safe travels, friends."

"Aye! Same to you."

CHAPTER 22

Jessa

"Shut up and get into the cell."

The irritating captive threw her arms out and grabbed the bars to keep from being pushed into the cell, "Do you have any idea who I am? I am Nassani, the granddaughter of the great Magi Rifin! You can't put me in a cage! The Magi are coming for me soon, I'm going to be powerful too! You'll regret this!"

Jessa kicked the woman in the stomach, as hard as she could. She hated when they got indignant.

Nassani shrieked as she fell backwards into the cell, and landed against the back wall with a dull thud.

"Well then this is our lucky day, Nassani. The granddaughter of a powerful Magi should leave a large puddle of mana when the worms are through with you."

Jessa sneered at the woman who was crumpled in a heap against the back wall. She was holding her stomach and trying hard to recover the breath that had been knocked out of her.

There was a loud bang as Jessa tossed the iron door closed, and it echoed through the halls of the dungeon. The noise startled many of the prisoners that were caged in small cells up and down the hallway, and it set off a series of gasps and cries.

She tuned out their pleas and shouts as she quickly walked down the hall to the stairs out of the miserable dungeon. This was her fourth capture in four days, and she was quickly growing tired of it.

Jalinox had instructed all of the apostles to make the harvesting of people with magic potential their highest priority. Some of the younger followers had been quickly gaining his favor because of how many captures they'd accomplished already. She hated competing with inferiors just to prove to Jalinox that she was an obedient follower. However, the politics of power was a part of what she'd gotten herself into and she was determined to play the game until she achieved her goals.

If that meant harvesting Magi before they learn how to cast spells, that's what she'd do.

From the dungeons she headed to the temple. She figured that she'd either find Jalinox there, or in his study, and the temple was closest so she'd start there.

As soon as she opened the door to the temple, she knew that she'd chosen correctly. Jalinox was on the stage speaking passionately. In the pews before him were about a dozen new worshipers. Some of them were probably prisoners who chose to avoid an unpleasant death by joining with their captors, and others were some of those particularly crazy people who joined Jalinox's followers by choice.

Throughout the empire, there were several temples dedicated to Viator, and Jalinox had apostles working in each one as the clergy. Membership in temples dedicated to the god of death was always pretty low, however every city had its underbelly of people drawn to those temples for one reason or another. She had been to a few of them recently, and it was always surreal seeing commoners casually worshiping Viator.

A few of the pupils looked back at her as she walked in, but Jalinox did not pause in his sermon. She sat down at the back of the room and watched patiently. She'd seen this sermon many times, and she knew that he was almost finished.

Once the sermon was finished, most of the pupils wanted to crowd around him to receive some sort of praise or ask him one dumb question or another. Several guards in the room walked around and gathered those individuals who were headed back to cells, and then the remaining students slowly trickled from the room after receiving a little attention from their master.

When the room cleared Jalinox walked to the back of the sanctuary and sat down next to her.

"I'm getting too old for this. Pretty soon I just might have to hand this duty over to one of my top acolytes." He flashed her a wicked grin.

"That sounds like a great idea, just so long as the lucky recipient of that honor is not me. I'm just as likely to kill them all as I am to teach them anything. You're much more patient with that nonsense than I am. And, you have dozens of apostles who'd do anything to win an assignment like that."

He sighed and then stood up slowly. "I'll keep wearing you down, eventually you'll agree to do it."

She stood up and followed him to the door. When they got outside, he turned to the left.

"Let's go and check on our prince."

"Is his soul still apart from his body?"

"When I last checked."

She shook her head slowly. "It's been days. When should we get concerned that he won't survive?"

"My dear, that has been a concern since before we even started. I told him not to leave the circle, he didn't listen." Jalinox didn't seem very worried.

"You didn't really think that a simple summoning circle could protect the prince from the patron-god? If this deity created our very souls, is a magical circle going to help?"

Jalinox chuckled, "Certainly not! I had hoped that it would prevent the prince's soul from leaving our realm, because I'm not entirely convinced that he'll retain his sanity if his soul is taken to the lowest planes of Khalius. But it seems that we'll know that answer soon enough."

They passed through one of the many doors that lead to the extensive underground complex beneath the compound. Several guards were posted at the various intersections as they snaked through the maze of corridors towards the vast room where she'd last seen the prince.

He pushed the door open, and she followed him into the room expecting to see the prince's body on the floor where it had been for days.

The body was not there, only the crumpled remains of discarded clothing.

Standing near the table was a naked man. His back was to the door, and he did not look up when they walked into the room. He appeared to be reading one of the books on the table.

She could hear the uncertainty in Jalinox's voice when he said, "Prince Edal?"

The person at the table turned and faced them.

Jessa gasped in shock. The person before her was the prince, but he had aged a decade or more. The prince who was just entering puberty several days before, was now a tall and skinny man. He had grown two feet, and his face looked mature and angular. Gone was the round and chubby cheeks of youth, they had been replaced by slim cheeks and several days of stubble.

His appearance wasn't the only thing that had changed, his entire demeanor was different. The prince planted his feet, crossed his arms at his chest, and raised his chin confidently as he looked at her and Jalinox standing in the doorway in shock. He looked proud and self-assured, and his lack of clothing did not seem to bother him.

In a deep voice the prince said, "How long have I been away?"

Jalinox replied, "Four days. Is there anything that you need? You must be hungry. Can I have my people bring you food or wine?"

The prince nodded once, "Yes, and some clothing, it is very cold here."

Jalinox called for one of the guards, and instructed the man to arrange for some food, wine, and robes for the prince.

Jessa couldn't resist the question any longer, "My prince, why have you changed so much? A few days ago, you were a boy."

"For you it may have only been a few days. For me, it was much longer. Several years at least. I do not know why my body aged while my soul was in Khalius, but my god blessed me with several years in his tutelage. I assure you that I am no longer the boy you knew."

Jalinox said, "Yes, that we can see. Have you completed the trials and given your soul to Wirmyntas?"

"Indeed, Jalinox. My soul is pledged to the patron-god, and I am his for eternity. However, I have another task to complete before he will accept me as his Archwarlock."

"I expected as much, my prince." Jalinox grinned widely. "If you will share the details of your quest, I will be happy to assist however I can."

With his chin still held high, the prince looked down his nose at the old necromancer. After a long silence, he replied, "Your assistance will not be required, Jalinox."

Jessa struggled to remain quiet, as the prince hinted that he was not content with being controlled. She stepped a small step to her right, to give herself a bit of space in case things turned ugly.

"As you wish, my prince." Jalinox hissed.

"I spent several years as a lord over Khalius, and I've spoken to the souls of many of your victims. My dear Tali, for example." The expression on Edal's face turned dark and he looked from Jalinox to Jessa.

She felt her heart drop to the pit of her stomach and she stepped further to her right. Suddenly it seemed that they would be battling the prince, and she wasn't entirely confident that they'd win. She had no clue what powers he might have gained, or what gifts the god had granted him, and she was certain that she didn't want to find out the hard way.

"Let's not be rash to jump to conclusions, Prince Edal." Jalinox held up his hands, palms towards the prince. She wasn't sure if he was trying to calm the prince, or if he was preparing to attack.

Edal did not look concerned, "I understand, completely. Tali was a tool in your quest for power, and I can respect your aspirations. Wirmyntas, however, finds you to be cowardly and presumptuous. You dabble with powers that you don't deserve, and don't fully understand. You bind his minor demons to do your bidding, taking the gifts meant for warlocks instead of having the honor to be satisfied with the gifts granted by the god to which you've freely pledged your soul."

The necromancer's cheeks flushed bright red, and Jessa was sure that he was on the verge of exploding with fury.

Jalinox took a deep breath, and let it out slowly. He smiled politely, and bowed slightly, "But of course, my prince. I should excuse myself, to make preparations."

"We have several stops to make before returning to Clornoss. During my time in Khalius, I encountered many souls of our soldiers who had died during Magi raids. I've learned much about their tactics, and we'll be sharing this information with the commanders of each of our garrisons. The Magi will find that our garrisons are not such easy targets when our troops know what to expect and how to prepare."

"Yes, my prince." Jalinox walked quickly out of the room.

Jessa turned to follow him, but the prince said, "Jessa, wait."

She turned, and bowed her head. "My prince?"

"Wirmyntas sees great potential in you. You are a strong and proud woman, and you could rule these lands at my side for a time, and then rule Khalius at my side for all eternity."

"But only if I submit to you and agree to be your subservient wife? Beget your children and pleasure you in bed? I think I'll pass, my prince." She stepped away from him.

Edal took several steps towards her. His laugh was anything but amused. "I would not desire a subservient wife, and Wirmyntas would not accept a weak warlock. Jalinox may believe your lie that you've given your soul to Viator, but I know the truth. You give devotions to Viator, and enjoy his gifts, but you refused to pledge your soul simply at Jalinox's orders. Wirmyntas approves, and would be happy to accept you as a warlock if you freely pledge your soul to him. As a separate offer, I would accept you as my empress, and my equal, once you've been accepted by the patron-god."

She was overwhelmed by the sudden shift of possibilities. So much had happened, and the power dynamics of her life were changing faster than she preferred. She needed time to consider her options. She bowed slightly, "Your offer is very generous, my prince. I will give you my answer soon."

"Don't wait too long, the door is likely to close without warning and then the choice will be made for you."

Jessa bowed, and hurried out the door. She ran to catch up with Jalinox. He was just exiting the stairs when she caught up with him.

She said, "Well, that was unexpected."

"I figured he'd be confident, but I expected him to be a twelve-year-old kid. I thought we'd have several years to mold him and shape what kind of a man he'd become. I must admit, these events are unexpected and potentially problematic." He didn't look at her or slow his walk.

"What are we going to do?"

"I'm still working on that. For now, we're going to go with the flow. Everything is still well in line with my original plan, we'll just have to see how things unfold."

- = - = -

A few hours later, Jessa and Jalinox returned to the prince's room. When they entered, she was happy to see that someone had brought the prince some clothes. He was dressed in robes of black and grey, and he sat on the desk in the middle of the room reading one of the books.

The prince stood up and walked quickly to the door. He said, "I'm anxious to get started, are you ready yet?"

Jalinox removed a wicket from his pouch. He said, "My prince, I'll open a hole and we can travel through the upper levels of Khalius to Clornoss."

The prince stepped between them. He said, "I told you, necromancer, we have several stops to make first." The prince reached out and grabbed them by the shoulders.

As soon as she felt his hand on her shoulder she instantly experienced the sensation of falling. She reached out to grab onto something, but there was nothing to catch onto.

Everything went dark and then streaked into a blur of colorless light.

She felt the prince let go of her shoulder, and the feeling of falling abruptly stopped. When she looked around she discovered that they were outside. It was cold, but at least there was no snow. They were standing near a road, and they were not far from a large military fort.

Edal walked away from them, heading towards the fort.

Jessa turned to Jalinox, and he looked as surprised as she felt. She had no idea how the prince brought them here. She suspected that they somehow travelled through Khalius, but it was different than anything she'd experience when travelling through the underworld.

Without waiting for Jalinox, she walked quickly to catch up with the prince.

When they arrived at the fort, they found the gate was closed and guarded by two soldiers.

The prince walked up to the men. He said, "I must speak to the commander of this garrison."

Neither guard moved. One of them said, "What do you want? If you're more conscripts, you're late and the general will have you flogged."

Edal reached out and gently touched the arm of one of the guards. Immediately the guard's eyes widened and flickered with fire, and his face contorted as if he was struck by crippling pain. The changes lasted but a fraction of a second, and then the guard looked as he had before. It happened so quickly that Jessa was left wondering if she had imagined it.

The guard said, "I'm sorry, my prince, I didn't recognize you. Please follow me." He opened the gate and slipped inside.

The remaining guard looked confused, and said, "Which of you is a prince?"

Jessa ignored him and followed the others into the fort. They walked to a small building, very near the entrance.

When they entered the small room a tough looking older soldier looked up from the paperwork on his desk. He studied them for some time, and then he stood up. "Who are you?"

The prince held out his hand, to give greetings. As soon as the general took Edal's hand, his eyes flickered with flames and his face briefly showed the agony experienced by the guard, and it faded just as quickly.

The general blinked several times, and then said, "My apologies, my prince. How can we serve you?"

"General, the Magi continue to raid our garrisons. You must be prepared for their diabolical tactics."

The general looked out one of his windows towards the gate of the fort. "I am not familiar with their tactics, my prince. But our defenses are formidable."

Edal replied. "General, the Magi will magically appear within the garrison, they'll murder everyone inside, and then they leave without a scratch. Using their vile magic, they have the element of surprise because they can appear and disappear at will. Instead of keeping you safe, your walls will prevent your escape. Your men must learn to guard the garrison from internal attack, and they should be prepared to respond at any time of day or night."

The general looked to the soldier at the door, and said, "Corporal, sound the assembly. I want every soldier armed and armored immediately, and then they should fall-in on the drill pad for further orders." When the soldier had rushed off to obey his commands, the general said, "My prince, we'll post archers on the roofs of the buildings and on the ramparts of the walls. Our cavalry will be on alert. The footmen will pull special guard duty in various overlook positions throughout the garrison where they can gain surprise on any Magi that might show up suddenly. If the sarding Magi want to ambush us, they're in for a surprise of their own."

The bell began ringing as the soldier alerted the garrison to assemble for orders.

The prince said, "May Wirmyntas grant you strength, general."

"Thank you, my prince. If you'll excuse me, I have orders to deliver."

As soon as the door closed behind the general, the prince said, "Our work here is done. Let's go to the next garrison."

Jessa couldn't contain her question any longer, "What did you do to those men? I saw the fire in their eyes."

With a small smile, Edal replied, "Perhaps someday I'll teach you."

She thoroughly regretted asking the question.

Without warning, he grabbed her shoulder. For a brief second she feared that she would be the next recipient of whatever he had done to those soldiers, and she braced herself for the agony that the others seemed to experience. Instead she felt the sensation of rapidly falling.

Before she could reach for something to grab onto, the streaks of grey ceased, the falling feeling vanished, and they were standing not far from another garrison.

CHAPTER 23

Ferth

Eleyne looked up from her book when the door opened, "That took much longer than I expected, what did he say?"

"The whole council was extremely busy today. I think half of the Magi Society was lined up in the council chamber, waiting to talk to them. I waited an hour or more before it was my turn. Eventually I talked to Cynia about it, and she said she'd ask Ranik to join us." Ferth closed the door and sat down in a comfortable chair near her.

Eleyne had been asking him for days if he would help her organize a raid on the garrison in Libur. That had been her city, before the Magi moved to the Stronghold, and her coterie had suffered significant losses while still stationed there. He could understand why she wanted to bring some retribution in the name of her old coterie.

Recently, Ferth had led several raids on imperial convoys and garrisons and each time he was joined by Zahr, Kyoso, and Bull. For this raid on Libur, Eleyne would be taking Zahr's place.

Ferth had been trying to find a time when Kyoso and Bull were available, so the four of them could pull off a raid on Libur. However, it never seemed to work out. All of the Magi had been busy with training and research, not to mention patrols and raids. Each time he thought he found a good time for a raid in Libur, something fell through.

With everyone very busy with their own missions, he went to the council to see if they wanted him to take a Society Magi or if there was another Order of Champions Magi who could take Bull's place.

Ferth was quite happy to not be a part of the grand council, because he would have little patience for so many people demanding his attention all day long.

Eleyne stood up. "Great! When can we get underway?"

"As soon as Ranik is ready. I stopped and told Kyoso on my way back, so he should be here any minute."

The two Magi talked for an hour or more before Kyoso and Ranik arrived.

When they entered, Ferth summoned his staff and gave Kyoso a confident grin. "Okay, Magi. Let's go raid some imperials!"

Kyoso hooted loudly, "Kyoso brings death today!"

He whispered the trigger word and teleported to Libur. When he arrived, he allowed the vertigo to subside, and then he looked around. He was in the country, outside of the city of Libur.

Not far to the south, he saw the garrison. Things looked normal, as expected, so he picked his location for his next port.

A quick spell and a whisper later, he was deep inside the Libur garrison. The area was clear so as soon as the vertigo passed he activated his ring and the portal appeared.

Eleyne stepped through first, followed by Ranik. Kyoso walked through last and the portal closed as he came through with the second portal ring.

"Kyoso will scout ahead!"

Before Ferth could reply, the Order of Shadows Magi vanished.

Ranik looked around, "It sure is quiet. Shouldn't there be sounds of a blacksmith hammer, or some sword practice? Something? The place seems abandoned."

"Yes, it does seem pretty quiet. But our last garrison raid was about like this. Let's look around." Ferth could go east or west, he decided to walk west so their shadows were behind them.

They walked down a wide walkway between buildings, and before long it opened into a large open drill area. The drill area was empty and eerily quiet.

Ferth looked to Ranik, and said, "Yeah, now I'm getting spooked. Something is wrong."

Eleyne pointed up to the top of the garrison wall across on the other side of the drill area. "Look there, I see an archer but he's not looking outside the fort. He's looking in here. Do you feel that? Like something is clawing at your mind, trying to take control?"

"Dammit, yes. Should we abort?" Ferth looked from Eleyne to Ranik.

"How can we abort without Kyoso, he's got the other portal ring."

From the far side of the drill area, he could hear Kyoso shouting.

"Kyoso brings death today! Die vile wretches!" The Magi began firing his magic arrows at guards on the tops of the garrison wall.

A horn blared from somewhere, and that was followed by several other horns. In seconds the entire garrison exploded into pandemonium. A door opened behind them, and several soldiers rushed into the walkway with swords drawn.

He shouted, "Krol'Zi Taldium!" Instantly a tawny mountain lion appeared at his side, and it rushed at the approaching soldiers.

Lowering the tip of his staff, he launched several fire orbs at the closest soldiers. There were too many of them, and he had to retreat into the open drill area to keep some space between him and the approaching soldiers.

Ferth regretted the move as soon as he made it. Several cavalry soldiers in full armor were galloping at full speed, directly at him. He had time to blast two of them with large balls of fire before they got close enough to strike at him with their swords.

A large tiger leapt at another knight, knocking him from his horse. However, that left a dozen or more still baring down on them.

He rushed to his right, and managed to blast two of them with a vicious volley of lightning as he darted back into the relative safety of the walkway between buildings.

The entire space was filled with sword-wielding warriors, several of whom were fiercely battling his mountain lion and the blue and white cloaked Ranik. The Order of Champions Magi was deadly with his sword, and at least a dozen imperial soldiers were dead at his feet as he stepped and blocked, parried and counter attacked. One movement led to another, and every other movement seemed to result in a dead soldier.

The knights had regrouped, and Ferth could hear them beginning their charge from behind, into the walkway between buildings. He turned to face them.

The aura was getting more powerful, and it wanted him to drop his weapons and surrender. He raised magical wards around his mind, and the powerful aura abruptly vanished.

The first arrow struck him in the back, and his magical cloak brushed it aside. He heard it zipping through the air, but he didn't fully realize what it was until he felt it hit him in the back. He glanced in the direction of the archer, and saw several of them on the rooftops taking aim.

To conserve his magewel, he continued to summon fire orbs through his staff. They wouldn't be as powerful as he could otherwise cast, but using the staff as a focus item allowed him to use much less magical essence and it looked like he'd need to use it sparingly if he was going to save enough magic to port out of this trap. Mainly he hoped they'd keep the cavalry at bay for a short while so he could focus on the archers.

Far behind the mounted troops, he heard soldiers erupt in raucous cheers. For a moment he could see several troops holding up the limp body of Kyoso, his grey and white cloak was whipping in the wind. The soldiers threw the body to the ground, and Ferth could no longer see it.

Standing alone in the middle of the drill area was an imperial officer, pointing and shouting commands to the troops. The soldiers seemed emboldened and energized by the officer's shouts.

Ferth cursed viciously, and then turned to his right. "Ranik we've got a sarding problem! Kyoso's down. He's surely dead!"

The Order of Champions Magi turned away from the warriors he'd been battling and rushed towards the open drill area, shouting, "Dammit, I'll get the ring!"

The mounted troops turned their attention towards Ranik as he rushed into the open area. The entire area was filled with soldiers, mounted and afoot, and Ferth feared the champion was sprinting to a suicide mission.

He turned to face the swarm of soldiers left mostly unoccupied when Ranik ran off after the ring. His mountain lion roared weakly and lunged at the closest warrior, but Ferth knew that the cat couldn't hold out much longer. It was bleeding severely from several gashes, and had several arrows embedded in its back and shoulders.

"Krol'Tu Salindi!" A large fireball raced from his outstretched hands, and plowed down the walkway between buildings. The screams from the nearby soldiers were brief, and as the smoke cleared he was happy to see that most of the enemy trapped in the confined space had been killed by the fiery ball of death.

He turned back to the open drill area. There was a horde of soldiers far off to his right, and Ranik's blue and white cloak could be seen briefly between gaps in the amassed soldiers.

The whole time the lone commander screamed orders.

Several zips buzzed the air, and a series of thumps against his magical cloak brought the archers back to the forefront of his attention. He spun and leveled his staff at the first archer. Before the orb had traveled halfway to his target he'd already moved to the next one. Orb after orb launched from the staff towards the tops of the buildings. He was certain he hit several of the archers, but many of them were able to duck away in time. He wasn't even sure that the ones he'd hit would be totally dealt with. However, that was all the attention he could spare.

Turning his attention back to the drill area, he looked desperately for the other Magi. The mass of troops around Ranik had mostly dispersed. The motionless form below the blue and white cloth, which was stained crimson red, blowing in the breeze confirmed his fears that Ranik was dead.

Far to his left he could see another mass of humanity, near the garrison gate. He knew that Eleyne must be the focus of that swarm. He began running in that direction. If he could get to her, he could try to port them both back to the Stronghold. He'd never done teleportation with another person without using the portal rings, but the second ring was on Kyoso's dead hand and it was unlikely that he could make it to Kyoso's body. Their only chance was a tandem teleport.

A huge growth of vegetation sprouted from the ground, in the midst of the soldiers near the gate. He recognized the Diviner spell and knew that Eleyne was close by.

His ability to run was being hindered by a nagging pain in his right leg. He refused to look, but he assumed that he'd been slashed or struck by an arrow, or something.

Several arrows rained down at him as he ran. Sharp jabs of pain proclaimed that some of the arrows succeeded in penetrating the protection provided by his cloak.

A dark form darted out of the mass of soldiers and plant life near the gate, and Ferth watched a battered tiger canter towards him. Seeing Eleyne in tiger form hurrying towards him was enough to drive him forward faster. She returned to human form as she leapt into his arms.

Arrows slammed into the ground all around them, and some of them bit hard into his skin as his cloak began to fail. She looked even worse than he felt. Some of the soldiers were able to break free from the aggressive plant life, and others scattered around the drill area rushed towards the two Magi.

Screams and battle cries were all around. Someone nearby screamed, "Die Magi!"

Ferth turned in time to see a group of soldiers already next to him on his left. His left hip and lower abdomen exploded into pain as the wide and heavy blade of a soldier's halberd cleaved deeply into his body. He could feel darkness clawing for him, even as he felt the bones in his hip shatter. A white-hot pain, like nothing he'd ever imagined, erupted from his lower stomach and he was certain that the mercy of death couldn't be far behind.

He could barely focus his mind to form the complex spell to freedom. He muttered, "Kur'Gezbar Duri."

Several weapons streaked towards them as he said the trigger word for the spell. If it fizzled, or if the imperials broke his concentration at the wrong time, they were both dead. He felt one blade dig deep into his left arm as everything spun out of control, and the world went black.

CHAPTER 24

Rissyl

It had been quite a while since Rissyl had ridden in a wagon, typically he either walked or teleported where he needed to go. The bouncy motion and gentle swaying of the wagon took him back to his first adventure with Cynia on their way to meet Randol. In some ways that seemed like a very long time ago.

She reached out and took his hand. Her smile could still brighten his whole day, and he couldn't help but smile in return. He squeezed her hand and gave her a playful wink.

She said, "I can't believe you were willing to leave Fort Randol with so many people lined up, wanting your attention."

He looked over at Kimly, and then back to Cynia. "I was pretty shocked to see Kimly walk into the council room. If the chancellor of Khardifar wants to meet with us to discuss how they can declare their autonomy from the Ryallic Empire, that is pretty momentous."

Cynia leaned back, and put one arm around him. "Yep, but you usually wanna talk for ages before deciding what to do."

"Instead, I brought the whole council with us." He gave her a grin, and leaned back against her arm and then nestled up against her.

Dalen, Sarasa, and Kimly sat on the bench across from them, and Tuknor sat next to Cynia. Up front, Favin drove the horses.

From the other side of the wagon, Kimly said, "I wasn't sure that you'd come. It was a bit of a risk, telling the Khardifar chancellor to travel to our meeting place before I'd even talked to you. Thanks for not keeping the chancellor waiting too long, Favin and I would have looked foolish."

Sarasa had been silent since they'd left the Stronghold. Rissyl didn't know if she was just in a bad mood, or if she held animosity towards Kimly. She'd been moody since her experience at Randol's home, so it was hard to say.

"You're in The Shrouded, aren't you?" Sarasa's question sounded more like an accusation.

Kimly simply replied, "Yeah."

Dalen turned to look at Kimly. "Were you in The Shrouded on the day we met at my grandfather's shop. Before you became a Magi?"

She nodded, but didn't say anything.

Sarasa pressed her point, "So your whole motivation for learning magic was to become a better thief? You used us, and then you vanished when we needed you most."

A heavy silence fell over the group, and Kimly sat quietly staring out at the countryside.

If he spoke-up on Kimly's behalf, Sarasa would be furious. Rissyl understood Sarasa's point but he wished that she would have chosen some other time to make it. Not that Kimly was around enough to work things out at a convenient time. Finally, he said, "Let's focus on the mission at hand. We can deal with the other stuff later."

He didn't know what they should do about The Shrouded group, but right now they needed all of the allies they could get.

Refusing to back down, Sarasa stated emphatically, "Riz, she's a liar and a thief! I have never trusted her, and I trust her even less now. I think it's just as likely that she's delivering us to the imperials so she can collect a fat bag of coins."

Kimly started to reply, and Rissyl quickly cut her off to keep things from escalating out of control.

He said, "Kimly! Rasa, please! If it's an ambush we'll deal with it. Until then, let's assume that things are as Kimly claims."

"I'll tell you one thing for sure." Tuknor stated.

Rissyl was surprised to hear his father join the conversation, but happy for any change of subject.

Tuknor continued without pause, "If Chancellor Bernold is involved, then there is a financial scheme of some kind. I've known the man for many years, and his own wealth is always his main concern. If he wants autonomy from the empire, he's not doing it to help the Denizens. He is looking to get even richer."

"What would he gain? He'd just anger the emperor and risk attack from the imperial army?" Dalen sounded skeptical.

Rissyl shared his skepticism, it didn't sound like a logical scheme for making coin.

His father rubbed his fingers together like he was playing with coins. "Taxes. Each city pays a fortune in taxes to Clornoss. If Khardifar and the surrounding towns and villages were autonomous, Bernold would

189

effectively be a king. All of the tax money from the region would stay in his purse instead of most of it being sent to the emperor."

This was why Rissyl asked his father to join them. As a lifelong politician, he knew the games being played.

Dalen crossed his arms at his chest. "Dammit! Now I dunno if this is a good idea at all! If we help them break away, then surely the emperor will attack them. That's a lot of death and misery just to prop up a different king and make him rich. Is that what the Magi Society is about?"

Everyone in the wagon started talking at once, and Rissyl tried to hold up his hands to get people quiet so he could speak.

Cynia shouted, "Shut up!" When things eventually quieted, she continued, "Listen, no matter what we do or don't do, someone's gonna get rich. That's just how life works. Maybe it's the emperor, maybe it's Bernold, or it'll just be someone else. The money ain't our problem. There should just be two things that the Magi Society cares about in this. Will this hurt the emperor and help the Magi Society survive? Will it help the people around here somehow?"

"They'll be dead if the emperor attacks, so that's not great for them." Dalen sounded unconvinced.

Rissyl knew that Cynia had made some very good points, and Dalen was too stuck on his own arguments to listen to them. "You're right, Dalen. If Bernold declares Khardifar and the surrounding region to be autonomous, it will surely bring war and bloodshed. But war is already happening in the streets of each city in the empire. The emperor's agents drag dozens of people to the gallows every day, falsely accused of being Magi. At least if these people are fighting for local autonomy, they'd be fighting for a cause and the hope for better days to come."

"They make a good point. I still don't trust Kimly, but I'm in favor of helping this chancellor even if his main motivation is his own greed." Sarasa didn't look happy, but she looked less likely to spring into attack mode.

From the front of the wagon, Favin hollered back to the Magi, "You're gonna have to make up your minds quickly, the manor is just ahead."

Rissyl looked up ahead and saw a huge manor off in the distance. Several horses were tethered near a small shed to the south of the manor. A large forest spread out before them, with the manor tucked back in a clearing and leaving a long wooded-area on both sides of them as they made their way towards it. If someone wanted to ambush them, it would be easy enough to hide in the forest on either side as the wagon approached the manor.

Apparently Sarasa was thinking the same thing, and she warned, "Stay alert. The forest would make a great hiding spot."

When they arrived at the shed, Favin stopped the wagon and jumped out to tether the horses to the hitching post. Several soldiers surrounded the wagon, and one held up his hand offering to help the Magi down from the back of the wagon. He said, "Welcome, Magi. The chancellor is expecting you."

The soldiers were not wearing the traditional tabards of the various imperial military groups. Instead they were all wearing some sort of short mantle, that only extended to their elbows. It was a loose sleeveless piece of cloth with a hood, similar to a cloak, but it was not opened in front. From the appearance, it was simply slipped over the head and it only covered the head, shoulders, chest, upper arms, and upper back. The mantles were grey with blue and white trim along the edges. Beneath the mantles, the soldiers wore a mixture of plate and chainmail armor.

As he stepped down from the wagon, Rissyl summoned his cloak and then prepared a spell to take out most of the nearby guards. He wanted to trust Kimly, but he wasn't going to take any chances.

If they were surprised to see his cloak suddenly appear, the soldiers were disciplined enough to refrain from commenting about it.

The soldier closest to him said, "If you're armed, you'll need to leave your weapons on the wagon. No weapons in the presence of the chancellor."

Rissyl held up his arms as the soldier patted him to ensure that he didn't have any hidden weapons. He said, "I have no weapons on me." He didn't mention that each of them could summon an arsenal of weapons at any time.

Once the soldiers had checked everyone, including Favin and Kimly, they were led over to the expansive manor.

- = - = -

He shouldn't have been surprised that the meeting with Chancellor Bernold felt less like a chivalrous plot for personal freedoms and liberty, and more like a shady business deal.

The chancellor seemed every bit as greedy and scheming as Tuknor had warned, and much of the beginning of the meeting was tense and borderline confrontational. Twice he expected Dalen to explode and storm out of the manor.

It didn't help that the chancellor flaunted his wealth in every way imaginable. The manor was furnished and decorated like a magnificent palace, with gold and silver featured prominently throughout the place. Elaborate marble sculptures lined the walls, massive tapestries and murals were plentiful, and even the smallest knickknacks looked expensive.

If that wasn't enough opulence, chancellor had a lovely cheirapsian woman attentively working on his shoulder muscles while he sat and negotiated with the Magi. Rissyl had heard stories of the charms and skills of the cheirapsians, but he'd never actually seen one at work and he knew that the services didn't come cheap.

Dalen had been pacing around the large room for most of the meeting. He stopped and looked at the chancellor. "We'll help your militia with the fort outside your city and help them deal with the emperor's troops in the city. But that's it."

Bernold nodded, "We'll also need Magi to do regular patrols in the cities and towns in the areas and the surrounding countryside, to assist our militia in keeping people safe and preventing imperial loyalists from causing problems, for at least the first year."

Sarasa and Cynia both laughed.

Dalen growled, "Not a chance."

Rissyl held up his hands, to encourage calm. "How about this? We'll identify all of the members of your militia who have the potential to become Magi. Any who are willing to take our oath and become full members of the Sovereign Magi Society will be brought into our ranks and trained as Society Magi. Although they will be full Magi and subject to our rules and laws, we'll agree to assign them to Khardifar to serve in your militia. They'll spend the majority of their time carrying out standard militia duties to keep your people safe."

"That's a really good idea, Riz. That could work nicely." Sarasa smiled and gave him a gesture of approval.

Even Dalen seemed to like the idea, judging from his slight smile and a raised eyebrow, but he remained quiet.

The chancellor considered the proposal, and then added, "I like it, but they're still under my command and must submit to my authority above all others."

Dalen stomped a foot, and grunted, "You're outta your sarding mind."

"Dalen, please calm down." Rissyl took a second to calm himself as well. "Chancellor, becoming a Magi is more than just learning some handy spells. It comes with a sacred oath and a tremendous amount of responsibilities, and a Magi's ultimate authority must always be the Magi Council. This is not negotiable."

"Yes, a Magi's ultimate authority must always be the Magi Council. Isn't that right, Kimly?" Sarasa's voice was filled with malice.

Kimly flashed her an extremely obscene gesture. No one else in the room seemed to notice, or care.

Tuknor stood up and moved towards the middle of the room. He said, "Chancellor, this is what I propose. Any militia members who are accepted as Magi will remain under your command in all matters that are not superseded by Magi Society laws or oath. Does that satisfy both sides?"

"I don't like it, but if it's the only way to get Magi into my militia ranks then I'll agree to it." The chancellor was visibly annoyed, and he motioned for the cheirapsian to stop rubbing his shoulders.

"This still don't address what happens when the emperor sends an army to Khardifar." Cynia sounded hesitant to bring it up.

He groaned a bit on the inside because he knew that negotiations were about to get unpleasant again. He was not mistaken. The conversation quickly turned contentious with both sides expressing their views passionately, and neither side willing to do any compromising.

Rissyl tried to see things from the chancellor's perspective, but it didn't help much. Ultimately, the Magi didn't have the ability to offer Khardifar any sort of protection against the full might of the imperial army. He tried to state that diplomatically, but the chancellor didn't believe it or didn't want to accept it as true. He was convinced that the Magi could cast some magic spell to place an impenetrable wall around the region, or selectively kill all of the chancellor's enemies without harming anyone that he favored.

Eventually the conversation stopped and everyone sat quietly, lost in their own thoughts.

Rissyl found himself looking at the mostly naked cheirapsian woman, and wondering if their skills were really as delightful as rumors suggested. After seeing one for the first time, he no longer doubted that they were every bit as skillful as the rumors claimed.

Cynia smirked at him, and whispered, "I see you looking at her diddies."

His cheeks reddened slightly at her teasing, but he didn't reply. Determined to conclude the uncomfortable meeting, Rissyl said, "Chancellor, we can't fight your war. It's as simple as that. We'll help how we can, but if you want to declare your autonomy from the emperor you must be willing and able to do it on your own."

For the entire meeting, Favin had sat quietly. When he started talking, the chancellor looked to him with genuine interest. "Have you considered hiring mercenaries to supplement your militia? If you institute a general conscription, and hire some experienced mercs, that might be adequate. I happen to know many people who can arrange for some mercenary companies."

"Mercenaries cost a fortune." The chancellor's voice, more than his words, expressed his frustration.

With a smile that Rissyl knew was not genuine, Tuknor added, "You could look at it as an investment in a lucrative future."

The chancellor seemed to accept that advice, and the conversation turned to more nuanced details of the agreement between the Magi and Chancellor Bernold.

Rissyl quickly lost interest and let his mind wander to other things, primarily centered around the cheirapsian and her skills of manual dexterity. Time got away from him and before long the meeting was concluded. Casual conversation was brief after the formal aspects were done, and soon all of the Magi were standing.

Bernold said, "Surely you won't be leaving without enjoying some time with my large selection of cheirapsians. Upstairs I've set up one of the best chambriums in all the lands. I insist that you treat yourself today. At no cost, of course."

"Thank you, chancellor, but we really must be going."

His heart dropped to his toes as Sarasa declined the offer so quickly. He didn't want to seem like the only one in the group who was overly anxious to experience the offered pleasures.

"Speak for yourself, Rasa!" Cynia squeezed his hand, and he fell in love with her just a little bit more. She always seemed to know what he wanted. She continued, "Some of us would love to accept the chancellor's generous gift."

In a soft and silky voice, the cheirapsian said, "We do insist that all clients observe proper chambrium etiquette at all times."

She went on to outline all of the rules and customs. The list was lengthy, but the main things Rissyl heard was that clothing other than a loincloth was prohibited, as was anything even remotely sexual. Everything else he missed as he impatiently sat there waiting for the fun to start. He felt like a kid anxiously waiting to open gifts while the adults were busy chatting.

Once they were invited to the chambrium he couldn't get up the stairs fast enough. The bath room was just as posh as the rest of the manor, and the huge pool of steaming hot water in the center of the room looked very inviting, but he had other things on his mind. He removed his clothing and placed them on a hook. He briefly considered going fully naked, but he knew that he'd feel uncomfortable if he was the only one in the group who didn't choose what little modesty they could claim.

The loincloth was tiny, and he didn't feel much more clothed than he had before putting it on. He adjusted it and headed out of the bath.

When he walked into the chambrium he couldn't believe how many cheirapsians were there. He only expected to see a handful, perhaps two or three. Instead there were more than two dozen of them, mostly women, and every one of them was stunning to behold. As he walked towards one of the stations he saw Kimly, Sarasa, and Cynia walking from their bath. Each of them was completely nude.

Sarasa caught him looking, and she didn't even try to hide her nakedness. What was it about this ancient custom that made people put aside accepted norms of behavior and act like being naked in mixed company was nothing unusual? At some point, he had stopped walking and simply stood and stared at her. He was suddenly very glad that he chose to wear the loincloth, to mask his involuntary violation of chambrium etiquette. He glanced at Cynia and instantly felt guilty for his wandering eyes. Her amused expression promised that she was going to tease him relentlessly when she got a chance, and that didn't make him feel much better.

He chose a mat with several alluring cheirapsians sitting around it. One of the women instructed him to position himself on his back, and close his eyes. Then two of them started working on his feet while two others began rubbing the backs of his hands. The woman at his head started applying gentle pressure to his temples. He almost sat upright when the final cheirapsian slid over him, straddling his stomach and began massaging his chest muscles. After the initial shock wore off, he allowed himself to calm down and relax to simply enjoy the experience.

After just a few minutes, he was completely engrossed in the indescribable enjoyment of the session. Abruptly the silence was disturbed by a gentle voice. At first, he thought it might just be his imagination.

"SOVRAN, I AM KILEA. CAN YOU HEAR ME?"

The velvety voice was in his head. He opened his eyes.

The cheirapsian who was straddling his stomach put her finger to her lips and made a hushing gesture. The voice in his head said, "DON'T SPEAK. OPEN YOUR MAGI VISION AND LOOK AT MY SOUL."

He didn't know how the woman knew about magesight, or that he had the ability to peer at someone's soul, but he did what he was told.

As soon as he opened his magesight, her soul drew him in. Over the last few years he'd gazed into many people's eyes using his magesight. Everyone's soul, or the image that his magesight presented to him that represented their soul, looked different. A soul appeared as an amazingly complex geometric object that seemed to float in space somewhere beyond the person's eyes. It was in this situation when he could also view a person's magewel to see how much, if any, magical potential the person possessed. Additionally, everyone had thoughts and ideas constantly buzzing around and they presented themselves in his magesight like rapidly moving gnats flying around the person's soul.

Diviners could see virtually every detail of a person's life and personality when they gazed at a soul with magesight. However, to Rissyl the person's soul was opaque and colorful, and it revealed few secrets to him.

The woman before him was remarkable, and he was surprised to see things that he'd never experienced before when gazing at someone's soul. The first things that he noticed, that were entirely unexpected, were hundreds of tiny strands of gold mist. Each one looked like a tiny golden string, but they were insubstantial. The strands spread out in all directions and most of them seemed to go on forever, but some were connected to other cheirapsians in the room.

The other thing that stood out as different was that she had a large and well developed magewel, but it was a shape and color that he'd never seen.

He spent several minutes just staring into her eyes, at her soul. The whole time she was still working on the muscles in the front of his shoulders, and the other five cheirapsians aggressively massaged other parts of his body. The physical pleasure, along with the intimate connection that came from viewing her with his magesight, was almost too much to handle.

An unusual tingling feeling in the back of his consciousness hinted that she was gazing into his eyes in a manner similar to the magesight that he was using on her. The sensation was odd, and a bit unnerving at the same time. He wondered what she could see, how he appeared in her eyes, and whether she could read his mind.

"OPEN YOUR MIND, SOVRAN. PLEASE LOWER YOUR WARDS AND ACCEPT MY BOND."

For a moment he resisted the idea, but he quickly pushed aside his concerns. He opened his mind to her.

Instantly he experienced a sensation like a warm stream rushing to the deepest depths of his soul, and it was euphoric. He moaned out loud, without realizing it.

She hushed him, verbally and mentally. "SHHH. YOU MUST CONTROL THAT, OR THE OTHERS WILL ASSUME YOU'RE BEING IMPROPER."

He wished he could tell her that he was sorry, and that he'd try to control himself better.

"DON'T APOLOGIZE, SOVRAN. THIS IS NEW TO YOU."

"YOU CAN HEAR MY THOUGHTS?"

"I CAN, NOW THAT WE'RE BONDED. YOU CAN CLOSE YOUR MAGI VISION, IF YOU WANT."

Before he shut his magesight, he focused on her soul one more time. He noticed a new golden strand that was much brighter than all of the others. It connected him to her soul.

"BONDED? WHAT DOES THAT MEAN?"

"OUR MINDS SHARE THIS CONNECTION, NO MATTER THE DISTANCE BETWEEN US."

"WILL YOU HEAR ALL OF MY THOUGHTS?"

"USING MENTAL WARDS YOU CAN CHOOSE WHEN TO OPEN YOUR MIND TO ME, AND I TO YOU."

He wondered why she had created this bond with him. Surely she didn't bond with all of her clients. He also considered whether the bond could be dangerous or a threat to him in some way.

Kilea felt amused, and he could feel it just as easily as he could feel any emotion within himself.

In his mind, he heard her say, "NO, SOVRAN, I DON'T BOND WITH MY OTHER CLIENTS. BEFORE TODAY I HAD ONLY EVER BONDED WITH OTHER DRUIDS."

His mind started racing with several questions at once. He didn't know anything about druids, other than some story he heard from Sarasa about a reclusive group of magic users from long ago. So, what are druids? Are they Magi, or something else? If Kilea was a Magi, that would explain the well-developed magewel that he'd seen in her.

"Slow down, Sovran. I can't answer your questions when you let your mind race like that. No, I am not a Magi. My magical gift wasn't given by Nalria, it comes from Dyranai the goddess of nature. In most ways my magical gift is different than yours. As the Magi are followers of Nalria, druids are followers of Dyranai."

He had a thousand questions, but tried to focus on one at a time, *"So, do all druids practice the art of cheirapsia?"*

"All cheirapsians are druids, but not all druids study cheirapsia. Like with the Magi and your Orders, there are several aspects to the magic of the druids and cheirapsia is just one of them."

"Then are the druids on our side in this war? Is that why you bonded with me, to help us defeat the emperor?"

She shook her head, *"The druids don't take sides. We value balance above all things. I have bonded with you in order to help maintain a balance."*

He was getting confused, and a bit annoyed, *"I don't understand? Balance? What's that supposed to mean?"*

"Druids strive for balance in all things. Take the art of cheirapsia, for example. It is the epitome of balance. We are neither clothed nor naked. Cheirapsia is conducted in a strict asexual environment and yet it seems sexual. Our techniques are at times very soft and at other times quite forceful, they can be fast and then slow. Sometimes we use rhythmic motions and other times there is no rhythm at all. We give great pleasure and also substantial pain. This balance brings an experience that is unequaled by other methods. It is but one of the ways that we live in balance."

"So, if you bonded with me, will you also bond with the emperor for a balance?"

"No, Sovran, you must understand that this isn't a war between the Magi and the emperor. At its root, it is a war between the gods. The gods have struggled to gain superiority over one another far longer than any human can comprehend, and the mortals are usually the tools in those wars. A century ago, a bitter war between the goddess Nalria and the god Viator led to the death of most of the Magi. Viator used the first Emperor Ryal as a puppet, and together they decimated the original Sovereign Magi Society and in the process Viator won a major victory against his rival Nalria and weakened her

SEVERELY."

He suddenly felt tiny and insignificant. *"SO, SINCE NALRIA HAS BEGUN TO REGROW HER POWER BY REBUILDING THE MAGI SOCIETY AND BRINGING MAGIC BACK TO THE LANDS, VIATOR IS ONCE AGAIN USING A RYALLIC EMPEROR TO WAGE WAR AGAINST HER AND HER FOLLOWERS?"*

"YES, BUT THIS TIME IT IS MUCH WORSE THAN BEFORE. NALRIA'S FATHER, THE DIVINE-SIRE KELEGAR, HAS JOINED THIS CONFLICT TO HELP HER REGAIN THE POWER AND INFLUENCE SHE ONCE ENJOYED. UNFORTUNATELY, VIATOR'S FATHER, THE PATRON-GOD WIRMYNTAS, HAS JOINED THE WAR TO AID HIS SON IN HIS GOAL TO DESTROY NALRIA ENTIRELY. THE ANCIENT GODS HAD BEEN DORMANT SINCE BEFORE DWARVES AND ELVES WALKED THE LANDS, SO THE RETURN OF THE ANCIENT GODS AND THEIR INVOLVEMENT WITH MORTALS MAKES THIS A VERY DANGEROUS TIME. IF WIRMYNTAS AND VIATOR SUCCEED IN KILLING NALRIA, THE RESULTING UNBALANCING AMONG THE GODS WOULD BE CATASTROPHIC."

Suddenly, so many things were becoming clearer to Rissyl. This explained Sarge's journey and re-emergence as the Azure paladin, and all of his talk of Kelegar. It also explained why Emperor Ryal I had been so fanatically determined to slaughter the Magi a century ago that he'd sacrifice so many of his people in the process. Rissyl felt like an insignificant participant in someone else's battle, and it made him angry at first.

Although, as he thought about it more, the goddess of magic had been up front with him from the very beginning. She warned that bringing magic back to the world would be dangerous, and he had consciously agreed to help in that quest. He treasured the magical gifts provided by Nalria, and the Magi Society that they'd worked so hard to rebuild.

Rissyl knew that Kilea heard his flurry of thoughts. He thought to her, *"THIS KNOWLEDGE THAT YOU BRING HAS GIVEN ME A GREAT DEAL OF CLARITY, MUCH TO CONSIDER, AND IT INTENSIFIED MY ZEAL TO MAKE THE MAGI SOCIETY STRONG EVEN KNOWING THAT OUR ENEMY IS MORE DANGEROUS THAN WE HAD IMAGINED."*

"BE WARNED, SOVRAN, THAT YOU HAVE NOT YET FACED YOUR MOST DEADLY FOE. I KNOW NOT WHAT IS COMING, BUT DYRANAI IS WARNING US OF AN IMPENDING UNBALANCING THAT COULD THROW NATURE OUT OF ALIGNMENT EVEN FURTHER IN FAVOR OF VIATOR AND HIS PATRON-GOD AND BRING US CLOSER TO NALRIA'S DOWNFALL. IT HAS NOT BEEN MADE CLEAR HOW THE DRUIDS MIGHT HELP RESTORE BALANCE, BUT OUR BOND IS ONE STEP TOWARDS THAT GOAL."

"YOU'VE ALREADY BEEN MORE HELP THAN YOU MIGHT REALIZE. YOU'VE GIVEN ME CLARITY THAT I HAVEN'T EVEN RECEIVED FROM NALRIA."

"HAVE YOU PRAYED TO HER, ASKING FOR ANSWERS OR GUIDANCE?"

He felt justifiably rebuked, *"WELL, NO."*

"PERHAPS YOU SHOULD."

He allowed himself to simply focus on the pleasures of the cheirapsians who continued to work on six different parts of his body, until another question came to mind, *"KILEA, WHY DO YOU CALL ME SOVRAN? IT'S NOT SOMETHING I'VE BEEN CALLED BEFORE."*

"SOVRAN MEANS LEADER, IN MENELIAN. NOW, HUSH YOUR MIND. OUR CONVERSATION WILL HAMPER YOUR EXPERIENCE, AND YOU DESERVE SOME PEACE BEFORE FACING WHAT'S AHEAD."

Rissyl closed his eyes and allowed himself to fully concentrate on the sensations being given from each of the cheirapsians.

CHAPTER 25

Sarasa

She had experienced a handful of things over the years that she felt needed to be remembered as defining moments in her life. Joining the fighting guild when she was still a young girl was certainly one of those, and taking the oath of the Magi was another.

Her experience with the cheirapsians may not quite rate as a defining moment in life, but it was surely something that she would remember fondly for a very long time. She felt more relaxed than she had felt in ages. Her body had so many aches and pains from many years of combat training that it seemed unusual to walk up the stairs and not hurt somewhere.

Sarasa smiled to herself and hummed a happy tune as she climbed the stairs two at a time on her way to her chambers. She couldn't wait to crawl into bed and enjoy the soft and warm comforts around her, as she slept completely pain free.

As she arrived at her door, the door to the chambers across the hall opened and Lasina walked out. Sarasa didn't know the young woman very well, because she was very new to the Order of Shadows.

Lasina became a Magi in Libur and had been a part of the Libur Coterie before all of the Magi came to the Stronghold. Before that, she'd been a prisoner at the Motlite compound. After being liberated from that camp, a couple of the prisoners became Magi and Lasina was the only one that Sarasa knew of who had gone on to be accepted into one of the Orders.

"Sarasa! How is Eleyne, will she survive?"

She was stunned by the woman's question, and the deep concern in her voice. "What do you mean? What happened?"

"You haven't heard? Something went terribly wrong during a raid! I heard that Eleyne and Ferth were hurt really bad! I think other Magi didn't survive, but I don't know for sure. I just know what I heard from some Society Magi who talked to someone who saw them port back."

"By the gods! No, I haven't heard anything, the council just returned from a mission in Khardifar. I'm going to get some answers, come along if you want."

She turned around and sprinted back down the stairs, and she could hear Lasina close behind. Once they got outside, she turned towards Sarge's temple. She wasn't sure where the injured Magi would be, but the temple was her best guess.

It wasn't a far run to the temple, but the low temps and light snow made it unpleasant. She ran up the stairs. The blood on the ground, and on the handles of the doors, were bad signs for Eleyne and Ferth but suggested that she was in the right place.

Sarasa pulled open the doors and saw a flurry of activity in the sanctuary. Several of the benches were pushed aside, and two large cots were set up in the middle of the room. Madalyn, Brielle, and even little Ayris were covered in blood which stood out brightly on their white robes. Sarge held a large bucket of water, and Brielle used it to rinse off a cloth.

On the cots were Eleyne and Ferth. Both of them were covered in blood, and Ferth had several arrows sticking out of his body. He moaned weakly as Madalyn worked to remove one of the arrows.

"Why can't we just heal him?" Ayris pleaded. She was kneeling beside him, holding a blood-soaked rag against his hip. Her voice sounded like she was on the verge of panic.

"Just hold the sarding rag on that hole. We can't heal him until we get these last arrows outta him." Madalyn's words sounded harsh, but her tone was calm and steady as she worked to remove an arrow from his upper chest.

Sarasa walked over to Sarge, and asked, "What happened?"

He sat the bucket of water on a bench. "I don't really know the details yet. These two haven't been very talkative. What I do know is that Ferth, Eleyne, Ranik, and Kyoso raided a garrison and the sarding imperials were ready for us. We were ambushed, and these two were hurt really bad."

The blissful feeling of relaxation that she enjoyed earlier was completely gone. She shook her head. "Dammit! Where are Kyoso and Ranik?"

"Dead. Left behind, as far as I can tell." He pointed across the room, to a person sitting on the floor with her back against the corner, quietly crying with her head buried in her hands. It was Ranik's sister, Firana.

Pointing at the cots, he continued, "These two barely made it back alive. Ferth took several vicious hits before they tandem teleported. It's a miracle that they made it back at all."

The door opened and Dalen came in, followed by Cynia. They looked as upset as she felt. They both looked at the two Magi in the cots for a long moment, and then they moved over next to her and Sarge.

Before she could say anything, she heard Eleyne speak weakly. Everyone knelt down near her.

Brielle hurried over with a cup of water, and Eleyne drank a small amount.

In a low voice, Eleyne said, "They were ready for us. Ambushed." She started coughing.

Sarge encouraged her to hush and rest, but she reached out and grabbed Dalen's hand.

She continued, "Imperial commander. My magesight saw him different. Presence inside him, leading and enthralling the troops to fight fearlessly. Savagely. Something evil."

"Theo, make the visitors leave. She needs to rest, she nearly died. They can talk later." Madalyn didn't even look up from Ferth as she instructed Sarge.

Sarasa was annoyed to be ejected from the room, by a girl that was barely an adult. However, she was impressed with the girl's poise and courage in such a bloody and gory situation. Before Sarge could say anything, she held up her hand, and stood up.

The others got Madalyn's point also, and Sarasa led them out of the temple to let the healers do their duty.

Dalen was last out of the door and he closed it softly behind himself. He said, "An evil presence, inside this commander? Enthralling the troops? Something's screwy at the Libur fort, and I wanna know what it is."

Sarasa frowned, "Yes, I have a theory, but I have to do some research before I'll know for sure."

"Of course you wanna read. This ain't the time for books, it's time for action!" Dalen placed his hands on his hips and looked defiantly from Sarasa to Cynia.

She raised an eyebrow, and looked at him. Then she looked to Cynia, "I already know what Rissyl will say, what say you?"

Cynia sighed, "Dalen, we gotta know what we're facing before we rush in blindly. I know Rissyl will agree."

"Of course Rissyl will agree with you! The Order of Champions ain't gonna sit back no more. It's time for offense." He looked at Cynia, daring her to argue.

Sarasa laughed. "The Order of Champions is simply five Magi! That's not exactly an army! We must proceed with caution, and knowledge! Besides, we promised to help the chancellor deal with the Khardifar garrison in two days. That has to come first."

Dalen turned to her abruptly, "Yes, but they're gonna do most of the work, the Magi will just be there to blast imperials from afar. And, the Order of Champions happens to be the biggest Order we've got. Even after Ranik's death we still got more than the rest of you. We've added several new Society Magi lately, and I've found a bunch of them worthy to be in my Order. Very soon I'm gonna invite over a dozen of them to join the Orders."

"Dalen, Society Magi are free to join whichever Order they want once they've been selected to become an Order Magi. You can't force them to join your Order." Sarasa couldn't hide the anger from her voice.

"No, I can't force them, but I've been working with them for a while. I'm sure most of them will want to choose my Order." He crossed his arms at his chest defiantly.

Cynia looked furious. "Why? Are you trying to take over the council? You know that Rissyl always tries to be fair and listen to all of us equally!"

"Rissyl ain't got the backbone to lead the council! But, no. I just wanna make my Order as strong as I can! I wanna make the Magi Society as strong as I can!" He started pacing back and forth, in front of the door to the temple. "Two of our Magi are dead, and two more are almost dead! The Rolimi are willing to teach us again, and I will be taking them up on that training! I'm gonna offer the Order selection to some Society Magi. If you wanna add to your Order's numbers, you got do the same. We must go on the offensive soon."

Without waiting for a reply, Dalen stormed off.

Sarasa couldn't believe what she had heard. Did her brother really plan to try to make his Order more powerful than the others? She looked to Lasina, "Make a list of any promising Society Magi who would make good Shadows. It seems that we need to go courting Society Magi to join our Order."

CHAPTER 26

Vendino

Everyone at the table seemed anxious to get through the routine matters of the meeting. The Council of Ministers had been in session for hours, and thus far the meeting had been fairly tame. The emperor was in a better mood than Vendino had seen in months and that made for a pleasant meeting.

When the meeting began he fully expected it to be miserable. Lord Jalinox was present, which was usually enough to throw the whole meeting into disarray.

Behind the scheming alchemist was one of his many attractive assistants who stood there silently, awaiting his orders. Vendino didn't know the woman's name, but it wasn't the woman who normally attended these meetings for Jalinox. That woman hadn't been around since her daughter had been killed by the Magi.

At his entrance, the emperor had announced that he had a special surprise scheduled for the end of the meeting. Vendino assumed that it had something to do with Prince Edal, since the entire palace had been abuzz with the rumor that the prince had been rescued. As far as Vendino knew, no one had actually seen the prince since his return.

His focus was brought back to the present when he heard the emperor change to a new topic.

"Minister Thorli, what is the status of our assault on the Magi through the dwarven mountain fortress?"

The former general looked uncomfortable. He shuffled through some papers, as if looking for some piece of information. Finally, he said, "Majesty, the new conscripts are just beginning to arrive and siege equipment is being built. The main assault should begin within the next few fortnights."

"I thought we ordered the units to attack long ago? I would have expected our best units to easily rout a band of dwarves."

"Yes, majesty, our troops have launched several assaults, but we've yet to break through their outer defenses. We must be patient and let them build the siege equipment they need, and get the new conscripts adequately trained. We'll be victorious very soon, your majesty."

The room grew silent, waiting for the emperor's response. Vendino was sure that the emperor would erupt, and possibly order the execution of who-knows-how-many military officers. Possibly even Thorli himself.

The explosion didn't come.

"Let's make sure it doesn't take long, I want victory soon. My patience is wearing out. I'm anxious to end this Magi problem so we can focus on more important matters."

He could hear several ministers release the breath they'd been holding.

The emperor stood up. "Ministers, it is time for my surprise! As I'm sure you've heard, my beloved son has been rescued and returned from the clutches of the wretched Magi! He is in my offices." He turned to the guard standing next to the door to his offices, "Please inform Prince Edal that we are ready for him."

The guard opened the door, and a man walked into the meeting room. The man looked vaguely familiar, but Vendino didn't know who he was. He was wearing robes similar to the ones usually worn by Jalinox, except they were black and grey where the alchemist wore robes of black and red.

"Council of Ministers, behold my son, Edal. The crown prince of the Ryallic Empire!"

Vendino's audible gasp was drowned out by the collective exclamations from around the room. He had seen the prince about a fortnight ago, and the prince had been a boy of barely twelve years. The man before them was easily double that age. Not only was the man tall and clearly fully grown, his face wore the lines and creases of many years of worry and stress. It was not the face of a boy raised in the shelter and carefree environment of the palace, it was that of a man who had known much pain and torment.

Aribeth, the Minister of the Treasury, exclaimed, "But this can't be! Edal is but a boy! Who is this man before us?"

The emperor stepped next to the man and patted him on the back. "This is my son, Edal. That much I can guarantee. The Magi have cursed him with some vile magic that stole his youth, but he is my son none-the-less!"

The Minister of Records, Minister Crawley, stood up and extended his hand towards the prince. "Majesty, this must be some sort of ruse!

Obviously this man is an impostor!"

Edal walked around the table, to stand next to Crawley. The prince stood several inches taller than the rotund minister. He said, "Minister Crawley, three years ago my sister and I accompanied your family on a trip to the shores of Varg. We spent the mornings fishing and the days swimming. By the evening time we danced to the music and watched your wife drink until she could barely sit without falling over."

The minister looked dumbfounded, and sat down quietly.

The prince then moved to stand behind Minister Aribeth. "My dearest Aribeth, how many times have you showered gifts upon me and my sister to remind us how loyal and important your family is to the empire? You've always favored my sister for her quickness with numbers, but your gifts and favors for us both have been innumerable over the years."

She lowered her eyes, and didn't reply.

"Each of the ministers in this room have spent years subtly trying to build themselves up in my eyes, knowing that one day I would replace my father as emperor. I didn't fully understand at the time. I just thought you were being kind because you liked me, but looking back I see through all of that now. My father insists that this is simply the way of things in palace politics, and perhaps that is true." The prince looked around the room.

Vendino stared at the prince in disbelief. He had trouble believing what he knew to be true.

The prince walked over to stand next to Jalinox's assistant. "I know that my abrupt aging is a shock, but it is a reality that everyone must come to accept. I am fully grown, and that is not all that has changed. I have chosen a bride." He placed his hand in the hand of the woman beside him, and then he raised her hand in his. "This is Jessa, and she is to become my bride and the princess of the Ryallic Empire!"

The woman's expression looked like someone had recently died. She certainly didn't look like a blushing betrothed future princess.

Vendino leaned his elbow on the table, rested his forehead in his palm, and gazed at the prince and his future bride. He no longer had any doubt that the man before him was in fact the prince. He was taller, but clearly his taste in low-class females had not improved any.

He glanced at Jalinox, and the psychotic man grinned at him sadistically. Vendino believed to the deepest recesses of his soul that the scheming man was somehow responsible for all of this.

The emperor clapped twice, "This is my surprise for you! My son has returned, and we're going to have a royal wedding!"

Everyone clapped unenthusiastically. Vendino assumed that they were all as shocked as he, and most of them were probably equally as appalled to have a low-born woman ascend to the level of princess.

Minister Thorli said, "My prince, I am elated to see you returned alive. May I ask how you escaped your captivity?"

Jalinox answered for him, "General Thorli, I was travelling with a contingent of my personal guards when we happened upon a Magi encampment. We rescued the prince and brought him here."

"You? Somehow you just happened to stumble upon the camp where the Magi were holding our prince captive and you managed to free him without the assistance of our armies or any of our agents? You really are a man of many talents, Lord Jalinox." Thorli sounded uncharacteristically confrontational.

"Our actions were truly guided by divine hands, there can be no other explanation. Good fortune led us to the right spot, when the camp was mostly empty. General Thorli, I would guess that the Magi were conducting raids on your garrisons and supply convoys at the time." Jalinox leaned back with a smug grin.

It looked like Thorli was about to respond, but the prince interjected before he could.

The prince said, "I'm afraid I must address some factual inaccuracies in Lord Jalinox's account of the situation. Jessa and I were both captives of the Magi, and together we escaped in the darkness of the night. We wandered the countryside alone for days without food or supplies. Depending on each other through this harrowing experience, we quickly developed a burning love for one another. Eventually, we happened upon a contingent of Lord Jalinox's guards who brought us to his compound for food and shelter. The remainder of his account is accurate."

Vendino could hardly control his mirth, it was not often someone was able to knock the freaky alchemist down a notch or two.

"Ha!" Thorli's abrupt laugh startled several of the ministers. He said, "Now that is a much more likely account of how the prince escaped the Magi. I commend you, my prince, for your bravery and determination in what I am sure was an awful experience."

The emperor sat down, and dropped his hands to the desk with a thump. "And I must offer my gratitude to Miss Jessa, for you obviously played an important part in bringing my son back to us!"

Emperor Ryal started clapping, and all of the ministers joined in. The prince put his arm around Jessa and pulled her closer. The woman smiled slightly, and seemed to be slightly less uncomfortable.

When things quieted down the emperor turned to Vendino. "Minister Vendino, begin preparations. Spread word to the people that the prince has returned and even though the Magi have cursed him with premature aging that he survived and will triumph over their wicked schemes! We will rejoice in his return and revel in his newfound love, in a royal wedding like the empire has never seen!"

He forced a smile, "Yes, majesty. The people will rejoice."

Prince Edal said, "I know that these things take time, so our invited guests can make travel plans and everything can be arranged. Jessa and I would like to see the Magi destroyed before we are joined in marriage, so everyone can rejoice with us without all of the worries and stress of a war." He looked to his future bride, and continued, "And there are other matters to attend to beforehand as well."

Minister Aribeth clapped excitedly, "A very mature decision, my prince! I am absolutely bursting with excitement for that joyous day!"

The tone of the prince's statement to his betrothed hinted that there was more to that story, but those things were none of Vendino's concern so he turned his mind to the huge ordeal of arranging an elaborate wedding. He started making a mental list of things that would need to be done and people who would need to be contacted.

That reminded him that he had received a note shortly before the meeting started. He pulled it from his pile of papers and held it up.

"Majesty, there was a message delivered a short while ago from the Chancellor of Khardifar. It arrived by fast-riders as we were about to begin this meeting." Vendino slid the sealed parchment over to the emperor.

Emperor Ryal inspected the scrolled message and then broke the wax seal. The expression on his face became angry and grew fierce as he read further. He wadded the parchment in his hand and started beating his fists against the table. "You impertinent swine! How dare you! I'll see your head impaled on a sarding pike for your insolence!"

Vendino stared at the monarch in shock, "Majesty, what does he say?" He couldn't imagine what the chancellor could have written that would sour the emperor's mood so quickly. He'd been prone to mood swings, but rarely so sudden or violent.

The emperor threw the parchment at Vendino and then stood up, grabbed his own chair, and began smashing it against the wall. His screams grew maniacal as the chair broke apart and he grabbed smaller pieces to break further.

The other ministers looked to Vendino expectantly, and he read the parchment quickly. Then he dropped it to the table in shock. He looked to Thorli and said, "Chancellor Bernold writes to inform His Majesty that Khardifar intends to secede from the empire."

Thorli's jaw stood agape, as the room burst into chaos. He said, "Secede? Is he insane?"

Throughout the room the ministers shouted to be heard over one another. Their shouts were still drowned by the emperor's enraged fit and violence towards the small pieces of his chair. Most of the ministers were standing and waving their hands wildly as they hollered.

Vendino pushed himself from the table, and leaned back in his chair with his arms crossed at his chest. Thorli rested his head between his hands with both elbows on the table and this thumbs on his cheeks and his fingers on his temples. They sat quietly as the others ranted and yelled at one another.

He had seen many angry outbursts in this room over the years, but never anything like this.

Eventually the emperor moved back to the table and slammed both palms onto the table with all of his might. The loud banging quieted the others enough to draw their attention back to the head of the table.

In a quivering voice on the verge of losing control once again, the emperor spat, "Thorli! I want that city razed to the ground, and every last person slaughtered. I want the heads of their entire council, especially that sarding louse Bernold, on a pike at the Clornoss gates. Do I make myself clear?"

In a hesitant voice, Minister Thorli said, "Most of our armies are well to the north, or headed there, to assault the dwarves. It will take time to issue orders and reposition them, majesty."

Emperor Ryal grabbed the end of the long and heavy table, lifted it almost a foot in the air, and then slammed it to the floor. All of the papers, goblets, inkwells, and other items on the table toppled over or fell to the floor.

He shouted, "I don't want to hear sarding excuses, Thorli! I want their heads on pikes!"

"Yes, majesty."

The prince's low voice reverberated through the room, drawing everyone's attention without him needing to shout. "Father, I would be most honored if you would let me lead the army that will bring this insolent city to its knees and remind the rest of the empire that we must remain united to defeat the hated Magi once and for all."

The emperor stood quietly for a very long time, and Vendino hoped that the father would deny his son's request. The prince had been a boy only a fortnight ago, surely he didn't have the skills to lead an army.

"Minister Vendino, I want you to arrange for a conferral ceremony with full honors, and be sure to extend an invitation to all of the appropriate Aristocrats, ministers, and magistrates. There, I will award Prince Edal with the rank of Captain General of the Imperial Army. Immediately following the ceremony he will lead a company of Wyvern Regiment to meet with the force that will destroy Khardifar and bring me the repulsive chancellor's head! General Thorli, you will be Prince Edal's second-in-command and his advisor. Minister Vendino, you will also accompany them as an advisor."

Jalinox looked irate. He crossed his arms and said, "Certainly you'll wish for me to go as well. Perhaps as a senior advisor?"

"My son, what is your opinion?"

"Of course Lord Jalinox should join us, but I think advisor might be a bit too much for him. Perhaps he could travel with us as a civilian observer?"

Jalinox turned to face the prince. "Edal this is an outrage! Observer?"

The prince said, "Observer."

Jalinox stormed out of the room.

Vendino sighed. Another trip of sleeping with the bugs? He was getting too old for this crap.

CHAPTER 27

Kimly

"I have to admit, the first steps of autonomy for Khardifar have gone much smoother than I expected." Favin grabbed a large slice of roast from the platter in the middle of the table, and then grabbed two large biscuits.

Kimly laughed, "That's because we can use the portal stones to travel to cities that still have food."

"Pass the honey. No, I'm serious. It was no small feat to expel the imperial troops from the garrison. I wasn't convinced that they could do it." He accepted the honey and began pouring a bit onto one of his biscuits.

She sat back in her chair and placed her hands on her stomach. "I'm so full, I might burst. If I wasn't a selfish wench I might feel bad for the miserable folks who are trapped in the city with no food."

Skoots pushed her plate away, and it was still heavy with food. She leaned against the table, and said, "I do feel bad, a little. At least for the people in our guild who aren't in The Shrouded and can't port somewhere for food."

Bernold had held true to his word, and shortly after the meeting with the Magi, he released Skoots.

The three rogues were in Bathok, about 150 miles west of Khardifar, at a busy tavern meeting with a local named Rymund. The man was a member of The Shrouded that Kimly had recruited several months ago. Like the others, he believed that The Shrouded was a large and ancient guild of rogues. He had been working hard to impress Kimly and often expressed an interest in moving up the ranks in the secret organization.

Rymund finished off another tankard of ale. "I don't understand how the city ain't got no food already. It's only been a couple days since Khardifar declared autonomy? The emperor might not even know yet."

Favin held up a finger, as he finished a bite. "Oh, he knows. I've no doubt about that. It's been three days since the imperial army was routed from the garrison outside of Khardifar, and probably four since Chancellor Bernold sent formal word to the emperor."

"Don't you mean Duke Bernold?" Kimly laughed out loud. The chancellor had wasted no time in declaring himself to be royalty and establishing his palace as the capital of the Duchy of Khardifar. She didn't know much about such things, but a single major city and a few dozen smaller towns and villages didn't sound like a nation large enough to be called a duchy.

He laughed along with her. "Yes, my mistake. Duke Bernold. Anyway, the duke's militia, a few Magi, and a mob of farmers and Denizens with pitchforks ejected the imperial troops from their garrison. It was a terrible battle and the duke's men suffered heavy casualties."

"We watched the whole thing from a safe distance, and it was the most fun I've had in ages! Once the Magi took control of things, the imperials lost the will to fight and soon they were running from the battle in a rout. Every time a straggling soldier would get separated from the larger group, the farmers and Denizens would drag him into the mob and beat him till he stopped kicking. I'd pay coins to see that again." Kimly grabbed a small chunk of roast from her plate with her fingers and started munching it.

"I still don't understand why the city don't got no food." Rymund looked confused, but fascinated by the story.

"I haven't got to that part yet." Favin showed no sign of slowing down on his relentless assault on his plate, snatching a quick bite between sentences. "So, as soon as the militia, the Magi, and the mob had taken care of the garrison they turned their attention to the city itself. For almost an entire day they went through the city door-to-door looking for imperial loyalist and troublemakers. It's been total chaos. Shops were destroyed and buildings burned to the ground. Anyone with strong ties to the imperials or the other cities have been killed, thrown in the dungeons, or banished from the duchy."

Kimly picked up the story while he paused for a bite. "It's been great for the thieves' guilds in the city. There's practically no sentinels around, life has been disrupted for everyone, and lots of folks are dead or gone and they've left treasure troves of stuff for the rest of us. I hated to leave the city at all, but we've got important business here today."

He added, "And we were starving, because there is almost no food in Khardifar. Most of the merchants have been killed or they've fled for their lives. The farmers are afraid to bring their food to the city, because the people who are left simply mob them the minute they bring their wagon through the gates. Bernold needs to get control soon, or the capital of the new duchy will be an empty city of fools who starved to death for autonomy."

Rymund grinned, "Sounds awful, so of course it's great for business. That brings us to the reason for your visit. Pipe tobacco, seasonings, and honey. I feel like a respectable merchant, smuggling this type of stuff. You guys are going to ruin my reputation if anyone finds out."

Favin grunted. "If anyone gives you grief, just tell them how much you charged us for this crap and your reputation will be just fine."

"The product is practically free. Most of the coins will cover my costs to transport this stuff into a war zone. Your people better be able to get my wagons through the city gates, and if my people get dead you owe me more. Is there anything else you're gonna want?"

Favin looked to Kimly and Skoots, and then shrugged.

Kimly said, "The duke is likely to get basic stuff moving soon. Fish, wheat, melons, and that sort of thing will get back to normal before long. It's the luxury things that will be scarce for a while, especially things brought from the other side of the empire. That's the stuff that the Gentry will pay dearly to get when they can't get it anywhere else."

"I'll keep my eyes peeled then." Rymund was quiet for a moment, and then added, "Kimly, before you leave could I have a private word with you?"

She motioned for him to keep talking, "You can talk Shrouded things in front of these two."

He looked at Favin and then Skoots, and then said, "I have found six people here in Bathok who would be good agents for The Shrouded. Do you have time before you return to Khardifar to bring them into the group and begin their training?"

She looked to Favin, and he nodded quickly. She replied, "I'm always happy to recruit new agents. This sarding war between the Magi and the emperor has been devastating on our numbers, so we need as many as we can get."

"Have you talked to Aeshlee, our agent in Orgrak? I was there recently and we met for drinks. She mentioned that she has several potential new members as well."

Kimly had forgotten all about the woman in Orgrak. She'd only met the woman once, and the whole thing had been fairly hasty.

A few months ago, Kimly had travelled to Orgrak with Rymund to smuggle some Dregs to a dancing establishment there. Kimly wasn't on a mission to expand The Shrouded, but everything just fell into place quickly. They ran into Aeshlee and Rymund already knew her. The three of them talked over some tankards of ale, and things progressed from there. By the end of the night there was a Shrouded agent in Orgrak, armed with a handful of useful magical spells, waiting to do Kimly's bidding when called upon.

By the time Kimly returned to Khardifar, she had completely forgotten about Aeshlee of Orgrak.

She said, "Oh yes, Aeshlee! I've been meaning to get to Orgrak. Sadly our top agents in that region have been killed by imperial troops, and so missions in that region have been light lately. I'll pay her a visit and get her new agents trained up." She thought of a great idea. "Actually, I think it's about time that you get that promotion you've been wanting! I'm going to promote you to a level two agent and place you in charge of Shrouded operations in Orgrak and Bathok."

Rymund looked like he might start glowing with pride. He grinned widely, "That would be great! Thank you!"

She took a long swig of ale, finishing off her tankard. "Of course, as a level two agent it really doesn't seem right that you're charging Favin so much for a simple shipment of spices and honey. He is a fellow Shrouded agent, after all. We must stick together, especially in these troubled times."

He sighed heavily. "Fine, I'll come down a few raptors."

- = - = -

Later that afternoon, Kimly was back in Khardifar with Favin. Skoots had something else to do, and she went her own way as soon as they were back in the city.

They were walking down the street near the bazaar, looking at the damage from the militia and the mob crashing through the city looking for imperials. Pretty much every building they passed had damage of some sort, but the vast majority of buildings had only suffered cosmetic damage. If this was the worst that the city saw, they'd soon have things back to normal.

There were few people on the streets, and all of the shops were closed. Even the forge in the blacksmithy was cold and the place was empty.

Favin said, "I appreciate you encouraging Rymund to reduce his price for me, since we're all a part of The Shrouded. You didn't have to do that, and I did notice."

She ignored his praise. "I have a mission for you, Favin. A Shrouded mission, if you are willing to accept it." She didn't look at him as they walked through the abandoned streets.

"Oh really? What's the mission?"

She kicked a discarded shoe out of the way. The streets that were usually fairly clean and clear of rubbish were now littered with debris and trash of all sorts. "The mission is to rob a warehouse in Bathok, and totally pick the place clean."

"What's special about this warehouse?"

"It's owned by Cletis Watters. He recently moved a fortune in foods, medicines, and other basic supplies there and he's planning to bring them into Khardifar soon."

He didn't reply right away, and she wondered if he knew that Cletis was her husband. Favin knew that she was married, but she'd never specifically mentioned who she was married to. It probably wouldn't be too hard for him to find out that she was the wife of one of the most powerful merchants in the city, if he had ever cared enough to inquire. If he had, he'd never mentioned it.

Finally, he said, "Why does The Shrouded want this warehouse targeted? Who gets to keep the goods that we take?"

His statement didn't reveal whether he knew that Cletis was her husband, and for some reason she hoped he didn't know. "Let's just say that they want Cletis out of Khardifar for a while. A major theft from one of his most important warehouses will certainly accomplish that. Besides, you get to keep a fortune in goods. Just make sure it happens three nights from tonight."

He asked, "That's not much time to plan, why so soon? Is this really a mission from The Shrouded, or is this a personal favor for you?"

Kimly cursed to herself. Apparently he did know. She didn't respond to him.

Favin added, "Of course I'll arrange for it to happen, Kimly. Why do you want him out of town in a few days?"

She smiled slightly, "Yes, it's for me. I'm going to leave him and I want to be able to get my stuff without a confrontation with him. I will be in

Tharrin for a few days, on business for The Shrouded. If Cletis could be in Bathok when I return from Tharrin, that'd be perfect."

"He is a very well connected and powerful man, robbing from him will be dangerous. But we'll make it happen." They walked in silence for a few blocks, and then he added, "When you leave Cletis, are you leaving Khardifar?"

She reached over and grabbed his hand, "I don't know what I'll do. I'm not planning to go anywhere, but right now I need my independence. Besides, you still owe me a second date."

"We haven't had a first date."

She grinned mischievously, "Well then, it looks like you owe me both." Her heart was beating wildly, and she felt like a naughty girl being entirely too flirtatious with a boy that her mother would hate.

He didn't reply, but he didn't pull his hand away.

Down the street she saw a group of militia escorting several wagons filled with food. It wasn't a great deal of food, but it was a start.

The militia were armored in the same sort of chain and platemail armor as the ones who met them at the chancellor's manor, and they wore the same grey and blue mantles. There were at least a dozen of them, and they were all walking with their swords drawn.

As they passed by, she saw a crowd of people following the wagons. Several of the duke's troops were walking slower to keep the crowd away from the wagons.

When they arrived at the bazaar, the militia soldiers spread out and guarded the area while the farmers stopped the wagons and began to set up a small marketplace.

By the time Favin and Kimly got close to the small market, the duke's troops had herded the crowd into a single line that extended far down the street.

One of the soldiers shouted, "Everyone in line gets one bag from each wagon, and no more!"

Someone in the crowd cried out, "What about my kids at home?"

"Only people in line get a ration! If they're not with you, they miss out this time."

The crowd went crazy, and Kimly squeezed Favin's hand in excitement. She led him closer so she had a perfect view of things if the crowd decided to riot or something fun like that.

Everyone was screaming and shouting about poor injured family members, their kids, the fact that they were Gentry, or whatever other excuse they could find to complain about life.

One of the soldiers stepped away from a wagon, and launched several fire orbs into the air. She then launched a few fire orbs at the ground near the line of people. Kimly noticed that the woman wore the mantle of the duke's militia over a brown and white Magi Cloak. Kimly was mildly impressed that the Magi had recruited and trained at least one of the militia as they promised. It also made her wonder how many of the Magi troopers the duke now controlled.

The display of magical power from the Magi militia soldier was enough to make the entire crowd grow quiet and obedient.

The Magi woman shouted, "One bag per wagon per person who is in line! That is the order of the duke! If you don't like it, get out of line and get nothing! When supplies improve, the rations will improve, but until then accept your handouts and be happy for them!"

Kimly wanted to start clapping. She loved to see masses of idiots being told to shut up and stop complaining about things. Although she'd hoped to see a riot, it was fun to see the masses told to take what they're given or get nothing.

Favin started walking again, and she walked beside him. Soon they were walking near the long line of people waiting for handouts. She could see the fear and uncertainty in their eyes, and many of them looked like they hadn't slept in a few days. The line was so long that she was sure that many of them would get no handouts today.

She pulled Favin closer as they walked, "Does the threat of an imminent attack from the imperials make you wildly randy, or is it just me?"

"You might be crazy, Kimly. You do realize that, right?"

She laughed, "Everyone's crazy, Favin. I just enjoy it more than most."

CHAPTER 28

Rissyl

Several Rolimi instructors worked quickly, bringing a number of tables and chairs into the council meeting room in Summit Hall. They also brought out a tall irregularly shaped table with four sides. It was placed in the front of the room near Mr. Pyllis.

Seeing the Rolimi hurrying around the room, and pulling furniture and things from the portal extended out of a small box on the floor brought back so many memories for Rissyl. It didn't seem like that long ago that he was the student, sitting nervously and about to choose his Order.

Now, as the Grand Evoker, he stood at the side of the room nervously waiting to see what the new students would choose for their Order. It was a different kind of nervousness. Instead of a fear of the unknown, and an overall fear that he might choose the wrong Order, he was now worried about the Society Magi who were about to make their selections. What would they choose? Would their choices change the power dynamics within the Magi Society since it was still so small? Most importantly, would they ultimately be making a choice that would end up costing them their lives in the war against the emperor or whatever more awful enemy awaited them?

Mr. Pyllis motioned for the large group of Society Magi who had been selected to join an Order to move over near him. He pointed to the tall table nearby. The table top was divided into four quadrants, and each quadrant was a different color. In the center of each quadrant was a small cup filled with a liquid that Rissyl remembered as terrible tasting.

In his fast and monotone voice, Mr. Pyllis said, "The Order of Evokers specializes in the Conjuration and Evocation schools of magic. It is represented by the color red."

He moved over to the green quadrant, "The Order of Diviners specializes in the Divination and Transmutation schools of magic. It is represented by the color green."

Then he moved over next to the grey quadrant, "The Order of Shadows specializes in the Illusion and Enchantment schools. It is represented by the color grey."

Finally, he moved to the blue quadrant, "The Order of Champions specializes in the Abjuration and Artificing schools and it is represented by the color blue."

It seemed like a lifetime ago when he made this choice. He looked to Cynia and she winked. She looked majestic in her green and black Cloak of the Grand Diviner.

Mr. Pyllis continued talking without pause, "It is time to choose your Order, and take the Covenant. I hope you've made your decision, because it's time to begin." He pointed at one of the Society Magi. He looked so young, and Rissyl had no idea what his name was or who had recruited him. The Rolimi said, "Sir, you're first. Walk over to the table, grab the cup of the color of your choice, and state that you choose whichever Order you are picking. Then drink the entire contents of the cup."

As Rissyl looked over all of the Society Magi, he realized that he didn't know most of them. The Magi Society had grown over the past year, particularly in the last few months. There were nineteen Society Magi selected, and their admission into the Orders would more than double the number of Order Magi in the entire society.

The first candidate selected the cup in the blue quadrant, and after making his statement and drinking from the cup the young Magi walked over to stand next to Dalen.

Over the next several minutes the Order of Champions and the Order of Shadows gained several new members.

He looked to Cynia and she looked about as nervous as he felt. It was silly, but in a way he took it as a personal insult that no one had wanted to join his Order yet.

By the end of the selection process, the numbers had evened out some and Rissyl was relieved to have four new Magi within the Order of Evokers. That brought their Order to a total of eight Magi.

Standing near Cynia were four new members for her Order, bringing the total number of Order of Diviners to eight as well.

Dalen looked annoyed, as always. He'd been hinting for days that he expected most of the candidates to choose his Order, so it seemed that he was unsatisfied that only five of the nineteen candidates were to become Order of Champions Magi. The new members brought that Order to ten Magi, so Dalen would still be able to brag that his Order was the largest in the society.

When he looked to Sarasa, she looked as happy as he'd seen her in a long time. She was talking excitedly with her new members. There were six young Magi that had joined the Order of Shadows, bringing Sarasa's Order up to nine members.

Overall, he was very happy to see that the Orders were all fairly even in numbers. He would have liked a few more new members, but at least none of the Orders had grown significantly larger than the others. He didn't like to think about politics within the society, but as they grew it was important to maintain a balance.

The Rolimi announced, "Alright, time for the Covenant!"

He didn't pay much attention while all of the new Order Magi recited the lengthy obligations. Before he knew it, Mr. Pyllis was beckoning them over to present the new members with their weapons and cloaks of their Order.

One at a time he presented a staff and a red and white cloak to the new members of his Order. All four of them seemed so young, and they all looked incredibly proud.

He hoped that he would not watch any of them die any time soon.

With a sigh, he pushed the depressing thought from his mind. He replaced it with a smile and addressed them all. "Now that the formal part of your initiation into the Order of Evokers is complete, let's head over to Evoker Hall and I'll show you around. You'll be assigned new quarters, and later today you'll begin your training."

Before he could lead them out the door, Dalen walked up and grabbed his arm firmly. He said, "Before you run off, I gotta talk to you while we got all four of us together."

Rissyl held up an apologetic hand to his new Magi, "I'm sorry, I'll be right back and then we'll get underway."

He followed Dalen to the front of the council chambers, where Sarasa and Cynia were already waiting.

Dalen abruptly said, "Kyoso's alive, barely."

Rissyl's jaw dropped in astonishment.

"How? I thought he died at that garrison?" Cynia sounded as shocked as he felt.

"We found him being held prisoner at that garrison. He was unconscious and nearly dead."

"Where is he now?"

"At the temple, under the care of our clerics."

"What happened, how did you find him?"

Dalen crossed his arms over his chest, "We found him when we raided the garrison, killed every last soldier there, and recovered Ranik's body."

"You invaded the Libur garrison without us?" Sarasa's question was phrased as an accusation, and it was shouted.

The rest of the council chamber grew quiet and everyone turned their attention to the four grand officers of the Orders.

He took a deep breath and willed himself to calm down before responding. It never did any good to argue with Dalen, because he would never admit that he did something wrong. He asked, "Who went with you?"

"Firana came to me, I guess she knew that I would wanna take action. She was our Evoker. Peke, Asha, and Bull demanded to come with us. We also took about two dozen Society Magi, including most of the candidates who took the Covenants today."

Rissyl shook his head in disbelief. He tried to keep his voice calm and quiet. "By all the gods, Dalen. You risked so much, when we knew so little about what was going on there. But thank the gods you were able to rescue Kyoso!"

He wanted to yell and scream, and lecture him about acting more responsibly. However, Dalen was the Grand Champion and it was well within his power to organize a raid. Plus, he had saved the life of one of their Magi. The council hadn't established any formal criteria or approval process for missions, so there was little that he could complain about.

The look on Dalen's face showed that he'd been preparing for a battle over the mission, probably since he completed it. He had most likely rehearsed his arguments and counter-points a dozen times.

With a defiant expression and posture, Dalen said, "It was the right move, we did it flawlessly, and Kyoso owes us his life."

Cynia asked, "What'd you face? Did you see the strange officer that Eleyne mentioned? Was he similar to the one killed at the Khardifar garrison?"

Dalen's demeanor changed as he moved from defending his actions to telling the tale of the battle. "Before we even ported in, Bull and I dropped a ton of protective spells on every Magi in the group. We also handed out bracers to defend against arrows and stuff. The other Order Magi were armed with several artifacts from their Halls, and I went in with more weapons than any five people might need. We were ready for a tough

222

fight, and that's why it went so well. The imperials fought like crazy people, and they had no fear. Even when their arrows didn't hurt us, and their swords bounced from our magical shields, they still didn't stop."

He paused, probably for dramatic effect, and then continued, "Peke, Asha, and Bull took on the commander. The Society Magi, Firana, and I took on the rest of the garrison. Really, I think we had the easier task. There was something unhuman about the commander. I didn't look at it with magesight, but it fought like a monster. I've never seen anything like it. It fought like that while it was shouting orders to the troops around the fort."

Sarasa still looked annoyed. She said, "That's pretty much what they said about the battle at the Khardifar garrison."

"Talk to Peke, he can tell you more. He said he would try to use his magesight to learn anything he could. If anyone's got answers, it would be him."

She walked off without replying.

Rissyl started to walk off as well, but Cynia held his hand and delayed his motion. He looked to her, and she motioned at Dalen with her eyes. He knew that she wanted him to give her cousin some kind of encouragement, or at least acknowledge that the man had done something positive. As much as he didn't want to admit it, she was probably right.

He turned to Dalen and said, "Thank you, Dalen. What you did was brave. You saved Kyoso's life and you brought retribution for the death of Ranik."

Cynia hugged her cousin, and then added, "You also made sure that they still fear sarding with us, and that's huge."

Dalen smiled at them both, turned around abruptly, and then marched over to his new Order Magi.

- = - = -

Later that evening, Rissyl sank down into his bed and pulled the covers over his chin. It had been a long and busy day. After getting the new Evokers settled and started with their training, he sat through several hours of meetings about an endless list of mundane matters. So many aspects of building a new city needed his attention, even though his father was dealing with the vast majority of the problems.

A few hours ago the council authorized the formation of a team of sentinels to patrol the streets of Randol City, and the city's first thief was condemned to a year in the Stronghold dungeon.

The Rolimi guardians had started patrolling the outer walls and inner streets of the Stronghold, and there had been a number of run-ins between the extremely strict Rolimi guards and the non-magical folks who had moved in to Randol City and sometimes needed to enter the Stronghold. He still wasn't sure how to deal with that situation, so he delegated that to Cynia to figure out.

The warm and soft bed felt fantastic, and he closed his eyes to enjoy the quiet for a while.

Shortly before drifting off to sleep, he heard Cynia walking down the hall towards their bedroom. It had been far too long since the two had enjoyed any quality husband and wife time. As he heard her approach, he started to make plans for a little bit of adult fun before going to sleep.

When she opened the door to the bedroom, he saw that she was carrying their son Chardy.

He sighed. So much for naughty fun. "Why isn't he in bed?"

"When I walked by his room he was crying. I thought I'd nurse him to sleep." She sat down on the bed and pulled off her shirt.

"Ain't he weaned yet, I thought he was eating solid foods now?"

"Yes, mostly. But I still like to nurse him sometimes."

He mussed his son's hair as she latched him on. "I think this little diddies-thief should go back to his own bed, it's Daddy's turn to enjoy those."

The door opened again and Ayris plodded into the room, rubbing her eyes. She climbed into the bed between Rissyl and Cynia, wiggled under the covers, and snuggled up to him with her nose buried against the side of his chest.

He pulled the covers down far enough to see her head. He said, "Hey Goblin-Ears, did you know that there's a special bed in another room just for you?"

She pulled the covers over her head again, and draped her arm over his stomach.

Rissyl pulled the covers down once again, so he could see the side of her face. He said, "Your mom snores like a troll. I'm sure you'll sleep better in your own bed."

"I'm sleeping right here tonight, papa. I'm still having that bad dream I told you about the other day."

He tried to remember the details of the dream. He said, "The one where scary monsters eat you from the inside out?"

"The one where the scary monsters eat YOU from the inside out. I'm gonna be right here beside you, to keep you safe while you sleep."

He rubbed her back gently. "Okay, you stay here and keep me safe."

Rissyl looked over at Cynia and she looked like she was about to cry.

She whispered, "That's so sweet!"

He closed his eyes and tried to fall asleep, but sleep was slow to come. Usually he could push things aside and fall asleep fairly quickly, but the events of the day demanded his attention.

Without warning he heard Kilea in his mind.

"ARE YOU BUSY, SOVRAN?"

"NO, KILEA."

He still hadn't mentioned his bond with the cheirapsian to Cynia or anyone else. In some ways he felt guilty, almost like he was keeping a secret about a lover or something. He needed to tell Cynia about it soon.

"I HAVE INFORMATION THAT YOU WILL WANT TO HEAR. THE ARISTOCRATS FROM THE CITIES AROUND KHARDIFAR ARE ABUZZ WITH GOSSIP ABOUT KHARDIFAR CLAIMING INDEPENDENCE FROM THE EMPIRE. THE IDEA OF AN INDEPENDENT SOUTHERN COAST IS RAPIDLY GAINING THE SUPPORT OF THE MOST INFLUENTIAL FAMILIES IN THE REGION."

He was shocked. He would have expected the prospect of war to terrify the Aristocrats and Gentry in that area. *"HOW DO YOU KNOW THIS?"*

"WEALTHY PEOPLE FREQUENTLY SPEAK TO EACH OTHER LIKE THE CHEIRAPSIANS DON'T EXIST. TO MANY OF THEM, WE ARE SIMPLY EXTREMELY EXPENSIVE SERVANTS. ALSO, THEY HAVE NO IDEA THAT CHEIRAPSIANS CAN SPEAK TELEPATHICALLY TO OTHER DRUIDS, SO THEY DON'T KNOW HOW QUICKLY THEIR SECRETS CAN BE SHARED. SO, AS FAR AS THE TALK ON INDEPENDENCE GOES, THE OVERWHELMING OPINION AMONG THE ARISTOCRATS THROUGHOUT THE SOUTHERN COAST IS THAT THEIR WEALTH CAN BUY THEM SAFETY, AND THAT FREEDOM AND THE PROFITS THAT GO WITH IT WOULD BE WELL WORTH THE LIVES OF A FEW THOUSAND DENIZENS."

It all sounded so dastardly, but he had to admit that having several major cities declaring themselves autonomous simultaneously would help the Magi Society a great deal, and it could also make it easier on Khardifar. If the emperor had to divide his forces even further, it would be a benefit for everyone.

"YES, SOVRAN, WE AGREE. IF THE MAGI WERE TO APPROACH THE CHANCELLORS THROUGHOUT THE SOUTH, YOU MIGHT FIND MORE ALLIES THAN YOU EXPECT."

"THANK YOU, KILEA. WE WILL TALK TO THEM."

"THERE IS ANOTHER THING I SHOULD SHARE WITH YOU. OUR CHEIRAPSIANS IN CLORNOSS HAVE BEEN HEARING SEVERAL CLIENTS TALKING ABOUT CHANGES IN THE PRINCE. THEY SPEAK OF SOME SORT OF MAGI CURSE THAT CAUSED THE PRINCE TO AGE MORE THAN A DECADE. THEY HAVE BEEN TALKING ABOUT THE PRINCE BEING ENGAGED TO MARRY, AND THAT HE WILL BE PUT IN CHARGE OF ALL OF THE IMPERIAL ARMY."

"MAGI CURSE? MORE LIES FROM THE EMPEROR, BUT THIS IS INTRIGUING INFORMATION. THANK YOU, I WILL DISCUSS THESE THINGS WITH THE COUNCIL. I SUPPOSE I SHOULD BE GETTING TO SLEEP, GOOD NIGHT KILEA."

"SLEEP WELL, SOVRAN."

He almost jumped from the bed when the door opened and Cynia walked back into the room. He hadn't even noticed her leaving.

"Chardy's asleep, and now it's my turn."

As she crawled back into bed, he said, "Have you ever heard of druids?"

"Yeah, don't they hide in the forests and commune with nature all day?"

"I don't know, maybe some of them. Apparently there are different types of druids just like there are different Orders of magic."

She looked over at him as she adjusted her pillow. "What about them?"

"It seems that all cheirapsians are druids, and they share some sort of telepathy."

Cynia was quiet and looked thoughtful. After a pause, she replied, "That explains some things, but how do you know this?"

"One of the cheirapsians at the chancellor's manor, a woman named Kilea, made a telepathic connection with me. She explained some things about the druids. She's also been giving me information that they obtained from Aristocrats around the empire."

"Riz, this is great." She sat up in the bed and turned towards him. "When I was a Dreg, most people ignored me unless they wanted something. They'd talk about private things that they'd never mention in front of their peers. If the Aristocrats are like that around cheirapsians, it could be very helpful to us."

He tried to adjust into a more comfortable position, without waking Ayris, but it was no use so he stayed in the same position. He said, "Tonight Kilea shared two interesting pieces of information. First, that the Aristocrats throughout the south are talking about their desire to see their cities follow Khardifar's lead and demand autonomy."

"I was wondering if that would happen. Maybe we should reach out to some of the southern chancellors and see if we can help that along any."

"I agree. The second thing she mentioned is that people are saying that the Magi cursed the prince. They say he has aged over a decade. There is talk of him being put in charge of the imperial troops, and even talk of a royal wedding."

"This is all very strange. I wonder what's really going on?"

CHAPTER 29

Jessa

The past couple of days had been a blur for Jessa. After Jalinox stormed out of the Council of Ministers meeting, she had accompanied the prince to his new suite in the palace. It consisted of several rooms in the emperor's wing of the palace, and it even had an adjoining room where she had been invited to live. As soon as they entered his new suite they had gotten into a huge argument. Actually, she had done all of the arguing and complaining, and he simply nodded and listened.

She had never agreed to marry him, and she still didn't know if she would. She was furious that he had made the announcement, because she assumed that he was trying to force her to do his bidding.

After several hours of listening to her ranting, he finally convinced her that it was still her decision and that he was simply trying to make her look good in the eyes of the Council of Ministers, establish her place within his father's court, and weaken Jalinox's position in the process.

She was suddenly in an uncomfortable position between the prince and Lord Jalinox. The necromancer lord was livid. She hadn't spent much time with him over the last couple of days, but in that brief time he made it clear that his aspirations had not changed. She worried that the new rivalry between him and the prince would spiral into something worse, and she was determined to be on the winning side of that battle when it happened.

Her reluctance to accept the prince's offer had nothing to do with loyalty to Jalinox, because she felt very little loyalty towards him. When she thought about it, she was using him as much as he used her. What she needed to decide was which way would give her the most power. Even though she had seen very little when it came to actual power from the prince, she was starting to think that he had the potential for far greater things.

She decided to go along with things as the prince arranged, at least until she made up her mind. To play along with that role, she ended up getting pulled into the planning and preparation for Edal's conferral ceremony. Several days ago she was abducting people and tossing them in a dungeon to be eaten by Manaworms, and yesterday she spent the day picking out fabric and choosing the flowers that would decorate the room for the prince's ceremony.

The absurdity of it all was enough to make her chuckle.

The ceremony had been as dreadfully long and dull as she suspected that it would be. The prince looked dashing in his new military formalwear, but the extravagance of the event and all of the pomp and circumstance annoyed her.

Her burning hatred for the emperor didn't help either. Every time she looked at the man she wanted to fill him full of Khalius Fire and watch him die so that she could raise him as an Awakened and then kill him again. She would never forgive him for causing the death of her brother, and it took all of her self-control to look friendly when all she wanted to do was bring chaos and death.

When the ceremony finally came to an end, she walked down onto the stage to stand near the prince. Everyone was gathered around hoping to congratulate him, and she had to squeeze between people before she could finally get close.

What she thought was the end was simply the beginning of the conversation segment of the ceremony. She ended up standing on the stage next to the prince, surrounded by rich people that she didn't know, for well over an hour. She lost count of how many hugs were given and how many people grabbed her shoulders to pull her into cheek kisses. It seemed that people were as excited about the upcoming wedding as they were about the conferring of the prince's new rank.

Then the prince suddenly announced, "I'm sorry everyone, but we must retire. Thank you for coming!" He led her by the hand and quickly headed off of the stage.

Minister Vendino hurried to catch them before they got away. "My prince, the wagons leave in fifty minutes!"

"We won't be long, minister."

They hopped off of the stage and then he led her down a hall and around the corner. He pulled a huge tapestry aside and stepped between it and the wall. She followed, but she felt rather silly facing a huge stone wall and standing behind a massive tapestry.

She heard a clicking sound, and a small section of the wall opened away from her.

The prince whispered, "Get in, quickly."

As she followed him into the secret passageway, he closed the concealed door behind them. They were in a very dark and damp corridor.

Jessa whispered, "A secret door? How'd you know about that?"

"I've played in these secret hallways since I was a boy. Listen, Jalinox is attempting a ritual to subjugate a Czelmic Demon. We've got to stop him before he completes that ritual."

The surprise on her face was genuine. She had no idea that Jalinox was so close to having enough mana for the ritual.

She didn't reply, and he reached out and grabbed her shoulder. This time she was prepared for the falling sensation and she made no attempt to grab for something to hold onto.

The falling feeling lasted only a moment, and then she was in the large room at Jalinox's compound where the prince had given his soul to Wirmyntas.

Jalinox was in the middle of the room. He was inside a large summoning circle, with both hands extended and he was screaming and cursing loudly.

His shouts were completely obscured by the terrible wailing and screeching coming from a massive demon trapped in a much larger summoning circle just to her left. The horrible creature was terrifying to behold and she found herself trembling in fear just from looking towards it. The demon was about twelve feet tall and at least that wide. Its powerful arms were long enough to drag on the ground if was standing upright. Its muscular legs each seemed to have two knees, one pointing forward and the lower one pointing to the rear. The demon's head was short and wide, with several horns along the top and an abnormally wide mouth filled with large teeth. It was scaly and deep red in color, and the scales smoked and burned with small fires in spots.

The demon flung itself wildly around the circle, beating on the invisible barrier with its head, kicking at it with its powerful legs, and trying to tear through it with its gigantic claws.

Some sort of shimmering light emanated from Jalinox's outstretched hands, and it shined on the demon.

Prince Edal sprinted between Jalinox and the demon, and thrust himself into the shimmering light. It encapsulated the prince and seemed to bind him. He stood in the light, facing Jalinox, with his arms outstretched. His body jerked violently as the light pulsated from the necromancer's hands.

With the light no longer shining on it, the demon calmed somewhat. However, it continued to kick and claw at the magical barrier trying to break through.

Jalinox was covered in sweat and his face was twisted in rage. His arms shook and it seemed like the light was surging from him of its own accord. He stomped his feet and pushed his hands forward and back slightly, and the pulsations in the light ebbed and flowed with the rhythm of the necromancer's moving hands.

Jalinox shouted, "Kill him, Jessa! Kill Edal now! This may be our only chance!"

She started walking towards the prince. His body continued to gyrate violently, trapped by the shimmering light. As she moved beside the prince, he looked to her. She thought that his eyes might be pleading with her, but felt that she was probably imagining it. He said nothing, and she doubted that he could speak as the light trapped his entire body.

It seemed likely that the prince would die if she stood by and did nothing. Jalinox sounded desperate for her to intervene, but the outcome didn't appear to be in doubt. Perhaps this was the answer she sought? She wanted to know which of them was more powerful, and that was playing out before her.

She started running.

Without further thought, she sprinted towards Jalinox and smashed into him with all of her might. The force of the collision sent them both tumbling to the floor in a heap. The light engulfed them both, briefly. The pain was intense, and then it was gone.

When she looked up, she noticed that the demon had vanished. She assumed that it returned to its rightful home.

Movement caught her eye and she saw Edal rushing towards them. He was unsteady on his feet, and she thought he almost looked like a drunkard trying to run somewhere. Jalinox was able to stand up fully before the prince got to him.

The necromancer lord screamed as he lobbed a huge orb of Khalius Fire at the prince. It hit the prince solidly in the chest, just as he got near. The attack staggered the prince, and caused him to yell out in pain.

As Jalinox extended his hand for another attack, the prince brought up both hands defensively. The massive purple orb shot from the hand of the necromancer and was immediately trapped and extinguished by the prince's outstretched palms.

Edal lunged forward to place his hands around Jalinox's neck. The necromancer produced a thick magical barrier of pure Khalius Fire around his entire body. The fire flickered fiercely, as if Jalinox was engulfed in purple flame, but the fires protected rather than harming him.

Jessa hear Edal's screams as he stood with his hands trapped in the purple flames, mere inches from the necromancer's neck. As he screamed, pulses of deep-purple fire began to erupt from the prince's palms and they instantly spread across Jalinox's protective shields.

The two dark lords stood locked in a battle of wicked clerical magic, and for a few seconds it seemed like it might be an evenly matched battle.

The onslaught of deep-purple fire from the prince intensified and slowly beat back the necromancer's fiery shield. The prince's hands grew closer and closer to Jalinox's neck, and even as Jalinox stepped away the prince followed and pressed ever closer.

Finally, Edal pushed completely through the shield. When the prince touched Jalinox's neck it was all over. Jalinox's body suddenly disintegrated to ashes and burst into a massive cloud, leaving only his skeleton. An instant later the skeleton crashed to the ground with a loud clatter.

The necromancer's ashes floated slowly to the floor, and Jessa thrust her sleeve over her mouth and nose as she scurried quickly backwards. She was repulsed by the thought of breathing part of the necromancer into her body.

She stood up and continued to back away from the jumbled pile of Jalinox's bones.

When she looked to the prince, he swayed as if he was about to collapse. Then his demeanor changed, and he stood up straight and tall. His rapid shallow breaths became more regular and controlled. He placed his fists on his hips and stood healthy and proud. There was an aura around him for a moment, and she knew that something about the prince had changed.

He smiled confidently and raised his hand, with his palm facing upwards. As he did, a dozen little demons popped out of the floor and started running around the room. They bounced and leapt, running in seemingly random patterns while they chittered and giggled. There were several types of demons rushing about, and she didn't recognize any of them. None of them seemed to notice her, if anything they appeared to be frolicking and playing chasing games with each other.

The prince pointed towards the pile of bones, and the demons instantly scurried over to them. They began breaking them and chewing on them joyfully. They tossed them in the air, and tried to tug them from each other. The snapping and grinding sounds of some of the demons eating the bones echoed around the room, and Jessa covered her ears.

When the prince lowered his hand, palm down, the demons popped back to Khalius. The room grew quiet.

Edal looked to her, and slowly extended his hand towards her. For a moment she was afraid that he was sending demons at her.

He said, "My quest is complete. I have slain Jalinox, and Wirmyntas has accepted me as the Archwarlock. His power is almost intoxicating. Take my hand, let us return to the palace. We have a city to destroy."

She walked to him. It seemed that she had made her choice.

CHAPTER 30

Rissyl

It felt like over-kill, bringing along so many of the powerful artifacts from Evoker Hall. Especially since they were just meeting with the chancellor of Tharrin to talk about the city breaking away from the emperor.

Rissyl was sitting in the shadows among some crates and barrels on the deck of a large boat, and none of the sailors or soldiers around him had any idea that he was there. The *Shadow Shroud* spell was one of the many simple spells available to all Magi. It wasn't a spell that he used very often, but he did see its usefulness. It was a bit surreal to be near so many people without them being able to see him. It was a good spell, but it had its limits. He had to be very careful to remain in shadows and avoid direct sunlight, and he had to be very quiet.

Since Kilea had mentioned the southern Aristocrats' favorable opinion of local autonomy, the Magi had moved quickly to take advantage of the information. In just a couple of days they were able to set up meetings with the chancellors of Tharrin, Bathok, Orgrak, and Gimzag.

Cynia had already led a cadre to Orgrak and tomorrow she would meet with the chancellor from Gimzag. This morning Dalen led a cadre for a meeting with the chancellor of Bathok. Sarasa was still trying to arrange meetings with the leaders of some of the other cities as well, but nothing had been set up so far.

Chancellor Tiyra of Tharrin seemed eager to meet with the Magi, but she insisted that they do it at sea where she could be sure that none of the emperor's spies could overhear things. The chancellor wanted the Magi to bring a boat of their own and meet her ship in the waters south of Tharrin.

Instead, Rissyl decided to sneak onto her ship well before they set sail. Once the ship dropped anchor, he would open a portal and let the other Magi join him on the boat. It seemed like it'd be an impressive entrance, and it would give him a chance to get a feel for the situation before bringing the others.

If he felt that it was a trap, he'd simply teleport back to the Stronghold and abort the whole mission. Everyone had been on edge since the death of Ranik. It seemed that the Magi had grown a bit complacent, and the death of that Magi had been a stark reminder that they needed to be more cautious in their routines.

The chancellor's ship was large, and he was looking out at a spacious deck in the middle of the ship. There were stairs up to higher level decks towards the front of the ship and back behind him in the rear of the ship. Several crew members were hurrying from place to place, pulling ropes, climbing masts, and doing other boat related things. He didn't know much about boats, but the crew seemed very skilled at their appointed tasks.

Rissyl had never been on a ship like this and had never been so far away from land, and the experience wasn't great. The constant rise and fall of the water and the swaying back and forth of the ship was enough to make his stomach queasy. He was glad that he wouldn't have to spend much time on board.

The chancellor was standing near the edge of the ship, looking out at the water. Next to her was an old man in fine clothing. They had been talking for a long time and Rissyl assumed they were looking out to sea expecting to see a boat filled with Magi approaching them.

He had seen a few soldiers on board, but there wasn't a huge contingent of imperial troops waiting to ambush the Magi. That was an encouraging start.

Being careful not to make noise, he stood up and moved a bit closer to the middle of the deck. The heavily clouded sky helped to maintain his veil of invisibility long enough for him to get situated. He didn't want to drop a portal around a bunch of crates and have the Magi tripping and stumbling around the ship as they made their grand entrance.

He raised his hand and activated the portal ring. Immediately a large magical portal of swirling colors appeared before him. Activating the ring disrupted his shroud spell, making him fully visible.

Someone behind him shouted, "Chancellor, look behind you!"

Rissyl reached in a pocket of his breeches and pulled out three ioun stones. He tossed them in the air and they instantly started spinning just above his head. All three of them circled his head slowly, about even with the crown of his head. Each of them provided him with magical protection from different forms of attack. One protected against piercing damage, one protected against cutting damage, and the last protected against slamming damage from hammers and such. The stones didn't make him impervious to injury, but they provided much more protection that just his cloak on its own. With these protective artifacts, and the various protective spells that Thon placed on him earlier, he was well prepared in the event of an ambush.

Zahr stepped out of the portal first. His skin and clothes were covered in a layer of thick bark, but as he moved the bark moved and bended as fluidly as skin so it didn't seem to hinder him any. The Diviner's green and white cloak blew freely behind him as he stepped to his left and stood ready for any attack from that direction. He held his staff out before him with the top pointed towards the front of the ship, and he looked anxious to take on any threats that arrived from the front of the ship.

The next out of the portal was Thon, and he looked like an armored knight ready to ride into battle. The Order of Champions Magi was covered in shiny platemail armor from his toes to the top of his head, and his huge broadsword was drawn and ready to taste blood. He turned to his right and stepped away from the portal. With his blue and white cloak waving behind him, he stood ready to deal with any threats coming from the back of the ship.

When Vora stepped through the portal it vanished, since she was wearing the portal ring that paired with Rissyl's. Vora was one of the new Order Magi who took the Covenants a few days ago. He didn't know her very well, but she seemed like a capable Magi and an eager learner. Sarasa was impressed with her, so that was good enough for him.

He would have rather brought an entire cadre of experienced Magi, but they had to make do with the people they had available.

Vora was using some magical artifact that caused her to appear semi-transparent. It looked as though he could put his hand right through her body if he tried to touch her. He didn't know enough about Shadow Order magic to fully understand the benefit of the semi-transparent effect, but it certainly looked impressive. She was standing with both hands on the hilts of her sheathed daggers, facing the chancellor.

Chancellor Tiyra took a step towards the Magi and clasped her hands before her. She said, "Well, you definitely know how to make an entrance, that's for sure. You can put away your weapons, unless you mean to kill me. Although, I doubt that you'd need weapons to do that. There is no threat to you here."

Rissyl nodded to the other Magi, and they all dismissed their weapons back to the plane of magic for storage. He stepped closer to the chancellor and bowed his head slightly.

"Chancellor Tiyra, thank you for meeting with us so quickly."

"How could I pass up an invitation from the Sovereign Magi Society? You're practically legendary. The honor is mine. Shall we have a seat?" She motioned towards the randomly stacked crates and barrels where Rissyl had been sitting earlier.

She was dressed in very simple, but well-made, robes of white and pale green. There were some patterns embroidered along some of the edges, but mostly they were modest robes. She walked over and sat down on top of a large crate, pulling her feet off the floor and crossing her legs before her. Her posture was upright and poised, although she was seated casually.

Rissyl and the other Magi followed her and claimed crates or barrels of their own to sit upon. He moved a barrel so he could face the chancellor without blocking the other Magi from seeing her. It was a much less formal arrangement than their meeting with Chancellor Bernold from Khardifar, and he felt at ease and comfortable already.

As they sat, Rissyl led introductions quickly.

After introductions, Tiyra said, "Before we get too far please allow me to be blunt and jump right to my first concern. Did the Magi curse Prince Edal?"

"I assure you, chancellor, the Magi did not curse the boy. To be honest, I don't know of any power that could cause someone to age like that." Rissyl was happy that Kilea had already warned him about that rumor, it would have been uncomfortable to be surprised by hearing that news from the chancellor.

Tiyra nodded, "I suspected as much. I don't know what is going on with the prince, but the emperor has been erratic and unpredictable for a long time. I've stopped trying to understand why he does the things he does."

"Does that mean that you're considering taking steps to break away from the empire?"

"I've been on the brink of that drastic step for months. Our Aristocrats have been pushing independence since the first time a Gentry hung from the gallows accused by the emperor's agents of being Magi. When Bernold established the Duchy of Khardifar, the fervor for a break from the empire rose to a whole new level within Tharrin. I think that most of the upper social levels of our city see a chance for fancy royal titles and the promise of lower taxes. I don't think they are considering the war and hardships that are likely to precede all of the benefits of independence. They assume someone else will have to fight the battles and suffer the inconveniences."

He was glad to hear that the chancellor seemed to already be considering both the positive and the negative implications of her decision. He said, "I must admit, Tiyra, that I am deeply torn about whether it's a good idea for the southern cities to stand against the emperor. Of course, it's extremely beneficial for the Magi, because it will divide the emperor's attention and make it less likely that he'll assault our home. However, if you go through with this you will make your city a target and make it much more likely that the emperor will assault your homes."

She looked sad, and she shook her head as she replied, "Oh, I assure you that it's a dreadful idea for Tharrin to claim autonomy from the empire. We're just a few days march from Clornoss and we will absolutely suffer attack from the emperor's legions very soon after we make that claim. So, let's talk about our options. Your missive suggested that the Magi could assist us were we to choose independence. What sort of assistance would you offer?"

"Primarily, we would help to clear out the garrison positioned right outside your city, and we would help deal with the emperor's troops and agents that are currently within your city. We could identify members of your loyal military forces who have the potential to become Magi and teach them how to use their powers if you desire. However, that's about the extent of what we could offer. There isn't much we could do to help defend you from a direct assault from the emperor's troops should he decide to attack your city with a large military force."

The chancellor looked thoughtful for a bit, and then said, "Our sentinels are completely loyal to Tharrin. When the conscription decree was issued, I ordered my sentinels to ignore it. That decision has pushed us towards independence more than anything else, as we've had to purge the city of imperial agents and troops who were clamoring for our sentinels to obey the emperor's decree. Our Dross is filled with the emperor's agents and other loyalists, where they'll remain locked-up indefinitely. As of right now, the streets of Tharrin are free of the emperor's forces. Our immediate problem is the garrison. The commander of the garrison doesn't know that we've imprisoned imperial agents and such, but he does know that our sentinels have not answered the conscription decree, and the commander has sent notice that we must comply with the decree or he'll be forced to take action. Even if we don't declare autonomy, the emperor's troops will likely be at our gates within days to punish us for ignoring the decree."

Thon cleared his throat, and then asked, "Will your people fight? Have they been armed to help defend against the emperor's forces? It is unlikely that your sentinels can do it alone, even against the small force stationed at the garrison."

"Our sentinels are unlike the city watchmen in most major cities. For many years now we've recruited some of the best soldiers to serve in the ranks of our sentinels. It's more of a regiment of experienced soldiers than a group of watchmen. They're skilled, well trained, and highly loyal to Tharrin. They may not be a match for the emperor's full army, but they are a good group of soldiers."

Rissyl wasn't sure whether to be happy or depressed. "So, your mind is made up, then? Tharrin is choosing autonomy?"

She frowned, "We really have no choice now. If we can get the help of the Magi to deal with the garrison, then we will handle the rest. Right now my people are issuing an evacuation order throughout the city. By the time we return many of the citizens of Tharrin will already be making their way east to Libur and some of the smaller towns and villages along the way."

Very slowly, Zahr said, "You're evacuating the entire city?"

It wasn't long ago that Zahr and his family had to flee Ront'El as the imperial army attacked that city. Rissyl could see the pained expression on Zahr's face, and he assumed the Magi was reliving the stress and pain of that ordeal. For him, this was all too familiar.

Tiyra nodded, "Oh yes. I am willing to sacrifice my city, and thus my power and position within it. But I am not willing to sacrifice my people. The sentinels will stay, and anyone who wishes to remain behind to help fight the emperor's forces will stay. Everyone else needs to flee while they still can. I hope that the Magi will help my sentinels deal with the garrison today, the sooner the better. Once the garrison is defeated, the fleeing people will have less to worry about as far as being attacked from behind. Also, when the garrison is defeated, our people can also flee to the west. People are being told that they should go east, because Khardifar could also fall under attack. However, if too many people go east it will quickly overwhelm those cities and towns with too many refugees. It's not like any place is really safe anyway."

She paused, and wiped a tear from her eye. She took a deep breath, and then continued, "All of our fishing boats, merchant ships, and anything seaworthy will be used to transport Gentry and Aristocrats to cities in the far eastern parts of the empire and even coastal Free-Cities in the far north beyond the empire. Even this is dangerous since elven pirate attacks continue to increase as the emperor focuses all of his efforts towards the Magi and ignores things like pirate raids."

Again she paused to compose herself. "Those who stay back to fight will hit the emperor's forces as hard as they can. If we can make a good stand in Tharrin, perhaps the emperor will decide to leave the other newly-independent cities alone?"

He hated the thought of another city being evacuated because of the emperor. The region around Ront'El was still trying to recover from the sudden influx of refugees from that city. Although, he had to admit that Tiyra's plan was probably wiser than what Chancellor Bernold was trying to do in Khardifar.

Rissyl looked to the other Magi, "Are we ready to help assault the garrison now? Is there anything else you need to do to prepare?"

They all nodded or shrugged, and Zahr said, "Let's do it."

Looking back to the chancellor, Rissyl said, "We weren't really planning to help assault the garrison today, but we can make it work. We arrived prepared for an ambush, so we might as well put these defensive spells to use."

Tiyra said, "If the emperor has sent troops to attack Khardifar, they're likely to pass right by Tharrin on the way. I would expect them to stop at our garrison as they pass through. We may only have days before things get much harder."

"Well then we shouldn't delay. Do your sentinels expect our help? Where should we meet them?"

She shook her head, "No, they have no idea that you'll be helping. However, this is Captain Kollen, the commander of our sentinels. He'll accompany you and inform the others that you'll be helping." She motioned to a soldier standing towards the front part of the lower deck.

Rissyl nodded in greetings towards the captain and said, "If you want us to get underway quickly, the captain could travel with us through our portal directly into your city. Then we wouldn't have to wait for the boat to sail back to town."

Vora quipped, "And we could stop with the dreadful swaying before my last meal comes back out."

- = - = -

The arrows started flying without warning.

Rissyl and the other Magi followed the main force of Tharrin sentinels towards the garrison, and they expected the imperial troops to warn them or issue orders to halt before they began attacking.

They were wrong.

The Tharrin footmen rushed towards the wall of the garrison while their archers returned fire at the imperial archers along the tops of the wall.

The Magi followed the footmen and as they got near the wall Rissyl shouted, "Stand clear!" He summoned magic and began shaping it for his first spells. When it was ready, he said, "Krol'Fe Salindi." A mint green sphere about the size of a watermelon appeared in his outstretched palm. It was an orb of pure magical force, and as he tossed it he cast another spell to shove it with incredible speed towards the wall. The large orb slammed against the wall and ripped a huge hole in the stones as it passed through. A small section of wall collapsed as he began the process again.

Over and over he tossed force orbs at the wall, and each time another small section of the wall crumbled before his magical onslaught. The Tharrin footmen poured through his first breech in the wall as he created more.

Several arrows slammed into him, and they ricocheted off or dropped harmlessly to the ground, as his magical defenses held strong.

When the foot soldiers stormed into the garrison the Magi followed closely behind.

Rissyl said, "Magi stay together! We can't retreat if everyone's doing their own thing. Stay on me."

He followed a large group of sentinels through a street between buildings, and then out into a broad open area in the middle of the garrison. Imperials and Tharrin sentinels were everywhere, in large groups locked in deadly combat. The imperials fought viciously, and the Tharrin troops quickly started taking heavy casualties.

Zahr shouted, "Rissyl, look over there! In my magesight, I see some sort of presence in that officer. Like two entities in one body, just like they described in those other commanders."

Off to the right an officer was yelling commands and directing several different groups at once. At the same time, the officer fought ferociously against two Tharrin warriors.

"Magi, that officer is our target!" Rissyl headed that way without looking to see if they would follow.

Thon quickly passed him, and his blade danced from one opponent to another as he battled his way through a group of soldiers.

Rissyl spun his staff in a butterfly pattern as he walked, and as it spun it produced streaks of lightning along the way. The energy coursed up and down the staff, and harmlessly over his hands, as he spun it. An imperial soldier lunged at him from his right, thrusting his large sword at Rissyl's side. He redirected the spinning staff, smacking the sword out of the way and then leveled the top end of the staff against the side of the soldier's head. When the staff connected, a loud clap of thunder erupted from the man's head as the lightning from the staff discharged into the unfortunate soldier's body. He jerked and shook as he dropped to the ground.

Without even stopping his forward progress, Rissyl brought the staff back into a butterfly spin. As it spun the lightning quickly regenerated along the wooden shaft.

It didn't take long for the Magi to make it to the imperial officer. The man had defeated several Tharrin soldiers, whose corpses were spread around on the ground before him.

Thon grunted a battle cry, and rushed to engage the commander. Vora and Zahr were right behind him.

He expected the fight to be brief, but the commander easily defended himself against the attacks from all three Magi. Vora's daggers moved quickly, and Zahr fought skillfully with his staff. Thon's relentless sword attacks at the same time would have been enough to best most any foe.

The commander took damage, as the Magi landed blow after blow. However he seemed oblivious to the wounds, and if anything they drove him to fight even harder.

Rissyl felt his mind getting foggy, as if something was trying to take control of him. He tossed up a ward to protect his mind. He had no idea what was trying to invade him, but he wasn't going to take chances. Other Magi had mentioned the same thing after the battles at the Khardifar and Libur garrisons.

The Tharrin sentinels continued to take heavy losses and the imperials were beginning to get the upper hand. The Tharrin's tenacity and will to fight seemed to be dwindling.

Twice Rissyl had to dispatch imperial soldiers who tried to catch him unaware, and arrows were once again coming in his direction.

He decided it was time to put an end to the commander. With a quick summoning of magic, he pointed towards the commander and said, "Krol'Tu Nari"

The thin column of fire burst from the sky and engulfed the commander, and the column immediately dissipated when it hit him. The imperial's skin burned away, and a creature appeared in his place. The monster was red and scaly, shaped roughly like a person with a grotesque face and horns all around its head and body. It screamed with rage and pressed its attack on the Magi even harder.

The Magi had jumped back from the fire as it appeared, and they clearly expected the commander to be dead. Thon barely defended against the creature's first attack after it survived the fire.

Rissyl was astonished. He had no idea what the creature was, or how it survived his fiery column.

Zahr's staff vanished, and was instantly replaced by a long and thin spear that seemed to be made of pure ice. Vora and Thon both pressed their attacks simultaneously, giving Zahr a brief opening for an attack of his own. He thrust the ice spear forward, and it drove deep into the creature's back.

The monster roared in pain, and desperately grasped at its back to try to remove the ice weapon.

It fell to its knees and shrieked loudly, and then dropped to the ground dead.

"What was that sarding thing?" Thon kicked the creature, to be sure it was dead.

The imperial soldiers immediately seemed to lose much of their ferocity. Several of them stopped fighting all together, and most of them appeared confused or disoriented. Those imperial soldiers who had combat experience continued the fight, but the Tharrin soldiers quickly gained the upper hand.

Rissyl and the other Magi turned their attention to subduing the last groups of imperial troops who were reluctant to surrender.

Within a few minutes of the creature's death, the last of the imperial troops yielded.

Captain Kollen grabbed one of the younger looking imperial troops and pulled him over away from the rest. He said, "Take a message to your emperor. Tell him that Tharrin is no longer an imperial city. We are an independent province and the imperial troops are not welcome here."

The captain practically tossed the soldier away, and the young man hurried to escape.

Turning to his sentinels, the captain shouted, "Bind all of the imperials, and drag them to the Dross!"

CHAPTER 31

Sarasa

Several riders galloped through the city gates and headed directly towards the abandoned barn where Sarasa and three other Magi were hiding.

Bull sat up and leaned against the dilapidated barn wall, looking through a gap between the boards. "Oh, here they come. There are a bunch of them headed this way."

"It took them long enough. How long should it really take to deliver a message to the chancellor, and then return his reply?" Peke was sitting on a large block of hay, in the middle of the barn.

"Well, let's just hope they're bringing a response from the chancellor and not coming out to collect on the emperor's bounty." Sarasa slid a dagger into its sheath and dropped a whetstone into her pouch.

Firana hopped off of a bale of hay, and brushed the stuff from her breeches. She grabbed three ioun stones from her pocket and tossed them in the air. They began spinning slowly around her head. She said, "I'm alright with either, as long as it gets us out of this smelly old barn."

Walking over to the wall, Sarasa looked through a broken board. There were at least a dozen horses, riding quickly towards them. She dropped an invisibility spell on herself as she drew two daggers. "Get ready, if they want death we'll give it to them quickly."

She watched Peke transform into a large golden eagle. He jumped into the air and spread his powerful wings in flight. Rising effortlessly, he perched in a large window towards the top of the barn.

Bull rolled onto his hands and knees and crawled across the floor, growling the whole way.

Firana laughed. "Bull, you can't transform into a bear! Get up, the soldiers from the city will be here soon."

He stood up and drew his longsword. "I was a wolf, Firana. A wolf. Not a bear. If you're going to squash my delusions, I'd appreciate if you'd at least get them right."

"You look more like a bear."

He flashed her a playfully rude gesture, opened the door, and walked out of the barn.

Firana and Sarasa followed him out.

The mounted soldiers arrived as the Magi emerged from the barn. Sarasa moved to flank them in case they tried anything unpleasant. She noticed Peke the eagle circling high overhead.

The riders dismounted and one of them approached Bull and Firana slowly. He had his hands slightly to the side with his palms facing them. He said, "You can sheath your weapons, Magi. You requested an audience with the chancellor?"

Firana dismissed her staff and Bull sheathed his sword but did not dismiss it.

The soldier motioned to a man behind him. The man wore simple riding clothes, a large overcoat, and a furry animal pelt hat.

He stepped forward and bowed to the Magi. "Gehrey Sullendris, chancellor of Rinamek City. It's a pleasure to make your acquaintance."

Bull and Firana bowed slightly and introduced themselves.

The chancellor said, "It's beginning to snow, perhaps we should move into the barn to have our discussion?"

The two Magi led the way into the barn and four of the soldiers walked in behind the chancellor. The other soldiers stood guard outside.

Sarasa followed them into the barn.

She dropped her invisibility as Peke soared through the window above, and dove towards the ground. He landed gracefully next to Firana, and transformed back into his human form.

"Simply remarkable! It seems that the Magi truly are as powerful as the rumors suggest." The chancellor looked genuinely pleased and intrigued.

"I am Sarasa, the Grand Shadow of the Sovereign Magi Society. It is a pleasure to meet you. Should I call you Chancellor Sullendris, or do you prefer Chancellor Gehrey?" These days, many people didn't use their family name at all, preferring only their given name even when used with their title. However, some people still preferred the old ways.

"Chancellor Gehrey, or just Gehrey is fine. There is usually something unpleasant about to happen when I hear my family name used."

She laughed, "I know how you feel. To be blunt, Chancellor Gehrey, I didn't expect you to come out here and meet with us like this. We were just asking to schedule an audience with you when it was convenient.

Magi aren't exactly greeted warmly by the imperial soldiers, so we have to be cautious."

"I was intrigued. I've never been handed a missive requesting an audience with Magi before. My curiosity was too strong, and I had to meet with you immediately. I apologize that I couldn't invite you as honored guests into my palace. All of the troops with me are my personal guards, and they are no threat to you. But, as you mentioned, the emperor's troops aren't fond of Magi and I'm afraid we have all too many of them in my city."

"We've seen some of them doing patrols. So, let's get right to the point. I'm sure that you've heard that Khardifar has declared itself to be an autonomous province."

The chancellor smiled, "The Duchy of Khardifar, if my information is correct?"

"Yes, that is what they're calling it. Other cities along the southern coast may be following the example of Khardifar. The Magi Society is offering to help cities that desire secession from the empire."

"Indeed, your missive did imply as much. Unfortunately, Rinamek City is not far from Clornoss and I won't risk angering the emperor. I don't support much of what he has done lately, but the danger is too great. My city will not be joining in this revolt against him. I'm sorry."

Sarasa was surprised at the chancellor's answer. She understood, and wasn't all that shocked that he would come to that decision. However, she was surprised that he would bother to meet with them if he wasn't interested in their help. She said, "If you don't want our help, why did you venture out into the cold to tell us yourself? You could have sent a messenger to tell us that, or you could have simply ignored our missive all together."

"Like I said, I was intrigued. Also, I wanted to give you some information. I was in Clornoss a few days ago, and I was surprised about how few troops are in the city. Even the palace stands mostly unguarded. Many of the troops have been redeployed to defend garrisons against Magi attacks, and very recently the emperor sent most of his elite troops, the Wyverns, on a mission. I'm told that some troops are being pulled from a large force that's been battling the dwarves in the far north, and they'll be deployed in Clornoss to bolster the defenses there. I thought you'd like to know that until those new troops arrive in Clornoss, the capital city stands vulnerable. The emperor is vulnerable."

"Well I'll be a troll humping chippie!" As soon as she said it, Firana clapped her hand over her mouth and apologized.

Sarasa barely noticed the vulgarity. She said, "By the gods, are you sure? How long do we have until the replacement soldiers arrive?"

"Hours? Days maybe? I have no way to be sure. The ministers I talked to made it sound like they expected the troops to arrive any day, and that was a few days ago. As far as I know it could already be too late, but I thought I would ride out here and meet with you and give you that intelligence in case it was useful to your cause."

She walked over and shook his hand, "Chancellor Gehrey, it was a pleasure to meet you. Thank you for sharing this information. We wish you and your city good fortunes."

The chancellor smiled as he shook her hand. "The pleasure was mine. Safe travels, Magi."

He left the barn, and his soldiers followed behind.

When the Magi were alone in the barn, Bull said, "What should we do?"

Sarasa shrugged, "I guess we go back and tell the rest of the council, and then we'll vote on what to do next."

Peke shook his head, "I don't know, Sarasa. There is no telling when the rest of the council will return from their various missions. Every hour we waste is one more hour for those reinforcements to arrive. If the emperor is vulnerable now, this could be an opportunity like we'll never get again."

She put her hands on her hips, and sighed. Sarasa didn't like the idea of running into the middle of things once again. As she thought about it, she did have a bit of a history of doing that and it didn't always turn out well. Memories of being almost dead, hiding in a box in the basement of a house in the Stronghold flashed through her mind. She said, "Or it could be a trap."

He shook his head again, "No, he was being honest with everything he said. I had my magesight open for most of the conversation, and I have no doubt that he was telling the truth."

Firana placed her hand on Sarasa's shoulder, "I say we do this while we can. You know that Dalen would agree."

Sarasa chuckled, "Yes he would. But I know that Rissyl would not agree. He would most adamantly disagree."

"Let's do this for Ranik and all of the other Magi and non-magical folks who have died because of the sarding emperor." Bull looked more serious than she'd ever seen him.

She sighed once again. "You're right. Let's do this. Bull, hit us with some defensive enchantments."

- = - = -

"I'm sorry I can't get us any closer to the palace. This is the closest I've been to Clornoss, so it's the only reference point I had where I could teleport."

Sarasa patted Firana on the back as she looked around at their surroundings. "Don't worry about it, this will work fine."

They were in the country, not far from the Clornoss portal stone. The walls of the capital city were visible off in the distance. She saw a farm close by, in the general direction of the city so she headed that way.

As they got nearer to the farm, it appeared to be vacant. To no one in particular she asked, "Why are so many of these farms empty?"

Peke replied, "I've been pondering the same question. I would assume it's because of the conscription orders."

"Look over there. These farmers left so quickly that they just abandoned their cows. Poor cows, they must be starving!" Bull looked distressed and made a sad mooing sound.

Firana smacked him with the backside of her hand. "Cows eat grass, goblin-brains."

"I've got an idea to get into the palace, let's see if they left their wagon." Sarasa picked up the pace.

They found a wagon stored neatly in the barn.

Bull looked at the wagon, and then out at the city walls in the distance. He guessed, "We're going to build a ram, attach it to the wagon, and bash our way into the palace?"

"Not quite. I'm going to cast an illusion of a bunch of produce in the back of the wagon, and then we're going to hide under a tarp and Peke is going to drive us right to the delivery area of the palace." Sarasa started arranging the tarp in the back of the wagon.

Peke looked thoughtful, "That's a really good idea. I'll transform myself into an old farmer so I don't look threatening."

"You know what's even less threatening? Old farmer's wives! You should transform into an old woman." Bull laughed exuberantly and gave

Peke a playful push.

"If I was going to transform into a woman, it would be a young farming wife with really big-"

Firana tossed a handful of hay at the two men. "Yes, Peke. We get the point." Her words were sharp, but her tone was playful.

Sarasa, however, sounded annoyed. "Yes, yes. Diddies are great fun. But we've got a palace to invade and an imperial leader to kill, could you please take this seriously?"

"Sorry, I get goofy when I'm about to go to combat. It calms me down." Bull didn't sound apologetic.

"We should take a minute to plan things. When we get to the palace, are we going to sneak in a side entrance and try to make it to the emperor unnoticed?" Peke looked to Sarasa with his question.

She shook her head, "I could sneak around easily enough, but stealth is not everyone's strength. Even a disguise would only get us so far once we get to the palace. I think, once we get inside we'll go in proudly as Magi. Let them know we're there. We'll deal with the guards as they come. Let's try not to hurt the servants if we can avoid it, but let them know we're there so they can spread the word. Let the people know that the Magi came and brought justice to the throne of the empire!"

Bull let out a woot, and the others joined in.

Once things settled down, they set about getting things situated. They pushed the wagon outside, and then started the task of getting the oxen hooked up to the front of it. It ended up being much more challenging than she originally expected.

Eventually they rounded up two large bulls and secured them in the yoke and to the wagon. The leather straps that went over the oxen's heads were also challenging, but eventually they got everything ready.

Sarasa summoned the magic for her illusion, and formed it into the proper shapes for the complicated spell. When it was just right, she touched the wagon and said, "Taln'Fo Denar."

The back of the wagon instantly became filled with dozens of baskets of produce, bags of wheat and flour, kegs of cider, and various other goods. She placed her hand through the illusion and lifted the tarp.

"Climb on in." Sarasa climbed under the tarp after Bull and Firana.

Before long she heard Peke say loudly, "Giddyap!"

The wagon jerked forward and they were underway.

The burlap tarp was heavy and scratchy. Bull said, "This sucks already.

If we're in an illusion, we do we gotta be under a tarp?"

Sarasa sighed, "Because, if we're moving around inside of the illusion it could cause the soldiers to see through it. The tarp will help protect the illusion."

He moaned, "Well, I shouldn't have had all those beans for lunch."

"I swear to the gods, Bull. If you break wind under this tarp, I'll stab you in the arse!" Firana scooted a bit away from the others.

It was like she was invading the imperial capital with children. Once again she sighed. "If I have to have Peke stop this wagon, you're both getting whooped."

Bull giggled, "Sorry mom!"

They all laughed, and the tension of the upcoming mission lifted a bit.

The ride to the southern gate of the city was rough and uneventful. Before long, Peke brought the wagon to a stop and Sarasa heard someone walk over to the front of the wagon.

"Where you headed, gramps?"

"Delivery, for the palace." Peke's voice sounded old and gruff.

"You're overdue, they're gonna be happy to see you. Hurry along."

The wagon jerked forward once again. Several minutes later the whole routine was repeated when they got to the internal gate between the Commons and the Garden District.

Eventually, Peke brought the wagon to a halt and she could hear him climbing out of the driver's bench.

There was a lot of commotion around the area, and she heard several people commenting about a delivery of goods.

Peke lifted the end of the tarp, and said, "We're here! But there's no sneaky way to get you out."

Sarasa stood up, dismissed the illusion, and tossed the tarp to the side. As she did so, she summoned her grey and black Magi Cloak and many of her weapons. With a quick spell, she activated the magic within her leather armor, causing her to appear mostly transparent. It was an effect called *Ghostly Displacement*, and it was an illusionary concealment that caused her to appear ghost-like and slightly away from her actual location. In training, the enchantment had been highly effective in helping her avoid blows from her attacker, even when she fought unarmed and without the ability to block or parry.

The disappearance of the goods in the back of the wagon, and the sudden appearance of people emerging from beneath a tarp, sent the people in the courtyard into a panic.

The wagon was stopped in a wide courtyard, in the back of the palace, near what was probably the servant's entrance. There were several people around the area, all of whom looked like cottars, scullions, and laborers of various types. None of them appeared to be a threat, and they all scrambled to get away from the Magi.

The other Magi followed Sarasa's lead and summoned their cloaks and weapons.

Bull drew the massive greataxe from its holder across his back, and held it menacingly in front of him as he hopped from the back of the wagon. He said, "The Magi Society has arrived, and we're hungry for vengeance!"

A porter at the servant's entrance to the palace took a step forward and held his arms to the side, trying to block the door. In a shaky voice, he said, "You may not enter! I'll call the guards!"

Firana hopped casually from the wagon, and pointed the end of her staff towards the porter's feet. She said, "Krol'Fe." A small mint green orb shot from the top of her staff and slammed into the ground right in front of the porter's feet.

The man screamed and jumped to the side as the *Force Orb* shattered, throwing dirt and rocks around the area. He ran along the side of the building, trying to stay as far away from the Magi as he could as he made his escape.

Bull walked up to the door and flung it open. As he walked in, he shouted, "Stand clear, imperials! The Magi Society is here to bust some arse!"

Sarasa followed closely behind him, and the other two Magi trailed her through the door.

They walked down a long hallway with doors on either side, and Bull continued to yell the whole way. Those servants that they encountered were quick to flee when they discovered the Magi.

A young man crossed their path at an intersection of hallways, and Bull grabbed him as he tried to rush away. He seemed to be in his early to mid teens and Sarasa guessed that the boy was a page. He dropped several letters and packages as Bull grabbed him.

In an intimidating voice, Bull growled, "Take us to the emperor, and I won't cut you into little chunks."

The young man tried to pull away, but Bull held him tight. He looked at the Magi defiantly, "Go sard yerself, Magi!"

Firana stepped up to the young man, and rummaged around in a pouch. She pulled out a platinum coin, and held it up. "We'll give you a raptor, if you take us to the emperor."

The page reached out to grab the coin, but she pulled it away.

She said, "After you take us to him."

He looked from her to Bull and back. Then he said, "Emperor could be most anywhere at this time of day. I'll take ya to his suites, that's the best I can do. If he ain't there, the servants there'll know where he is."

She nodded and put the coin back in the pouch. "It's a deal. Take us to his suites, and we'll give you the raptor."

Bull released the young man and he didn't move. He said, "Make it two raptors and I'll take ya through the servant's halls, so you miss mosta the guards."

Firana hesitated and Sarasa said, "Yep, kid. Let's do it. Lead the way."

The page led them through a maze of narrow hallways, up some stairs and then back down others. Bull stopped yelling and focused on following the fast young man through the palace. After a number of twists and turns, Sarasa was completely lost. As they walked the hallways, alarm bells started chiming throughout the palace.

The page said, "Someone alerted the guards, they now know you're here."

Bull grunted, "Good!"

"Keep going, kid." Sarasa pushed the page in the back, gently, urging him along faster.

In some areas the servant's hallways intersected with wider corridors used by the rest of the palace occupants, and the page led them back into the more narrow hallways meant for staff. Along the way they encountered a couple of patrols of palace guards, but Bull dispatched them with little effort.

Eventually the young man stopped at a large door. He said, "The outer room of the emperor's suites is on the other side of this door. There'll be guards in there." He held out his hand.

Sarasa and Firana both placed a platinum coin in his hand.

He looked down and inspected the coins, and then he rushed off down the hall the way they'd come.

Without warning, Bull opened the door and rushed through.

The room was filled with at least a dozen palace soldiers, who were all wearing the blue and black tabard of the Wyvern regiment. The soldiers fought bravely, but they were no match for four fully prepared Magi.

The flurry of flashing blades and streaking magical spells lasted only a few seconds. Sarasa's blades dispatched two of the skilled soldiers and when she looked for her third, they were all dead.

Bull didn't wait. As soon as the last guard fell, the Magi was rushing on through the double doors to the next room of the emperor's suites.

The room was empty.

He continued from room to room, and the next several were either empty or had only a servant cowering in a corner begging to be spared. They ignored the servants and kept going from room to room, looking for the emperor.

When Bull kicked through the elaborate double doors leading to a grand library, he was greeted by several Wyvern soldiers. He was off-balance, from kicking in the doors and the first attack slammed hard into the breastplate of his armor.

He roared and brought his greataxe slamming down onto the head of the nearest guard.

A grey Rolimi dog climbed out of the floor and rushed at the nearest soldier. Sarasa's Rolimi dog was small and it had shaggy fur, short legs, and a short furry snout.

A series of force orbs streaked passed Sarasa as she prepared to throw a dagger at one of the soldiers. Firana continued to lob sphere after sphere of the mint green orbs into room.

In the corner of the room, with his back pressed up against large bookcases, the emperor screamed wildly. "Kill the Magi, dammit! Kill them all! How dare those vile filthy wretches foul my palace with their presence! Kill them!"

The emperor's maniacal screeches were muffled by the battle cries and death screams of the warriors.

The Wyvern soldiers battled bravely to their last breath, but soon after bursting through the door the Magi had killed every soldier in the room.

Bull rushed forward with his greataxe poised high, ready to crash down into the emperor's head. He shouted, "I sentence you to death for your many crimes!"

Sarasa suddenly had second thoughts about killing him. She could almost hear Rissyl arguing to take the emperor and lock him in the Stronghold dungeon until they could hold a trial. She rushed over to Bull and grabbed one of his large arms. "Wait! We can't kill him!"

The large Order of Champions Magi was incredulous. He turned slightly, so he could see her. "What!"

She turned to Peke, "Firana and Peke, guard the door!" Then she turned to the emperor. "Emperor Ryal III, as the Grand Shadow of the Sovereign Magi Society, I am taking you prisoner for crimes against me and countless others! If you resist I will kill you where you stand."

The emperor thrashed his hands about wildly, as if batting at a swarm of bugs, trying to keep the Magi away from him. He bellowed, "Get away from me! Guards! Guards! Kill these sarding Magi!"

Bull swung the huge greataxe horizontally at the emperor's head. For an instant she thought that he intended to decapitate the hated man, and she wouldn't have blamed him if he did. Instead, he smashed the flat side of the massive weapon up against the emperor's head.

The emperor slammed up against the bookcase, and slumped to the ground like he was dead.

Peke shouted, "I think we have more coming, get ready!"

Sarasa replied, "Let's get out of here. Bull, carry the emperor! Firana, take us directly to the Stronghold's dungeons!"

"Kur'Gezbar!" Firana vanished.

Moving to the middle of the room, Sarasa activated her portal ring. The portal appeared in front of her outstretched hand and within seconds the swirling colors merged into an image within the hallways of the dungeon.

Bull rushed through the portal, carrying the unconscious leader of the empire.

As soon as Peke stepped through the portal, Sarasa stepped in behind him.

The dungeon was fairly dark and very cold.

With the emperor still in his arms, Bull walked into an empty cell. He dumped the unconscious man on the ground unceremoniously, and then walked back into the hall.

Sarasa closed the door with a loud crash, and made sure that it was locked securely.

"By the gods, Rasa. We really did it!" Firana embraced her in a tight hug.

"And I didn't end up almost dead in a box. What a refreshing change. Now I need an ale." Sarasa patted her on the back, and then stepped away from the embrace.

Bull cheered loudly, "The war's finally over! And I'm the hero! Woo hoo! Let's go celebrate!"

She had her doubts that the war was over. They had the emperor, but there were still plenty of people to take his place. This was a major victory, and she fully intended to celebrate, but she'd be very surprised if the battles were over. She followed the others down the hall and out of the dungeons.

CHAPTER 32

Jessa

For three days they had been marching, and Jessa was beginning to wonder if they'd ever arrive in Khardifar. Traveling with an army was even slower than walking on her own, because there were heavy wagons and supplies that had to be brought along.

She spent most of her time in a fancy covered carriage with the prince. The two ministers rode in another carriage, and there were several wagons carrying various officers and their servants and helpers.

The vast majority of the army was marching on foot, in long columns of four and at the front of the army were dozens of horsemen in full armor.

A couple of days ago, their force met with a larger group of soldiers traveling from the west and headed to the capital. The prince ordered them to merge with his troops, and the army's size more than tripled that day.

Edal hadn't mentioned Jalinox's death since they left his compound. When they arrived back at the palace, Minister Vendino was unwilling to wait even a minute when Jalinox didn't arrive as expected. He seemed almost giddy to see the army begin its journey without Jalinox. She wondered how happy the minister would be to hear of the necromancer's death. He'd probably throw a party.

A commotion up ahead broke the monotony of the trip, and she looked to the window of the carriage with interest as a rider on horseback approached.

He said, "My prince, we've encountered someone walking up the road. He is a soldier from the Tharrin garrison. We're bringing him to you now."

The prince opened the door, hopped out of the slow-moving carriage, and started walking beside it. She climbed out after him.

Several other riders approached as Jessa walked at the slow pace of the army. A man climbed down off a horse from behind a knight. He nervously saluted the prince. The soldier seemed very young and his uniform was tattered and bloody.

He said, "Sir, there has been an uprising in Tharrin. The Magi helped the city attack our garrison. Our entire company is dead, other than me. The Magi sent me to tell the emperor that Tharrin is no longer a part of the empire."

Ministers Thorli and Vendino walked up as the soldier delivered his message.

The prince smiled wickedly. He said, "Go to the mess wagon and eat something. Then take a horse and continue on to Clornoss and deliver your message."

Thorli shook his head, "This is terrible news. The secession problem is spreading, we need to get a handle on things before they get completely out of control."

"I don't think it's terrible news, General Thorli. Tharrin is much closer than Khardifar. We're less than a day away. We'll make an example of Tharrin and then march on to deal with Khardifar as well. When we're done, no other city will dare defy us!"

- = - = -

The next morning the army arrived at the city walls of Tharrin. The army had stopped for the night a few hours after encountering the soldier from the Tharrin garrison. Like normal, the bugle sounded much earlier than Jessa would have liked, and the army was back underway before the sun was fully risen.

After just a few hours of marching this morning, the prince called it to a halt not far from the city's walls.

She could see the archers along the wall, scurrying from place to place. They were surely raising the alarm and alerting the city's troops that the imperial army had arrived. She imagined that the Tharrins were afraid as they looked out at the large army gathered outside their walls. They should be afraid, for they had no idea what they were really up against.

Jessa followed the prince to the minister's carriage.

"General Thorli, have your captains report to me. I'd like to give a brief talk to the command staff before we break ranks and spread out for the attack."

The old general saluted his prince casually, and hurried off to carry out the order.

Several minutes later he returned with four officers trailing behind him. One of them wore full battle armor and the tabard of the mounted troops. Another one wore the lighter armor and tabard of the Wyvern regiment from the palace. The other two wore footmen's armor and tabards that she didn't recognize, they were blue and black like the others but the silhouetted animal emblazoned on one was a tiger and the other was a panther. They were the tabards worn by troops that the army met along the road outside of Clornoss.

Those troops had been under orders to reinforce the capital, but the prince had ordered them to join his force for the attack on the southern city.

Thorli stopped before the prince and saluted once again. He said, "Captain-General Edal, these four captains are the commanders of the four regiments currently in our army."

The captains saluted and stood at rigid attention before the prince.

The prince walked up to two of them on the right side of the line and placed one hand on each of their shoulders. He said, "May Wirmyntas guide your way and lead us to victory!"

The two captains gasped briefly. Their faces twisted in anguish and Jessa saw small flames flicker in their eyes for a fraction of a second as the demons took possession of their bodies.

The other two captains shifted their weight nervously, as the prince stepped over to them and placed his hands on their shoulders. Once again he said, "May Wirmyntas guide your way and lead us to victory!"

Like the others, the incredible pain ripped across their face as the flame danced in their eyes. It only took a moment for the demons to inhabit their bodies. An eye blink later the torment faded, and the captains looked like nothing strange had occurred.

She could hear murmuring between the two ministers, but neither of them spoke aloud.

The prince stepped away from the captains, and then faced them. In a commanding voice, he said, "Go now, and prepare your troops! Inspire them to victory in Wirmyntas' name!"

As the captains rushed off to address their troops, Jessa felt something strange happening to her head.

It was as if something was calling out to her, beguiling her somehow. She felt a sense of rage and a primal desire to battle and kill. These were not unusual feelings for her, but they were building with an intensity that she'd never experienced. The longer she stood there, the foggier things became. She felt herself slowly losing control, like another entity was slowly gaining influence over her.

When she took a step against her will, she knew that something nefarious was at play and it was gaining control of her. She gathered all of her will, and threw up a *Spell-bane Aegis* ward around her mind. As soon as the spell took effect she felt the fogginess begin to subside. It was a simple Society Magi skill that she learned long ago when Rissyl and the others first accepted her as a Magi, and it was meant to protect her from spells that affect the mind. It was something she practiced sometimes, in preparation for a battle against the Magi. She never imagined she'd need it to protect against her allies.

The prince looked at her for a moment, and smiled wickedly. He said, "You surprise me, princess. I didn't expect you'd have the ability to shield your mind from the demons' *Dominion Ripple*. Most impressive, you will indeed make for a worthy wife and a powerful warlock in your own right."

She had no intention of arguing with him at the moment about whether she would become his wife. Instead she watched as the army began to spread out in preparation for the attack on the city.

Edal walked towards the city, and as he walked he raised his hand with the palm towards the sky. Dozens of small demons popped out of the ground and began running alongside him. He continued walking with his hand raised, and demons continued popping up behind him. They spread out to the sides and soon there were a hundred or more of them. They leapt and hopped as they scurried along beside him.

The snow melted as the legion of demons pranced over it, leaving a wide swath of scorched brush and dirt in their wake. Small fires burned briefly and then extinguished, leaving small trails of smoke drifting in the air.

The ministers walked passed her, and she moved in step with them. Both men looked as entranced as the other people around them. They sneered and marched towards the city with weapons drawn. Even Vendino brandished a small dagger and looked ready to kill the first enemy that approached him.

If they noticed the legion of demons, they didn't mention it. She assumed that they were completely enraptured by the demons that now possessed the four captains. Or perhaps Edal had gifted the ministers with demons of their own, without her noticing. It surely wouldn't surprise her.

As soon as the approaching army was within range, the Tharrin archers unleashed several volleys of arrows. Some of the first troops dropped to the ground, dead from arrows, but the rest of the troops pressed on as if they didn't even notice. The army didn't run, it simply marched towards the city at a fast pace.

The legion of demons rushed through the troops and soon moved to the very front of the army. When they reached the city walls, the demons easily leapt up to the tops of the walls and attacked the archers.

By the time the first soldiers reached the walls and leaned ladders against them, all of the archers on the tops of the walls were dead. The soldiers began streaming up the ladders and onto the walls.

It didn't take them long to open the city gates for the mounted knights and the main portion of the army to enter the city.

When the prince got close to the imperial soldiers who had been killed by the archers, he turned to Jessa and said, "Your Awakened Spawn await, princess."

She said a quick prayer to Viator, and raised a dozen of the recently slain troops to be her undead minions. They climbed to their feet and started ambling towards the gate.

When she got near him, he said, "Let's take a better look at the city, before it's destroyed. Shall we?" He reached out and grabbed her shoulder.

The falling feeling lasted only a moment, and suddenly she was standing on the top of the city wall.

Down below the battle was intense and it spread throughout the city.

The Tharrin soldiers were losing badly. Most of the demons had already spread out through the city, leaving the enraptured imperial soldiers to battle the few remaining Tharrins.

Jessa could see the demons smashing through doors and entering the houses looking for the living. Several of them were spitting streams of fire at the houses as they entered, and the city burned in many places.

The prince began pointing around the battlefield below him, and the dead began to rise to do his bidding. She could see their eyes glowing bright green, and she knew that these were not like her Awakened Spawn. These were the Drudges reanimated in the name of Wirmyntas.

Her Awakened, with their red glowing eyes, required a mostly intact body in order to animate them. They would be destroyed if their heart was destroyed, and she had to concentrate on each of them to maintain control over them.

The Drudges didn't require an intact body. Even just the skeletal remains of a person or creature could be reanimated as a Drudge, needing only a skull to remain animated. From what she'd been told the Drudges didn't need to be individually controlled. They were given a simple mission when they were animated and they would single mindedly follow the simple instruction until given different instructions. This would give the prince the freedom to raise many of them.

She watched as each of the dead warriors below them, both imperial and Tharrin, rose from the ground and shambled off in search of a victim.

If the tremendous display of power was draining him somehow, the prince didn't show it. He stood proud and tall, looking out over the battle.

It struck her as odd that there were almost no civilians running about, or scattered dead along the streets. If they were hiding in their houses, then many of them were dead already.

The fires were spreading quickly and a dense smoke was billowing from many different sections of the city. Even the palace, far on the other side of the city, was engulfed in flames.

The ministers stepped off of a ladder, onto the top of the wall and stood next to the prince.

For several long minutes they stood and watched the city burn. Most of the demons, soldiers, and Drudges had moved far into the city and she could only see a few of them.

Eventually, the prince looked over to Thorli and said, "General, sound the withdrawal. Our work here is done."

Even before the general lifted the bugle to his lips, the prince's legions began obeying his commands. General Thorli blared the retreat tune through his bugle, over and over. The sound was echoed by several other bugles scattered around the city.

Soon the demons began to pounce down the streets and out of the gates, followed by the beguiled troops, and eventually the slow moving Drudges.

Fires were spreading quickly, and by the time the final Drudges were moving out of the gates, most of the city was a roaring inferno. The flames were even starting to lick up towards the top of the wall near them, as it consumed nearby buildings.

Jessa didn't even realize the prince had placed his hand on her shoulder, until the falling feeling grabbed her unexpectedly. An instant later, she was standing in the field outside of the city. They were in the middle of the army, and it was marching intently away from the city.

She asked, "Where are we going?"

"Khardifar, of course."

"Don't you think the complete destruction of this city will get your point across and bring the other cities in line?"

"Father wants the heads of the Khardifar chancellor and its Council of Ministers on pikes outside of Clornoss. I intend to animate them as Drudges and have them walk themselves back to the capital with us while their city burns to the ground."

She looked at him, wondering if it was stupid to ask her next question. "What will the Denizens of Clornoss think, seeing the dead walking and demons frolicking among the troops? Surely you won't possess them all with demons or enrapture the entire capital city, will you?"

"Sadly, no. It would bring order to the heathens of our city, but no that is far beyond my powers. Even this army before us is approaching the extent of my powers and I must dismiss most of these demons or risk losing control of them. That would be devastating, indeed."

He reached his hand out, palm down and lowered it towards the ground. All of the demons began popping back into the ground, retreating back to Khalius. Before long, they were all gone.

She asked, "What about the demons in the captains. Have you dismissed them as well?"

He shook his head, "No, when I release them the captains will of course drop dead. Then I'd be left with no one to lead the regiments. I'd need to promote people to replace them, and then possess them with their own demons when we get to Khardifar. Instead I'll just maintain them until we're done with this messy business."

"How long is this march to Khardifar going to take? I'm growing weary of sleeping with bugs. I really hate bugs." She shivered, thinking back to the awful bug incident on her trek through the mountain to the Magi Stronghold.

"Several days, I'm sure. Twice as long if we take the Drudges along, but less time if we force the army to march there without sleeping."

She groaned. "Why don't you just use your warlock powers and zap the army to Khardifar, like you and I have been traveling from place to place?"

"That ability is limited to the number of people that I can grab, so me and two others. Not an army."

"Dammit. Well, lose the Drudges and make the troops keep walking until we get there. I want to get this over with, so I can go home."

He turned to her, "So we can go home and get married?"

She didn't answer right away. "I thought you wanted to wait until after the war with the Magi was over?"

"If the destruction of an entire city doesn't bring the Magi out of hiding, then they're truly cowards. No, I suspect that the Magi will rally to the defense of Khardifar now that Tharrin has been destroyed. The battle at Khardifar will surely go down in the histories as the final battle of the war against the Magi."

"And if it doesn't?"

"If they don't come to the defense of the people in Khardifar, then we'll leave those smoldering ruins and march directly to the Mazbakhar Halls. We'll meet up with the main imperial army there. Then we'll vanquish the dwarves and march right to the Magi Stronghold and kill the cowards behind their own walls."

She looked away from him. "And then we can get married."

"Then we can get married, after you've completed the rites to become a warlock and you've pledged your soul to Wirmyntas."

CHAPTER 33

Kimly

The flames continued to burn unhindered throughout most of Tharrin. Kimly was sitting on the third-floor balcony of a large villa in the countryside not far from the city. Her feet were propped up on a hassock and she was snuggled back into the most comfortable chair she'd ever found. In one hand she had a large silver goblet of delicious wine and her other hand was buried in a bowl filled with dried fruits and nuts.

When she was a young girl she used to love sitting near a big fire and watch the flames flicker and dance before her. She found it soothing and a bit mesmerizing.

The view of Tharrin burning to the ground was no different. The smoke was thick in places, and it obscured her view of the fire sometimes so that was a little disappointing. However, for an event that was probably pretty tragic for a lot of folks, she found it wildly entertaining and even fairly relaxing.

It started out much less enjoyable.

She had come to Tharrin a couple of days ago to try to meet with Shrouded members, and bring on a few new people. She hadn't planned for Tharrin to defy the emperor, and she really hadn't expected the imperial army to burn the city to the ground.

While she was teaching some new Shrouded members, everything was turned upside down. When the Decree Callers rushed through the city announcing mandatory evacuation of the entire city she decided to stay around to see what happened.

By nightfall the vast majority of the people had fled the city. There were several troops and foolhardy Denizens who wanted to stay behind to fight, but most of the streets were empty. The people evacuated the city in such a hurry that they left many of their valuables locked in their houses.

It was a dream of a lifetime for a rogue.

When the imperial army arrived, she knew that the treasure hunting had come to an end. She figured she'd have plenty of time to stash away some goodies and then sneak out of the city before the fighting reached the Gardens District. She certainly didn't anticipate the army pouring into the city so quickly, and she didn't imagine that there would be an army of vicious little monsters.

She barely got out of the city alive. The painful cuts on her arms, legs, and back were a brutal reminder of how close the little fire monsters had come to completely ruining her fun.

Sadly, she lost most of her treasures in the wild flight from the city and the battles that happened along the way. She was able to get a few nice trinkets and knickknacks, so it wasn't a total loss.

Kimly wasn't the only enterprising thief who tried to profit from the evacuated city. She saw several of them killed when the imperial army arrived, and she had been forced to kill a couple of them when she claimed this villa as her temporary lodging.

As she watched the fire burn her mood turned a little melancholy. The fire was fascinating, and its warmth was definitely appreciated. However, it was hard to enjoy watching the city burn to the ground and not be sad about all of that fantastic treasure that was being destroyed in the intense fire. It was such a terrible waste.

She finished the wine in her goblet, and then emptied the bottle as she refilled the silver vessel. The owners of the villa could have at least left behind a Dreg or two to fetch her another bottle of wine. Now, if she wanted another bottle, she'd have to go to the wine cellar herself.

She sighed in annoyance.

The fire was beginning to burn lower. It wouldn't be long before all she could see over the city walls was the thick smoke, which would probably pour from the city for many more hours.

She took several large gulps and finished off the wine. With any luck, the army had moved far enough away by now to give her a clear path to the portal stone. If she was going to save any of her favorite things, she probably needed to get back to Khardifar pretty soon.

Most likely there wasn't a lot of time to waste, but she couldn't resist looking through the villa for a few minutes to see if there was anything fun left behind.

It would take several days for the army to get all of the way to Khardifar, but she would like to get there and hire a few wagons before word of the destruction of Tharrin arrived in that city. By tomorrow or the next day some of the refugees on horseback would probably arrive in

Khardifar. Once the people realized that Khardifar was doomed there would be mass hysteria and it would be dreadfully expensive to find someone to transport her favorite things from the city.

The main bedrooms in the villa seemed pretty well cleaned out, as she poked around. Either looters had beaten her to the prizes, or the owners took the best stuff with them when they evacuated.

She grabbed a couple of cute little golden statues on her way down the stairs, and stuffed them into one of her many already overly-full pockets.

There was a large dappled horse in the stables behind the villa, and she walked up to the large animal. She'd never been great with horses, but maybe she could convince the creature to carry her to the portal stone. That would save her several minutes of walking.

The horse was well trained and patiently waited for her to pull herself onto his back. She didn't bother with a saddle, since she wasn't sure how to put it on properly anyway.

The ride through the open fields was exhilarating, and she spent the whole time holding the animal's neck for dear life. After a bit of difficulties guiding it, she found that if she leaned to one side or the other, the horse would turn in that direction.

Far too quickly they arrived at the portal stone. She slid from the back of the horse, and stood there admiring it. For the first time, she saw what made some people so crazy about the animals.

She gave it a hug around its large chest, and said, "I'm glad you weren't eaten by fire monsters. Thanks for the ride. You're free to run and play, but don't go that way, the army went that way. Bye!"

She smacked the large animal lightly and shooed it to the east. Then she activated the portal, causing it to raise from the ground. The obelisk was three feet tall when it emerged fully from the dirt. The magical runes down the sides of the portal stone started glowing as she touched it. She summoned the magic for the spell and then said, "Tryz Uni Ac'Tovik."

The vertigo from teleporting, and a whole bottle of wine, combined to make for an unpleasant arrival outside of Khardifar. She held the portal stone for a few minutes until the spinning stopped.

The walk into Khardifar went fairly quickly. She debated whether to go home first or see Favin first, and after a bitter internal argument she decided to talk to Favin first.

It felt odd to walk down the streets of Khardifar and for everything to seem normal compared to what she saw in Tharrin. The people went about their evening business completely oblivious to the fact that Tharrin was a smoldering ruin. When the first riders from Tharrin arrived the streets would be chaos and this sense of normalcy would evaporate quickly.

When she walked into the building used for the headquarters of Favin's guild, she took a deep breath. The place had a distinct smell and she'd never really noticed it until then. It was a mixture of several scents, and she was going to miss it when the place was burned to the ground.

She found Favin in his office with Scoots. They were sitting on either side of his desk, discussing something quietly.

When he saw her come in, he said, "Welcome back, Kimly. That mission that you assigned has been completed without any complications."

She sat down on a crate next to Scoots. "That's good, thanks Favin."

"You don't sound very happy about it. Are you having second thoughts about leaving him?"

Kimly shook her head, "No, I'm not having second thoughts. It's been a rough day and I've had way too much wine."

He made a sour face, "Yes, I can smell the wine. Scoots took care of things at the warehouse. Everything went flawlessly."

She barely listened to his word, and instead of responding to him she simply said, "Tharrin is gone."

Favin looked at her with an expression that showed he had no clue what she meant. He said, "Huh?"

Kimly shrugged. "Burned to the ground by the imperial army."

The other two both cursed out loud in surprise.

He leaned back in his chair in disbelief. "What about all of the people?"

"Burned to death, I'm sure. Well, at least the ones who weren't eaten by the fire monsters or slaughtered by the troops. I suppose the good news is that a lot of the people were evacuated before the army arrived, so we'll be flooded with refugees pretty soon."

Favin placed both palms against his temples and leaned back further. Scoots buried her face in her hands.

Everyone was quiet for a long time.

Finally, he said, "Fire monsters? We've got to warn people, and get the guild members as well-armed and armored as we can. When the army arrives, we need to be prepared!"

She looked at him like he had grown a second head. "Get them armed? Are you stupid? We've gotta get out of this sarding city before the army burns it to the ground!"

"Without warning people? Kimly, even you can't be that heartless. Can you?" His words were barely more than a whisper, and they were filled with disbelief.

She stood up, waving her arms angrily. "Heartless? It ain't heartless, it's called survival! That's what I do, dammit! I survive because I look out for myself first!"

He crossed his arms at his chest, and raised his voice. "Then why are you here? Why not flee and not bother telling anyone? You've got plenty of money and you can use the portal stones. You could go anywhere you want."

"Because I didn't want you to be eaten by fire monsters! I thought we could relocate together, make a new start somewhere."

Scoots looked up at her. "What about me, and the rest of the guild?"

Kimly sat back down, "You could come with us, of course! All of The Shrouded could come, and we'll build a new guild in a different city, far from the war."

He lowered his voice back to normal. "I don't know, Kimly. My heart tells me to stay and fight. We're rogues but we're not cowards. I can't just abandon our guild. Besides, surely the Magi will help us?"

She was growing more annoyed that he wouldn't see reason. "Dammit Favin, you don't know what this army is like! Everyone who stays in this city will die, including the Magi if they try to get involved. When I say fire monsters, I mean really horrible creatures like something straight outta Khalius. Hundreds of them!"

He was quiet, and she continued, "And there was this aura that I can't explain, this feeling of dread and horror that threatened to take control of me. I ended up needing to raise wards around my mind to finally make it go away. I don't know what it was, but it felt like it would suck my free-will from me."

Scoots was the first to reply, "Where would we go?"

Favin sat forward and looked to Scoots, "You'd flee, and leave most everyone you know behind to die?"

"Kimly is right. We can stay here and be dead heroes, or we can survive and build a new life somewhere else. I plan to survive. With the exception of you two, no one in this city has ever given me anything. Since

I was little I've had to take anything I needed. I refuse to become a dead hero for a city that has given me nothing." Scoots opened a coin purse and started counting coins.

He dropped a hand to the desk. "Okay then, where would we go?"

Kimly said, "Over the last year or so I've purchased a few smallish houses in other cities. We could go to any of them."

He looked dumbfounded, "Why would you buy houses that you don't need?"

"I dunno? I like to have options. Besides, sometimes I like to have someplace quiet where I can just sit and be alone. Now that I'm rich my quiet hiding place doesn't have to be a musky mausoleum in a dreary cemetery, or hiding in someone's warehouse. My quiet place can be any of the nice houses that I own. They're quaint and have a few Dregs to keep things tidy and take care of my chamber pot."

Scoots smiled slightly, "Which one is your favorite?"

Kimly thought for a while, and then replied, "Thudo. The house isn't nearly as nice as some that I own, but it has a great view of the sea. More importantly, Thudo is far from all of this war and death. It's the largest city east of Clornoss, so there should be plenty of opportunities for enterprising rogues such as ourselves. The house is kind of small, but there are eight or nine bedrooms. It should be enough for all of us, until you get places of your own."

Favin smiled, "I think Viper spent some time in Thudo before he joined us. He might even have some contacts there. I think I am growing fonder of this idea. Should we at least warn the chancellor? He's been good to us."

With a playful smirk, Kimly shook her head. "And spoil the surprise? No, let's just get our affairs in order and get out of here before the chaos starts and the streets get flooded with people. I really don't want to get stuck in a mob of idiots wailing in despair. If we get split up, the Thudo portal stone number is twenty-eight, which is Tov Oxt in the language of magic."

He nodded, "Fine, I'll gather the other Shrouded so they can come with us, and I will be telling the members of the guild that they should evacuate anyway they can."

"Okay, do it quickly. Other than the jewels, coins, and my favorite hats there ain't much at home that I'll need to grab before I'm ready to go. I'll arrange for a wagon to bring the rest of my favorite things to Thudo if they can get them packed up and on the road before the killing starts."

CHAPTER 34

Sarge

The candles throughout the sanctuary flickered in the cold wind, when Sarge entered the temple. He closed the door quickly, and removed his heavy robes.

Madalyn rose and turned from the altar as he walked towards her. "You weren't gone long. Did you find them?"

"No, the army ain't made it to Khardifar yet."

"My prayer time is plagued with an overwhelming sense of foreboding. Great evil is already walking the lands."

He sat down in a pew in the middle of the sanctuary. "Yes, it's the Archwarlock. When I was in Khardifar, Kelegar spoke to me. My purpose in all of this is clearer."

She suddenly looked frightened, and she sat down next to him. "Archwarlock? What are you going to do, Theo?"

"What I must, sweet one. I've already talked to Rissyl. He says I'm a fool, but he won't try to stop me. I've come here to make sure you know that I'm proud of you, and that even if you were my own daughter I couldn't love you any more than I do." He wanted to say more, but his voice was already on the brink of revealing how close he was to tears.

"Don't talk like you're about to die! Now tell me what you're planning."

"Rissyl said that the imperial army destroyed Tharrin. They're surely marching to Khardifar right now."

She covered her mouth in shock and despair. "What about all of those people?"

He shook his head, "Most of the people were evacuated before the army arrived. The defenders are dead and the city is in ruins. Khardifar will be next if we don't do something."

"I hoped that since we captured the emperor the war would be over."

He patted her on the leg, "Me too."

Madalyn looked at him expectantly, still waiting for him to answer her question.

272

"The Magi are gonna attack the army. I've gotta go now and do my part. It's Kelegar's will, and my duty as his paladin."

She stood up and straightened her new robes. "Alright, but I'm coming with you."

"Absolutely not! You'll be staying right here, where you're needed."

"You mean I'll be staying here where I'm safe? Well, I most certainly will not be staying right here."

He stood up and hugged her tightly. "This is my destiny, not yours. You are meant for much greater things."

Sarge walked away so she wouldn't see his tears. He grabbed his heavy robes and stepped out the door into the cold.

As he was closing the door, he heard her say, "You've been like a father, and I love you too. You'd better come back to me!"

The door slammed harder than he intended, as he pulled against the strong winter winds.

His trek to the portal stone was mostly a blur, as he thought about the events of his life and how much things had changed in the last few years. Before long he was standing outside of Khardifar, holding tight to the portal stone there.

When the queasiness wore off, he walked over to the simple wagon parked nearby. He had left it there earlier.

Rissyl was probably right, he was a fool. As he urged the oxen forward, he reached into an interior pocket of his robes and pulled out his recorder. If he was going to be a fool, he'd be a fool who was enjoying a happy tune on his favorite instrument. The simple woodwind instrument whistled merrily in his practiced hands as he blew into it.

It was difficult to play while the wagon bounced down the road, and occasionally he had to pause his song to grab the reigns and redirect the cows when they got distracted or simply stopped walking all together. However, mostly he played his happy tune and tried not to think about the task ahead.

After a few hours of traveling, the sky began to darken and he stopped to set up camp for the night. The wagon was stocked with the things he'd need for a few days of travel, and the night passed quickly and uneventfully.

The next morning the driver's bench of the wagon seemed more uncomfortable than before. He was stiff and sore from sleeping on the ground. For years he had lived a nomadic life, sleeping under the stars and living off the land. He was surprised how quickly he had become soft, and how much he had grown to enjoy a warm bed and a soft pillow.

He wondered if he'd ever get to enjoy a wonderful bed again?

For much of that day he traveled silently, without song or instrument, just the creaking of the wagon and the occasional mooing of the oxen.

It had only been a couple of days since the destruction of Tharrin, and an army travels very slowly, so he expected to travel east from Khardifar for several days before he met up with the army.

He was wrong. By mid-day the imperial army appeared far off in the distance as they crested over the gently rolling prairie to the east.

Sarge's heart began beating heavily in his chest as he saw it for the first time. He was all alone, and before long they would be upon him. He said a quick prayer to Kelegar, asking for the strength and courage to go through with this.

It didn't take long and he was very near the army. He steered the wagon off of the road, to give them room to pass unhindered, as a merchant would likely do.

The army was larger than he expected. The Magi believed that most of the imperial army was amassed outside of the dwarven kingdom, so he didn't expect a huge force this far south.

Four mounted knights broke away from the rest of the formation and moved to intercept him. They marched in perfect step and turned in precise unison as they approached. The knights halted their horses before him and one of them said, "Where you headed, Denizen?"

Sarge waved and smiled, "Greetings soldiers! I'm a merchant from Bathok, on my way to Libur to trade my wares. I've got a great selection of jerky and smoked meats if you'd like some."

Something was coming for him, and it wasn't just the knights. It was a feeling deep inside, there was a powerful aura in the area, and it was calling to him. It wanted him to obey. The others had mentioned experiencing the same thing at the garrisons.

The knight replied, "You've been drafted, Denizen. Welcome to the imperial army. You will come with us."

Two of the knights dismounted and walked over to him.

He raised his hands, "I'm sorry, you've picked the wrong man. I'm a humble trader, not a warrior. Do these look like a warrior's hands to you? I'd make an awful soldier."

The two knights helped him down from the wagon.

The aura was insistent and it urged him to submit. He could feel his anger rising, and his nerves were on edge. He craved battle and he could sense the aura building that desire.

"Service to the emperor is every Denizen's duty. Follow us."

The knights remounted their horses and they all surrounded him. They led him into the heart of the army, weaving between many different columns of soldiers who marched along at the pace of the advancing force. He was surprised at how quickly they marched, for such a large army.

The aura was even more powerful as they moved through the troops, and he knew that he could wait no longer or he'd lose himself to the overpowering will of whatever was feeding that aura. He had hoped to gain a better understanding of the aura before blocking it, but he could not. He raised the wards around his mind. Instantly his head began to clear and he felt his temper calming.

As they led him through the midst of the army, he was astonished at how synchronized everyone was. He could hear some men calling out a simple marching cadence.

"Left. Left. Left, right, left. Left."

Over and over the cadence was called, and the entire army marched perfectly to the quick beat of the cadence.

He had been in the military long ago, and they hadn't been nearly this precise in their marching. Obviously, the soldiers of this army were under the influence of the aura, and it was guiding their movements. He wondered how much control the aura had over them.

When they arrived at a long line of wagons traveling two by two, the knights fell into the quick pace of the army. One of the knights said, "The quartermaster here will get your gear, and then you'll report to Sergeant Wilmer over there. You belong to him now."

The knights didn't wait for an answer, they hurried back towards the front of the army.

The quartermaster threw him a longsword in a scabbard attached to a belt, and a blue and black tabard with a tiger silhouette on the front and back. He didn't pay much attention to it, he simply slipped it on and buckled the sword around his waist.

As he walked to his new sergeant, he noticed a single soldier that was slightly out of step with everyone else. The man was in a company near the one led by his new sergeant. The man's timing was only slightly off, but it was enough to make him stand out in Sarge's mind.

While he walked, he casually looked at some of the soldiers around him. They looked angry, but they also looked tired. The bags under their eyes suggested that the men hadn't slept in days. The commanders must have pushed the men to march day and night since leaving Tharrin. That would explain how they made such good time, but he didn't think they'd be very effective in battle if they were never given any chance to sleep. He doubted even the aura could keep a man going when he was ready to drop from exhaustion.

He approached Sergeant Wilmer, and the man simply pointed towards the rear end of his company.

Sarge slowed his walk until he arrived at the back of the company of soldiers, and then he fell into step at the back of their line.

Then he marched.

The marching was at a very quick pace but it was monotonous. He did his best to march to the exact beat of the cadence like everyone else, so he didn't stand out. The last thing he needed was for someone to notice that he was out of step. He was a skilled fighter, but he wouldn't stand a chance all alone against an entire army if things turned ugly.

As he marched along in the midst of the army, he once again acknowledged that Rissyl and Madalyn were right about him being a fool. He knew that Kelegar wanted him within this force for some reason, but that's all he knew. What was he supposed to do? That was still a mystery. Originally he figured he'd be taken prisoner by the army, or maybe they'd simply pass him by. He didn't figure that he'd be sucked into it.

His only choice now was to keep marching and trust that Kelegar wouldn't simply lead him to slaughter for no reason.

He kept an eye on the soldier in the other company that had been slightly out of step. Most of the time he kept pace with everyone, but every once in a while Sarge noticed a slight alteration and it wasn't happening with any of the other soldiers.

Somehow that man had blocked the aura. When Sarge had passed him, he hadn't recognized him so he was fairly certain the man wasn't a Magi. However, he didn't know how else the man could block the aura.

He had plenty of time to ponder the curious situation, and his precarious predicament, as they marched on towards Khardifar.

He estimated that they would be in Khardifar by morning if they marched through the night. That was much sooner than the Magi expected. He said a little prayer to Kelegar that the Magi didn't spend too much time planning and preparing or it'd be too late.

The sun dropped low in the western sky, and Sarge mentally prepared himself for a long walk in the darkness.

Then, without warning, the cadence callers said, "Company. Halt!"

Every soldier within sight, with the exception of Sarge and the one soldier in the other company, stopped perfectly with the command as if they'd anticipated it.

Sarge had been deep in thought, and almost missed the command altogether. He almost smacked into the soldier in front of him, but he did manage to stop without any major incident.

He heard several leaders say, in unison, "Set up camp for the night!"

What had been a very precise and orderly formation of disciplined troops turned into the organized chaos of many men going in different directions to get the supplies and set up camp. He followed the men in front of him to a wagon and grabbed some of the things needed to build their temporary camp.

Many of the soldiers seemed a bit confused and disoriented, and they all looked exhausted. Some of the battle frenzy was gone from their eyes, but they still worked together efficiently as they set up camp.

He wondered if the power of the aura was still in place, so he lowered his wards. The aura was still there, but it felt much weaker than before. Whatever was controlling the army, it seemed content to give them some freedom for the time being.

Several soldiers from his company started working on a campfire.

A short man with a pointy nose said, "Where are we, anyway?"

A man with the name Surra tattooed on the back of his hand replied, "In the middle of nowhere, on our way somewhere. What does it matter?"

"When was the last time we slept? I'm about to drop." The man moved away from the smoke, as the campfire grew. He was tall and lanky, with long braided hair.

A soldier walked up with a waterskin and the men passed it around, each taking a long drink. Another man tossed them a small chunk of meat and a dry biscuit.

"By the gods, it's like I haven't eaten in days! Anyone want to share their portion?" The pointy nosed man looked around the group hopefully.

The man with the braid laughed, "Go sard yourself, troll humper! We're all hungry."

Pointy nose threw a stick in the fire. "Where are we going? I thought we were headed to Clornoss, but I can smell the sea. We're nowhere near Clornoss."

Tattooed man finished a long drink from the waterskin and then passed it along. He said, "You ask alotta questions. We're going where they say to go, that's what soldiers do. We march here and we march there. Sometimes we sit in a garrison and drill all day, and sometimes we march all day. Get used to it and stop asking so many stupid questions. If they wanted you to have an opinion the quartermaster would have issued one to you."

The conversations all around Sarge were much the same. Some of the soldiers were confused and curious about their surroundings, but most were simply content to accept that they were wherever they were, and they were doing what they were supposed to be doing.

As the meager dinner ended, some of the soldiers wasted no time in going to sleep. Others huddled around the fires to get warm and chat.

There didn't seem to be much organization to the camp, and many of the soldiers were walking about, so he risked moving around to find the soldier who seemed to be able to block out the aura.

It took quite a while, but eventually he found the man. He was sitting a bit away from the nearest fire, and Sarge walked up and sat down near him. The man just sat and stared at a campfire.

"I'm Sarge, what's your name?"

The man didn't look at him. "People call me Floppy."

Sarge raised an eyebrow, "That's an odd name. How'd you wind up out here, Floppy."

He was large and muscular, and his curly black hair was very short. He said, "I was drafted, and I don't want to chat."

In a low voice, Sarge said, "Want to tell me how you ain't affected by the aura that's gripped the others?"

Floppy looked at him for the first time, with an expression of concern and suspicion. "Who are you?"

For some reason he felt like he could trust the man, and he decided to take the chance. It was dangerous, but he always trusted his instincts. In a very soft voice, he said, "I told you, I'm Sarge. And I'm a Magi."

The big man's jaw dropped wide open, and then he looked all around the encampment to see if anyone had taken an interest in them. "That ain't funny! Are you trying to get us both killed?"

278

"I am telling the truth. Now it's your turn."

He shrugged. "Let's just say that I'm an agent with an ancient secret guild. The ability to shield my mind is one of the perks."

Sarge wanted to press him for more details, but most of the soldiers were already asleep and if he spent too much time talking to Floppy it would raise suspicions. He said, "If things get ugly, you've got an ally right here."

Floppy looked at him for a few seconds before replying, "I ain't in a position to turn away allies. I've got your back as well."

With a quick nod, he stood up and returned to the campfire near the soldiers from his company. Most of them were already asleep, and he found a spot as close to the fire as he could get.

CHAPTER 35

Rissyl

"Alright, let's take it from the top and walk through the plan one last time." Rissyl thought that the room filled with Magi might grumble about being asked to go over things once again, but everyone seemed intent and focused.

Almost every Magi was in the large council chambers on the top floor of Summit Hall. Even the elderly Magi from the Free Cities were in attendance, and would be participating in the ambush.

Initial plans for the attack started soon after Kilea whispered in Rissyl's mind about the horrible devastation of Tharrin. The debate in the Magi Council had been loud and passionate, although it didn't take long for them to agree that the Magi had to do something to try to save Khardifar and stop the bloodthirsty army.

It was a long march between Tharrin and Khardifar, so it would take the imperials several days to reach their next victims. The Magi had spent the first day and a half planning and preparing. That should still give them plenty of time to meet the imperial army a good distance from Khardifar.

The Magi had asked the Rolimi to help in the battle, but they flatly refused. They were willing to guard the Stronghold to keep it safe from invaders, but would not participate in the human's quarrels.

Dalen said loudly, "I'm gonna lead the Western Unit, and we'll have a Shadow Magi from each of the other four units with us. At first light tomorrow morning we will go to the Khardifar portal stone and meet up with some of the militia from that city, and some mercenaries that they've hired. We'll go east on foot until we get close to the army. The goal is to meet them as far from the city as we can. We might be traveling for a couple of days before we find them. We wanna use the militia from Khardifar to act as scouts and to do other things like hunting for food as we go."

He was standing on the west side of the room with Firana, Eleyne, Vora, four of the other new Order Magi, and about a dozen brown and white cloaked Society Magi. Those twenty Magi were the West Unit.

He continued, "Once the scouts have them in sight, I'll send a nexus stone message to all stones saying that the assault is gonna start. The Shadow Magi from the other four units will be carrying the destination portal rings for their unit. When the army is spotted, the Shadows will go to locations on the far east, north, and south sides of the imperial army using *Invisibility* to get there unseen. The Shadow Magi for the Healer's Unit will go about a mile west, keeping us between them and the imperials."

Rissyl said, "While the West Unit is traveling, the rest of us will be back here in this room waiting for word that the assault is about to begin. Once your unit's Shadow Magi has activated their portal, everyone needs to port to the battlefield as quickly as possible. Remember, leave the portal and get out of the way so the next person can go through."

He was standing on the east side of the room near Zahr, Asha, Bull, four new Order Magi whose names he didn't remember, and about a dozen Society Magi. They would make up all of the East Unit.

Dalen added, "The Shadow Magi need to get into the location for their unit, and get their portal ring activated, as fast as they can. It is likely that the imperial army will spot us soon after we spot them, and they're gonna attack as soon as they see us. By the time the other units are deployed, the West Unit will probably already be fighting. As soon as I send the nexus stone message, get all of your defensive spells cast quick so all that is done before the portals are opened."

On the north side of the room was Sarasa and her North Unit. It consisted of her, Brandam, Peke, Thon, as well as a dozen Society Magi and four new Order Magi.

She said, "As soon as the flanking units arrive on the north and south, we'll rush in to engage the army from those sides. According to Brandam, it's quite likely that the army will try to send the mounted troops far to the sides to try to flank our West Unit. So, our first goal is to take out the mounted troops."

Cynia spoke from the south side of the room, "All of the Diviners should use their magesight a lot. If you see an imperial commander that's got some kind of monster inside him, make sure everyone knows. We gotta make them a priority, because they might be controlling the soldiers. Zahr found that they can be hurt by frost or ice, so use those if you can."

She was standing next to Ferth, Lasina, Alin, four new Order Magi, and about a dozen Society Magi. They were the South Unit.

Rissyl spoke up again, "Don't forget your mental wards! The monster commander thing that we encountered was giving off some nasty aura of control, but your wards should block it if you start to experience that."

Gimroe, one of the elderly Magi from the Free Cities, said, "I'll be leading the Healer's Unit. The Society Magi in my unit will be running around the battlefield and bringing back those who need healing. Our clerics will set up some cots at our base and we'll provide care to anyone that we can help."

Standing next to him were a couple of other elderly Magi from the Free Cities, Thain and Makah, as well as Ayris, Brielle, Madalyn, two new Order Magi, and about half a dozen Society Magi. They were the Healer's Unit.

There had been a huge debate about the Healer's Unit, and after over an hour of arguing Rissyl finally agreed to allow Ayris and Brielle join the Healer's Unit. If he had his way his step daughter and his little sister would stay safely at home at the Stronghold. However, he gave in after fierce protests from those girls and encouragement from several Magi. The Order Magi in that unit were under strict orders to evacuate at the first sign of danger to the clerics.

Rissyl said, "Remember, there are less than one hundred of us. It's likely that we'll be terribly out numbered. Fight smart, and force them to fight in a way that gives you the advantage. Make use of the magical artifacts that you've been given, and all of the spells that you've been practicing so hard. We knew a day like this would come. The emperor is in our dungeons, and we're about to take on a large force of the imperial army. Victory is at hand, but it won't be easy."

Sarasa pointed at several crates in the middle of the room. She said, "Everyone take two flasks from those boxes. Those are elixirs that will restore your magewel! Don't drink them until you feel yourself running low on magical essence. Once you drink it, your magewel will refill quickly. This won't give you unlimited magic, but it'll keep you going if things get rough. I want to thank Dalen and the other Champions for brewing so many of these so quickly!"

"Me? You're the one to thank for these beauties!" Dalen smiled and pointed at his sister. "You and your silly books are the reason that we finally figured out how those casks of elven herbs were brewed."

Moving out to the middle of the room to grab a couple of flasks, Rissyl said, "Alright Magi, I think we're done for the night. Good luck West Unit, and safe travels! I'll see the rest of you back here first thing in the morning to begin our long wait for Dalen's message."

As the other Magi filed out of the room, Kyoso walked over to Rissyl. He moved very slowly and it was obvious that he was still weak and recovering from his ordeal at the garrison.

He said, "Kyoso wants to aid in the attack. Those imperials need to die, and Kyoso is just the Magi to do it!"

Rissyl smiled and patted the quirky Magi on the shoulder. "I know you want to help, but you're going to stay here and recover."

Kyoso started to object, and Rissyl shook his head and walked away.

CHAPTER 36

Sarasa

Shortly before dinner the next day, Sarasa's nexus stone began glowing green indicating that it had a message for her. She looked around the room and saw other Magi holding stones that were also softly glowing green.

She held the stone to her ear and activated it. Dalen's voice sounded anxious, "They're coming! Get ready!"

Sarasa stood up. "Get ready, South Unit! It looks like they met the army much quicker than we expected! Ennis and Master Thon, get those defensive enchantments going!"

The two Order of Champions Magi began casting defensive spells on all of the Magi in the North Unit.

Sarasa raised her hand and activated the ring. The portal emerged before her. It would stand there and swirl with random colors until Tynissa activated the destination ring. Tynissa had only been a Shadow Magi for six days, but she was a very skilled fighter and Sarasa said a quick prayer to Nalria that she'd get the portal opened without complications. All of the new Shadow Magi had trained hard with Sarasa and with the Rolimi instructors for the last several days. She hoped it would be enough to see them through this battle.

The room had been quiet for the last several hours, as the Magi sat scattered around the room in quiet contemplation about the things ahead of them. No one expected the nexus gems to start glowing today, so suddenly the room was abuzz with nervous chatter and last minute instructions.

The minutes dragged by slowly, and with every passing minute she got more nervous. The whole plan depended on the Shadow Magi making it to their destinations and activating their portal rings. If something awful happened to any, or all, of the Shadow Magi the whole assault would go horribly wrong very quickly.

Nerves turned to agitation. "What's taking them so long?"

Thon stepped behind her and started rubbing the muscles of her

284

shoulders and neck. He had been her fighting guild instructor for many years, and he always knew how to keep her focused.

He said, "There will probably be plenty of opportunities for hardships today, don't invent new ones before they happen. Calm your mind."

"You're right, master. Thank you." She took a deep breath and then let it out slowly. The rough kneading of his fingers helped to lessen the stress.

On the other side of the room, she heard Cynia say, "There we go, South Unit! Through the portal, let's go!"

Sarasa watched as the South Unit stepped through their portal, one at a time. After all of the others were through, Cynia stepped through and the portal vanished.

With a sigh, Sarasa looked over to Rissyl. He looked anxious, and didn't glance her way.

She began to pace in a small area near the portal. The nervous energy was building, and she needed to move around. The whole time she kept her eyes on the portal, and with each step she cursed their long wait to get into the battle.

The swirling colors suddenly morphed into the image of a field in the countryside.

She said, "Sarding finally! Let's go North Unit!"

One at a time her Magi stepped through the portal. It seemed to take ages, but finally it was her turn. As she stepped towards the portal she raised the wards around her mind to protect against the aura that Rissyl described.

The relative silence of the chamber room was instantly replaced with a battering of sounds that momentarily rattled her senses. The quick thumping of horse hooves was seemingly everywhere. Behind her and off to the left were the zips, pops, and explosions of magical spells. The grunts, gasps, battle cries, and screams of war created an audible backdrop that brought back too many horrible memories.

Still trying to get her bearings after teleporting, she turned to her right to assess the battlefield.

A large horse was almost on top of her, and it was galloping at full speed. The knight on its back was leaning out of the saddle and was already in the middle of his attack. The evening sun shined brightly on the deadly blade as it rushed towards her midsection. The knight wasn't content to wound her, he intended to slice her in two.

Before she fully recognized the danger, she was already leaping to her right. Muscle memory took over, and she let her body do what it was trained to do. She felt the knight's blade smash into her left foot as she dove through the air. The protective spells saved her foot from serious injury, but the force of the blow significantly disrupted her leap and caused her landing to be dreadful. Instead of hitting the ground softly with her hands, and then rolling gracefully over her back and then onto her feet, she instead hit the ground solidly on her back and tumbled roughly along the ground until she came to a stop face-down in the dirt.

She was in a large pool of blood next to a motionless body. She stood up quickly, looking for the next attacker. When she didn't see any immediate threat, she glanced down and saw a lifeless Society Magi on the ground at her feet.

There would be time for grieving later, and she looked around to assess their situation. Mounted troops were scattered all around the area, and they were racing around the battlefield making deadly attacks at the Magi whenever they got close. A large fireball exploded, off to her left. Magical orbs of every size and color zipped this way and that all around her, as the Magi fought to overcome the deadly knights.

The Magi were scattered around the area, most likely because they dispersed as the knights thundered towards them as soon as they exited the portal. Not far to her right she saw Thon and Brandam fighting side by side against a knight that had been knocked from his horse. As soon as she noticed them, she saw that three mounted knights were riding directly towards them.

She knew she couldn't get there before the knights did. With a shout of warning she started shooting *Force Orbs* at the nearest knight as she rushed forward. The first orb hit a knight in the side, and the next several hit him in the head, arm, and side. The fourth knocked him from the horse.

Loud hoofbeats behind her hinted that her original attacker had swung around and was coming for another chance to kill her.

She spun around and held up both hands, shouting, "Taln'Fo Denar!"

Instantly a large brick wall appeared before her, and it stretched out to her left and right for a dozen feet in either direction. It was just an illusion, but she hoped the knight would believe it was solid.

The steady hoof-thumps turned into a jumble of random thumps as the horse struggled to stop in time to avoid the wall. Suddenly the knight, having been thrown from his saddle, fell through the illusionary wall and crashed hard onto the ground not far from her.

She summoned a large orb of force over the knight's head as he struggled to regain his feet. As the orb began to fall towards the warrior, she summoned the magic to slam the orb to the ground with tremendous power. The horrific sounds of metal bending and bone crushing, mixed with a very brief cry of agony, told her that the knight would no longer be a threat.

Without pause, she looked back to Thon and Brandam just in time to see one of the thundering knights drive his longsword deep into Brandam's side. The Magi screamed and dropped to a knee.

Sarasa screamed and rushed towards him. Before she could get to him, Thon had already dealt with the two other knights nearby and the one who had injured Brandam had already rode far out of range.

She grabbed Brandam's hand as soon as she got close, and he looked up at her with panic in his eyes. He held his profusely bleeding left side with his arm. She could see him struggling to keep his innards from falling to the ground, and she choked back a sob.

Weakly, he mumbled, "I love you, Rasa."

She'd never heard that from him before, and she'd never said it to him either. She didn't love him, at least not in a romantic way. She opened her mouth to reply, but she was interrupted by Thon behind her.

He shouted, "Look out!"

When she looked behind her she saw a knight on foot rushing towards them. Thon ran around her left, but the knight was already raising up for the death strike.

Rage filled her as she summoned a huge amount of her magical essence and molded it with fury. Hatred filled her eyes as she hissed, "Myr'vur Salvi!"

The knight's sword clattered to the ground as he stumbled and then fell to the ground beside it. With no visible wounds, man died without even crying out.

Thon whispered, "By the gods."

It was the first time she'd used the *Death Whisper* spell. It was extremely powerful but it was also tremendously draining on her magewel. However, in a twisted and sadistic way she found it quite satisfying.

She looked back to Brandam and he stared lifelessly towards the sky. No longer holding them in, his insides were beginning to spill on the ground.

She didn't get a chance to tell him those three words, and it was too late. With a scream of fury she stood up and sprinted to the knight she'd just killed. She kicked the body in the head with all of her might. Over and over she kicked until the helm flew off, and then she kicked some more.

Thon grabbed her roughly, and spun her around. "He's plenty dead! Let's go!"

Sarasa pulled away from her old teacher forcefully. He was right, and that just bugged her more. She looked around to find her next victim.

Two Order Magi a few yards to her right finished off the last knight in the area. However, many of the footmen from the main part of the army were headed towards them.

"Beware! Footmen from the south!" She pointed towards the advancing army.

The Magi began moving towards the army, and casting spells to try to slow the approaching warriors.

A large section of land came alive with plant life, directly in front of the troops. The writhing vines wrapped around legs and torsos, holding tight to many of the soldiers. Some were even pulled to the ground in their struggles. Sarasa silently thanked Peke for the plant spell.

Several large animals, including wolves and tigers, rushed towards the imperials. She knew that some of them were the summoned companions of Evokers, and some of them were Diviners who had shape-changed.

The space between the Magi and the imperial soldiers streaked brightly with many magical orbs and several of the soldiers lost their lives to the spheres of deadly colors.

She quickly reached into a pocket and pulled out one of the elixir flasks. With a flick of a thumb she popped out the cork, and she guzzled the content as quickly as she could. The stuff tasted worse than it smelled, and that was an accomplishment, but she could feel her magewel recharging as she walked towards the enemy.

With a quick word, she dropped an *Invisibility* spell on herself and continued towards the enemy.

Someone screamed off to her left and she looked that way in time to see one of the knights attacking one of the new Order of Champions Magi. The knight was on top of the Magi, and he was pummeling her with his armored fists.

Movement further to her left drew her attention that way, and she realized with horror that most of the dead knights had risen as Awakened and were moving to attack the Magi from behind. Behind their visors she could see green glowing eyes.

She yelled, "Dammit! Behind you! Green-eyed Awakened Spawn! You've got to smash their heads!"

The hollering disrupted her invisibility, but the spawn could see through that anyway so she didn't bother recasting it.

Two of the dead-but-walking creatures were coming at her, so she moved to engage them.

After her experience with these things when she was all alone at the Stronghold, she decided that she needed to have a spawn head-bashing weapon handy at all times. She had selected a really nice warhammer from the Shadow Hall artifacts. It had a dark brown wooden handle and a steel grey head that was engraved with a variety of runes. Although the hammer was a beautiful weapon, it was the magical properties of the hammer that most attracted her to it. When she struck an object with the hammer, an equal and opposing force struck the object from the other direction as well. It created a stabilizing effect, and greatly increased the amount of force delivered to her target. If she struck a foe in the head, for instance, it would be the equivalent of two people striking the head on either side with two identical hammers.

She had affectionately named the weapon Squashem. A month or two ago, with Dalen's help, she tied it to a location in the Plane of Magic allowing her to summon and dismiss the gorgeous weapon at will.

The creature snarled as she approached, and she summoned Squashem with a sneer. The first creature swiped its armored hand at her, but she easily ducked the attack. When she stood up she slammed her hammer into the creature's knee as hard as she could. The reverberations shot up her arm, and it felt like she slammed the weapon into a stone wall.

The creature's knee shattered and it stumbled to the ground.

She turned her attention to the other one. It swung its sword wildly at her head. With a quick step forward, she dropped into a forward roll avoiding the attack and quickly stood up behind the spawn. She turned to face it, and used the momentum from the turn in her ferocious hammer-strike at the spawn's head. The force of the blow almost shook the weapon from her hand, and the creature's helm smashed completely flat with a gut-wrenching crunch. Blood and goo splattered everywhere as the spawn fell to the ground.

The first Awakened spawn awkwardly crawled at her with its broken knee. She stepped over and casually slammed Squashem onto the back of its head.

She felt the blood splash onto her legs as she looked around for the next dead thing that needed re-killed. Unfortunately, the other Magi had already dealt with the other spawn. She looked back to see if the prone Magi still needed assistance, but the Magi had overcome her attacker and was already moving towards the south.

The main part of the imperial army was much closer, and several of the Magi had already turned their attention back to the advancing troops. The battle cries were growing louder, and the troops seemed fearless even though they were taking heavy losses from the Magi's spells as they advanced.

She dismissed Squashem and summoned The Pricks. It was another silly name, but she'd had a bit too much wine when she named them and the names amused her.

The Pricks were a pair of long daggers. Like Squashem, they were artifacts that she found in Shadow Hall and they were both adorned with runes and imbued with magic. She drew the daggers and lightning danced up and down the blades. When these little beauties bit into a victim, it also delivered a deadly electrical burst.

Although she could toss some fire orbs and damage the enemy from afar, her most deadly skills needed the enemy to be closer. Being that close to the foes was dangerous, especially with hundreds of them. So, she summoned the magic for another spell. She mumbled, "Taln'Fo Duri." A dozen illusionary copies of Sarasa appeared all around her, each one about a foot or more from her in random directions. As she moved, the copies of her moved as well. Some of them moved along with her and some lagged behind her movements by a second or two.

The anger had cooled slightly after the satisfying smashing of spawn-heads, and she took a deep breath before rushing forward to engage the enemy. All of her illusionary copies rushed along with her.

A large eagle swooped down from the sky, and launched a series of fire orbs from a bracelet around it's talon as it dove. A line of fiery explosions engulfed many soldiers directly in front of her, but it barely slowed the crazed troops that were near the smoldering victims.

Peke was not far to her left and an Order of Champions Magi was to her right. Other Magi were spread out to either side, and they all braced for the onslaught of the foot soldiers.

A huge fireball erupted from Peke's outstretched hands and exploded impressively, taking out numerous imperial troops. The heat was intense, and she stepped to her right out of reflex.

Several troops came at her at once, and she turned into a swirling and rolling blur of motion, with a dozen illusionary copies of herself mimicking her movements all around her. Everywhere she turned another soldier died. She sank one of The Pricks into one trooper, and then turned and smashed the other Prick into someone else. At times she had her weapons deep in two different soldiers at the same time.

Occasionally she felt a weapon slam against her body, but so far her defensive spells and her Magi Cloak were preventing the worst of the attacks.

Screams, explosions, fire from the sky, flashes of steel, and victim after victim became a blur in her mind. Always moving and ducking, never staying in the same spot for more than a second or two before she darted to the next spot.

A few times she needed to throw out a magic shield to stop an attack that would have probably broken through her enchanted protections. However, most of her effort and movements were devoted to killing and moving.

Soon the number of living troops nearby dwindled so that she had to go looking for her next target.

Then the dead began to rise.

"Dammit!" She screamed in renewed fury. "I hate these sarding things!"

She slammed The Pricks back into their sheaths and dismissed them, quickly summoning Squashem once again.

Her moving and killing dance resumed as the field of dead soldiers rose up to continue the work they started while still alive. Now, instead of stabbing them to death, she had to squash their head until they were re-dead. At times she even scampered up the backs of the taller spawn so she could reach their head.

Seconds turned into long minutes, and still the battle continued. All too many of the creature's attacks managed to make it through her protective spells, and some of them were starting to nag at her and slow her movement.

When the soldiers were dead and then killed a second time, she finally had a moment to catch her breath. She looked around quickly and saw that Peke and Thon were still standing. They were both bloody and looked like they had been trampled by oxen, but they were standing. Only one other Order Magi in the North Unit was still standing, an Evoker. None of the Society Magi were still standing, but the moans and cries around her suggested that some of them might be alive.

She didn't look for them. Instead, she started walking towards the rest of the imperial army. The main part of the imperial army was several dozen yards ahead of her, and they were engaged in fierce battles from the east, west, south, and even from several Magi attacking them from the air.

There was still a huge group of imperial troops to deal with, and suddenly it felt like they'd barely made any progress at all.

Then things got drastically worse.

Creatures started popping out of the ground. At first it was just a few, but they just continued to appear. Some of them were springing from the ground between the North Unit of Magi and the remaining force of imperials, but she could see the creatures bouncing and jumping scattered throughout the army.

She sighed and remembered what Rissyl had said about the creature that had been inside the imperial commander. Kill it with frost or ice. She just happened to have the perfect weapon for killing with frost.

She dismissed Squashem and summoned Mr. Chilly.

CHAPTER 37

Bull

"Please... stop." The man's voice was very weak.

Bull paused and picked up the injured Society Magi, and carried him quickly to the ditch where several others had gathered to tend their wounded and await the arrival of the medics.

He placed the man on the ground near Asha. Then he said, "How ya doing, Asha? Try to stay awake! The medics'll be around soon, and they'll carry ya to the clerics to fix you up."

Kneeling next to her, he placed his hand on her cheek. She didn't look good. She'd lost a lot of blood and she seemed to be slipping in and out of consciousness.

A less injured Society Magi was kneeling next to her, keeping pressure on her wounds.

Things had turned ugly, shortly after the unit of Magi in the east ported into the battle. The entire scene was chaotic, and Asha ended up with horrendous wounds almost immediately. Moments after she was injured, Bull suffered a deep slice along his left leg. Rissyl had ordered him to retreat and get the wounded somewhere safe.

That was done.

Bull stood up, preparing to head back to the battle. He grabbed some rags from the ground near Asha, and tied them around the large gash in his left leg to try to stop the worst of the bleeding. That would have to be good enough for now.

Off in the distance, he saw several dwarven lizard riders approaching at full speed. The large lizards covered the ground between them quickly.

Gruknor jumped down from his mount before it was fully stopped. "Well met, Bull! Me feelin's are hurt. Why weren't we invited to yer party?" He pointed to the massive battle taking place off to the west.

"Marshal, what are you doing here?"

The dwarf ignored the question, rummaged around in one of his packs, and pulled out a vial of some kind of paste. He pulled the bandage from Bull's leg, and smeared a large glop of the foul smelling goo all over the wound.

Bull cried out in pain, "By the gods! What is that trollshit? That kills!"

Gruknor tied the bandage back onto Bull's wound, and said, "Stop actin' like a babe. It'll only hurt fer a bit!" He turned and looked to the other dwarves. "Get these Magi patched up, then time fer some fun!"

Bull watched as the dwarves quickly tended to the wounded Magi. They certainly were not as gentle and caring as the Magi's clerics. However, the salve that they applied to his leg was already starting to provide some relief. He asked, "Can your goo keep her alive?"

The marshal shrugged. "It'll numb the pain and help stop the bleedin'. It can't perform miracles."

"Why are you here? I thought you would have headed back to the mountains by now."

"We're still lookin' fer our last captive clansman." The dwarf pointed to the east. "We gotta new base over there. Scout saw the imperials pass by. When we saw yer attack, we didn't wanna miss all the fun!"

He held out the vial, and Bull took it.

The dwarf slapped him on the back, in a good natured farewell. He said, "Care fer yer wounded! We got imperials to slaughter!"

All of the dwarves climbed gracefully onto their lizards, and Bull had to move out of the way to avoid being trampled.

He watched them draw their weapons as the large creatures rushed towards the battle.

Movement from that direction caught his eye, and he noticed two wounded Magi staggering towards him. He hurried over to help them over to the ditch.

CHAPTER 38

Sarge

For most of the battle Sarge had been trying to avoid combat. When the fighting started he systematically made his way over to Floppy, and the two of them had been doing a pretty good job of staying out of trouble.

Both flanks of the imperial army had taken some losses, but it was starting to seem like the overwhelming size of the army, and the crazed battle-frenzy created by the aura, might be more than the Magi could handle.

He and Floppy were in the rear of the formation of imperial foot soldiers who were advancing towards the west. As they inched forward, Sarge discreetly cast a series of protective spells on both himself and Floppy, in preparation for the impending combat.

Marching towards the west and avoiding combat, while all around his Magi friends were battling, was almost more than he could bare. He felt terribly guilty that he wasn't with one of those groups of Magi fighting against the imperials. However, he knew he must be patient and obey the wishes of Kelegar.

The sounds of the battle changed slightly, and he looked to the right to see what was going on.

Not far from him a small demon popped up out of the ground. It was about two feet tall, covered in smoldering scales, and was a deep red in color. As soon as it landed, it bounded away from him heading towards the Magi in the north.

Another demon jumped out of the ground, a little further away from him. It scurried and jumped, moving quickly through the formation of imperial soldiers.

The troops didn't seem at all phased as more and more demons leapt from the ground all around them, and Sarge expected it was because of the controlling aura.

Beside him, Floppy whispered, "What are these sarding things?"

As soon as Sarge saw them, he knew exactly what the creatures were and he finally understood why Kelegar wanted him in the middle of the enemy.

A deep voice from behind him called out, "How are you two not following the *Dominion Ripple*?"

Turning quickly, he saw that a large group of Wyvern troops and two imperial captains were baring down on him. His disguise had finally been discovered.

He tossed aside the inferior sword that the imperials had given him and summoned his azure armor and his magical weapons. The armor was made of plate and chainmail, with Kelegar's symbol on the chest. It was highly polished, and had a slight blue tint to it. The helmet had small wings on the sides, and it was open face.

After summoning his weapons, there were now a number of weapons in sheaths and scabbards around his body. Two axes were strapped to his outer thighs, a greatsword was strapped to his back, a dagger was sheathed on each forearm, a weighted chain was clipped to his belt on the right side, and a pair of steel reinforced short clubs were strapped to his belt in back. That was in addition to a variety of throwing spikes, caltrops, brass knuckles, and other useful toys stashed in nooks and crannies throughout his armor and boots. All of these weapons were enchanted with numerous magical properties ranging from fire damage to magical poison.

He didn't draw any of those weapons. Instead he pulled his simple divine longsword from the scabbard on his left. It was given to him by Kelegar's zealots on the Dinbera Island. The sword was beautifully crafted and was always razor sharp, even after fierce battles and long practice sessions. However, he had never seen the blade glow with a pale blue radiance until this moment as he held the holy weapon before him.

He slowly advanced towards the imperials.

As the first Wyvern trooper rushed forward, he began to pray out loud, "Divine-sire Kelegar, you have shepherded me to my emergence as your azure paladin,"

Somewhere nearby to his left he barely noticed a brilliant explosion of light, as lightning descended from the sky and smashed through two demons as they raced across the battlefield. The thunder was tremendous, but Sarge tuned it out with most of his attention on his prayer and the foes before him.

The first Wyvern Regiment trooper thrusted his sword towards Sarge's midsection, and the paladin casually parried and counter-thrusted. The holy sword cut through the elite soldier's armor like it was paper. As the large warrior fell, Sarge yanked his sword free and readied for the next assailant.

As he moved, he continued praying loudly, "and brought me from ignorance to knowledge."

Two more elite troops advanced at him, trying to attack simultaneously and catch him in their trap. His large sword spun and danced before him, as he side-stepped both attacks and brought his sword down through the sides of both blades of his two attackers. The imperial steel snapped, and he halted the sword's momentum. Two quick movements later, and two more elite soldiers dropped to the ground at his feet.

All around him, bright flashes of lightning and booming thunder brought death to more demons.

He had to shout his prayer to even hear himself over all of the thunder, "I beg that you forgive our people and our ancestors for their disobedience and ignorance."

The events around him became a blur of motion, brilliant flashes of lightning, explosive thunder, and spraying blood as he made his way through the elite troops to get to the commanders.

"Give us the power to defeat this unholy evil, so that your holy name and glory can be praised throughout the lands!"

A powerful blow hammered into his back, causing Sarge to take a step forward to maintain his balance. When he glanced back he saw the man who attacked him, his weapon was extended out before him and his body was gyrating like he was being electrocuted.

The final three nearby Wyvern rushed forward. Sarge was vaguely aware of Floppy at his side, fighting against a couple of opponents on his own.

Step, parry, thrust and an elite soldier met the hilt of Sarge's glowing blade.

Parry, step, spin, and slice sent another enemy to meet Kelegar's judgement.

Step, block, step, parry, and finally a thrust finished the third Wyvern.

"By all the sarding gods! Look at that!" Floppy pointed towards one of the commanders.

The man stood with his arms clutching his chest and his face twisted in a horrific expression of agony. A pair of red scaly claws had erupted from the man's chest, and they were pulling the commander apart. A demonic face appeared in the hole of the man's chest between the clawed hands. Suddenly, the demon heaved and the officer ripped completely in half. Skin, muscle, and bone dropped to either side of the creature and blood soaked the ground at its feet.

The demon roared as it dropped to all fours, and raced towards Sarge.

He tossed up a magical shield, just as the demon pounced at him. The fiery creature crashed into the shield, and ricocheted to the right.

A second demon discarded his imperial commander host and rushed at Sarge as well.

Sarge raised his holy sword towards the sky in both hands. Lightning continued to flash, and thunder crashed, all around him. In a loud voice, he roared, "In the name of Kelegar, I smite thee!"

A massive bolt of lightning struck Sarge's sword and forked into four smaller bolts. One bolt obliterated the demon that had just crashed into his magical shield, and another struck the other advancing demon as it leapt towards him. The bolt slammed into the demon and shredded it into tiny pieces that pelted into Sarge and smoldered against his azure armor.

The other two large bolts shot out across the battlefield, one shooting towards the rear and the other racing to the south.

The concussion of the thunder from the massive lightning strike was strong enough to drop Sarge to one knee.

He felt drained and weak, but the huge army advancing from all sides was not content to let him rest.

Sarge forced himself to his feet, with help from Floppy.

A maniacal scream from the east warned him that the battle was far from over. He looked that way and saw a tall man in black and grey robes. Beside him was a woman in black and red robes, and they were both moving towards him.

He knew at once that he was finally looking at the Archwarlock. Something deep inside him cried out that the man must be destroyed.

Unfortunately, there were dozens of elite Wyvern Regiment soldiers between him and his enemy. It would be a daunting task to get through them.

The Archwarlock pointed at him and screamed something.

A large bulbous demon oozed out of the ground in front of him. It was at least five feet tall, and more than five feet wide. The grotesque demon was covered with long tentacles that wiggled and writhed all around its fat body.

Sarge groaned, "I'm getting too old for this crap."

The rotund demon was surprisingly quick, and several of its powerful tentacles propelled it forward and several more reached out for him. He slashed at one, and moved to avoid another.

A large tentacle caught his leg. As Sarge brought his sword down to free his leg another tentacle wrapped around his right arm.

Within seconds the demon had ahold of him. It lifted him off the ground and several more tentacles snaked around his body and limbs.

CHAPTER 39

Rissyl

The battle in the east had started out terribly. Rissyl estimated that half of the Society Magi and at least four of the Order Magi in his unit had been severely wounded or killed within the first few minutes.

He had watched Asha get skewered by two different imperial soldiers and dropped shortly after they had entered the battle. Bull was wounded early as well and Rissyl had ordered him to pull the wounded Magi to the east to wait for help.

They were so far from the healers that he doubted that help could make it in time, but he was hopeful.

Not long after that, a surprisingly large group of dwarves joined the battle from the east. There were a dozen dwarves mounted on large lizards. He didn't know where the dwarves had come from, but he was very happy to see them.

With the imperial cavalry mostly destroyed, and the eastern side of the imperial troops consisting of mainly archers and footmen, the dwarven cavalry had a distinct advantage. The dwarves proved to be an extremely valuable ally to help the East Unit of Magi get the battle under control in that region.

Shortly after Rissyl saw the first fire monster pop out of the ground, the sky filled with lightning. It was the most incredible thing Rissyl had ever seen. For several minutes an intense lightning storm raged directly over the imperial army. Dozens or hundreds of individual strikes streaked from the sky, and everywhere the bolts hit, another one of the bouncy creatures was destroyed.

Rissyl continued to launch *Force Orbs*, *Fiery Columns*, and *Fireballs* at the imperials spread out before them.

When the huge bolt of lightning struck in the middle of the imperial army, it seemed that the entire battle paused for a moment. The massive thunderclap caused his ears to ring, and he was not all that close to where the lightning struck. The unusual bolt hit something and broke into parts.

After that, the sky quieted. The lightning strikes had stopped, but the imperial troops all seemed momentarily disoriented. Just like in the Tharrin garrison once the monster inside the commander had been killed, the troops lost their ferocity and some even looked confused.

A pair of large lizards galloped past him and the dwarven riders rushed a group of imperial warriors before him. They quickly cleaved their way into the heart of a thick squad of them, sending imperials scampering to get away.

Rissyl launched a series of *Fireballs* towards any troops that started to look his way, and he moved forward after every spell to make progress towards the heart of the army.

Off in the distance he saw Tiberos running across the battlefield. The enemy might not be able to see him, but they certainly felt his bite. He'd seen the big Rolimi dog bite a large chunk out of a soldier's leg just a bit ago.

Up ahead he saw a pair of large birds diving down, launching orbs at the troops as they flew.

Just beyond them, a glow of color caught his eye. The color was over on the north side of the army and it was cutting a path towards the center of the troops. At first he didn't know what it was, it just looked like four large green and brown lights. Then the lights moved some, and Rissyl recognized them as four large Rolimi creatures. They were shaped like large bears with heads and beaks of hawks, and they were mostly transparent. Their features were outlined in green and brown colored light.

He had seen one of these creatures when the Magi were helping to evacuate Ront'El during the imperial invasion last year. Ayris had called the creature from the plane of magic when her parents were killed.

If these Rolimi were roaming the battlefield, Rissyl had the heart-wrenching suspicion that Ayris was not far from them.

"Dammit!" He swore in fear and frustration.

He looked around to see if anyone in his unit was in extreme peril and needed his assistance. They were spread out to the south, and they were making progress against the imperials. He saw a handful of Society Magi as well as an Evoker and a Champion battling alongside dwarven warriors against several imperial troops.

Off to his left, he saw Bull rushing forward. The Order of Champions Magi had a blood-soaked bandage on his left leg, but he looked determined to get back into the fight.

Rissyl shouted, "I thought I said to retreat with the other wounded!"

"It's justa scratch. I don't wanna miss all the fun." The Magi's words sounded like typical Bull comments, but his voice was weak.

"Fine, that Evoker and Champion to the south need your help, go join them!"

Bull didn't answer, but he started limping in that direction.

Rissyl summoned several small Fiery Columns at a group of imperials who were rushing towards Bull.

Then he pulled his last elixir flask from his pocket and quickly drank the contents.

There was a warm rush throughout his body and he could feel his drained magewel quickly replenishing.

In a nervous voice, he uttered, "Kur'Gezbar."

The battlefield changed, as he teleported over to the spot with the Rolimi creatures. He tossed out his arms to balance himself, as the dizziness took hold.

All three clerics, as well as a handful of other Magi were gathered between the four Rolimi creatures. They were all moving fairly quickly towards the center of the army. The large Rolimi creatures rushed from one imperial soldier to the next, and the several Magi between them shot a steady series of magical orbs at any warriors that approached.

As soon as he was able to take a few steps without fear of falling down, Rissyl staggered towards the clerics.

He shouted, "What are you sarding doing? You were supposed to stay in the west, far away from the sarding battle! Yet, here you are in the middle of it!"

He tossed a fireball at a large group of imperials. It exploded on top of the nearest, and bodies were tossed in all direction as the force of the blast emanated out. As his anger grew, he tossed two more fireballs to either side at troops in those directions that might think about advancing at his sister and daughter.

Ayris shouted, while pointing defiantly to the south, "Madalyn's gotta get to Sarge. Kelegar is calling her to him!"

He lobbed another large ball of fire at troops regathering before them. Then he snarled, "Kelegar should find an adult to save Sarge, and leave the children in the back of the battle where I told them to stay!"

"Kyoso has kept them safe!"

Rissyl looked over and saw the Evoker launching one magical arrow after the next with his enchanted bow.

"Dammit, Kyoso! You were supposed to stay at the Stronghold!" Rissyl continued tossing fireballs as he shouted.

"What's that?" Brielle yelled in surprise.

Rissyl's last fireball had cleared a path between them and some sort of big fat creature with dozens of wiggly tentacles dancing around its disgusting body.

Sarge was caught in the creature's many appendages, and it was smashing him against the ground. There was a large imperial soldier alternating between attacking the monster, and fighting against other imperial soldiers.

The Rolimi creatures rushed forward, attacking warriors along the way. Madalyn ran along with them, in a dash towards Sarge and the creature.

Rissyl and the others hurried to keep up. Magical orbs streaked past him on both sides as the Magi fought to keep the cleric safe.

Suddenly, several purple necromancer orbs flew directly at Madalyn from their left. Each orb slammed against an invisible barrier around the cleric, the bubble was roughly six foot in diameter with Madalyn in the center. Each time another necromancer orb slammed again the bubble it glowed briefly with a soft blue radiance.

When he looked to the left to find the source of the necromancer attack, his heart sank as he recognized Jessa walking towards them. She walked next to some tall evil looking man.

Jessa was the little sister of Rissyl's friend Burga. They'd grown up together, and now he would have to kill her.

He shouted back to Kyoso, "Keep the clerics safe!"

As he turned to make his way over to Jessa and the tall man, he held both hands out before him. He murmured, "Krol'Ak Fruli." A large spray of icy shards shot from his out-stretched hands and struck several of the troops between him and Jessa. The deadly spikes of ice smashed against some solid pieces of armor, but slid right through the chainmail links and into the exposed faces of many soldiers before him.

Each step brought another spray of ice and another group of dead or badly injured soldiers. The other troops before him rushed away in panic, clearing a path to Jessa and the man.

Dead soldiers were scattered around his feet as he hurried towards her.

The tall man beside her grinned at him evilly as he watched Rissyl approach. The man held his hand out towards him, and the dead soldiers all around him began to move and rise to their feet.

"Die Magi, so I can raise you as a Drudge too!" The tall man screamed.

Rissyl saw Jessa hold out her hand to shoot her necromancer fire at him.

A large raptor screeched as it swooped in from behind, and clawed at Jessa's head with its sharp talons.

As Jessa batted at the raptor, Tiberos ran up and started biting at her legs.

The first Awakened creature grabbed at Rissyl's arm, and another grabbed him from behind and tried to bite him.

He yelled, "Krol'Fe!" A mint green Force Orb shot from his outstretched hand and crashed against the side of the closest creature's head. A loud pop, and a disgusting splatter, sent the creature back to the ground.

Rissyl could barely move because the creatures were all around him. He continued to shoot orbs at them, but the creatures were coming faster than he could destroy them.

CHAPTER 40

Sarge

One of the monster's tentacles was wrapped around his throat, and he could no longer breathe. It slammed him hard against the ground once again. A loud pop, and an explosion of pain in his chest, promised that he'd just broken another rib.

His sword was on the ground out of reach, so he was wielding one of his axes. As he swung the magical weapon a trail of frost floated in its wake. The ax cleaved deep into one of the monster's tentacles, but Sarge knew that it was a losing battle. At this rate he was going to pass out long before his ax did any serious harm to the creature.

The dizziness intensified and darkness clawed at him, demanding that he submit.

He heard Madalyn's voice and knew that he must be hallucinating. She said, "Return to the place from whence you came!"

His breath returned with a desperate inhale and for several moments he breathed heavily and scrambled to get away from the monster. When he opened his eyes, the creature was completely gone. Madalyn rushed over and knelt beside him.

In a weak voice, he asked, "Have you gone crazy? What're you doing here?"

She placed a hand on his forehead and gently pressed his head onto the ground, "Hush, Theo, you're badly hurt."

"Where did that creature go?"

She ignored his question, and placed two fingers on his lips to quiet him.

Fighting raged all around them, but he saw some large Rolimi creatures and several Magi all around him keeping him and Madalyn safe for the moment. Floppy was also nearby, desperately fighting against imperial troops and Awakened spawn.

Madalyn placed both of her hands on his chest and quietly, but passionately, prayed to Kelegar for healing.

Almost instantly he felt a warm sensation fill his body, it was a feeling a joy and serenity that lasted only a moment. When it passed, he was able to breathe normally and the most excruciating pains were gone.

He sat up, grabbed Madalyn gently on both sides of her head, and pulled her close. He kissed her on the top of the head and then let go. "Thanks kiddo, now you need to get back to safety. I've got to get to the Archwarlock."

"Most of the damage has been healed, Theo, but you need to rest. Your body is not ready for more battles."

"My body's just gonna need to get ready quickly." He stood up and gathered his weapons, replacing them in their sheaths and straps.

Madalyn looked to her left, and said, "Kyoso take Brielle, Ayris, and the others back to the north where it's safer. I'm going with Theo."

Kyoso raised his bow in the air, "Kyoso will keep them safe! Follow closely!"

"By the gods, Madalyn! You've brought them into the middle of this nightmare?" Sarge was practically shouting, although his voice was still scratchy and faltered at times.

"I couldn't have got here without Ayris and her Rolimi friends."

Kyoso, Brielle, Ayris, a handful of older Magi, and four large Rolimi creatures moved off to the north.

Before he could demand that the young cleric retreat with the others, several Awakened with green glowing eyes rushed towards them.

Madalyn stepped between Sarge and the approaching undead creatures. She flicked the end of a metal scepter towards the creatures, and water sprayed from the end of the weapon. The water droplets hit the creatures with a sizzling sound, and each Awakened spawn hit by the water dropped to the ground instantly.

She stepped forward, praying loudly as she walked. With every step she flicked the scepter once again. Each spray of holy water disrupted the enchantment of more of the creatures.

He watched in disbelief. As he stepped along behind her, he asked, "Where'd you get that?"

Madalyn flicked the weapon again, and said, "It's a great story for another time. Where is the Archwarlock?"

Sarge looked around the battlefield. There was chaos everywhere. The Magi and the Khardifar mercenaries in the west were getting closer, and several mounted dwarves could be seen to the east. Magi were locked in deadly combat in every direction, and the number of imperial troops had been diminished significantly. However, they were still outnumbered badly and it didn't help that the dead kept rising to fight again. Several of the little bouncy demonic creatures were scurrying around the battlefield once again, attacking Magi along the way.

Pockets of intense combat were all around, and streaks and explosions of magic seemed to be everywhere.

Then he saw the purple light of necromancer magic and focused his search there. He saw the Archwarlock and a necromancer woman fighting desperately against Rissyl and several other Magi, and they weren't far away.

He pointed in that direction, and shouted, "Over there!"

Sarge stepped in front of Madalyn and led the way, with Floppy close behind her. The three of them fought their way towards the Archwarlock. Holy water continued to spray from her scepter with each flick of her wrist, and the Awakened quickly fell at their feet.

Those attackers who were not undead monsters were quickly dispatched by Sarge and Floppy as the trio advanced to the heart of the battle.

A volley of purple necromancer fire raced at them, and shattered against some protective bubble that seemed to be centered on Madalyn. Each time the purple orbs hit the bubble, it glowed blue briefly and then vanished once again. He pressed forward, careful to stay close enough to her so that her sphere of protection would continue to defend against the deadly purple fire.

The prince was wielding a large halberd made of pure fire of a deep-purple color. The weapon spun around his body, darting this way and that, and making many blocks, parries, and attacks with blurring speed and engaging two Society Magi at once. Although the fiery halberd was being wielded by the prince, and it moved along with him, he wasn't actually touching it. The weapon fought on its own, as if it was being controlled by the prince but it was not in his hands.

Rissyl shot several force orbs at the prince, but each was intercepted by the spinning fiery halberd.

The necromancer woman near the prince continued her onslaught of purple fire. There were several Awakened spawn around her, preventing three Magi from reaching the woman.

One after the other, both Magi fighting the prince were cut down by the relentless attacks from the fiery halberd.

Floppy got to the prince before Sarge could get there. The large man lunged in with four powerful strikes at the Archwarlock, but the fiery halberd easily blocked each one. Then the prince's fire weapon hooked behind Floppy's head and yanked him quickly towards Edal's outstretched hand. Before Floppy could recover his weapon from his previous blow, the prince reached out and grabbed Floppy by the shoulder.

The large warrior turned to ash.

Sarge felt like he'd been punched in the gut by an ogre. He watched as the ash of Floppy's skin and muscle floated in the wind and his bones dropped to the dirt with a brief clatter that was mostly drowned out by the sounds of battle all around.

The Archwarlock looked at Sarge with hatred, "You're next, paladin." He spat the word paladin as if it was a curse.

Sarge heard Rissyl shout the trigger word to a spell. The Magi was nearby, to his left. A large bolt of lightning streaked at the Archwarlock.

He wasted no time, rushing towards the prince to try to time his attack as the Archwarlock recovered from Rissyl's magical attack.

The lightning raced forward, and slammed into a deep-purple orb. The impact of the two magics exploded in a violent scattering of lightning and warlock magic.

Pushing through the discharge of magic, Sarge thrust his holy longsword at the prince. The blade cut through the fiery halberd with ease, and landed a solid blow deep into the side of the Archwarlock.

With a scream, the prince lashed out with several attacks at once. Deadly deep-purple orbs shot from his palms, some aimed at Sarge and some at Rissyl. At the same time, several large demonic creatures rose up from the ground all around the prince.

Sarge screamed out as several of the warlock's death orbs passed through Madalyn's protective bubble and struck Sarge in the chest. He could feel the life being stolen from his body with each one.

Creatures came at him from both sides, and he quickly impaled one through the chest with his longsword.

The prince screamed as he continued the blitz of warlock magic pummeling them.

Madalyn cried out behind him, and he glanced that way as a series of deep-purple orbs crashed into her. She staggered back, dropping to a knee.

As desperately as he wanted to rush to her aide, he knew that his only choice was to finish the prince before the man could kill them all.

One of the demonic creatures clawed at his back, and grabbed the side of his face tearing flesh with its burning talons.

Sarge spun the sword quickly, changing to a reverse grip. Then he thrust the sword backwards, sliding the side of the blade against the side of his own chest as it passed deep into the heart of the creature behind him.

He spun quickly, bringing himself closer to the prince. Edal retreated, trying to put more demonic creatures between himself and Sarge, but it was too late.

The first blow struck the Archwarlock in the left arm, the second slashed deep into the right side of his face and practically separated his jaw from this skull. Sarge's final blow sent the glowing holy weapon deep into the Archwarlock's chest.

Deep-purple fire shot out in random directions as the prince waved his arms around and lashed out in a final attempt to defeat his enemies.

Edal dropped to both knees and then fell face first into the dirt.

The remaining demonic creatures retreated back to Khalius where they'd come from, and all of the green-eyed Awakened spawn fell to the ground lifelessly.

Sarge staggered over to Madalyn. She slowly stood up and fell into his arms when he got near her.

The strain of the battle, and the life-stealing effects of the Archwarlock's magic, sapped his strength. He wasn't sure of he was holding up Madalyn, or if she was helping to keep him standing.

He rested his forehead against the top of her head, and tried to get his breathing under control as he hugged her tight.

CHAPTER 41

Rissyl

He couldn't believe that the wicked prince was finally dead. Rissyl had started to doubt that the man could be killed. He stood for several seconds, looking at the motionless body of the prince.

Jessa raised her arms into the air. There were more than a dozen Awakened spawn around her, still battling Magi. The green-eyed spawn dropped when the prince was killed, but these were controlled by Jessa.

She said, "I surrender!" Each of her Awakened dropped to the ground, as she released her unnatural animation of those corpses.

Rissyl walked towards her. He lifted his hand to summon a pillar of fire to kill his childhood friend.

She clasped her hands before her in a pleading motion. She said, "Rissyl, please forgive me! The prince, and Lord Jalinox before him, controlled my mind and forced me to be their servant! You've freed me from their bondage!"

The large raptor, that had attacked Jessa earlier, glided to the ground and quickly transformed into her original form. Cynia crossed her arms, and looked at Rissyl expectantly.

Sarge and Madalyn approached from his right. They both looked like they were about to collapse at any moment. She struggled to help support him, which would have been a challenge for her even if he wasn't in heavy armor and burdened with an arsenal of weapons.

In a very weak voice, Sarge said, "You ain't gonna believe those lies, are you?"

Rissyl shook his head in sorrow. "Jessa, you've given your life to evil. I tried to save you once, and you turned away."

"Riz, I was compelled by necromancer magic! I was unable to resist, but now I'm free! You've got to believe-"

She stopped talking mid-sentence and cried out in surprise.

Sarasa became visible behind her, and she held a dagger forcefully against Jessa's throat. She whispered, "Just give me an excuse."

Rissyl looked to his wife, and pointed towards Jessa. "Please, read her."

Cynia walked over to the necromancer. She looked into the woman's eyes for several long seconds and then looked up at Sarasa. Rissyl had no idea what horrors he had just asked Cynia to experience. If there was any other way to be sure of Jessa's intentions he wouldn't have asked her to do it.

In a low voice, Cynia said, "Kill her."

A fraction of a second later, Cynia was covered in Jessa's blood as Sarasa slid her dagger quickly across the necromancer's throat. The Shadow Magi let Jessa slump to the ground with a thud.

Rissyl turned away quickly and shielded his eyes, but it was too late. He couldn't unsee the brutal end to his childhood friend. There had been so many fun moments as a child with Burga and Jessa, usually with Brielle tagging along. Several childhood fun-times flashed before his eyes, intermixed with the sight of Sarasa ending Jessa's life.

Sarasa gasped, and said, "The prince!" She pointed at the ground.

Rissyl looked and realized that the prince's body was no longer there. It had vanished. He looked to the others, "Where'd it go?"

"Wirmyntas must have dragged it down to Khalius to begin an eternity of suffering for his defeat. Good riddance!" Sarge spat on the ground where the body had been.

Rissyl stared at the dirt where the prince had been.

Cynia said, "The battle ain't over, we got an army to defeat."

He looked around the battlefield and found that Cynia was partly right. Many of the soldiers of the imperial army were still alive, but most of them were either running away from the battlefield or simply surrendering.

Sarasa walked over and took Sarge by the arm. She said, "You two need to sit down before you fall down." She helped them to the dirt slowly.

Rissyl and Cynia began walking around the battlefield looking for any soldiers who refused to surrender. A row of wagons stood off to the south and they extended off to the east. As they walked past them, they found several imperial soldiers huddled between the wagons. All of them looked injured, and most of them raised their hands when they saw the two Magi approach.

He said, "Stand up slowly and keep your hands in the air where I can see them if you want to live."

311

One of the men, an old man in an extremely elaborately trimmed tabard stood up and grabbed a sword from the ground as he stood.

An older man behind him grabbed him and said, "Thorli, you old fool! Drop that sword. It's over!"

The old warrior pushed the old man away, and said, "Leave me alone, Vendino! The emperor will have our heads if we surrender!"

Rissyl raised his hand, ready to summon something deadly if the old man advanced. He said, "The emperor has been captured. The war against the Magi is over. This is your only chance to surrender."

"Did you say Thorli?" Cynia stepped forward, and most of the injured imperial soldiers moved out of her way.

The old warrior placed the tip of the sword into the ground, and leaned on the handle like a cane. He said, "I'm General Thorli." He took a deep breath and looked around the battlefield. He let the breath out slowly. "We surrender."

Cynia walked up to him and looked him in the eyes. Then she said, "You once owned a Dreg named Molia Dodisen."

Thorli nodded slowly, "Yes, a long time ago. How do you know that?"

"She was my mom."

He looked at her in surprise and then the realization shown in his eyes. He said, "You look so much like her."

She looked over to Madalyn, and said, "Dear, do you have the strength to heal this man?"

Madalyn nodded and walked over slowly. As she got close, in a quiet voice she asked, "What is special about this imperial?"

With a sigh, Cynia said, "He's my father."

CHAPTER 42

Rissyl

The crowd continued to grow, and the atmosphere in the huge courtyard was tense and quiet. Earlier the crowd had been boisterous and Rissyl feared that things would turn confrontational between the Magi and the Denizens of Clornoss.

The Magi were spread out across the stage of the gallows, looking out at the growing crowd. Rissyl and Cynia were on the left side of the stage, and Dalen and Sarasa were on the right side. Between them were Minister Vendino and Minister Thorli. The Magi were dressed in formal blouses and breeches with their Magi Cloaks flowing proudly in the gentle Late-Winter breeze.

Spread out behind them were about a dozen other Magi, including all three clerics. Sarge stood in the middle in his shining azure paladin armor, and he held onto the arm of Emperor Ryal III. Zahr was holding his other arm.

The emperor was bound tightly at his ankles and wrists, and he was gagged. He was still wearing his royal robes, but they were tattered and dirty after many days of living in Fort Randol's dungeons. Around his neck was a thick rope tied into a noose. The end of the noose hung down the emperor's back.

It had been over a fortnight since the battle outside of Khardifar, and Rissyl had been anticipating and dreading this event since the end of that battle.

For several days the Magi had been posting notices all around Clornoss and the other major cities of the empire. The notices announced that the emperor would be hanged for his crimes in the Clornoss courtyard on the 2nd of Late-Winter at mid-day.

Now that the appointed time had arrived, he hoped that they weren't making a mistake. Large crowds were sometimes unpredictable, and if the Magi were forced to harm Denizens of Clornoss because of some sort of riot it could complicate things and possibly make the war against the Magi drag on.

Rissyl looked back at the Magi flanking the emperor, and Zahr gave him a slight nod. In a loud voice, Rissyl spoke to the crowd. "Ladies and gentlemen of Clornoss. Behind me stands Emperor Ryal III, the heartless tyrant who relentlessly hunted down and killed many Magi for no reason other than his own jealousy and fear! He has ordered the slaughter of hundreds of innocent people from his own empire under the excuse of waging war against the Magi! For decades he has sent his troops to attack and destroy the peaceful Free Cities in his thirst for expansion of his already vast empire. In punishment for these crimes, the Grand Council of the Sovereign Magi Society has sentenced him to death by hanging."

Zahr raised his hand and the end of the noose shot up into the air, pulling the emperor off of the ground by his neck. Once the emperor had been lifted about four feet off of the stage, the rope stopped and remained stationary in the air. Emperor Ryal struggled and thrashed around against his bindings for several long minutes, and then eventually stopped moving.

His body gently swung from side to side, with the top of the rope still attached to nothing, held only by Zahr's magic.

The crowd stood in shocked silence as the body slowly rotated on the end of the rope and swung back and forth.

Suddenly the silence was broken by a single voice, somewhere in the middle of the crowd. "Praise the gods, he's dead!"

A huge cheer broke out throughout the crowd. The cheering turned to dancing and cries of jubilation, and it carried on for a long time.

Rissyl released a deep breath of relief and Cynia grabbed his hand. She leaned her head against his shoulder and they waited for the crowd to calm down and give its attention once again.

After at least fifteen minutes of joyous celebration throughout the crowd, Rissyl held up his hands and asked for silence. They didn't respond right away, but eventually the gathered people grew quiet and listened once again.

Finally, he was able to announce loudly, "Standing next to me are Ministers Vendino and Thorli, who have spent many years on the Council of Ministers for the Ryallic Empire. These men have-"

The crowd began jeering and cursing at the ministers, and Rissyl held his hands up once again.

"Listen! Magi have the power to read a person's soul and know if they're telling the truth. We have tested these two ministers and know

314

them to be fair and competent leaders. With the death of the emperor and his son, Prince Ryal, the leadership of the Ryallic Empire falls to Princess Anoria. Since the princess is still a child, Minister Vendino has been appointed to be her regent. As the acting leader of your empire, Regent Vendino has something he would like to say."

The handful of curses and foul comments came from the crowd, but mostly they were silent.

The new regent stepped forward slightly, and interlaced his fingers before him. Rissyl had spent many hours chatting with the man over the last few days, and he knew that he was extremely nervous to speak in front of people especially in this circumstance.

In a loud but wavering voice, Vendino said, "I've been a minister and advisor to the emperor for many years, and I've carried out many orders that I didn't approve of and would never have made myself. To be honest, I do not feel worthy to serve as regent and feel that justice would be better served if I were hanging next to the emperor right now."

The crowd was completely silent listening to his poignant words.

As he continued, a single tear streamed down his cheek. "When I think of the lives that have been taken, I am filled with great sorrow. I implored the Magi to choose a different regent. For reasons I'll never understand, they were insistent that the duty should fall to me. If I've learned anything over the years, it's that this empire is too vast to be ruled over by one person. The power is too great, as is the potential for corruption. Therefore, as my first and only decree as acting regent for the Ryallic Empire, I hereby declare that the empire is dissolved and disbanded. Each major city is free to govern themselves and their surrounding province in whatever manner that they see fit as independent nations. I will stay on to serve as Princess Anoria's regent over the newly formed Kingdom of Clornoss until she reaches the age of adulthood."

By the time the new regent stopped talking, he was being drowned out by the crowd. Some people were cheering, and some were shouting and jeering.

There was uncertainty throughout the gathered people, and Rissyl could understand their trepidation. People naturally fear change, and suddenly the most powerful and influential city in the empire had become just another city in a land filled with minor kingdoms. It would take time for them to adjust. He assumed that the reaction within the other cities would be much more favorable when those people learn that their province was no longer under the control of an all-powerful emperor.

Dalen called for quiet, and then said, "The Magi Society will work with the ruler of each new nation, to give support and ensure that things go smoothly when they set up the new government. We will demand that the ruler of each new nation agrees to these two conditions if they want support and trade with the Magi. First, people will no longer be enslaved as Dregs, this must end completely and immediately. Second, the ruler must agree to live peacefully with all other nations and Free Cities."

Once again the mass of people erupted in cheers, and this time it seemed unlikely to calm down quickly.

- = - = -

"The clerics and I wanna start preaching about Kelegar throughout the lands. Eventually we wanna build Kelegarian Temples in every city." Sarge leaned back in his couch, next to Madalyn.

Rissyl smiled, "That's great, surely you'll usher in a great Kelegarian revival."

"I certainly hope so."

He looked around the room and took a moment to appreciate the things that he had. The final battle against the imperial army had been terribly costly. Many Magi had died, and the grieving period was just getting started. However, they had been victorious and they could begin to rebuild the Magi Society.

Ayris and Chardy were in his arms and Cynia sat next to him. They were in the lounge in Summit Hall with Rissyl's parents, sister, and a number of other Magi.

Tuknor said, "When you have a few minutes, there are a number of logistical things that we need to discuss about Randol City."

Before he could reply, the door opened admitting Sarasa and Dalen. They walked over and took a seat near everyone else.

Rissyl said, "I'm glad that you're here. Cynia and I have been kicking around an idea, and we want your opinion. Do you think we could build a large permanent portal in Randol City, big enough to transport wagons and horses?"

"That's a great idea. Where would we put the other end of the portal?" Dalen looked intrigued.

"I don't know?" Rissyl shrugged. "We'd have to find a nation interested in being the trade center between the Magi and the rest of the known-lands."

Sarasa nodded, "I'm pretty sure it can be done, but it'll take some research and the combined magic from all of the Orders."

With a grin, Rissyl said, "You're our greatest researcher. Will you figure out how to make that happen?"

She sighed, and for a moment he thought that she would be unwilling to do it. After a long pause, she said, "Yes, I will do the research. However, once the research is done, I'll be leaving."

Rissyl sat foreword. "Leaving for where?"

"I don't know yet. I will be resigning my position as the Grand Shadow and then I'm going to take a long break from all of this. I don't know what I'm going to do yet. Maybe I'll travel around and see the sights, or find a deep cave and sit in quiet contemplation for a long time."

"You can't leave! We can finally rebuild the Magi Society like we've dreamed since we were little! How can you leave after all we've gone through to get here?" Cynia sounded angry.

Sarasa looked forlorn, and Rissyl knew that she hadn't seemed truly happy in a long time.

She motioned towards the children on his lap, and said, "You two have a beautiful family, and you can now finally settle down and raise them without fear of being hunted by the emperor. I..."

Her voice broke and she took a moment to dry her eyes, then she continued, "I need to figure out life, and my place in the lands. I can't do that here. I will be back eventually, but right now I have to focus on me."

She stood up and walked towards the door. As she walked, she said, "I should get started on that research."

Cynia nudged him, and motioned for him to follow Sarasa out the door.

She was outside and several steps away from the building when he caught up with her. She turned to face him, gave him a gentle kiss on the lips, and whispered, "I will always love you."

He didn't know what to say, and when he opened his mouth to say something she put her finger up to his lips to silence him.

She turned and walked away. For a while he stood there and watched her leave. Finally, he turned around and went back into the lounge.

As he walked back to his couch, Dalen said, "She told me a few days ago that she was leaving. I tried to talk her out of it, but she is determined.

Maybe it's for the best, she's been different since the attack at Randol's place. She needs to do whatever will bring her some happiness."

Ayris jumped into Rissyl's lap as he sat down, and Chardy crawled off of Cynia's lap to claim part of his dad's lap away from his sister. A brief sibling-war ensued and he had to adjust them to ensure that they both had plenty of his lap.

He was sad to see Sarasa struggling to find herself, and very disappointed to hear that she would be leaving. He reached over and put his arm around Cynia and pulled her against him. He was a very fortunate man to have such a wonderful family, and he thanked all of the gods, especially Kelegar and Nalria, that his family made it through the war mostly unharmed. He hoped that Sarasa would eventually find whatever she sought. Hopefully the gods had something wonderful planned for her too.

www.ingramcontent.com/pod-product-compliance
Lightning Source LLC
Chambersburg PA
CBHW060520180626
46817CB00002B/434